To Sue
Have a great read.

E.Y. Reegen

FOOSA!

Primal Instinct

FOOSA!

Primal Instinct

- a novel -

Edward Joseph Begen

www.ivyhousebooks.com

PUBLISHED BY IVY HOUSE PUBLISHING GROUP
5122 Bur Oak Circle, Raleigh, NC 27612
United States of America
919-782-0281
www.ivyhousebooks.com

ISBN: 1-57197-418-0
Library of Congress Control Number: 2004101677

Printed in the United States of America

To my sons, Paul & Michael

Luke Dollar holding a sedated fossa named Tina.

Many thanks go to Luke Dollar, Ecologist/Biologist, of Duke University. His work in the field of carnivores inspired this manuscript.

ACKNOWLEDGMENTS

To my wife, Linda, LPN, for her patience, love and support.

To Darrel Demers, NREMT-P.

To Lorraine Morse, for her editing and critique.

To Dr. Timothy Janz, MD.

And to all those who offered encouragement throughout the writing of the manuscript, especially Joan Peters, my biggest fan. I thank you.

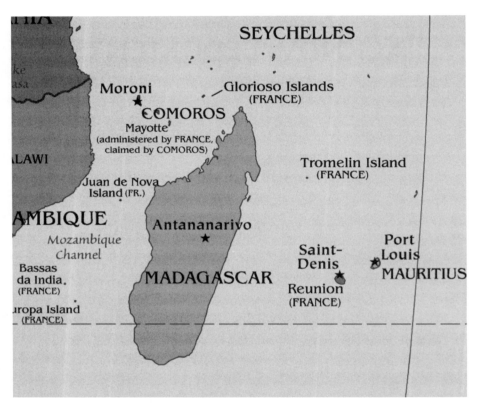

Map showing Madagascar's position just off the eastern coast of Africa.

Courtesy of exxun, www.exxun.com.

INTRODUCTION

Madagascar, or "The Big Red Island," is officially known as the Malagasy Republic. It's the fourth largest island in the world and sits in the Indian Ocean, separated from continental Africa on the west by the Mozambique Channel.

When civilization first arrived on Madagascar about two thousand years ago, the people began clearing the land to plant rice paddies, using a technique called slash and burn—a technique still being used today. At that time, the island was populated with giant specimens of fauna that have since vanished or disappeared into uncharted rain forests. Most of the unique plant and animal life that exists today is endangered because of the continued destruction of their habitat by human hands. Eighty-five percent of the natural forests have been lost over the last 20 years.

Presently, there are tremendous efforts underway to save this unique ecosystem, but poverty, poor education, political corruption, cyclones and flooding continue to take their toll. This deforestation and occurrence of the most terrifying storms imaginable, are exposing some areas to strange ecological imbalances and eradicating many of the unique animal species.

Today on this island there prowls an animal that can't be found, according to biologists, anywhere else on earth in the wild. In proportion to its size it is the meanest and most bloodthirsty of any other known to modern man. Very little is known or even written about this fantastic killer of the forest. Its scientific name is *Cryptoprocta ferox*, better known as the fossa.[1] Its bloodlines are a mystery in a sense, but believed to be a mixture of ferret and mongoose which makes it as good a description as any.

It has retractable razor-like claws and 32 very sharp teeth, well suited for any task. Its agility in the trees, as well as on the ground, makes it a most formidable predator of lemurs (ape-like animals) and any other animal it chooses for a meal. The fossa's mode of attack is quick and fatal, usually biting into the head to hold its victim and then tearing it to pieces with its claws. When this animal decides what it wants to eat, it's all business going after it.

No one has actually witnessed a kill, but the sanguinary evidence at a kill site has allowed biologists to recreate the scene. It weighs about 20 pounds and is approximately three feet long with a proportionate size tail. Now for an animal this small, some of the feats described may sound unbelievable.

What I am about to propose will certainly stretch your imagination even further. There are many who believe the ancient ancestor of this animal still survives somewhere on Madagascar's eastern coast. This forbidden area is known as the "Jangala Reservation."

Because of its density, disease carrying insects and other barriers to man, few choose to venture into its tangled vegetation. It's an area that has never been charted nor explored, at least by anyone who has ever lived to tell about it. Fossa's ancestor, known scientifically as *Cryptoprocta giganta*, would be longer than six feet with an equally long tail and weigh in at well over 250 pounds with more ferocity and agility than the largest African feline.

---

[1] For clarification to the reader the word "fossa" is spelled "foosa" in some instances to mainly express the Madagascan pronunciation and to add a bit of aura and superstition. Foosa refers mainly to the *ancient* one.

With the massive amount of deforestation occurring in Madagascar, there is a dwindling food source. Many believe the ancient fossa, if it does exist presently, will most certainly become extinct or be forced into migration and a change of diet. So here we are in a time with natural disasters on one hand, and on the other, human-induced destruction on a scale unparalleled anywhere in history, aiming at astoundingly untouched and, in some cases, uncharted magnificent rainforests.

And so this story . . . let's say it's merely a conjecture of what may soon become a reality.

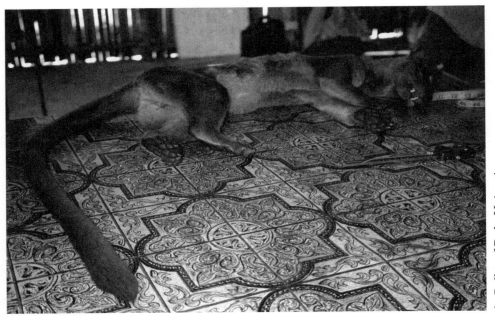

A sedated fossa named Ginny.

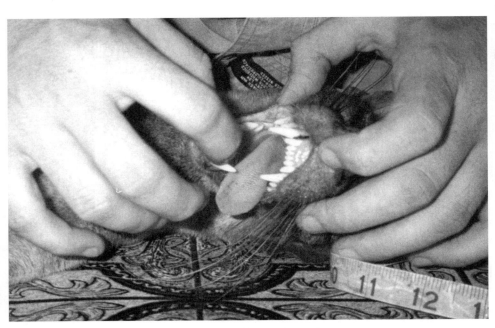

A close-up of Ginny's teeth.

CHAPTER ONE

Batrambady Research Station

Tsarafagundi Forest, S.W. Madagascar
July 1996

"She's beautiful, Dad," said Blaine. "I wish I could take her home," he continued as he stroked the soft fur of a maroon and white Sifaka lemur. Sheena, as she was called by Blaine, is a primate with big eyes and soft fur and endemic to the island of Madagascar.

"She's taken quite a shine to you since you've been here," said his father, Sheldon. "You're a real natural in the field. I know your mother's very proud of the way you've handled yourself on this trip. By the way, where is your mother?"

"I believe she's packing, Dad."

"Speaking of packing," said Sheldon, "I think it's time you've gotten your gear squared away also. Six A.M. comes early, and we don't want to be searching around for stuff at the last minute."

"Here's Mom now," said Blaine as he pointed toward their tent.

"Sheldon, can you come here for a moment?" asked Sharon in a sexy tone. Sheldon sort of skipped toward her singing an old song called "I'm Yours" or something to that effect. When he stood before her, she kissed him on the nose and said, "Do you have any room left in your suitcase?"

"I knew it was something devious, and I thought you loved me," said Shell, as he was called most of the time.

"But I do . . . I do. More than you'll ever know," said Sharon. "now what about the room in your suitcase?"

Shell just nodded his assent and asked, "Will you be all set for tomorrow's departure?"

She returned the nod and then sadly said, "I'm going to miss this place this year. It's the first time in three years this Gibbons family has shared a vacation together. I'm so glad that you gave Blaine the O.K. to travel with us this summer."

"Well, honey, you know how it is with diseases around here and all the inoculations one needs just to travel in this country. I guess I just felt he was ready."

"From my observation point," said Sharon, "your feelings were correct. Our son is turning into quite a young man."

Blaine was eavesdropping and laughingly added, "I agree wholeheartedly, and besides, you're only saying it because it's true." They all shared the laugh, and then Blaine said seriously, "All kidding aside, Mom and Dad, this has been a fantastic learning experience and a great vacation, and it isn't over yet. We've still got a visit to Paris and three whole weeks in Florida with Aunt Linda and Uncle Ed." Then walking away as if in a world of his own making, he raised his hands high and shouted, "Fishing, boating, swimming. It'll be heaven!"

Shell exclaimed, "You don't suppose the fact that my brother has a boat on the bay in Florida has anything to do with his excitement, do you?"

Sharon just laughed again and thought, "I couldn't be happier if I'd have planned it myself." Then she continued out loud, "Shell, should we tell him it's taken us three years to save for this trip?"

"No need, hon, his appreciation is written all over his face. Besides, how many other people get to take a two-month vacation?"

"Other teachers like us, hopefully," she added.

Shell and Sharon Gibbons are both high school teachers. They both teach biology in different schools in Massachusetts and were both ecologically brainwashed by the same professor in college from whence they had taken their first field trip to Madagascar. That was about fifteen years ago, and they've been going back whenever time and money allow. Having most summers off from teaching gives them the time, but money sometimes becomes tight, especially raising a young one.

Shell went straight into college after the Marine Corps, wishing he'd done it in reverse. He said life would have been a little easier as an officer rather than a "grunt" (mud marine), but usually insisting it was a good experience.

At five feet, ten inches tall, medium build and weighing in at 190 pounds, he never considered himself anything like a poster-type marine. His nose is a little off center to the left due to being broken a couple of times while playing ball and amateur boxing. Not once has he considered seeing a plastic surgeon, though Sharon hints at it occasionally and always insists it gives him character. Honesty is blended in with *Semper Fidelis*, and the Corps always gets the credit for his character makeup. His dirty blonde hair is worn on the short side, blending in handsomely with the deep blue eyes that seem to penetrate to the soul when he looks at you. Casual dress is his motto, and he seldom wears a tie outside of school. Many of his pupils joined the Corps because of his influence, though he doesn't hold sway over his own son in that department. His older brother, Ed, claims that particular honor, and not because of his age, but because he's all Navy, and Blaine loves boats. Shell has himself to blame, for on a few occasions when he and Sharon went on a field trip to Madagascar, Blaine spent the time with his Aunt Linda and Uncle Ed in Florida on the Gulf Coast. Naturally, Ed began teaching him all he knew about boatmanship and fishing. He and Ed are close. Blaine is the son that Ed never had.

Sharon at five feet, ten inches seems to be constantly watching her weight. Though she maintains a very good figure, she loves to "pick" on occasion and has a tendency to add a few pounds. Her dark brown hair and hazel eyes tend to project a very sexy but intimidating appearance to most men. She was never the outdoorsy type 'til she went on her first field trip and was introduced, not always formally, to every insect imaginable. Madagascar has some very rare beauties in that department. Her facial features are average with slight dimples, noticeable only when she laughs. She has to work constantly on her voice tone for its tendency is to be on the masculine side if she gets overexcited or angry. Otherwise, her normal speaking voice is low and smooth.

She and Shell dated in college and were married a year after they graduated. Now, you might ask what kind of offspring would these two foster. Well, Blaine does have blue eyes and light brown hair, and it seems that's where the resemblance ends. He's definitely his own man, in character as well as appearance. His father hates boats, but Blaine's content whether on the water or in it. Joining the Navy and then someday owning his own boat are his constant dream.

When he first told his folks about his aspirations, his father just stared at him with his deep blue eyes and said, "And you'll join the Navy on the Marine Corps' birthday, I suppose!"

Sharon just shrugged her shoulders and said, "He knows what he wants."

"Yeah, Dad, like good food, clean sheets and a rolling deck beneath my feet," offered Blaine.

"Can't argue with that," said Shell, and they all looked around at each other and laughed. They are a close family.

One of Blaine's traits is to clasp his hands behind his back when confronted by a problem and then raise them over his head toward the heavens when the solution comes to him. This has been going on since age four, and there's not another person on either side of the family whom he could have emulated. So when his parents see him do this, they know he's in deep thought.

At age 13, he's of normal height and weight, according to their physician, and waxing strongly. He runs like a deer, and his balance aboard ship is uncanny. Uncle Ed just says he's a natural. Ed has had him tying knots in boat lines since he was able to walk. At age four, he tied his first sheepshank.

His free time is always taken up with fishing, boating, playing baseball (another of his passions) and reading everything he can find on oceanography. His passion for playing third base has already rewarded him with an M.V.P. at school along with a broken finger and a broken nose. After the nose was broken, he said to his father, "See Dad, I'm taking after you!" Shell told Sharon afterward he didn't know whether to whack him or hug him. In any case, there wasn't any deformity to speak of, and not wanting to discourage his attraction to the game, they allowed him to pursue his goals. Watching children grow while keeping feelings and emotions in check is definitely a reason for the early growth of gray hair. Shell's father always said, "Better on the ball field than hanging on the corners." In this case, Shell applied this philosophy to Blaine and he's not sorry for it.

Blaine also asks a lot of questions. He questions everything and everybody. This started in the seventh grade when his history teacher instilled this in the whole class. He always told them not to accept anything as fact without proof or unless spoken by someone they knew to be absolutely trustworthy. "Don't ever be afraid to ask why, what, who, when and how," he told them. Blaine took this as gospel and has been practicing it ever since, especially when he discussed it with his parents and they agreed wholeheartedly.

Blaine is prone to occasional chicanery, but his manners are impeccable and a delight to his parents. Many times word of his good deeds crossed their ears, as did the tomfoolery, though the latter was rare, thank heaven.

"Are you really going to miss this place, Sharon?" asked Shell. "No indoor plumbing, sleeping in a tent, rocks in your rice . . ."

"Ah, rocks in my rice. That I'm definitely going to miss, along with the bones in my stew and all the other goodies I've grown to love!" Shell started to laugh, and Sharon picked up her hairbrush as if to throw and said, "If this venture that we make on occasion was just your idea, I'd have something to complain about. But it's always a joint decision. Tell me we're doing some good here."

Shell took her in his arms. "We were told from the start that it would be difficult, sometimes dangerous, and the only satisfaction derived may be the thought we tried to make a difference. There are so many others here and throughout Madagascar probably feeling the same way you are."

"And you?" she asked.

"Yes, counting myself as well."

The operation of this forest station is jointly controlled by World Conservational Trust and World-Trek International. Here researchers work on a number of projects from captive-breeding programs of rare tortoises to the study of wide-eyed primates called lemurs, to birds, other exotic animals and insects. There are many volunteers from around the world of which the Gibbons family are just a few. They've been assisting primatologists with the various lemur species capture-and-release programs, fitting them with radio transmitters so that they can monitor their health, primarily with parasitic exams and weekly physicals. There's not a great deal that can be accomplished in two to three weeks by volunteers, so it may seem to the individuals, but all efforts when combined, offer a world of needed information.

"What time's our flight out?" asked Sharon.

"We're scheduled to leave Mahajanga at 10:50 A.M. day after tomorrow," answered Shell.

"You seem a little nervous, Shell, what's bothering you?"

"So I'm a little jumpy about flying, and I'm not too nuts about that damn bumpy road into town," said Shell.

"You'll be fine, dear. Besides, you're a Marine. You can handle anything with improvisation, at least that's what you've been telling me all these years. So improvise!"

As he reached out to grasp her hand, she eluded him and ran for the safety of the tent, trying to hold back the laughter, but he caught her at the entrance. They kissed. He pulled her inside and closed the tent flap.

A short time later, when they both had finished packing, he said, "We better check on Blaine to make sure he's ready to go in the morning. The van is leaving at eight o'clock."

Blaine was bunked in with one of the other younger volunteers, and when they looked in on him, he was fast asleep with both his bags packed and sitting by the entrance. "You know, honey," said Shell, "that boy never ceases to amaze me."

"Let's get some sleep as well," she suggested. They both retired.

Everything in the compound quieted down as all settled in for the night, at least 'til three A.M. or thereabouts. Shell sprung up in his sleeping bag, near terror. Every soul in the area was awakened by the sound of death shrieks. It was a sound that most had never heard before. Shell threw on his pants, told Sharon to stay put, and then headed for the commotion. As he passed Blaine's tent, he cautioned Blaine and his tent-mate to hold fast. Several other men moved in the direction of the sounds also, including two of the Malagasy assistants.

When Shell had reached the perimeter of the compound, he turned to one of the others and said, "What's that ungodly odor?"

One of the Malagasies muttered, "Foosa!"

"What the hell is foosa?" asked Shell, as he was looking around. His voice trailed off, "Oh, no . . . who's got a flashlight?" Someone flashed the light in his direction toward the ground.

There was blood everywhere and pieces of what appeared to be lemur fur scattered around.

"What could've possibly done this?" asked one of the others.

Once again the Malagasy guide uttered, "Foosa."

"Foosa . . . foosa, isn't that some kind of local superstition or myth?" asked Shell.

"It's not a superstition or a myth," said one of the researchers. "It's a predator indigenous to this island and in lieu of any better description; it's a cross somewhere between a ferret and a weasel. It just may be one of the fiercest animals on earth."

"I've been coming here for several years and have never heard of it," said Shell.

"Few have, and actually there's not a lot written about them, but I do believe it's called a fossa in the book I read," added the primatologist.

The Malagasy guide assured everyone that the animal in question has not been known to be dangerous to man except way back in time when they were of much larger size. They feed mainly on the lemur population.

Shell looked over his shoulder and saw Sharon and Blaine coming toward him. Someone had turned on the compound lights. He walked toward them, turned them around and said, "Let's head back. I'll explain later." On the way back to the tenting area, he told them a predator had killed one of the lemurs, and when Blaine showed a feared concern, he assured him that it wasn't Sheena, his adopted, temporary pet.

Getting back to sleep was a problem for most, including Shell, who made a mental note to read up more on this fossa character. He had never witnessed a kill site like that, nor knew of any animal that was that sanguinary. He fantasized all night over what this animal would look like.

CHAPTER TWO

Mahajanga

Morning came early and naturally the conversation around the breakfast table was over the night's rude awakening. Just about every native had something to say about the history of the carnivore in question, but nobody had ever seen one except for the camp guides, who both claimed to have encountered the animal.

After bidding farewell to all, the Gibbons family boarded the van for the 70-mile trek to Mahajanga where, hopefully, there awaited hot baths and a comfortable night's sleep. They were facing a long flight to Paris.

"Where will you be staying?" asked the driver as they came within sight of the town.

"We're at the Roches Rouges," said Shell.

A short while later the van pulled up in front of the hotel. The driver had the bags taken care of, and the Gibbons entered the lobby to check in.

"Dad," said Blaine, "could we take a walk down to the dock later on this afternoon? I'd love to see some of those big fishing boats up close!" He followed up quickly, "Mom, would you mind?"

Shell answered, "Let's get settled in first and have some lunch. I've also got to secure us transportation to the airport."

"Hot shower for me first or I don't go anywhere!" said Sharon.

Shell and Blaine looked at each other and nodded their assent in unison.

After a light lunch of lasopy, a vegetable puree, crackers and salady voankazo, fruit compote with lichee nuts and topped with vanilla flavoring, they were off to see the town.

Mahajanga is the second largest port of Madagascar and is situated on the Betsiboka River. It has a population of over 100,000 people of various backgrounds being mostly of Indonesian, Polynesian and European descent. The newer section of the town is centered mostly on the city hall. There is a giant tree called a baobab, a symbol of the founding fathers, on the main thorough fare bordering the seashore.

The town's old sector is confined mainly to the harbor quarter and has some nineteenth-century Arabian houses. There are Christian churches and mosques, and the city has its own university. There's an airport nearby and coffee plantations and rice paddies abound. Other industries include fishing, raising cattle and lumbering. Mahajanga in Swahili means "town of flowers," well represented by its shady arcades and flowering bougainvillea.

"Hey, you guys!" said Sharon. "It's hot and dusty and my feet are killing me." They had been walking around for a while.

"Oh, Mom, can we just see the fishing boats before we head back?" asked Blaine, at the same time looking at his father like a dying calf going to the slaughterhouse. He added, "Please?"

"C'mon, honey, I promised him," said Shell. "We'll take a taxi back to the hotel." Applying the familiar expression of surrender to her face, she proceeded to the docks.

Blaine was in his element. He loved the atmosphere of men mending nets and unloading fish from the boats. There were cargo ships loading coffee and vanilla, and as Blaine looked toward the other end, he noticed a crowd gathering and was anxious to see what was going on. He grabbed his parents' hands and hurried to join the crowd.

"Oh, wow! Look at that!" Blaine said, as he pointed to a large fish that was winched up by the tail with its nose touching the dock.

Shell exclaimed, "It's a shark!"

One of the locals added, "Yes, it's a Tiger." This was the first time Blaine had ever seen a real shark up close except in an aquarium. "Seventeen-footer; it looks like," continued the local.

"Do these boats go out just to catch sharks?" asked Blaine. Blaine's query caught the attention of a man standing nearby. Actually, he was the captain of the fishing boat, *Tolura*.

"Excuse me," said the captain. "I could not help overhearing your inquiry and if you will permit me to respond . . ."

"By all means," answered Shell.

"Occasionally," offered the captain, "we are forced to entertain a big brute like that one, who chops our nets to pieces and renders them unmendable. Fortunately, in this case, we were able to sell off the fins and jaws and along with the carcass, we will obtain a few francs, so it will not be a total loss. Oh, forgive me. Permit me to introduce myself. I am Rijah Andrianaivo, captain of the *Tolura*."

Shell reached out his hand and said, "Pleased. My name is Shell, this is my wife, Sharon, and the inquisitive one is my son, Blaine."

"Are you a fisherman, young man?" asked the captain.

"Not yet," answered Blaine. "But someday I'll have my own boat," and his voice trailed off as if in a trance. "Someday . . ."

"I believe you will, young man, but bear in mind it's a tough way to make a living," said the captain.

Blaine countered, "But if you love what you're doing, it's worth it."

"Spoken like a true seaman," replied the captain. Turning to the parents, he asked, "You are English?"

"American," they both responded at the same time.

"American, of course," echoed Rijah. "Are you on vacation?"

"Not exactly," said Sharon as she made an attempt to move a little further away from the shark and the pressing crowd. "We're both high school teachers in America, and we come here for a few weeks each year as volunteers for research work at Batrambady Forest."

"What do you research?" asked Rijah.

"The lemur population," she continued. "This is our last day here and Blaine just had to see the boats."

"I would love you to meet my wife," said the captain, with excitement in his voice. "She loves company and she loves to cook."

"We couldn't impose on you like that. You don't even know us," said Sharon.

"I can tell by your well-mannered son what kind of people you are. The fruit does not fall far from the tree! But forgive me for being so presumptuous. Did you already have plans for dinner?"

Shell paused, "Well, no . . ."

"Good then, it is settled. Is six-thirty a good time?" he asked. They all looked at each other and nodded affirmatively. "Good," he continued. "And I'll collect you . . . where?" he asked looking at them questioningly.

Sharon, feeling swept off her feet, replied, "Les Roches Rouges."

"Great choice," said Rijah. "The owner is a friend of mine."

"And what's your wife's name?" Sharon asked.

"Yvette," was his reply. He continued, "I must get back to work, and I must call my wife if I am to be on time. Until this evening?"

"Six-thirty," Shell replied. After one more look at the shark, Blaine was ready to return to the hotel.

It was still early when they returned to the hotel. Plenty of time for a dip in the pool and a short poolside nap before dinner.

"I've never eaten in a Malagasy home," said Sharon. "Have you Shell?"

"No, but the meals are probably on the same line as the hotel with a little more embellishment. Anyway, let's just go and enjoy ourselves. It will all fall into place."

"You know folks," Blaine spoke boldly; "I'm all riced and beaned out. What I wouldn't give for a hamburger and fries."

Sharon laughed in agreement, and Shell asked, "I thought you guys were really keen on the zebu stew?"

"It had bone shards that almost choked me the first time," said Sharon.

Blaine countered, "Yeah! And the rice was laced with rocks. I'm surprised we still have teeth." In Madagascar, rice is served with every meal. In some places, it's dried on the road, hence the rocks. Good cooks serve good rice and boneless stew.

"You don't suppose they all speak English," asked Blaine.

"Most likely a combination of Malagache and French," replied Shell. "In any event your mother speaks fluent French, and I . . . well, I can dabble in a little Malagache. Besides Blaine, your French is coming along a little."

"Very little!" replied Blaine.

The Gibbons family was collected at six-thirty by Rijah and whisked away to the outskirts of town. They arrived at a simple but beautiful terraced home, adorned with flowers, and were greeted at the door by Yvette, Rijah's wife and their 14-year-old daughter, Sirana. The night was getting interesting for Blaine already.

"Welcome to our home," said Yvette graciously, and when Sharon offered her apologies for the last minute imposition, she continued, "No, please. We love company, and we have never dined with Americans. I have so many questions to ask. I may be apologizing to you before the night is over."

Introductions were given all around. Sharon just stared in

admiration at the furnishings and the way everything was so meticulously arranged. "Your home is quite beautiful, Yvette, and the flowers . . ." Her voice trickled off, as she smelled the fresh floral arrangement.

Rijah interjected, "So tell me, have you ever eaten in a Madagascan home?" Looking at the three, as they nodded no, he continued, "You are in for a real treat, for I'm married to the greatest cook in all of Mahajanga." He thought for a second and added, "Maybe of the whole island."

"Please don't pay attention to my husband's flattery. I think sometimes he could charm the scales from a fish."

"And fish is what I know best," said Rijah.

"You must understand," Yvette implored, "we have two homes. One is his boat, where he lives most of the time, and the other is here where he eats. I decorate this home the way I choose, and the boat, well he won't let me near it because his idea of decoration is oil, grease and fish guts."

The Gibbons were amused at the chatter back and forth and really made to feel at home. The conversation became alive from all sides, and Sirana and Blaine were hitting it off quite nicely. As a matter of fact, he had, momentarily, a hard time separating his eyes from hers.

Yvette is a small woman, about five foot, two inches, quite attractive, dark complexion and very soft spoken. Rijah, on the other hand, is sturdily built with a ruddy and somewhat wrinkled face, most likely earned from all his years at sea, and a very robust and outgoing personality.

Sirana lies somewhere in between. She's outgoing and quite soft spoken while carrying on a great conversation. Her eyes are large, hazel-colored and quite sexy, probably because of the way she wears her long black hair over one side of her face. She's a couple of inches taller than her mother, medium built and very buxom, considering her age. It was no wonder Blaine became infatuated with her. Yvette is of French descent, while Rijah is the offspring of an Indian father and Malayan-Polynesian mother. The combination is obviously apparent in Sirana's attractiveness and vibrant personality.

The traditional Malagache meal is usually served on a mat on the floor, but in the cities, tables are used. In this household, Yvette insisted upon it. When dinner was ready, they all entered the dining area, and Sharon was immensely impressed with the table treatment. The large round table was covered with a yellow tablecloth. Yellow napkins were placed on white serving plates, each adorned with a bright orchid flower. The centerpiece was a bowl of fresh fruit interspersed with some of the same flowers on the plates.

"This is absolutely beautiful, Yvette," commented Sharon.

"You are most kind," Yvette responded.

Rijah with his tactful elegance announced, as he glanced at his wife and daughter, "Dinner is being served."

"We begin with the *lasopy*, a veal-vegetable puree, thick and hearty," said Sirana.

Shell spoke up, "We tried some lasopy at the hotel this afternoon; it was plain vegetable."

"Did you care for it?" asked Rijah.

"Yes, it was very good," replied Shell. "But there wasn't any veal in it."

"He uses Yvette's recipe," Rijah commented, "but lacks the fine touch. He also uses her recipe for the verenga and seems somehow to spoil it. This *verenga*, shredded beef baked in the oven, is beautifully browned. This large bowl is *vary minanana*, steaming hot vegetables."

Pointing to another dish, he described it as the *lasary voatabia*, tomato and scallion salad. Then he continued, "And naturally, the rice, but interspersed with fresh-caught curried fish."

"Please forgive my husband's praise for my cooking; he sometimes becomes overbearing, and besides, you have not yet eaten. Please enjoy!"

Rijah interjected once again with, "I do want to caution you on this particular bowl. It's called *sakay*, a very hot red pepper dish that may give you a bite, if you are not used to it."

The feast began and Blaine couldn't get enough of the verenga and hot vegetables, even though his mother urged him to try all of the dishes. To Sharon's surprise, Shell was enjoying the hot sakay on just about everything.

The dinner was topped off with *salady voankazo*, the same dish that Blaine had had for lunch but didn't hesitate to have again.

After complimenting for a dinner that was wonderfully cooked and so graciously and beautifully served, Sharon asked, "Why would you go through all this trouble for people like us whom you hardly know? I'm speaking for the family when I say we most certainly feel graced."

Rijah spoke up and said, "You are strangers in a strange land with a need for friendship and refreshment. I am a good judge of people, and after speaking with your son and hearing his enthusiasm for the sea, how could I not invite you to my home and share you all with my family? It is you who have graced our table." The Gibbons family was humbled.

They all shared information about each other through conversation, and this gave Rijah a chance to dabble in a little braggadocio about his 20-year-old son who is attending college. His name is Aurelien, and even when Rijah speaks his name, he beams with pride.

Just before it was time to leave, they exchanged addresses and phone numbers and vowed promises to use them. It was a very good evening for all.

Just before Rijah dropped them at the hotel, Shell asked, "What do you know about foosa?"

"Foosa?" Rijah replied surprised. "Where have you heard of

the foosa?" So Shell filled him in on the incident at the campsite and expressed his desire to find out more about it.

"Well, I have not seen one myself," said the captain, "but when I was a child I would hear the elders as they sat around the camp-fire speaking of such a one which would eat children and kill the cattle. They would raise their arms, face the sky and shout "FOOSA!" We, as children, were told never to enter the forest alone and if we smelled something real bad to run all the way home. To this day, sometimes when I smell rotting fish or meat, I think of these tales."

"What I smelled last night," said Shell, "was brutal."

The captain continued, "Because of the fear instilled in us as children, few venture into the deep forests. Maybe that's why I stay on my boat!" He laughed heartily and the Gibbons joined him in the laughter.

"Well, here we are my friends. Good luck and bon voyage," stated Rijah as they pulled up in front of the hotel.

"We had a wonderful experience and a great time," said Shell. "I only hope that someday we may reciprocate in some way."

"You have a family to be very proud of Rijah. We could never thank you enough for your hospitality and friendship," added Sharon.

"And you, young man," said Rijah, as he rubbed Blaine on the head, "hang on to your dreams of the sea and they will come true."

"I will, captain, I will, and thank you. You're very kind."

"God is good," said Rijah. They all shook hands and parted.

CHAPTER THREE

The Journey Home

All had a good night's rest, and morning seemed to come very early. The yawning seemed "catchy" as they sat down to morning repast. "Oh, goody," said Blaine, "more rice for breakfast."

"O.K. wise guy," cautioned Shell. "Knock it off!" Sharon just shook her head smiling, for she'd had her fill of rice as well. In Madagascar, rice is served with every meal and not as a side dish, but as the main course with other dishes used to complement the rice.

"I have no idea what food, if any, will be served on the plane nor can I predict an unscheduled layover. So I suggest you both eat a good breakfast," said Shell, sounding like a scoutmaster on an overnight bivouac.

Sharon countered with, "And you, our fearless leader, why do you not partake of nourishment?"

"I think it's the sakay. I kind of went overboard on the hot stuff last night, and I don't want to hear 'I told you so' from either of you." Sharon and Blaine just looked at each other and had all they could do to keep from bursting into laughter.

So Shell settled for a cup of coffee and a couple of antacids, and when breakfast was through, they packed and checked out. Promptly at 8:30 A.M., they were picked up and whisked to the airport. Within an hour, the bags were checked in, and with no hang-ups, they were seated waiting for the 10:50 A.M. flight to "Tana," the short term used for Antananarivo, the capital city and also the hub for connections to all destinations. Air-Mad, short for Air Madagascar, is the local carrier and flights are usually on time, having an excellent safety record and an air fleet consisting of mostly Boeing 737s.

"Now I can relax a little," said Shell as they were boarding. "I always have the jitters until the bags are checked and we're seated."

"Shell," remarked Sharon, "you're always jittery when you fly. When we land, you'll worry about the luggage and connections for the next flight. Try to remember, dear, the joy is in the journey."

"I'm glad I'm not a grownup yet," said Blaine. "I don't worry about anything."

"Your day's coming," answered Shell.

The plane taxied out and shortly they were airborne. Sharon always enjoyed traveling and very seldom became concerned with air safety, but for some strange reason, she was getting edgy and couldn't put her finger on the cause. Sharon and Shell were sitting together and Blaine was seated across the aisle. Sharon whispered to Shell, "I feel a little edgy."

"Hey, the joy is in the journey, remember?"

"Seriously, Shell, I have this strange foreboding sensation that's giving me the creeps. You know I never get this way on a flight."

Seeing Sharon was somewhat alarmed, Shell tried to calm her down. "Honey, you know how I get. I'm always nervous flying, sometimes downright scared, but it always turns out O.K."

She grabbed his hand and held it tightly saying, "I hope so."

The remainder of the flight wasn't long, and as they touched down, she began to relax, letting loose of Shell's hand. "Ah, circulation at last!" he quipped.

"Don't mention my feeling to Blaine," she said.

"Of course not," he answered, adding as he rubbed the circulation back into his hand; "I may never write again."

She stared darts at him, and then they all deplaned. He was doing everything he could think of to keep her spirits uplifted, but he sensed something was amiss.

They retrieved their bags only to find out that the flight to Paris was being held up due to mechanical problems.

"I knew it," she said. "I knew it."

"Calm down," said Shell.

"What's wrong with Mom?" asked Blaine of his father.

"She's just a little nervous, that's all."

"But Dad, she never gets nervous."

"I know," he answered. "Let's see if we can work out the problems here." Shell went to the airline desk to get more information, and just then, they announced there would be at least a four-hour delay. That did it for Sharon. No way was she getting on that plane.

"What do you suggest we do?" asked Shell. "It's a long swim from here."

"Please don't be sarcastic," replied Sharon. "I just can't get over this damn feeling."

"Wow," exclaimed Blaine, "Mom is serious!"

Shell asked Blaine to take a short walk for a minute while he tried to figure out a solution with his mother.

"What do you want to do, Sharon?"

"Let's go home," she said.

"Home? Home where? You mean Peabody, Massachusetts? What about Paris? My brother's house in Florida? What do we do . . . just chuck the whole vacation out the window?"

"I guess I'm not making much sense, am I?" she responded. He just held his hands out in an "I don't understand" gesture. She continued, "Couldn't we skip Paris? When we get to Atlanta, we can decide whether to continue on to Florida or go home to Peabody."

"How do we explain this to Blaine? He counted on Florida being the highlight of the whole trip."

Sharon thought for a minute and came back with, "You see what kind of flight arrangements you can make. I'll speak with my son. Cancel the Paris flight in any case." Shell took a deep breath and blew it out while nodding his assent.

Blaine was very understanding about bypassing Paris, but urged his mother to carefully reconsider Florida for his sake. She agreed. Meanwhile Shell returned with good news. They accepted cancellation of the Paris flight while giving full reimbursement toward the flight to Johannesburg, South Africa with connections to Philadelphia, Pennsylvania, USA. Sharon felt a little more at ease and well pleased with the cooperation she received from her two guys.

They had time for some lunch, and this time Shell needed something on his stomach and decided on rice.

"God bless you!" said Sharon. Blaine closed his eyes and envisioned biting into a juicy hamburger but kept it to himself. Good judgment.

The flight to Johannesburg was restful and uneventful, causing Sharon to be a little more laid back. They had a choice of catching the morning flight out to Philadelphia or getting a little rest and leaving in the early evening. They decided on the first flight out, knowing they'd be sleeping on the plane anyway. There wasn't any sense hanging around South Africa if you weren't going to see any lions. At least, that was Blaine's opinion.

Shell was very concerned about Sharon for he had never seen her this way. He was just hoping she'd get over this thing by the time they touched down in old Philly. He was not one to disregard a woman's intuition. That much he had learned in his years on this planet, and he had also learned never to try to understand a woman. To do so would be folly for any man, so said a wise old friend from years ago. He believed this and practiced it.

Sharon got some good rest on the long flight to Philly, and they touched down without incident.

"How're you feeling, Mom?" asked Blaine.

"Much better, thanks," was her reply, and Blaine just stared at her, waiting for some sort of decision on the trip to Florida.

Shell interjected, "What do you guys think of staying over here tonight, getting a good meal and heading to my brother's house in the afternoon?"

Sharon began feeling a little guilty because her guys were trying to make concessions to cheer her up. She made a decision. "Let's continue on to Fort Myers today."

Blaine let out a loud "Yahoo!" But then he got control of himself and said, "Oops! Sorry. Are you sure it's what you want to do?"

Shell repeated the question. She nodded and said sighing, "Yes, I'd like a good lunch and see if we can get a mid-afternoon flight."

"Done," said Shell. He made all the arrangements.

Boarding time was set for 3:30 P.M. They all had salads for lunch in contemplation of a huge steak dinner in Florida, even though the aroma of the fast-food burger was driving Blaine crazy.

They arrived at the gate, ready to board at three. Although they usually start boarding a half hour before take-off, by 3:10, nothing was happening. "This is the right gate, huh Dad?" asked Blaine.

"Let me see what's going on," said Shell. He spoke with the girl at the desk, and she told him there would be a slight delay. "For how long?" he asked. She wasn't sure. She was waiting for word.

Finally, word came, "All passengers assigned to flight 2290 out of concourse B, gate nine are to proceed to concourse B, gate 16 for boarding to Fort Myers, Florida." The message was repeated.

"I don't like this," said Sharon.

It turned out there was mechanical difficulty beyond immediate repair, but not of a critical nature. It seems that one of the toilets was unserviceable, so they said. The replacement flight was due out at 4:30 P.M.

Luggage was transferred, the plane was boarded and liftoff took place at 4:35 P.M. Sharon's jitters subsided for the time being, but there was something deep down inside she couldn't shake or explain away. "What's wrong with me?" she uttered to herself.

Blaine was sound asleep 10 minutes after takeoff, and Shell was five minutes behind him with light snoring. Sharon cuddled up next to Shell and soon after, she was asleep as well.

"Arriving in Fort Myers in 15 minutes," was the next voice they heard. They were grateful to the stewardess for not awakening them for the snack. She explained they looked too comfortable to disturb.

Blaine looked out the window as the setting sun caused a mixture of blues and reds in the sky. The sun looked as if it were sinking into the Gulf of Mexico. Sunsets in southwestern Florida are indeed quite breathtaking. Fishing, boating, dolphins, sharks, manatees and all the other things his Uncle Ed wrote about were rushing around in Blaine's head.

It had been three years since he'd seen his Aunt Linda and Uncle Ed. That was just before they moved to sunny Florida, and he missed them a lot. He spent many hours fishing with his uncle when they lived in Peabody, but then again, the two families were very close for that's all there were. Everyone else had died off. There were no other children in the family, and Ed and Linda treated him like their own son.

"And, ah! Yes! Tarpon season in Boca Grande pass," he said out loud. No one seemed to pay attention. Tarpon are large game fish that sort of "stack-up," as Uncle Ed puts it, meaning they're abundant a short distance from his home. Of course, in the mind of a boy like Blaine, he would most certainly catch the world's record.

As he came back to reality, he leaned over to his parents and said, "I could really use a comfortable bed."

They both answered, "Ditto." Then his mother added, "But first, a nice juicy steak, baked potato with oodles of sour cream and butter and a Caesar salad!" He and his father just looked at each other and licked their lips in agreement.

"One other thing," added Blaine, "key lime pie!"

The plane touched down and taxied in to the gate. "See, honey, I told you it would be all right."

"I know, Shell," said Sharon. "I'm sorry I put you through all that trouble."

"No trouble dear, for what other reason am I here but to serve you." She whacked him on the arm.

CHAPTER FOUR

Englewood, Florida

Linda called out, "Ed, do you remember your brother's arriving tonight?"

"Yes, dear," answered Ed. "But he said something about maybe staying a night over at a hotel in Fort Myers."

"But shouldn't you at least be ready in case he calls?" Linda was just trying to lure Ed into the house for dinner. "You've been working on that boat since after breakfast."

"What time is it now?" he asked.

"Five-thirty P.M. Will you be dining with me tonight?" she inquired, displaying a little sarcasm in her soft, somewhat crackly voice.

Ed has a loud voice, even when speaking normally, and Linda is always cautioning him to hold it down, especially when he gets excited in a conversation. He blames it on all the loud machinery he had to work around for the past 30 or so years. Speaking in his normal tone from the dock to the back door of the house, about 50 yards, he said, "Honey, this engine is humming right now. You know I promised Blaine that teaching him seamanship and saltwater fishing would be the priorities on this vacation."

She just stood with her arms crossed staring in his direction.

"All right . . . I'm coming," he said and started walking toward the house. "You know," he thought, "Blaine's 13 years old now. Where's the time gone?" He looked at Linda again, still standing there. "I know you're hungry . . . just let me wash a little."

Ed is Sheldon's older brother, who unlike his brother, decided to be a blue-collar worker. Linda was pregnant at the time, and money became a huge consideration. Even though he had completed two years of college, he sought and gained employment as a welder on nuclear submarines for General Dynamics. The work was hot and dirty, but the pay was good. He planned on continuing his education later on, but that never came to pass.

When the time came for Linda to deliver, complications set in. She was 32 hours in labor, and instruments had to be used to remove the child. Four days after the birth, the baby died of brain damage. It was a tremendous blow to the both of them, and also left Linda unable to bear any more children.

A short time later, Ed was able to land a job with General Electric in Lynn, Massachusetts, welding on jet engines. This brought him much closer to home. He and Linda owned a modest house just over the Lynn line in Peabody.

Linda worked as an L.P.N. at the Union Hospital in Lynn for many years. She was an only child, and at age 50, became parentless when her mother died. Ed's parents had also been deceased for a few years. Their only relatives were his brother Sheldon, sister-in-law Sharon, and nephew Blaine.

They all spent as much time as possible together, and in the summers when Blaine's parents could afford to go to Madagascar on their field trips, Ed would use three weeks of his vacation and spend it with Blaine. He and Blaine became very fond of each other, and any spare time Linda could get away from work, she'd join in on the fun. He became the son they never had.

When Ed turned 55 years old, General Electric asked him if he'd be interested in early retirement. He'd carry the same insurance until he was 65, both life and medical, and would receive a monetary supplement until age 62, when he would be eligible for social security. It was definitely something to consider. A great number of welders never make it to retirement age. Linda thought it was a good deal, and Sheldon told him he'd be crazy if he turned it down.

So, at age 55, Ed retired and Linda said, "What now?"

"We sell the house and move to Florida. We buy a boat and live happily ever after," answered Ed.

"What about my job and our friends and our family?" asked Linda.

"We have to start thinking of the future and those damn snowy and icy conditions around here. We're not getting any younger."

After much thought, consideration and planning, the house was sold, and they settled in southwestern Florida. There hadn't been a hurricane disaster in that area for 30 years, and that was a prime consideration for locale.

Linda remained somewhat homesick for the first couple of years, even though she'd made many friends and worked part time in a local doctor's office. Many other women had told her to be patient for they went through the same experience. "Two to three years," they'd say, "before you really accept the lifestyle."

Ed loved it from day one. He very seldom thought of New England, and he only missed his brother and family. Now his family was coming here for a long vacation, and Ed was hoping his brother would become so impressed with the area that he would want to relocate as well. Linda knew what was on Ed's mind.

As a matter of fact, she knew what he was going to say sometimes before he'd say it. "So, you're thinking of having them as neighbors, right?" asked Linda.

"Having who as neighbors?" Ed questioned.

Linda just stared at him as if to say, "I know what your scheme is."

"Well, I thought it would be a great idea. The high school

needs teachers, and you know Blaine would absolutely love it here."

"So you say," Linda retorted. "What makes you think you know what's best for everybody? They may love to vacation here or maybe they won't. This place is not for everyone 'cause if it were, we'd be awful crowded and congested here, don't you think?"

"I guess I am being a little presumptuous," said Ed, "and maybe a bit selfish as well. My intentions are good."

"They usually are," replied Linda. "And so are most of your ideas, but you have no tact and most times fail at getting them across. Just be patient and allow them to enjoy themselves, and maybe they'll come to that conclusion on their own, just like we did."

"I hate it when you're right," said Ed, smiling. "Let's eat!"

CHAPTER FIVE

An Evening in Fort Myers

The word exhausted seemed more suitable for the state of the Gibbons family rather than merely tired. It had been a long, arduous trip.

"I think I'll give my brother a call," said Shell, "and let him know we'll be staying over around here for this evening." Pulling a slip of paper from his wallet, he looked at Sharon and asked, "Do I need to dial the area code before the number or just one and the number?"

"Just dial the way it's written. I already inquired before we left," answered Sharon.

"Oh, you're so efficient, my love," said Shell as he dialed the number.

Ed answered the phone in his usual thundering voice, knowing it would be Shell. "Eddie's Lounge, manager speaking."

"Hi, brudda, it's me," said Shell, fooling around gangland style.

Ed laughed. "Where are you?"

"We just landed," said Shell. "We're going to collect our bags, rent a car and get a steak."

"What do you need to rent a car for?" asked Ed. "I'll come pick you up."

"We're really tired, Ed, so we'll rent a room here, as well, and drive over to your place in the morning," replied Shell.

"Okay, shweetheart, you're the boss," said Ed while sounding like Humphrey Bogart. He added, "May I make a recommendation?"

"Please do!"

"Well, there's a good place for steaks not far from where you are, the Sanibel Steakhouse. You just come out of the airport heading towards downtown Ft. Myers 'til you get to Route 41. Go straight across and it's on your left."

"Gotcha," said Shell, "Sanibel Steakfest."

"Steakhouse!" repeated Ed.

"I know. Just testing."

"Yeah, just testing my sanity. You want a hotel also?"

"Why not?"

"Best Western, North Ft. Myers. After the steakhouse, you get back out on Route 41 north, and it's just over the bridge on your left, next to the beautiful Caloosahatchee River."

"Is that one 'e' or two?" asked Shell.

"You are a pain in the ass, young brother," said Ed. They both laughed. "You have the directions to my house, I hope."

"Sharon has them. No sweat. See you in the morning."

After loading the luggage onto a cart, Sharon and Blaine proceeded over to the rent-a-car area where Shell was already signing the contract and getting redirected to his brother's hotel and dining choices. Reservations were also made for the hotel.

"Here, honey, you read the directions and I'll drive." Shell made his way out to Daniel Webster Parkway and headed toward Route 41.

"I'm starving," said Sharon. "I really couldn't make it on airline food alone."

"Yeah, and I don't want to look at another bowl of rice for a long while," added Blaine. "A long, long while."

"Your ingratitude baffles me," said Shell. "But I will expeditiously have you both in front of a choice cut of Black Angus."

Blaine sunk back into the seat and began thinking about the whole experience, so far, and all the wonderful moments he was having with his parents and said to himself, "How lucky can a kid get? Boating, fishing and swimming yet to come. Wow!"

As they neared the intersection of Webster and 41, Sharon said, "We go straight through here. It's just a little ways down on the left."

"Check," said Shell and pulled into the parking lot.

During dinner, which was proving to be outstanding, Sharon asked Blaine, "Well, son, how's it going so far?"

"You guys are the greatest!" said Blaine. "I had no idea what Madagascar would be like. It was nothing near what I'd pictured it. I've learned a lot on this trip, and I really appreciate the time we're getting to spend together."

"You've really grown up on this trip, son," said Shell. "You surprised us with your maturity and the way you handled yourself. You didn't complain when things got a little tough and uncomfortable, even when the spring kept popping up through your mattress."

"What mattress?" asked Blaine. "We were in sleeping bags."

"Just seeing if you're paying attention, son."

"I just followed the example of you guys and especially, Mom, who didn't complain at all," added Blaine.

"That's true," said his father. "But we've done this several times. Now, your mother wasn't so gracious the first time she experienced the Big Red Island."

"All right, hold it right there, Mr. Gibbons," said Sharon. "That was the trip into hell, and I don't even want it mentioned."

"I was just making a comparison, dear, but you've been great on all subsequent trips." She gave him that "watch-yourself" stare, and he continued, "Truly, you have."

"I love you too, dear," she replied.

"By the way, what was the name of that animal that killed the lemur outside of base camp?" Shell asked.

"I believe it's called a foosa or fossa or something like that," answered Blaine.

"I believe I'm going to focus some study on that animal next trip," Shell said as he eyeballed the waiter approaching with their dinner.

"Oh, gross!" said Sharon. "You two have to bring up that subject just when the steak arrives, but I swear nothing, absolutely nothing will deter me from my appointed and chosen task."

"Well spoken," said Shell. "Let's eat!"

After dinner, they drove out to Route 41 and headed north toward the Best Western hotel. "My brother was right about that steakhouse, wasn't he?" asked Shell.

"It was excellent!" answered Sharon. "Watch the road!"

Shell was driving in the inside lane doing the speed limit of 45 miles per hour. He noticed the bridge up ahead but failed to see that the lane he was in exited before the bridge. Sharon saw it and warned him to get in the center lane. Shell quickly glanced in the rear and side view mirrors, and upon not seeing any danger, jerked the car into the outside lane. He didn't see the sports car rushing up on his blind side in the middle lane, heading over the bridge at breakneck speed. The two cars collided. Sharon screamed as their car skimmed the side of the concrete abutment divider and rolled over three times, slamming into the divider on the other side of the road and coming to a stop after sliding 50 feet in an upside-down position.

The sports car went head on into the abutment. The driver was sent through the windshield and hurled in the air for quite a distance. The sounds of crunching metal, broken glass and screams filled the previously normal quietness of a warm Florida evening.

Permeating the air was a combination of smoke, gas, oil, radiator fluid fumes and the stench of death. For a short while, the whole area became completely still. One of the witnesses in a following car recovered his senses long enough to dial 911 on his cell phone, still in a state of semi-shock. It seems it's always that way for a witness to a catastrophe. In spite of seeing what they know they've seen, believing comes hard.

The witness jumped out of his vehicle, but quickly found there was nothing he could do. Others joined him and they felt helpless as well. All involved in the accident were either unconscious or dead. The sports car had burst into flames, but was void of occupants. The bridge had then taken on the appearance of being freshly painted, in blood as it were. Within a few short minutes, the scene was filled with flashing lights and sirens reporting from all directions.

Darrell Demers, NREMT-P, the life support coordinator, was dispatched and en route to the accident scene. He is a rather large but sensitive guy whose presence would be intimidating to someone who didn't know him. His partner, Jamie Brennan, is somewhat opposite in stature and frame of mind. Nothing seems to bother him. On the way, they were told there were four victims: two obviously dead and two critical. Darrell called for one additional paramedic unit and then called Incident Command, usually the highest-ranking fire officer on the scene.

"Paramedic One to Incident Command," said Darrell.

"Yes, this is the I.C., Lt. Orozco."

"Where do you want us to set up?" asked Darrell.

"Come right onto the bridge, north side," said the I.C. "We have everything blocked off."

Jamie looked at Darrell and said, "It must be a bad one!"

When they arrived at the scene, Darrell was told where the victims were. He immediately assumed responsibility of triage officer and assigned his partner, Arthur "Jamie" Brennan the task of confirming both obvious deaths. He then assigned the other two paramedics of Unit Two the duty of evaluating the criticals.

Jamie approached Darrell first. Darrell looked at him questioningly, and Jamie gave his confirmation of death as follows, "I checked the carotid pulse of both victims and putting it mildly . . . they're screwed. Driver of car number one, patient—pardon me— victim number one, male, Caucasian. Injuries as follows: avulsed left ear, protruding left eye, facial deformities concentrated on left side. Left arm degloved from elbow to fingers. Chest badly bruised. Bilateral deformed lower leg fractures. No respiration, no pulse. Victim apparently traveled outside driver's window during the roll, then fell back inside of the vehicle.

"Victim number two, driver of car number two, sports car. Injuries as follows: male victim found approximately sixty feet from or forward of car number two. No obvious injuries except for light lacerations to the face and obviously deformed neck. Victim's chin completely over left shoulder. Skin very cold and pale. Use of seatbelt non-apparent. Victim apparently ejected through windshield on impact and fractured neck on making contact with the ground. That's it!"

"Thanks, Jamie," said Darrell. "Let's see what we can do over here."

When they arrived at the criticals, the other unit reported as follows: woman, Caucasian, approximately 40 years old, found just outside the vehicle. Unresponsive, gurgling respirations, weak, thready pulse, blood from mouth and nose. Severe right side chest bruising. Right side, sucking chest wound, skin very pale and cool. Blood pressure 88/42. Pulse 110. Respiration 24 shallow. Diagnosis: Right-sided hemo pnemo thorax, beginning to tension. Shock due to blood loss in chest.

"We've taken cervical spine precautions with collar. Maintained an airway with jaw thrust. We suctioned blood from airway and intubated with 7.5 endotracheal tube. Listened for bilateral breath sounds . . . no sounds on the right. Very hard to ventilate with ambo bag. Sealed sucking chest wound with bio-occlusive dressing. Started two 14g IV ringers . . . lactate wide open."

"Good work!" said Darrell. "Let's get her on a long board and into the ambulance. How's the boy?"

"We've designated him patient number two. The woman by the way is patient number one.

"Patient number two, injuries as follows: male, Caucasian approximately 14 years old, unresponsive. Large depressed skull fracture to right side of head. The only other injury is open tibia, fibia to right lower leg. BP 150/94, pulse 62, respiration 28, diagnosis: subdural hematoma with right lower leg extensive orthopedic injuries. We've taken cervical precautions, same as patient number one. Maintained airway with jaw thrust, intubated with 6.0 endo tube, ventilated with ambo bag. Positive bilateral, equal breath sounds, soft, non-bruised stomach, pelvis intact. Left leg okay. Straightened right leg. Marked pedal pulse and splintered with air splint. Two 16g IVs ringer lactate, one KVO, second wide open."

The whole report took less than a couple of minutes, and that as the woman was being loaded into the ambulance. "Okay, he's on a long board as well. Strap him down. Let's get them in!" shouted Darrell. "Keep the vitals monitored!"

Lee Memorial Hospital and Trauma Center was only minutes away, but as the ambulance was leaving, patient number one became very hard to ventilate. Jamie yelled out to Darrell, "There's bright red blood coming up the tube! BP is 50/20. Pulse 160. Patient's in ventricular fibrillation."

"Shock her!" shouted Darrell. They shocked her three times, started CPR and gave Epinephrine IV with Lidocaine IV. Darrell called into the trauma center,

"Paramedic Unit One en route with 40-year-old female patient who just converted to V-fib. CPR started. ACLS protocols will be followed." Nothing more could be done. She died just as they reached the trauma center.

The trauma center received the following call immediately after the first. "Paramedic Unit Two to Trauma Center. We are en route with male, approximately 14 years old. Unrestrained passenger in high-speed rollover. Patient unresponsive to all stimuli. Large depressed skull fracture, left side. Right pupil slow to react, left equal. No chest, abdomen or pelvic trauma. Only visible injury, open tibia, fibia to right lower leg. BP is 150/94, pulse 62, respiration 28."

They dropped the body of Sharon Gibbons at the hospital, and when they started out the door, the other ambulance was just pulling in with Blaine.

"How come you look so upset over this one?" asked Jamie of Darrell. "It usually takes a lot to rattle your cage."

"I was just thinking," said Darrell, "I wouldn't want to be the one to tell this kid both parents bought it. That's if he makes it himself. Right now it doesn't bode too well."

Jamie put his arm around Darrell's shoulder. "We did all we could do."

"Yeah, I know," said Darrell, "but I'm still going to need a stress debriefing after this one."

"Our shift is over in a half hour," said Jamie. "What say we get a couple of beers and leave this in God's hands?"

Darrell sighed deeply and said, "And to think I'm stuck with you as my brother-in-law as well. No wonder I'm stressed out! But I'm sure glad you're here."

CHAPTER SIX

The Morning After

Ed was back out tinkering with his boat when, all of a sudden, he got an upsetting feeling in his stomach. He just sensed something wasn't right. He called out, "Linda, has Shell called yet?"

"Give them a break, Ed. They had a long trip and they're exhausted. I wouldn't doubt they slept in. A big breakfast would be in order, as well," offered Linda.

"I guess you're right, as usual, but I feel a little uneasy this morning." Ed went back to his tinkering and Linda said she'd give him a yell when they called.

It was sometime after noon when Linda made her way out to the dock, and when Ed saw her, he asked, "Did they call?"

Linda just shook her head to the negative and said, "I'm getting a little concerned myself. Why don't you go in and call them?"

Ed called Best Western and asked for the Gibbons' room. "I'm sorry, sir. I can't seem to find any record of them ever checking in," said the clerk.

"This is the Best Western on southbound Route 41, North Fort Myers?" asked Ed.

"Yes, it is, sir," answered the clerk.

"Is it possible they could have checked into a different branch by mistake?"

The clerk checked the records again and then went to the computer. "We have another facility over on Business 41. Our computers are tied in. Let me check again." The clerk double-checked and still there wasn't any information on the Gibbons or any notice of cancellation. The clerk went back to the phone. "I'm sorry, sir, at no time were they registered as our guests."

"Thank you," said Ed and hung up.

He looked at Linda in bewilderment and said, "There's something screwy here . . . they never checked in."

"Call the state police!" said Linda. "They could've been in an accident!"

"But even if they were at the hospital, they'd call." Just as Ed felt the words leave his mouth, he got a godforsaken stab in the pit of his stomach. As he glanced at Linda, she mirrored his face of fear. Ed reached for the phone.

"Hello, state police, Sgt. Corts speaking."

"Sergeant," said Ed, "I'm Ed Gibbons of Englewood. I hate to sound panicky, but my brother and his family were due to check in at the Best Western in North Fort Myers last night and failed to do so. They were also supposed to call us this morning . . . no call. I hope you can understand my concern."

"Please hold, sir. I'll check the accident reports." A short time later the officer returned. "Did you say your name is Gibbons?"

"Yes, I did," said Ed apprehensively.

"Is your brother named Sheldon?"

"Yes, he is," replied Ed.

"May I have your address, sir?" asked the officer.

"What's the problem, Sergeant?"

"I'm sorry, sir. I'm unable to discuss this matter over the phone." To prevent any further time lost, Ed gave his address. "Thank you, sir. We'll have someone over to see you shortly," said the officer very politely, and then hung up.

Ed hung up thinking the worst, and Linda looked at him and asked, almost hysterically, "Speak to me . . . what is it?"

"I don't know," he mumbled. "They're sending someone over." They sat down next to each other in silence, held hands and waited.

Within 15 minutes, the doorbell rang and Ed answered. "Please come in." A plain-clothes lieutenant showed his badge and entered.

"Is your wife here with you?" he asked. Ed nodded affirmatively and led him into the living room. "Please sit down," the officer urged. Then continued, "There's no easy way for me to tell you this . . ."

Linda, realizing her worst fear was about to become a reality, sobbed out, "Oh . . . no."

Ed just clenched his teeth in fearful anticipation, waiting for the lieutenant to continue. The officer explained the whole accident in detail without becoming gross or offensive to the loved ones. Linda stared out the window in shock and disbelief.

Ed asked, "You say the boy is still alive?"

"As of this morning," the officer answered. "But he's still in a coma."

Ed put his arms around Linda. "I'm going to really need you this time. Stay strong."

As he looked back at the lieutenant, the officer said, "I'm going to need you for a positive identification at your earliest possible convenience. Give us a call when you're ready and we'll take you over."

"Of course," replied Ed and, thanking him, showed him out. He then turned to Linda and couldn't hold back the tears any longer. It was as if all the sadness of eternity entered his soul and he just slumped to the floor.

When tears were no longer available to either of them, Linda indeed became strong and helped Ed up to the couch. "We need to be at the hospital."

Ed looked at her and answered, "You're right. There is someone that needs us now. It wouldn't be good for someone else to have to tell him when he awakens."

They were silent all the way from Englewood to Lee Memorial Hospital in Fort Myers, holding hands and trying to cope, as reality continued to gain the upper hand. Never did reality pay a closer visit than when they entered the intensive care unit to see Blaine covered in bandages and tubes running out of just about every orifice. They went to his side, kissed and spoke to him. No response was forthcoming. They then stepped out of the room, spoke to the charge nurse and had the attending physician paged.

"Mr. and Mrs. Gibbons?" inquired the doctor. When they nodded, he reached out and took their hands in his. "I'm terribly sorry. There's no way or manner anyone can share your grief over the loss of your loved ones, but we'll do everything in our power to save the boy."

"How bad is the boy?" asked Linda.

"Well, right now," said the doctor, "there are no major decisions to make. Forgive me, I'm Doctor Ronald Tredge." He shook their hands and continued, "He has a fractured skull. There was massive swelling, and we had to ease the pressure on the brain. We're hoping when the swelling subsides, his comatose state will subside as well. I was the neurosurgeon called in to treat the boy.

"There's also extensive damage to the left leg. Dr. Gail Droney of orthopedics can bring you up to date on that condition, though I understand all went well. I believe she's on call this afternoon, if you'd care to speak to her.

"Where we are right now concerning the boy's condition is letting time and nature take their course. He'll be under constant monitoring and you'll be advised of any changes."

"So, there's really nothing we can do right now. How about visitation?" asked Linda.

"Anytime you wish," said the doctor, "twenty-four hours a day. Speak to him often. Though he may not respond, we find this helpful in many instances. Are there any other questions?"

"There's just one problem, Doctor, that's a slight hindrance. We live in Englewood, and it's quite a ride over here every day. We'd like to spend as much time with the boy as possible."

"Give us a few days, Mr. Gibbons, and when we're sure the patient is no longer critical, maybe it will be possible to move him to the Englewood Hospital. I make rounds there once a week. We'll also have to clear it with Dr. Droney. I don't foresee any problems. Do you have anyone in mind to administer treatment at that facility?"

"We hadn't even thought about that," answered Ed.

"You'll have ample time to decide. If I can be of service in any way, please feel free to call." The doctor once again offered his condolences and left.

Ed turned to Linda and said, "What do we do now about Shell and Sharon?"

"What do you mean?" asked Linda. "Do what?"

"Well, we have to make arrangements, make decisions . . ."

"The rest of the day," said Linda steadfastly, "we spend with Blaine. We hold his hands, we talk to him, and somehow he'll know he's not alone."

"You know," said Ed, "that doctor's okay. I could understand everything he was saying. He didn't try to baffle us with all that medical jargon." As he was speaking he was looking out the window into space, and Linda realized he wasn't with it. She was wondering if he actually heard what she said.

"Honey," she said, "are you all right?"

He just looked at her a little befogged and answered, "Oh . . . yes. We need to be with my nephew. I'll sit for a while. Do you have any gum?" Ed never chewed gum but Linda supplied him with a piece anyway, after removing the wrapper.

"Let's try to relax . . . we'll be okay," she said. He followed her to intensive care.

They sat with Blaine until 10 o'clock that evening, and Linda had many of her questions answered by the attending medical personnel. She began to feel a lot more comfortable with the treatment that was being administered. She was definitely concerned about the prognosis for the leg injury. Dr. Droney said he would need rehabilitation for some time, and still there would be a chance he would entertain a slight limp. If he didn't come out of this coma, what difference would it all make? She rolled all these questions around in her head, offering herself all the possible solutions until she caught herself daydreaming about how things used to be.

"This isn't helping anyone. Let's go home and get some rest. We'll handle things one at a time . . . one day at a time, starting tomorrow."

"You're right, honey. Let's head home."

The shortest way home to Englewood was Route 41 north and that would bring them right through the accident scene. Ed went straight across 41 and headed out to Route 75 north. Linda glanced over at him, as if to ask what he was doing, and then just bowed her head in full understanding.

At breakfast the next morning, Ed said, "I'm really not looking forward to this, and I don't want you to come with me. I'll be okay."

"If I had to identify someone close tomorrow, I'd want you with me," said Linda.

"This isn't tomorrow . . . it's today and besides, I want you to remember them the way you last saw them. That'll be a comfort to me."

When Ed returned, he was very silent, and Linda waited until he felt the need to converse.

"That was the toughest thing I ever had to do," he said. "I had triplicates made of the death certificates. I think the first thing I need to do is contact their lawyer and read the wills to see what their specifications are for burial, if any. Plus Blaine's . . . er . . . condition . . . er . . . makes it hard for any kind of decisions. We don't know how long he'll be in that damn coma."

"We know the lawyer well and much can be accomplished over the phone and by fax," Linda offered. "And remember, think twice, act once. That's what you always advise me." He gave her a gentle pat on the behind and shook his head in agreement. They headed out for the hospital.

Over the next few days, they consulted with doctors, clergy, lawyers, friends and undertakers. They decided to have Shell and Sharon buried up north, per their wishes and not hold a memorial service until Blaine was well enough to travel. All agreed that when Blaine surfaced from the coma, he'd have enough to contend with without having to go through burial services as well. The last part of the plan was to bring Blaine to Peabody, Massachusetts for the memorial service and allow him to "lay the ghosts," as it were. A very tough thing for a boy of any age to be pressed into.

Blaine was in the 32nd day of the coma when one of the aides heard him speak. She ran for the nurse who immediately notified the doctor and family. She then came to his bedside. "Young man, you've been giving us quite a scare. You've been asleep a long time."

"Could I have a glass of water, ma'am?" he asked. As the nurse was pouring the water, he spoke up again, "What happened to me anyway?"

The nurse informed him, "You were in a bad accident. The doctor will explain when he arrives."

"That's strange," he said, "I don't remember any accident." The nurse asked if there was anything else he required, and he said he was fine.

When Ed and Linda arrived at the door of the room, the doctor was waiting for them. "I felt it best if we all went in together," he said. Ed disagreed. He thought it would be wise if they had a few moments alone with him first.

They entered and in an upbeat tone, Ed said, "Hey, young man!"

"Uncle Ed, Aunt Linda, what are you doing here?" Blaine asked.

Linda responded, "You're in the Englewood, Florida Memorial Hospital. It just makes sense that we're here. We live just down the street a mile or so."

"Englewood, wow. But where's Mom and Dad?"

Ed was about to answer when the doctor entered the room. Ed looked at the doctor with the expression that said, "I'm ready to tell him."

"Let me check you over for a minute, my young friend," said the doctor.

When he was through, he stepped back, and Ed, glancing over at Linda, sadly said, "You've been in a bad accident. You were hurt badly and your parents . . ." He hesitated looking back at the doctor and Linda.

"What about my parents?" Blaine shot back, almost sensing the answer.

The doctor spoke, "They didn't make it, son."

Blaine stared back at him in shock. "You mean they're dead?" Blaine shifted his gaze to Linda, to Ed and then back to the doctor.

"That can't be . . . tell me it's not true, Aunt Linda!" She came to his side to comfort him, and he buried his head in the pillow and shouted, "No! No! No! This isn't real. This isn't happening!" He pushed his head deeper into the pillow and wept bitterly and loud. All those at the nurses' station out in the corridor cried as well.

Much time passed and the physical healing was well on its way, but the mental, emotional and spiritual wounds went much deeper, making full recovery a long road ahead. It was months before Blaine was up to handling the stress of a memorial service. But he did it and Ed and Linda were very proud of him.

The service was held in Peabody, Massachusetts at the South Congregational Church, presided over by the Reverend Richard Farnum. The pastor's wife and Linda were good friends. Tina was also a friend of Sharon. Their friendship and assistance through the whole ordeal was invaluable. There was a huge turnout of friends at the service. Just about everybody connected with the teachers' association was there. This, most certainly, helped the family to cope with grief.

Property matters were settled and a trust fund was set up for Blaine. Then it was off to Englewood, Florida where, hopefully, a new life would be established.

CHAPTER SEVEN

Modamanjari Rainforest

Southwestern Madagascar
June 1997

Chester Whalton, accompanied by his guide and assistant, Randrian, was screening an unfamiliar section of the Modamanjari rainforest in search of a newly reported lemur family.

The indri lemur is an apelike creature that prefers to live most of its life in an arboreal setting in Madagascar's shrinking forested environment. It makes a sound like a low note of a trumpet quite loudly and echoed by the rest of the family in slightly different tones when sensing danger or intrusion. To a real nature lover such as Chester Whalton, the sounds are like music played with symphonic gusto.

Chester or Chett, as he prefers to be called, is an ecologist/biologist assigned to the research center of environmental studies sponsored by World Conservational Trust and World-Trek International. For many years he and his wife Pamela Chase were volunteers involved in almost every phase of conservation, from the study of tortoises and birds to their present full-time employment of tracking and cataloging various types of lemurs.

Their present project involving the indri population brought them into areas of the forests they had not encountered before.

"I don't understand this," said Chett to his guide, "this family was never seen in this section of the forest before, at least it had never been reported 'til now. I suppose the poaching and encroachment by man is causing them to move around more."

He no sooner finished speaking when they heard a loud scuffle. They rounded the bend and in a small clearing lay the shredded remains of an adult lemur almost made unidentifiable by the blood-soaked splatter of viscera and other parts of the victimized animal. Some fur was still floating in the air, a sign they had obviously scared off the perpetrator with their arrival.

"What in God's name could have accomplished something like this? What's that unholy odor?" exclaimed the biologist.

Randi, as he was called by friends, spoke one word, "Foosa!"

"Foosa . . . what's a foosa?" Chett waited impatiently for the answer.

Randi sat down and calmly tried to impart to his boss all of his limited knowledge on the subject of the mysterious carnivore.

"My grandfather once spoke of an animal with a strange taste for blood that would terrify the villages, especially at night. The livestock was always guarded and the children were forbidden to leave their homes after dark. We, as children, were also cautioned. It is said this animal could choke off one's breath with the odor of its anal glands."

With that remark Chett began to laugh but Randi cut him short and said, "No . . . no . . . 'tis true. We were made to promise never to go in the forest or we could become like one."

"That sounds like a lot of superstition to me," said Chett, "how come I, or Pam for that matter, have never seen one and we've been researching these forests in Madagascar for years?"

"They are very secretive and seldom seen in the daytime. Some say the giant ones have retreated into the forbidden forest, the area known as the Jangala Reservation," whispered Randi

"Giant ones? How big do these things get?" asked Chett.

Randi answered again in a whisper, "No one knows for sure. The ones that are in these forests are about the size of the lemurs they chase. They are vicious but I know of not one soul who has been attacked." When he finished speaking his eyes scanned the perimeter of the clearing very carefully.

"Have you ever seen one?" asked Chett.

Randi nodded and answered, "Yes, but only a glimpse. You see, foosa is as fleet in the trees as he is on the ground."

Chett looked at Randi straight in the eyes, trying to fathom the whole tale, and murmured in a loud whisper, "It's arboreal as well. What sort of animal could this be?" Then in a normal tone of voice he asked, "How do you know it was a foosa you saw if you only had a glimpse?"

"There is nothing else like it in these woods. When you see one you will know and never forget. Your nose will always remember." Randi looked around again after he spoke.

"So the awful odor that's lingering here now is the foosa?" asked Chett.

"It can be much worse if you are near when it is upset. That is the rumor."

Chett was filled with questions that couldn't be answered on the spot. Pam was on sick-leave tending to her sick mother in the States and he would be following shortly. He knew he had a lot of research to do to check out Randi's tales. Not that he didn't trust his guide and friend, but knew the Malagasies could get caught up in their superstitions.

Upon his return to the States he discussed the happenings with Pam and mentioned his desire of researching this creature. She had never heard of the animal either but she did read an article about a

Professor Lansing that was associated with World-Trek International. He had accumulated the funding for a carnivore research project in Madagascar. He was presently recruiting people for staff positions and volunteer service.

Chett went to the library and found that information on this beast was hard to come by. He did discover that the scientific name was *Cryptoprocta ferox*, better known as the fossa. Apparently it was first discovered and named by someone in the 1800s. They described it as being a mixture of cat and ferret. Then he thought to himself, "Why does Randi call it a foosa?"

He read old journals that spoke of a blood-thirsty weasel-like animal that could feed on oxen. Then one phrase he read jumped off the page: *To be dreaded when at large.* "What exactly did they mean by that? Does this thing really come into the villages?" He was becoming very infatuated with the idea of directing his research toward this strange carnivore.

Upon returning home his wife handed him the article describing the project of Doctor Lansing. He didn't waste any time making the call and was able to secure an interview. He confided to the professor his lack of knowledge concerning the fossa. Lansing was quite taken by this eager young man and very impressed with his honesty, qualifications and knowledge of Madagascar's interior.

"You're married, you say?" asked the doctor. Chett just nodded and added, "Yes, but my wife works in the field as well. We're both employed by World-Trek."

"So am I," replied Lansing, "and the problem I'm having as director of this project is time. There's never enough of it. Now if I had someone to act in my behalf at the research station who would report to me at regular intervals . . ."

Chett spoke right up, "Sir, I'm your man!"

"That's a coincidence," said Lansing, "I was thinking the same thing. You see, Chett, I'm hoping to create a program that will give us greater insight into the fossa as well as the other Madagascan carnivores. We need to know more of their habits, peculiarities and interactions with other animals and their environment. In view of the massive deforestation occurring now, we'll need to know what we can do to help conserve them. Do you have any other questions about the project and its goals?"

Chett thought for a moment and asked, "Will I be working out of the same station that I'm assigned to now? Lansing answered in the affirmative and Chett asked for one more favor, which was to retain the same assistant and guide. "Your call. You're now in charge," answered the professor.

As Chett was leaving the building he noticed an election poster, which read in part, COUNCILLOR-AT-LARGE. The words "at large" stood out and rang a bell in his head and he recalled that part of the old journal that stated, "when at large," speaking of the fossa. "This should be quite an exciting adventure," he thought.

CHAPTER EIGHT

Road to Maturity

Englewood, Florida

Blaine's recovery was swift, and though rehabilitation went well, it still left him with a slight limp, which for all intents and purposes, did not restrict his physical activities.

His Uncle Ed taught him everything he knew about seamanship and boat handling, and he was an avid pupil. He loved the sea. Linda taught him gentleness and courtesy, and though she knew it wasn't the same as his real mother could give, she offered her constant love and understanding.

Considering all that he had been through, Blaine was comfortable and happy. His second love was playing baseball and he excelled. In his fourth year at Lemon Bay High School, as their star pitcher, he was offered a scholarship to play for the Gators at the University of Florida in Gainesville.

Ed and Linda were very proud of him, but he wasn't sure it was what he wanted. He wanted most to be at sea. Ed and Linda tried to persuade him to take the scholarship and pursue his ambition by becoming a marine biologist. Ed said, "Even if it's not all you want, at least you can go in the Navy as an officer and not a swab-jockey like I was."

Then Linda spoke up, "You know if your parents were here, they'd want you to go after that degree."

"Yes, I know," answered Blaine. "But look at what my father did. He got his degree after the service. He became a Marine first."

"All we can do is counsel you," said Ed. "You have to make the choice."

Blaine decided to speak with the Navy recruiter, feel him out and see what kind of a deal he could make. Blaine wanted sea duty. They told him they had four years of it waiting for him. They were looking for men like him. He felt seven feet tall and bulletproof.

All went well until the day of the physical. This is where they check your body from stem to stern to be sure you're strong enough to serve in their beloved Navy. Blaine was turned down. He was informed that he couldn't be accepted due to the disposition of his leg. He was classified as handicapped.

Blaine was not only disappointed, he was furious. He paid a visit to the recruiter and wrote a stiff letter to the Department of the Navy. The recruiter gave all the help he could but to no avail. That was that. Linda told him that maybe it was a blessing in disguise. Everything happens for a purpose. It just didn't take away the sting of being called handicapped.

He had kept in constant contact with the captain in Madagascar and his daughter, Sirana. From the first day they had heard of the accident, their prayers went out for his recovery and for peace for the deceased. They were very taken by the Gibbons on their visit to Mahajanga and saddened beyond words by the news of their demise. Many times they invited Blaine to visit, but he just couldn't bring himself to go. There were too many memories. They understood. Blaine told them of the rejection by the Navy and how it crushed him. Rijah, the captain of the *Tolura*, then reminded him of what he'd said when they last spoke in person, "Stay with your dreams. Let nothing deter you and they'll come true."

It was time to pursue a different avenue. He accepted the scholarship. The catch was he had to play ball, which called for many practice hours on the ball field. Home games plus the travel to the away games didn't leave a lot of time for sleep, at least not if you were planning to add in some heavy studying. A degree in marine biology doesn't come without hard work and dedication. There are many hours of field research besides, and though Blaine was physically up to the challenge, mentally he was wearing thin.

His third year at the college was coming to a close and he felt the need to spread his wings, as it were. He wasn't sure where he wanted to fly to, but it was a definite fact that he needed a change and a break from the grueling regimen he had set for himself. He had always managed to get out with the boys for a few beers and also dated occasionally. He was by no means a prude. His dates were usually with Judy Timmor, who had a crush on him since they were freshmen.

He was very fond of Judy, but she seemed to be getting just a little too serious and he was feeling pressured to make a commitment he wasn't ready to think about as yet. Beer with the boys was less demanding, though not as satisfying.

His three buddies, Bill, Earl and Larry, had been with him since registration in his freshman year. Many times when the going was rough, they'd find some humorous way to cheer one another up, either with a joke or some foolish prank. One time, when Blaine felt like beating his head against a wall, Earl thought of a joke about getting beat on the head.

"One time I was stopped for speeding by a state trooper down in Alabama. At least I thought it was for speeding until I pulled over, and he asked why I went through the stop sign without coming to a full stop. I explained that I sort of eased up, and then continued on. He reprimanded me and said easing up is not the same as coming to a full stop. I continued to disagree with him until he finally pulled out his club and commenced to rap me on the head with it. 'What are you doing?' I exclaimed. He answered, 'Do you want me to stop or do you want me to ease up?'"

Here it was May 2003. The four of them were of like mind, which wouldn't shock most people, and all felt the need to bury the books and do something of a different nature, far away from school and duties.

"So what are you guys doing for the summer?" Bill asked the other three.

Blaine just shrugged, "I don't know," for he had no other plans besides boating, fishing, swimming and just plain taking it easy with his aunt and uncle in Englewood. He missed them anyway. Ed was pushing 65, and Blaine would help out around the house and dock . . . a dab of paint here and some caulking there. Though Ed was no slouch, he still appreciated the help.

Blaine used to talk so much about Lemon Bay that one previous summer the three buddies came down for a two-week vacation. After they got through raising hell on Lemon Bay and nearly tearing up Manasota Key, the local authorities and Ed convinced them it would be in the best interest of all to cut their vacation short. So after three days, they bid everyone farewell and left.

So it just followed that when Blaine mentioned Lemon Bay this year, they all looked in his direction. "No way in hell!"

"Aw c'mon Blaine," they all said in unison, and Larry kicked in with, "Where is your sense of humor?"

Blaine answered, "Buried somewhere in Englewood Beach where they took us all into protective custody. You fellas do remember that little stint, don't you?"

Bill added, "Those cops don't have a sense of humor, either." Getting serious, Bill continued, "All kidding aside guys, I do have a place to go this summer. Jill and I just became engaged, and I'm flying out to Utah to meet her folks and spend some time there."

"Good for you, Bill," said Larry. "You notice, I said it was good for you. It surely would not be good for me!" He laughed.

They all offered their congratulations and then Larry spoke up again, "I also have a place to go this summer. You all know my older brother, Paul, hasn't been doing very well physically, so I'll be in Long Beach, California trying to help out wherever I can, but I'm sure I'll still get a few hours on the beach for sightseeing and the like."

Earl was the only one who hadn't said much. He was saving his vacation plan telling 'til last. Now the attention of the other three turned to him, and he just blurted out, "I'm going on an expedition to South America."

Blaine became very curious and asked, "Expedition? To where?"

"Far up the Amazon," Earl answered. "I signed up for an archeological trek to Brazil for field research. Get this, there have been recent sightings of large hairy hominids far up the river. I'm excited as hell!"

"Right," Bill joked. "Don't you know those rumors were started by cannibals, making plans for next month's menu?"

Everyone found that remark humorous, except Earl. "No, seriously, guys, the deforestation that's taking place throughout the whole world is forcing many species of wildlife to migrate. There are some animals believed to be extinct and making their presence known. Check out the Net. There are a lot of strange sightings taking place."

"So, where did you find out about this expedition?" Blaine asked.

"On the Net!" replied Earl. "World-Trek International has trips going all over the place."

"That would definitely be something different to do this summer!" exclaimed Blaine.

Larry added, "I checked into that stuff last year. Some of those treks are only for short durations of two to three weeks. They don't carry you through the whole summer and, in most cases, you pay your own expenses."

"That's a bummer," said Blaine. "You're doing them a favor and end up paying for the privilege."

"Well, I guess the view they're taking is that you're only paying for school in the field, and it's usually just airfare anyway," offered Earl. "You bring a sleeping bag and some clothes, and they supply the food, and in some cases, a cot and tent. Running water is iffy."

"In any event, I think I'll jump on the computer in the morning and see what I discover, if anything," said Blaine, while popping open the last beer.

The next morning, Blaine tapped into the Net, and scanning through "Select an Expedition," saw there was one entitled "Tracking Carnivores with Chester Whalton."

This really caught his eye, for the base camp for this expedition was located at Batrambady Research Station, where he was with his parents seven years ago. They were directing their research to the *Cryptoprocta ferox*. "Fossa!" said Blaine excitedly. "My God, this brings back memories with a rush."

Blaine started talking to himself nervously, trying to make excuses not to go. But what a perfect situation, he thought, to face the fears of the past and to visit the captain and his family. "All I have to do now is sell my idea to Uncle Ed and Aunt Linda," thought Blaine. "I know they wanted to spend the time with me. They'll understand . . . so I'll download the particulars and lay it all out for them."

The following weekend, Blaine was in Englewood and off for the summer. "Hi guys!" Blaine shouted as he opened the door to the house.

"Blaine!" said Ed excitedly. "Good to see you home and safe. The boat's ready and waiting. Use it anytime you wish."

As Linda was giving Blaine a hug, he spoke over her shoulder to Ed, "Thanks Uncle Ed, but I may not be using it much this summer, and you, Aunt Linda seem to get younger and more beautiful every time I see you."

"Whoa! Young man," said Ed. "Run that by us again. You're not going to be using the boat? Is the world supposed to end tomorrow? What's this all about?"

"And yes, young man," added Linda, "why all the flattery?"

"Well," answered Blaine, "it's like this. I decided to do some field research, at least for a few weeks."

Linda released her hug and moved him to arm's length and asked, "Field research where?"

"Madagascar!" he replied. "It's expensive and I'll need to know how my trust fund is holding out. Will I have any problem meeting next year's tuition if I blow, say $5,000 on this expedition?"

"There's no money problem," answered Ed. "Now let's get back to this trip or expedition, as you so aptly put it. When did you come up with this idea?"

"Oh, I was chewing the fat with the guys, you know Bill, Larry and Earl," replied Blaine.

Ed interjected, rolling his eyes back in his head, "Now there's three of a kind that could beat any full house!"

"Be kind, Ed," said Linda.

"Be kind," Blaine continued. "Anyway, Bill is getting married, I mean engaged, and going to Utah. Larry's visiting with his sick brother in L.A., and Earl is going on an expedition up the Amazon. Actually, he's the one that steered me to the website that posts the field trips. I don't know if I ever mentioned this, but my father was talking about getting involved in this study just before the accident, when we were in the restaurant." Blaine related all that had transpired at the campsite in Madagascar, back in July, 1996, as best as he could remember and expounded on what they had learned of the fossa from the locals.

"So you see, it's imperative I go for two reasons. It's the last place we were all happy together, and I may have a chance after the research time to get some experience on a real working fishing boat with Captain Rijah."

"Have you made any definite plans yet?" asked Linda.

"I was waiting to hear what you guys thought first," replied Blaine.

"We can't stop you from growing or making adult decisions," said Ed. "I was in the Navy at 17. If you feel this is what you want to do, go for it!"

"I agree!" added Linda. "It's just that you've never been away from us except for school."

"I promise I'll be careful and I'll write. It's approximately a 19-hour, 9,200-mile trip, not counting possible layovers, to Antananarivo, the capital. Then a short hop to Mahajanga, where I'll call you. Then a 60-70 mile jaunt by beat-up van to the research station."

"Sounds like fun," quipped Ed. "How long will you be gone?"

"The fossa research is only for 12 days, and then I hope to spend a few weeks in Mahajanga, if the Andrianaivo family will have me. I need to touch base with them before I make any definite plans."

Blaine laid the downloaded brochures on the kitchen table and went to the computer to set up the trip and e-mail the captain. The reply was returned quickly stating that he was welcome for as long as he cared to stay. So he went to the World-Trek online booking center and became a member of team #2. The team size was limited to 14, and he had registered as number 11. His project dates were from June 24th to July 6th, and members' share cost was $2,895.

While he was on the computer, Linda was scanning the project brochures and spotted this sentence underlined, "the fossa (*Cryptoprocta ferox*) is one of the most ferocious predators that walks the earth." She panicked, but Blaine assured her not one of them had been implicated in a human death, as far as anyone knew.

For the next two and one half weeks, he and his aunt and uncle spent many quality hours together. They all knew too well how quickly happiness can end, and so they made the best of it, caring and sharing, one day at a time. The time went by quickly and the day of Blaine's departure arrived.

Blaine made a loving and explanatory call to his distant girlfriend, Judy, who also was disappointed he wouldn't be spending any appreciable time with her in July as planned.

When he hung up, Ed came over to him and whispered, "Your aunt's worried already, so be sure you keep us posted on your progress and send some postcards."

"I'll call you from the rendezvous site, and after that I'll be in the bush where communication is a premium," said Blaine. "So it may be a couple of weeks between phone calls."

After some teary goodbyes and a couple of hugs, it was off to Madagascar!

CHAPTER NINE

Rendezvous

La Piscine Hotel
Mahajanga, Madagascar

The team of 14 college students was milling around in the lobby of the hotel, waiting for the orientation by Chester Whalton's right-hand man, the Malagasy guide Randi. With only a short night's sleep, Blaine couldn't understand how everyone else seemed to have so much energy after so long a trip. After all, they didn't arrive from the airport until after 10:30 P.M.

Blaine turned to one of the others and said, "I'm dragging!"

"So am I!" said the coed. "I think some of the others arrived day before yesterday."

"Well," said Blaine, "that would account for all the piss and vinegar."

"All the what?" asked the coed.

"Oh, I'm sorry for the use of that vernacular. Marine Corps language seems to rub off on you after so many years. It means full of energy," answered Blaine.

"You were in the service?" asked the coed.

"No, my father was but never used that sort of term in mixed company. He was a schoolteacher, you see."

"Why do you say that in the past tense?" she asked.

Just as Blaine was about to answer, Randi spoke up loudly to get the group's attention, then began the orientation.

Blaine whispered, "Talk to you later."

The guide gave a brief explanation of things needed and not needed. Then made sure everyone had sleeping bags and answered all pertinent questions. It's a distance of 106 kilometers or 70 miles to the research station. Amazingly, the whole group, after being separated between two rusty vans, was loaded without a hitch and was on its way.

Even after seven years, Blaine thought the road looked familiar. "I remember Dad hated this drive up to the camp. He always said that Madagascar had the nicest people and lousiest roads in the world. Anyway, I hope this Chester Whalton is someone you can speak with and not just a reclusive order giver. I really want to learn something on this trip," Blaine thought to himself.

"Where are you at?" said the person sitting next to him.

"Oh, hi," replied Blaine, somewhat startled. "Just daydreaming, I guess." He held out his hand and introduced himself.

"Bob," said the other, "Virginia Tech. So what brings you here?"

"Recapturing some memories and hopefully creating some new ones."

"You've been here before?" asked Bob.

Blaine just nodded and said, "With my parents, observing lemurs, about seven years ago."

"Do your parents come here often?" asked Bob.

"They're both dead now." As Blaine said the words, a deep sense of emptiness crept inside of him.

"I'm really sorry," said Bob. Both were silent the rest of the way.

Pamela Chase greeted everyone as they disembarked from the vans and thanked them all for coming. "She seems very personable," thought Blaine. "I wonder where this Chester Whalton is. I expected him to meet us. He's got some very good credentials and I should be able to learn quite a bit while I'm here."

He glanced around the area and found that little had changed since his last visit except now they had running water. "That's a big plus in this place. I wonder if they serve the same food."

Just as that thought cleared his mind Chester appeared and shook hands with all and introduced himself as Pamela's "better half," or "Chett," as he preferred to be called. They appeared to be both in their early thirties to Blaine and in a way they reminded him of his late parents. They seemed to be really enjoying each other and their work.

Chett spoke: "Once again, I want to welcome you all here and maybe, for the present time, satisfy your inquisitive natures. First of all, my wife heads up the program on lemurs and will not be working closely with us but she'll be available for any questions you may have on the other fauna. I have the carnivores. Many of you may not know what a fossa is, but I assure you by the time you leave here . . . well, you'll be sure of its existence. Please pay heed to our warnings, especially when venturing into the bush. There are dangers. All of our guides speak English as well as French and Malagache. If you have any questions at all, please don't hesitate to ask. There's no such thing as a dumb question out here. I'll do my best to impart to you all I've learned in my research and hopefully you'll retain some of it. You'll be assigned tent sites for your entire stay, and meals are at the same time every day as per schedule."

One of the students asked, "Do we get any free time?"

"Of course," answered Chett, "you'll have regular breaks throughout the day and evening assignments are voluntary, otherwise, free time. Are there any other questions?"

"When do we eat?" asked a portly youth.

"Lunch will be in one hour and then we'll assign teams. Right now, you'll be assigned tent sites where you can settle in. See you at lunch!"

They all got settled in, found out where the restrooms were and where to wash. Then, after a lunch of fresh fruit and lasopy with crackers and rice, they gathered together at the tables where they shared names, schools and/or occupations and hometowns in a round table fashion. This helped them all to relax, and the introduction of the camp mascot, a common brown lemur named Fifi, added a little pleasure to the relaxation.

"Petting this animal makes me feel so comfortable," said Sarah, the coed from Utah State. She was the one that spoke with Blaine at the hotel.

After introductions, Blaine found a way to maneuver himself to a position next to her. "I know," he said. "It always seemed to have that same effect on me, as well."

"You've petted one of these before?" she asked.

"Seven years ago, only then the mascot's name was Sheena." Sarah looked at him questioningly. So he continued, "I was here with my parents who were volunteers for lemur research. They were both ecologists and biology teachers who had me along, hoping to influence me into joining in their endeavors."

"And did they influence you?" she asked.

"Well, somewhat," he responded. "Here I am doing fieldwork in Madagascar, when actually, I'm in my fourth year majoring in marine biology."

"Aren't you kind of far from the ocean?" she queried.

Then he explained his father's last visit here, and how curious he had become of the fossa and why. "So, I thought I'd check out this animal, strictly out of curiosity mind you, and sort of lay the ghosts to rest."

"That's taking a lot of courage, I imagine," said Sarah. "And I admire you for that. I hope it all turns out well."

"Thanks," said Blaine and with enthusiasm, asked, "When do I hear your story?"

"Later," she whispered quite sexily and then left to mingle.

Everyone sort of milled around, getting to know each other, and by late afternoon, all were schooled in the use of radio transmitters and other pertinent paraphernalia dealing with the project. Assignments were given out for the next day, and the rest of the afternoon was free time.

Blaine wanted to get a few words in with Chett, and the opportunity arose when they were both reaching for a soda at the same time. "Hi, I'm Blaine Gibbons."

"How do you do? I'm Chett. There's some colder ones in that other chest."

"You mind if I ask you a couple of questions?" asked Blaine.

"Shoot!" said Chett.

"I was here seven years ago, researching lemurs with my parents, and on the last night we were here, there was a bit of excitement. A lemur was killed right outside base camp and my father was first on the scene. He said he couldn't believe the carnage. The guide kept repeating, 'Foosa, foosa,' and there was a terrible odor in the area. Could this have been what we're here to conserve now?"

"Sounds about right," he answered. "Did you see the kill site?"

"No. My father helped squash the panic and had my mother and I return to our tents. The next morning the only topic of conversation was fossa, but it seemed the Malagasy guide was the only one with any information on the subject. Only one of the conservationists had ever seen one or for that matter ever heard of one. One of my father's last comments was that he would do some research on this animal next trip. It was never to be. He and Mother were killed in an accident soon after we left here. Anyway, it's been on my mind for a long time, and when I saw your page on the Internet, I decided to come. I want to learn all I can about this animal."

"You're in the right place," said Chett. "The best spot in the world to learn, actually, the only place where they exist that we know of."

"Off the record, Chett, what are they really like?"

Without hesitation Chett spoke right up, "Fossa is a quick and efficient killer. It's equipped to take on anything it encounters and moves up and down trees as quickly as it does on the ground. It's tenacious and will eat anything, anytime."

"And humans?" asked Blaine.

"None on record," replied the leader, "but its great-granddaddy would've been capable."

"Would you expound on that a little?" asked Blaine with great curiosity.

"Let me see how to put this. The animal we're all researching right now is the *Cryptoprocta ferox*. It weighs about 20 pounds, is about three feet in length with a tail of the same size, probably accounting for its great agility in the trees. Great-grandpa, *Cryptoprocta giganta*, would probably have weighed in at over 250 pounds, more than six feet long and with a six-foot tail. It would have enormous strength and its ferocity would be unmatched. Some Malagasies believe they still exist in seclusion."

"Not around here, I hope," said Blaine.

"Over on the northeastern coast there's a place nicknamed the 'forbidden forest.' The Jangala Reservation is what it's called and the alias is quite apropos. It's so unfriendly to man that a detailed map of the interior has never been made. I was there once!" Chett said with obsession in his eyes. "The forest in that area is very dense . . . twice as bad as here. We didn't get very far. My malaria started acting up so we packed it in and headed back. Cutting through that bush was almost an insurmountable task. We never saw so much as a track that bore any resemblance to a fossa."

"Then you also must believe they exist," stated Blaine.

"I didn't see any sign of one, but in that tangled forest, tracking is near impossible. There's a shortage of footpaths to follow. It's like the land that time forgot. Boy, you really got me on a roll. Forgive me."

Blaine was just staring at Chett with mouth agape and finally muttered, "Why do you keep coming back here?"

Chett responded by saying," Hopefully by the time you leave here, you'll understand. Get some rest. I'll see you in the morning."

CHAPTER TEN

The Beginning

Jangala Reservation
Tomboiana Province
June 25, 2003

During the months of February, March and April, northeast Madagascar was hit by two major cyclones, a tropical storm and heavy rains, causing wide scale flooding.

On February 17th, Cyclone Eline ravaged the area with winds up to 125 miles per hour. About 100 villages were flooded and isolated.

March 2nd saw Tropical Storm Gloria dump 11 inches of rain, driven by 70 mile per hour winds, causing river flooding and extensive road damage, as well as the loss of human life. A large toll was taken on animal life also.

On April 2nd, Cyclone Hudah, one of the most powerful in years, struck with a force of 190 miles per hour. The violent winds and strong rains that accompanied these storms had very destructive effects on the forests. Trees were uprooted and the heavy rains caused erosion of the hilly areas, creating landslides.

Tomboiana Province lies at the foot of the forest cliff, between the highlands and the Indian Ocean. This area, with its tropical climate, is home to unique flora and fauna. Following the devastation by the storms, strange phenomena have been noted, including unusual migration of endemic animal species. On June 25, near the village of Ariandiro, located on the edge of the Jangala Reservation, an eerie occurrence is being investigated:

"What is all this commotion?" asked the local gendarme.

One of the villagers spoke up. "An ox has been slaughtered!"

"That is not an unusual occurrence in these parts," offered the gendarme. He then inquired, "Who is this man?"

"He is the owner of the ox," answered the villager. The officer was looking over his eyeglasses and peering at an elderly gentleman who was staring into space and mumbling in low monotones, apparently in a state of shock.

The bystander continued to speak, "He came stumbling into the village a little while ago, and with a rather raspy voice, kept repeating something that sounded like foosa, but I can't be sure. Then he pointed to the edge of town."

"You people and your superstitions," bellowed the officer. "Foosa is an old wives tale. Where is this dead ox?"

"It has not been my desire to see it, but I am told it can be located on the west side of the village," said another. The officer told one of his subordinates to accompany the old man to his office and hold him for further questioning, and then he started up the trail.

About three quarters of a mile outside the village, just around a bend in the road, he came to an abrupt halt and started to gag. The gendarme had all he could do to keep from barfing. He had never seen such carnage. Blood was splattered on the ground, in the bushes and as far up as eight feet onto one of the trees. There were body parts strewn all around, and he could barely make out the form of what was once, apparently, an ox. The cart it was pulling was knocked onto its side and laid in a ditch.

"Mon Dieu! This can't be true. There is neither man nor animal around here capable of performing such a deed." He turned and ran back to the village in an attempt to question the old man, but after 30 minutes, he still hadn't received a response.

"I'm going to lie this in the hands of Inspector Areben," said Gendarme Ratsira. "Get him on the line for me!" he ordered his subordinate.

The inspector listened intently to the tale of the gendarme, for they have been friends for many years. "Mon ami! Are you losing the grip on yourself? Why do we have all this panic over a dead ox?"

The gendarme, in defense of his pride, answered, "René, I have been a policeman for many years and never have I seen a thing such as this!"

"Seen? Are you saying you witnessed the kill?" asked the inspector.

"No, I haven't, but obviously the old man saw something that put him in shock! It was his ox! The cart was turned over and the ox butchered."

The inspector again queried, "So are you saying you suspect a gang of some sort?"

There was silence for a moment and then the gendarme spoke softly and said, "I believe it was an animal. The villagers are saying it was foosa."

"Bah!" retorted René. "That's a fairy tale told to children!"

"All I'm saying," said Ratsira "is that something overpowering drove that old man to madness."

"Isn't it possible," offered René, "that he was hit on the head by someone and wandered around for hours before he stumbled into the village? God only knows how many other animals may have fed on the carcass. Now be reasonable, my friend, those people don't need to have their imaginations and superstitions all stirred to a frenzy. Calm them down and calm yourself. I'll be there soon. I want to see this for myself."

"Thank you, Inspector, I am not worthy of your trouble," said the gendarme. "I'll await your arrival."

When the inspector arrived a few hours later, people were still milling around on the street in front of the gendarmerie. "I thought I asked you to calm these people down, Ratsira?" said René.

"I tried," answered the gendarme, "but there is so much fear, they are afraid to travel outside the village."

"Take me to the kill site!" commanded the inspector.

On the way up the trail, Ratsira told René about an American biologist who had attempted travel into the Jangala Reservation but was forced to turn back. "He came through this village asking many questions about the foosa and the forbidden forest. He's made an extensive study of the animal in question."

"Where is his base camp?" asked René.

"I believe he said he's in Tsarafagundi at the Batrambady Station," replied Didier Ratsira.

"Mmmm . . . That's interesting, though anyone who would venture into the Jangala Reservation must be missing something of value in his brain."

Just as he finished speaking, they came upon the blood-splattered ground. As the inspector looked around, he reached for his handkerchief and covered his mouth. He turned away from the sight and said, "Let's get back to the office!" With his attitude and tone much subdued, he asked, "Do you know the name of this biologist?"

Didier replied, "His name is Chester Whalton. He left his number with me in case anyone wished to report a sighting." As they walked into the office, Didier went into his desk drawer and after shuffling around a few papers said, "Here, I found it! You know, René, there is an old saying that applies to the fossa." He paused for a second, and when he saw he had the inspector's attention, he added, "Absence of evidence is not evidence of absence."

"Oh, my friend," said the inspector, "you'll always have the heart of a farm boy!" And with a little lilt in his voice said, "Make that call to the American. Maybe he can put these superstitions to rest. In the meantime, see to the old man and disperse the crowd."

Much earlier that same day at the research station, before the need for sunglasses, the 14 volunteers were awakened for their first full day in the field. Though most were still tired from their travels, all were excited and anxious to get started. Blaine was quite at ease and taking it all in stride. He'd ventured into this forest before.

Rice is served with every meal and not being his favorite sustenance, Blaine chose not to rush to breakfast. This morning he would opt for some fruit and a little chocolate. The chocolate is made here in Madagascar and, some say, is the best in the world. "Why not?" he thought. "Everything else is unique!" He knew the temperature would be rising into the high 90s and plenty of fluids were in order.

They were each assigned to teams and given their assignments. Chester Whalton and his Malagasy assistants were to be the team leaders. He spelled it out for all to understand, "For your safety, we lead, you follow. I don't want anyone venturing off by themselves and getting lost. Do we understand each other?"

In unison, they all shouted, "Yes, sir!" The teams headed out in different directions.

A little ways up the trail, about 300 yards or so, Sarah shouted, "Damn, it's hot!"

"You got that right!" said Bob, echoing the sentiment.

Blaine stopped to wipe the perspiration from his brow and with a knowing grin said, "You haven't seen anything yet!"

Blaine was elated that Sarah and Bob had been assigned to the same team because he felt very comfortable with both from day one. As they continued up the trail, he said out loud, "Do you believe this? Here we are in Madagascar, one from Utah, one from Virginia and I, a Floridian Bostonite, searching for an animal few have ever heard of, much less seen, and to top it off, I'm in search of an oceanographic degree. The closest water is Lake Manjara."

"Yeah," interjected Bob, "with 14-foot crocodiles, hungry crocodiles."

As he thought about it for a minute, Blaine reasoned, "Maybe I am better off with you guys!"

"Well, for now anyway," Sarah added.

As they worked their way through a tangle of lianas, tough shrubs and other growth, they approached an open field, called a savanna. Chett pushed through first and scared up millions of locusts. Sarah, following close behind, wasn't the least bit squeamish, and this really impressed the two guys. On the other hand, Chett was getting frustrated, not with the team but over the fact they had covered 10 miles or more, mostly off the beaten paths, with nothing to show for it. In spite of cuts and bruises, not one had spotted their quarry.

"I've had some positive signals on this radio," said Chett. "But they get broken up because of the deep ravines and impassable ridges. Look at this area up ahead. We can't even get around."

"How much of a range do these radios have?" asked Sarah.

"Supposed to be two miles, but the fossa can cover up to 12 miles a day and doesn't like company. We might have some luck at the traps."

Bob spoke up, "I had read that the fossa was only a night hunter."

"That's a fallacy," said Chett. Then he went on to explain, "We've tracked them in the daytime and it's my belief they'll eat whenever they're hungry." As he finished speaking, he pointed up the trail. About 50 yards ahead near a ridge, a shadowy figure appeared. It looked both ways, like a child who'd been taught to cross the street in safety, and dashed to the other side in a flash.

"Did you all see that?" whispered Chett. The others just nodded, hearts pounding, and followed the leader on the run to a nearby trap. The trap had been baited with a live chicken, but when they arrived, all that was left were a few feathers and a lot of blood. The fossa had escaped with the bait. "Let's head back," suggested Chett. "The others may have had better luck."

When the team arrived back at base camp, Chett was handed a message to call an Officer Ratsira of the Ariandiro Gendarmerie. He headed for his office, wondering what this could be about. The others just collapsed at one of the tables that had been used to carve meat for the evening meal . . . stew. They were too tired to care and just wrapped themselves around cans of cold Maddy's Pilsner beer. "Wow," exclaimed Blaine. "They have an ice machine now!"

"Officer Ratsira," the officer said as he picked up the phone.

"This is Chester Whalton."

"Oh, Mr. Chett, I'm so glad you returned my call!"

"How can I help you, Officer?" Chett asked curiously.

Officer Didier Ratsira conveyed the happenings of the day and described, in detail, the gory kill site. He finished by asking, "Could this be the work of a fossa?"

"Why do you ask that?"

"Because the old man who's in shock was heard to have muttered the word foosa."

Chett thought for a moment and answered, "All I can tell you at this time is that the animal that I've been researching for the last six years, in my opinion, would not be capable of killing a cow, much less an ox of the size you describe."

"Could it be several of them? Do they travel in packs?"

"Not to my knowledge," answered Chett, and then offered, "have you considered wild dogs?"

"There's been no report of wild dogs anywhere in this area. I even checked out the logbooks over in Tomboiana. Nothing of this nature has ever been reported."

"Well, I really haven't any other suggestions at this time, but if there's another occurrence, rope off and guard the site immediately, then call me. If I encounter any such happening in this area, I'll contact you." The officer agreed, thanked Chett for his time and expertise, and then hung up.

Randrian had just returned with his team and stopped at the office to check in. Chett imparted to him the story as he had heard it from the gendarme. "Sound like foosa to me!" said Randi.

Chett looked him straight in the eyes and asked, "Have you ever seen a fossa kill an ox?"

"No, not personally. I heard long-ago stories of when big foosa was here. He could kill anything!"

"That was long ago, and most of those stories were made up to keep children out of the woods."

There was silence for a couple of minutes and then Chett spoke again, "A few years ago, I read an article from an old journal . . . " He scattered some papers around his desk, then checked one of the drawers. "Yes, listen to this!" He then read: "When at large, the fossa can be a very formidable predator."

His eyes rolled around the room, and when they came to rest on Randi, he asked, "This ox killing this morning, could it have been granddaddy fossa? Those first words in the article, 'when at large,' did they mean that it rises from obscurity on occasion? That was written just over a hundred years ago, yet it was supposed to have been extinct. Is it still surviving in the Jangala Reservation, and if so, why would it leave the relative safety of the forbidden forest to come out to kill an ox?"

Randi said, "Some things are better left unknown. Let's get some food!"

At supper, everyone sat around and shared their experiences of the day, but Chett was uncharacteristically silent. The warning to eat carefully was issued. Bone splinters could be found in the stew and the rice harbored an occasional rock. A few minutes later, one of the girls let out a scream and pointed.

"It's just a *Gromphadorina portentosa*, a hissing cockroach," said one of the guides. "Some have them as pets."

The girl in question took a second look and said, "I'll stick to the usual cat or dog for a pet, if it's all the same to you." The rest of the volunteers filed by for a quick look, but none offered to pet it. It was much bigger than any roach they had ever seen.

The next few days were routine and uneventful and, though all covered much ground, fossa remained elusive. Early on the eighth day, July 1st, long before sun-up, there was a loud ruckus at one of the perimeter traps. By the time anyone arrived at the sight, whatever it was had escaped back into the woods with its prey, leaving splattered chicken blood behind. The traps needed to be re-worked and made stronger.

Chett became very disappointed at the way the trappings were going so he decided to hold a lecture to keep the volunteers from being bored. He passed around many photos to assure everyone the animal in question really existed. Blaine moved in real close to Sarah. She was getting the hint that Blaine was interested in her. "Somehow," he said, "I feel I'm going to be a part of this animal's history."

"And you want to be part of my history, as well," she said.

"The thought had occurred to me, but I sort of put it aside."

"Why is that?" she asked.

He just looked at her dreamily and said, "Exhaustion."

She laughed then examined one of the pictures closely. "It most certainly looks like a cat," she noted, "Check out these huge paws!"

"I can't get over the size of the tail," said Blaine. "It's as long as its body! It appears as though it should belong to the lion family."

They were all staring in admiration at the photos of an animal with a mostly white under belly and a mixture of black and brown over the rest of its body. Its whiskers were longer and much more numerous than animals in the cat family. The teeth and claws were quite formidable. At least now they had a better idea of what they were seeking.

Chett ended the lecture with, "Hopefully we'll have better luck tomorrow. Sometimes, as a few of you know, we may get a glimpse of one and then it could be weeks before another sighting. This happens and it's what constitutes our work here. If we can establish patterns of behavior, we'll be better able to assist in its survival. Your help is most certainly needed and appreciated. Now I believe it's time to eat."

A short while after dinner, the ringing of the phone pierced the stillness of the warm evening air, and he was summoned to his office. "Hello, Chett here."

"Mr. Whalton, I am Inspector René Areben of Tomboiana Province. How are you this evening?"

"I'm well," replied Chett. "How may I help you?"

"I believe an associate of mine was in touch with you a few days ago, concerning a certain incident. Is this true?"

"Yes," said the biologist. "An Officer Ratsira called. But I'm afraid I didn't offer him much help with his problem."

"Well Mr. Whalton, at the time I was pleased that you couldn't because I, myself, did not place much faith in this 'fossa' theory. Recent events have forced me to at least explore the possibility of its existence."

"Oh, it exists all right," said Chett. "I held one in my arms recently."

"Yes, I'm sure that is true, but the animal under consideration, according to superstition, would be a much larger specimen. Let me be more specific," said the inspector continuing, "There's been another incident 35 miles from Ariandiro in a small village called Bolamsika. We're investigating the disappearance of a herdsman, as well as the gross mutilation of one of his cattle. The kill site is not unlike the last one.

"The villagers are terrified and are convinced the 'ancient one' has returned to exact some sort of punishment or some other foolish thing. Their superstitious minds run wild with fear. They say it's a foosa!"

"And what do you say, Inspector?" asked the biologist.

"I say it's rubbish! But I told them I would call in an expert on the fossa to dispel these ravings."

"I'm assuming you're asking me to come over there?" asked Chett.

"By all means and the Ministry will cover your expenses," replied the inspector.

"That's very generous of you, but I'll be glad to help all I can. Isn't that area on the edge of the Jangala Reservation?" The reply was affirmative. Chett continued, "Those roads are difficult to travel in the daylight hours, and I don't believe I would want to attempt the journey at night."

"This is true," said René. "Could you possibly leave at first light?"

"That will be arranged," said Chett. "That type of carnage will draw other predators. It would be of great importance if the site was protected and untouched."

"I have already given the order. I may expect you?" René asked questioningly.

"We should be there by late afternoon, and may we dispense with the formalities? My name's Chett."

"And I'm René. We'll meet tomorrow?"

"See you then," said Chett and hung up.

CHAPTER ELEVEN

What If?

Late afternoon of July 2nd found Chett and one of his assistants just outside the village of Bolamsika. He had left Randi in charge back at the base camp with instructions that all the teams going into the forest carry communication radios. They were to check in at regular intervals. Too many odd things were taking place in the whole area. Known animal behaviors of many of the species, especially among the lemur populations, were changing dramatically. Just in the past couple of weeks, migrations of some animals were recorded that were not known to have migrated before. Biologists and ecologists that have had ongoing research here for years were baffled.

As they pulled up, just outside the gendarmerie, the smiling face of Officer Ratsira greeted them, "Good afternoon, Mr. Whalton."

"Good afternoon, Didier. This is Philibert, my assistant." They nodded to each other.

"Come inside," said Didier. "Let me offer you some cold refreshment. . . . Beer?" They both gave an affirmative answer. "I'll let the inspector know you are here."

René came out from the inner office, reached out his hand in a warm welcome and said, "Glad you're here, Chett."

They shook hands and Chett responded, "My pleasure. This is my assistant, Philibert." They shook hands as well.

"Please, gentlemen, sit down."

The inspector was staring at Chett for a moment making the biologist feel a little uncomfortable. "Is there something wrong?"

"No, no, I just pictured you to be a much older man. Your reputation is senior to your years," stated René.

"Why thank you, René, my boyish features help hide the stress marks." Chett figured René to be in his mid-forties, light complexion for someone who lived and worked in Madagascar. He probably spent most of his time behind a desk, and judging the size of his belt, had to assume he liked double helpings of rice and beans.

"So how was your trip?" asked René.

"Tiresome. But you have me very curious. Since your call yesterday, I've tried to stay focused on what I know to be reality, but my mind keeps wandering into the what-ifs."

"What if what?" retorted René. "Let's not let our imaginations get carried away. Let's stick to the facts. You're here to help me quell these superstitions, not pour fuel on them. I agree to keep an open mind, but let's stick to the facts!"

"You're the boss, Inspector; show us what you've got!"

René led them to his vehicle, and after a short drive, they arrived at a roped-off area, overseen by two gendarmes. Philibert scanned the area in amazement. He had never seen an animal, which appeared to have been in large proportion, torn to pieces in this manner. There was no shortage of blood. It was soaked into the ground and splattered all over the brush. What was left of the carcass didn't leave a whole lot for examination.

Chett conferred with Philibert for a few moments and said to René, "This is definitely the modus operandi of a fossa but on a scale far beyond my scope."

Philibert added, "When I was a child, I heard tales of happenings such as this, but never since then. As I grew older, I passed off those stories as myth. But this . . ."

As they gathered scat samples and checked tracks, the biologist was almost convinced that this carnage was the work of granddaddy fossa, *Cryptoprocta giganta*. His emotions were see-sawing between the excitement of discovery and the fear of meeting it face to face.

"So, what are your thoughts, Chett?" asked René.

"Well, sir, I'm afraid my what-ifs may be coming close to fact. The tracks are huge and almost the size of North American black bear and there were possibly two attackers. Scat samples are slightly different and much larger in size than I'm use to dealing with. That's most likely due to a difference in diet. Lord knows what they've been eating in that forbidden forest."

"Exactly," asked René somewhat disturbed, "exactly what are you implying?"

"I believe we have a couple of giant fossa on our hands," was the reply.

"Ridiculous!" shouted René. "You're dabbling in fantasies. Do you expect me to bring these tales to my superiors? Couldn't poachers have done this and made it look like the work of wild animals?" snapped René.

"I suppose anything's possible," he answered, "but until I find evidence of the contrary, my opinion stands."

Philibert joined the conversation. "You know, Inspector, if we're wrong, nothing is lost. On the other hand, if we're right, we've got ourselves a couple of killing machines, capabilities unknown."

"Any word on the missing villager?" asked Chett

"Nothing yet," mumbled René, trying to fathom the depth of the situation.

"You know, René, even though this animal was written off as

extinct many moons ago, there's been a suspicion among many that it has been existing all along in the forbidden forest."

"If that's the case," asked René, "why has it waited until now to show its face?"

"My God!" Chett exclaimed excitedly. "René, look what's been happening in this country! The weather's been unusually severe, the forest is disappearing thanks to man, and the food supply is getting scarce. We have no way of knowing what kind of damage the Jangala Reservation experienced from all the storms and flooding. There's no way of telling how many fossa there are, but my best guess is that they're on the move, possibly migrating."

"To where?" asked René.

"Who knows? But if my hunch is right, there'll be another killing soon."

"There is one other possibility," offered Philibert. "They might have wandered out for a look-see and a quick meal and are heading back from whence they came. Time will tell."

"It's a good thought," said René. "But, if your theory is correct, would they have a taste for human blood?"

Chett thought for a second and answered, "They like eating apes and monkeys and lemurs. If you believe that man evolved from ape . . ." and then smiled.

"This is no time for humor," René rebutted.

"Sorry," said Chett on a serious note. "Actually, I've never heard of a human being attacked or killed by a fossa, though there's not a lot written on the subject. There's still some daylight left. Let's look around and see if we can pick up a trail."

The tracks led them off the beaten path, so Chett and Philibert split up. René went back to his truck, locked the doors and cracked the windows; strange behavior for a non-fossa believer. The other two gendarmes stayed near the kill site as a back up. About a hundred yards into the bush, Philibert heard a moaning sound. "Chett! Over here!" he shouted.

When Chett arrived on the scene, Philibert was cradling a badly wounded man in his arms. He shouted back to the gendarmes for a medical kit. A few minutes later, René showed up with the bag and excitedly asked, "Is he alive?"

"He's breathing," said Philibert. "That's about it."

"What could have done this?" asked René.

Chett just turned back and stared at him as if to say, "You don't know?" Then he observed, "He's been clawed up quite severely, but there's no sign of animal feeding on the flesh. The slashes are deep and he's lost a lot of blood. We've got to get him to a medical facility."

"The closest one is in Ariandiro," offered René.

"Hell! That's 40 miles from here!" shouted the biologist. They made a makeshift stretcher and carried him back to the van.

"He needs antibiotics," said Chett, and René went into a side pocket of the medical kit and produced a syringe and a small vial.

Traveling on the back roads of the interior at night is suicidal. But with the help of a bright moon and a gendarme who was familiar with the terrain, they arrived safely at the field hospital. Thank God they radioed ahead because the whole town was asleep when they pulled up in front. The doctor on call, actually the only one within a hundred-mile radius, was obviously not used to treating wounds of this severity, but proved to be very adept with a needle and thread. The patient was infused with three pints of blood, cleaned up, sewed up and left to rest with an intravenous of antibiotic drip. He was still unconscious.

Chett and Philibert were barracked at Didier's house and welcomed the thought of a good night's sleep. Philibert slept well, but Chett couldn't close his eyes. He kept trying to picture a fossa that was 10 times larger, in every way, than any he had seen. "Oh, my God . . ." he thought. Then, he dozed off.

During breakfast the next day, René summoned them to the

hospital. Miraculously, the patient had pulled through and regained consciousness, but with no idea of where he was.

"How are you feeling this morning?" asked the doctor.

"I'm very sore and weak. Who are you?"

Then René stepped forward and said, "He's the one who patched you up. I'm Inspector Areben. We found you in the bush, badly wounded, and brought you here."

"Where am I?" the patient asked.

"You're at the Ariandiro field hospital," answered the doctor.

"I need to get home!" said the patient, as he tried to sit up but fell back down again from weakness. "My family . . ."

"Don't worry," said the inspector. "We'll notify your family, but first we need you to answer some questions." Just then the biologist and his assistant entered the room. They introduced themselves and asked if they could sit in on the questioning.

"By all means!" permitted the doctor. "He's out of danger."

"Tell us what happened to you last evening?" bid René.

"Evening?" the patient answered hesitantly. He then continued, "It wasn't evening . . . maybe four o'clock. I decided to take a shortcut home for the evening meal. Yes, I remember now. I heard this terrible sound."

"What kind of a sound?" asked Chett excitedly?

"A screaming cow . . . I don't know how else to describe it. Something was in great pain. As I ran toward the commotion, a dark figure came out of the trees and knocked me backwards with great force."

"See!" interjected René. "I told you. It was poachers."

"Then what happened?" asked Chett of the patient.

"That's all I remember, until I awoke this morning."

"Okay my friend," René said to Chett, "what is your theory of what happened?"

"I believe this herdsman arrived shortly after the kill. The fossas heard him coming and retreated to the trees to guard their meal. The herdsman wandered in too close. It's possible they had never encountered a human being before. One of them leapt out of the tree to warn him off."

"That's one hell of a warning!" shot back René.

"If they meant to kill him, they would have," cautioned the biologist, "Their next meeting with a human could be fatal."

"So, you're still convinced it was two animals?" asked René.

"What's your version?" asked Chett.

"Simple. One or two poachers were carving up the cow, when along came our friend, the herdsman. One of the poachers climbed the tree, and when he was close enough, the poacher jumped out of the tree, knocked him down, slashed him with a razor and left him for dead."

"Doctor," questioned the biologist, "could those slash marks have been made by a razor?"

The doctor thought for a moment and not wanting to offend the inspector answered, "It's possible, quite possible."

Chett turned to Philibert and said, "We may as well head back home. There's no sense in hanging around here."

As they were getting into the van, René came over to thank them for their trouble and assured them he would apprehend the perpetrators in short order. Chett's response was, "I guess we'll just have to wait and see."

As they were driving away, the inspector echoed the same phrase, as he was rubbing his chin, "Mmmm, wait and see . . ."

The journey back to the compound from out in this backcountry is endured, seldom enjoyed, and painfully long. Chett once again was silent and full of what-ifs. As they pulled into base camp, they found themselves in the middle of a mini-celebration.

"What's going on?" Philibert asked Randi.

"Uncle Sam day!" replied the assistant.

"Of course, the Fourth of July," mumbled Chett, and he and

Philibert joined in by having a couple of beers and some rice and beans.

Later on, as Chett was trying to sleep, he kept wondering what he would do if René called him about another incident. "I should call Dr. Lansing," he thought. "But not 'til I have absolute proof of my convictions. I know I'm right. I don't care what René thinks!" Then he fell asleep from exhaustion.

It was still early evening, and outside Blaine and Sarah found themselves alone at one of the picnic benches. "Okay, Sarah, this is a good time to tell me about *you*. We've been so busy; I haven't had time to hear your story." Sarah was very attractive and Blaine was sort of semi-infatuated with her.

"Not a lot to tell," she said, and then went on. "I attend Brigham Young University as ecology major and I'm a real stickler on conservation, obviously. I live in Provo, right near the school, and this is the first time I've ever been away from home. I was supposed to travel with a friend, but she broke her ankle mountain climbing, two weeks before it was time to leave. My parents were opposed to my coming alone, but I assured them I wouldn't be alone, and besides, they knew they couldn't change my mind. My boyfriend couldn't deter me either. As you can see, I have a mind of my own."

"A boyfriend, huh?" he said. "I never entered that item into the equation."

"Oh, and what equation is that?" she asked.

"Well, I've been thinking of hitting on you all week. I just haven't mustered the courage until now." After he said it, he smiled in such a way that she didn't know if he was serious or not. Then he touched the back of his hand against her cheek. She responded to his touch by pressing her head firmer against his hand. Her lips came close to his. He quivered as their lips pressed gently together.

As he attempted to fondle her thigh, she grabbed his hand and said, "No! This isn't right. I mean . . . it's not you, Blaine. I was given a marriage proposal the day before I left, and I promised I would give it serious consideration while I was away. Until now, I was positively going to accept."

"And now?" asked Blaine.

"You're not helping matters any, but even though I'm on the other side of the world, I've got to be honest . . . I've just got to be honest."

"He's a very lucky guy. I just hope he knows it," Blaine said, as he started to walk away.

"What about you?" she asked. "Don't you have someone at home pining away for you?"

"Not exactly; what I mean is . . . I date on occasion, but keep it on the light side. I'm not quite ready to make that total commitment."

"Some girl is missing a wonderful opportunity. When you meet the right one, you'll know it. Goodnight."

He bid her a goodnight and thought to himself, "At this very moment, no one could be more right for me than Sarah." But he had to admit that he was in lust and not in love. Blaine tried a cold shower, but the thoughts of what might've been kept him awake for most of the night.

Morning came and as Blaine was getting dressed, he realized that this was his last full day at the complex. All the volunteers from various places would be heading home in the morning. All, that is, except him. He would be visiting the Captain and his family in Mahajanga.

His team spent the day checking traps, and Blaine noticed that Chett was very silent, only speaking when spoken to. At the evening meal, Blaine still hadn't noticed much of a change in his demeanor. He was forcing himself to be sociable and trying hard to enjoy the company of the 14 that were leaving in the morning.

The first chance he got, Chett stole away to an isolated bench, apparently in deep thought. Blaine gave him a little while alone and then hesitantly approached. Chett looked up and said, "Mr. Gibbons, have a seat."

"Are you sure I'm not imposing on your thought process?" asked Blaine. "I noticed the wheels turning all day."

"No, not at all; actually, I wanted to speak with you personally, before you left in the morning. I want you to know how much my assistants and I appreciated your efforts since you arrived. You're a natural conservationist."

"That's odd that you should say that," said Blaine. "My parents said those exact words, right here, seven years ago."

"They had great insight," responded the biologist. He then continued, "Randi lauded your enthusiasm, especially while I was away. He's never done that before. It seems you're always there with a helping hand or a good idea, just when one is needed. That's a rare quality. I understand you're a senior at the University of Florida?" Blaine just nodded the affirmative.

Chett continued, "Have you given any thought to making fieldwork part of your career? We could sure use you around here."

"That's quite a compliment, especially coming from you," replied Blaine. "My parents, were they alive, would be pushing me in the same direction. I guess I'm marching to a different drummer. I love the sea and my parents wanted me to be a biologist, so I fused them both together and study oceanography. I'll be a marine biologist. I have a friend in Mahajanga who runs a fishing boat. I'm hoping he'll take me on as a deckhand for the rest of the summer. I need and want some hands-on experience."

"Well," offered Chett, "should you ever change your mind, you know where we are."

"Chett, do you mind if I ask you something personal?"

"What is it, Blaine?"

"I know you're deeply troubled about something; I thought maybe I could help. I haven't seen your wife around lately."

"You're very observant!"

"There's nothing observant about it. Your pet zebu could see it in your face!" said Blaine.

Chett smiled, thought for a moment, wondering if he should share his concerns, and finally said, " First of all, Pamela had to make an emergency trip to the States. Her mother's health is deteriorating rapidly. It's definitely one of my concerns but I'm sure she'll be stabilized. This has happened before. My other concern has to do with the fossa. Do you remember the mini-safari that I had gone on, to Jangala Reservation? I mean the one I told you about?"

"Yeah, the forbidden forest . . . where granddaddy fossa lives," replied Blaine.

Chett then explained to Blaine the sequential happenings of the past week. He also conveyed the inspector's theory without disclosing his own hypothesis.

"So what kind of animal was it?" asked Blaine.

"I believe it to be *Cryptoprocta giganta*, but I can't substantiate it just yet."

"Hold it right there!" shot back Blaine. "Are you suggesting that a supposedly extinct animal is back in circulation from some place unknown?"

"I'm stating," retorted Chett, "that an animal, which has existed all along in that deep forest, has been forced into migration by a combination of natural disasters and human infringement. I should go to Dr. Lansing, my sponsor, with this, but I need more than droppings and blood samples. If my hunch is correct, fossa will leave a trail of blood. I just pray they don't take to eating human flesh." His voice trailed off as he finished the sentence.

"If what you say is true, where would they be heading?"

Chett paused for a long while before he answered, "I wish I knew. Inspector Areben wouldn't accept my hypothesis either. I hope I'm wrong, but all we can do is wait and see. You know, on one hand we could be on the verge of a fantastic zoological find, and on the other, we could be dealing with killing machines 10 times larger and deadlier than their modern day offspring."

"And you wanted me to stick around?" Blaine said with a chuckle, trying to keep it on the light side.

"I'm sorry. I guess my head is just buried in the what-ifs."

Blaine suggested quickly, "What if we have a farewell beer together and talk about something really important, like my love life!"

Chett just laughed and said, "Thanks. See, another key idea at the right time."

CHAPTER TWELVE

The Tolura

During breakfast, Chett made one last appeal to Blaine. "Sure you won't change your mind and stay on?"

Blaine took a sip of coffee, feigning contemplation, but remained adamant. "Sorry Chett, the sea beckons and I must answer the call."

They wished each other the best of life, then shared farewells, good wishes, and in some instances, hugs and kisses with the rest of the volunteers.

They packed into two rusty vans and headed for Mahajanga, where they would make connections for their flights home. Blaine, on the other hand, had a reservation at the La Piscine hotel for a couple of days until he could find suitable, long-term accommodations. After checking in and stowing his gear, he went for a walk.

"The town hasn't changed much at all," he thought, as he strolled down near the shipping docks. Retracing the footsteps of seven years ago was painful but necessary. He stared out over the water in deep thought, and the pleasant memories of his parents caused him to sigh. "I miss them terribly," he said to himself.

He continued to walk and when he spotted the *Tolura*, he became very dismayed. She was in dry dock, set up for repairs. "I guess I can kiss the thought of a job goodbye," he voiced out loud and then noticed someone stirring in the wheelhouse. He approached the boat and yelled out, "Ahoy there!"

A young man in his late twenties came to the hatch. "What can I do for you?" he asked.

"I'm Blaine Gibbons and a friend of the captain. For a moment, I thought you were Rijah."

"You're American," stated the stranger and continued. "That name sounds familiar. I'm Rijah's son, Aurelien, but most people call me Aury. Are you looking for my father?"

"Yes, I am . . . well, I wasn't . . . but I was going to. What I mean is that I was going to call on your family later today," answered Blaine.

"You're in luck!" said Aury as he glanced at his watch. "I'm just on my way over there for lunch and you're invited."

"I don't want to impose."

"No imposition. My mother makes enough for an army to eat and forces me to sample everything."

"I remember," said Blaine. "You're mother and your sister are very good cooks."

"How long has it been since you've seen them?"

"Oh, it's been about seven years. I visited with my parents, and you were away at college."

"That was a lifetime ago!" responded Aury. "My sister's a nurse now and doesn't cook anymore, and I'm married and have my own home. I usually have lunch with them on Thursdays, so here we are!"

It was a short drive to the house and nothing looked familiar to Blaine. Aury's mother answered the door, gave her son a hug, and as she looked over his shoulder at Blaine said, "And you are?"

"I'm Blaine . . . Blaine Gibbons."

"I can't believe it!" exclaimed Yvette, as she released the hold on her son and grasped Blaine's right hand with the both of hers. "Come in, come in. Rijah, come see who's here!"

By the time Rijah rose from the chair, they had all entered the room, and he stared inquisitively at the stranger, unsure of whom it was.

"Blaine," said Aury.

"Gibbons . . . Blaine Gibbons?" asked Rijah. Blaine just nodded and held out his hand, but Rijah gave him a hug and held him at arm's length and said, "Where does the time go? You're a grown man! Welcome . . . welcome."

Looking at both parents, Blaine apologized, "I'm sorry I didn't call first, but I decided to take a look at the docks and the *Tolura*. That's where I met Aury and got the invitation to lunch."

"That's right!" said Yvette. "Aury was in school when you were last here. We were very saddened by the passing away of your parents. Many prayers were said."

"Thank you. I needed every one. Where's Sirana?"

"She's at work in the hospital as a registered nurse. We're very proud of her!" replied Yvette.

"No doubt," said Blaine. "That's quite an achievement."

"And you, young man," asked Rijah, "what are you doing with your life?"

"I'm in my fourth year of college, majoring in marine biology. I told you once, someday I'd have my own boat."

"I remember," said Rijah. "By the way, my daughter will be home for the evening meal, and you'll be here to greet her, as well. We will not take a negative reply graciously."

"That sounds like an order. I obey!" said Blaine laughingly.

While they were having lunch, Blaine dominated the conversation with details of the volunteer work at Batrambady with Chester Whalton and the fossa.

"And I thought it was just a children's story," exclaimed Aury. "They really exist. Have you seen one?"

"I've never had the pleasure," said Blaine. "But I've got a picture in my bag back at the hotel. I'll bring it next visit."

"Not seven years from now, I hope," replied Aury.

Blaine changed the topic and asked, "What's wrong with your boat, Rijah?"

"Not my boat anymore, Son," said Rijah. "Aury's the new captain as of July 1st."

Yvette spoke up. "It was my idea. It was time to pass the torch. Injuries were becoming too frequent, and besides, it's a young man's trade."

"She's right in one respect," said Rijah. "By the time you learn all there is to know about your mistress, it's time to retire."

"Mistress?" asked Blaine.

"The sea," said Aury. "Getting back to your question about the boat, she only needs some minor repairs; we're actually waiting for the nets to be mended. We should be seaworthy in a couple of days."

"So how long are you here for?" asked Yvette?

"Well, I was kind of hoping I could land a job for the rest of July and all of August, on a fishing boat. I need the hands-on experience. You can't learn it all out of books. Anyway, now that Rijah's retired . . ." His voice trailed off in disappointment.

"Don't be so downcast," said Aury. "I might be able to use you. Have you any experience on a working fishing boat?"

"Not on one the size of the *Tolura* and not commercially," answered Blaine. "My Uncle Ed was in the U.S. Navy and taught me a lot about seamanship and fishing, but unfortunately, our boat was only a 19 footer. I've also learned quite a bit at school and have been out on their research vessel twice."

"What type of research?" asked Rijah?

"It was mainly on waves and tides . . . and bottom sounding."

Aury nodded his head in approval, and then asked, "How are you physically? I noticed you walk with a limp." And before Blaine could answer, he added, "You can't be nursing an injury when you're working a slippery, pitching deck with cables and lines all around, not to mention the other crew members and waves awash."

"I can appreciate your concern," said Blaine. "But this leg is completely healed. It's a result of the accident seven years ago. I walk a little gimpy, but it's strong, stable and never gives me any trouble."

"Do you have any computer skills?" asked Aury. Blaine nodded affirmatively. Aury's tone then softened and he said, "Excuse me for being short with you, but I had to see if you easily lost your temper. I have two other hands, Sabastien, whom we call Sab, and Haji, whom we refer to as Haj. We keep the names brief so we can communicate quickly in case of trouble or danger, and we always know where the others are. I repeat . . . we communicate! I'm big on safety."

"If you take me on, what will be expected of me?" asked Blaine.

Then Aury read him the riot act. "All my deckhands have to know how to shoot and haul nets, operate the winches, mend nets, splice rope and wire, pack and stack fish and on occasion, stand watch. Of course, if something happens to me, somebody has to know how to get the boat back to port. Still think you want to work on the *Tolura*?"

"Positively!" answered Blaine.

"We won't expect you to learn everything overnight, but we do expect you to apply yourself. I won't tolerate any goofing off," said Aury sternly. "You're going to need some gear, personal gear, which will come out of your first paycheck. You'll need gum-soled boots and your own wet weather gear, and maybe a belt with knife and harness. The rest we supply, including the insurance."

"It sounds great to me. When do we get started?" Blaine was ecstatic.

"Don't you want to know what the job pays?" asked Rijah.

"I know you'll treat me fairly," answered Blaine. "Now all I need is a place to stay."

"That's settled," stated Yvette. "You'll take the room Aury vacated when he married."

"I don't know what to say," Blaine remarked in gratitude.

"Just say yes," suggested Rijah.

"Only if you allow me to pay my own way."

"Okay," answered Yvette. "You'll pay what Aury paid when he was here."

"Excellent idea!" added Rijah.

Blaine looked at Aury and asked, "Will I make enough to cover expenses?"

"Room and board are 200 francs," offered Aury.

"But that's only around $50 U.S.," said Blaine.

"So it is, and it includes laundry service, as well as pleasant conversation at dinner. Your gear payments are extra, and yes, you'll make enough to cover expenses. Bear in mind, you'll only be making apprentice wages until you start to pull your own weight. Pay is based on shares of the catch; the more the catch, the more the pay."

"So, it's settled then?" asked Rijah.

"Settled," said Blaine. He shook hands with father and son and gave Yvette a big hug and whispered in her ear, "Merci beaucoup!"

So Blaine settled in and unpacked the few things that he had, and reluctantly surrendered his dirty clothes to Yvette for laundering. He had this thing about women washing his skivvies, even his Aunt Linda. Later he joined the boys on the veranda for a beer.

"Are you coming back for dinner with your wife?" Rijah asked his son.

"No, Papa," answered Aury. "Moira has another commitment tonight, and I've a ton of paperwork to catch up on."

"I thought Moira handled that stuff?"

"She usually does, but it's mostly insurance forms I need to get out of the way, including the new applications for our new crewman here."

Blaine appreciated the implication of himself as a crewman. Somehow he felt like he finally found his station in life, at least for the time being.

As Aury finished his beer, he said, "I've got to check on the nets. With any luck, we'll be ready to shove off by Tuesday. Blaine, I'll pick you up around 5:00 A.M. on Monday. I want you to meet the crew and familiarize yourself with the doings."

"I'll be waiting for you, and once again, thanks for everything." Aury just nodded and shook his hand.

A little after 4:30 P.M., Blaine unsuspectingly greeted Sirana at the door. She just stared at him and asked, "Who . . . ?" and was answered before she could get another word uttered.

"It's me, Blaine!"

"Oh my God, but you're so grown up and handsome!" she said excitedly.

"Thank you. Mind if I give you a hug?" he asked.

"Of course, of course," she answered as she fell into his arms.

Then very seriously, Blaine said, "I want to express my deep appreciation for all those letters you wrote, and all the prayers that were said. There's no way to tell you how much they helped. Look at you. You're a nurse! And a beautiful one, may I add."

"Yes, you may. Compliments are always welcome. When did you get here?"

"Why don't the two of you come inside," said Yvette. "After such an auspicious start, I want to hear what's coming next!"

They both laughed and Blaine answered, "I arrived in Madagascar two weeks ago."

"Two weeks ago?" asked Sirana sternly. "You've been here two weeks, and you just got around to visiting us now?"

"Give him a chance to explain, Sirana," said her mother.

"I'm sorry, Blaine, please continue."

So he continued, "I was assigned to a research team before I left the States. Right from the airport we were shuttled to the La

Piscine Hotel, and after a brief orientation, we were whisked away to Batrambady forest station in a rusty van. There wasn't any time to call then, and at the station, the phone was strictly for business or emergency use."

"So what were you researching?" asked Sirana.

"The fossa," answered Blaine, and he could tell from her expression that she also thought fossa was a children's story. He added, "I'll expound on it later. Right now, tell me about yourself. You look great in that outfit!"

"Thank you again," she said. "But I've the need for a shower, and I'll be helping with dinner."

"Your brother told me you didn't cook anymore," he said.

"Oh, you met him? Well, I only help when there's company. We'll talk later."

At dinner the conversation was light with Sirana describing her life and the reasons for her career choice, one of the big reasons being the lack of adequate medical facilities and personnel throughout the whole island. Having a degree made her someone very special indeed.

Blaine detailed his experience with the island's carnivores and bragged about his new status as a deckhand on the *Tolura* and the new boarder of the Andrianaivo household. Every time their eyes came into full contact with each other, they would both hold the stare for a moment, then turn away quickly, so as not to be overly obvious of their attraction for each other, though it was quite apparent.

"Blaine, would you like to see what the town looks like at night?" asked Sirana.

"I think I'd like that!"

"Mother, Papa, we're going for a walk into town. We may be gone a couple of hours," said Sirana.

"Enjoy yourselves!" her parents answered in unison.

For the first few minutes, they walked in silence, he with his hands in his pockets and she with her arms crossed, then Blaine said, "You know, you were very instrumental in my recovery and helping me back to sanity."

"It must have been terrible for you," said Sirana. "I would often try to put myself in your position and it would be unbearable. Many nights I would just cry myself to sleep. Even though I only knew your parents for a day, they will always be in my thoughts and prayers."

"You're truly a good friend," said Blaine, and added, "Sometimes when I awake, I feel as though they're still alive. It's strange."

"Not so strange," she said. "In our culture, the dead play a role in the lives of the living. We regard the dead with awe and reverence. You see, to us, the afterlife has as much importance as the present. If we believe, in any way, the dead have been displeased; we have a ritual called 'famadihana' or 'turning of the bones.' The dead are exhumed, entertained, talked to and re-buried with gifts and new shrouds."

"Now that my parents are gone, I can understand that. I went to the burial site a few times and sort of held my own memorial service. I spoke with them and even asked their advice about a few things. Somehow I feel they can hear and sense my presence."

Sirana kissed him on the cheek. He put his hand on her shoulder and kissed her on the cheek. They gazed into each other's eyes for a long moment, and then Sirana muttered, "I like the old sector of town the best, the harbor quarter with its old Arabian-style houses."

"That's my favorite also," interjected Blaine. "I guess I'm just partial to boats and docks and anything connected with them. Let's walk along the beach."

In the background, they could hear some vaky soava, a rhythmic style of singing, accompanied only with hand clapping, and

Sirana advised him there are some styles using musical backgrounds that weave themes of poverty, love, loss and hope.

They talked and talked about thoughts and dreams, and Blaine couldn't believe he had so much in common with someone who lived on the other side of the world. As they walked, Sirana loosened the bun her hair was tied up in, and shook her head, allowing her jet black hair to flow over her shoulders and yellow lace blouse and come to rest just below her full breasts. Blaine took a deep breath and also admired the way her eyes flashed in the evening light.

The rest of her figure, he noticed for the first time, was pleasing to the eye and with his limited experience, guessed she was 5'4" tall and weighed about 125 pounds. Her lips were full and her teeth just sparkled against the background of her smooth dark skin. Her features were average, according to the world's standards, but to Blaine, at this moment, she was the most beautiful woman in the universe.

"Blaine, are you okay?"

"Sorry, Sirana, I guess I was just daydreaming. I've been up since 5:00 A.M. It's been a long day." He didn't know what else to say without giving himself away. He never felt this way before and it frightened him.

"I should have been more thoughtful," she said. "Let's head back to the house."

He wanted to reach down and take hold of her hand, but decided it wasn't a good move just yet. "How does your father like retirement?"

"It's only been a week, but I actually believe he's going to enjoy it. Mom says he meets with some of his old cronies for coffee, and he gets involved in their projects. They take advantage of his trade knowledge and willingness to help."

"You have real nice parents. Look what they've done for me already!"

When they arrived home, Blaine bid all a goodnight, thanked them again for their hospitality and retired to his room. After a shower, he laid in bed staring up at the ceiling. His thoughts were all on Sirana at first, then drifted to fossa, then to the sea and finally came to rest on his Aunt Linda and Uncle Ed. Reminding himself to call them in the morning, he fell asleep.

The phone began ringing in Englewood, Florida. "Honey, would you get that?" asked Ed. "I'm up to my . . . er . . . elbow in grease!"

"Hello," said Linda softly, as she put the phone to her ear.

"Guess who?" quipped Blaine.

"Blaine! You're not hurt, are you?"

"No, not at all; I'm fine. How are you guys?"

"We're okay, just a little concerned, and after all, this is the first call since you left. No matter, it's just so good to hear you. Are you still doing research work?"

"I finished up yesterday," answered Blaine. "It was very interesting and, at times, quite adventurous."

"You didn't run into that fossa, bloodthirsty thing, did you?" she asked scarily.

"They're truly beautiful, and from what I've observed, are really no threat to man. They're not easily caught for study or even seen, for that matter. The closest I got was a glimpse of one and seeing the havoc they create with chickens."

"So what are you up to now?" she asked hesitantly.

"Aunt Linda, you won't believe how lucky I am. I'm at Captain Rijah's house and listen to this—they're putting me up for the rest of the summer, giving me a job on the boat. I'm going to get paid for it!"

"I'm really happy for you," she said. "I know it's something you've been wanting a long time. Promise me you'll be careful.

I know you're a grown man now, but I can't help feeling like a parent."

"You are a parent. You've been a mother to me for a long time," he said. "And Uncle Ed's been nothing short of a father. I love and appreciate you both."

The tears welled up in Linda's eyes, and she said softly, "We've tried so hard . . ."

"Oh, there you go," he said, "getting emotional on me. Is Uncle Ed around?"

Linda called Ed to the phone. "How goes the battle, Blaine?" he asked with his somewhat thunderous voice.

"I'm hanging in there and your wife will update you on my travels. I just wanted to hear your voice and let you know how much I appreciate everything you've done for me. I love you both dearly."

"You're loved as well," replied Ed.

"Well . . . er," Blaine hesitated for a second, "it's time to go before we start getting mushy. I'll try to call you every week. I should be leaving here the 30th of August. If there's any change, I'll let you know. Oh, take down this phone number." He gave his uncle the number in case of emergency and said goodbye.

CHAPTER THIRTEEN

A Taste of Blood

Savutanana Village

One hundred and fifty miles from Jangala Reservation, the sun was setting over a sleepy, inland village. Somewhat reclusive, the town was almost completely surrounded by dense forests and vegetation, except for several oxcart trails that fingered out into the wilderness.

To the north side of town, there at the forest's edge, Sifaka diadem lemurs were socializing and feeding on the flowers of the tamarind trees. Just overhead, the screech of a kite, a predatory bird, came as a warning but went unheeded. The lemurs continued to feed. The kite made a second pass, seeming to screech louder, but it was too late. "Pffft" . . . The sound came from a blowgun, 50 feet below on the forest floor. A large adult Sifaka, hit by a poisoned dart, wavered back and forth slowly, and as it started to tumble from the branch, a second dart was on its way. "Pffft" . . .

Several large branches broke the first victim's fall, landing only five feet from the poacher who was crouched behind the brush. The second fell unobstructed, landing with a loud thud. The rest of the lemur family, as though just becoming aware of the danger, scattered through the trees with great commotion. The poacher stood up, and sensing that it was not he but another danger that spooked the lemurs, scanned the area around him.

As he looked over his right shoulder, he was set upon with such great force that his neck snapped, and he was allowed one scream before he was literally torn to pieces by carnassial weapons. Two animals, one from the trees above and behind the poacher and one from the dense, ground-level vegetation, attacked simultaneously, tearing his insides to shreds before he even landed on the ground. Blood and guts were strewn all over the area and some visceral remains clung to the surrounding shrubs. The forest became silent.

Two children were playing no more than a hundred yards from the scene. Upon hearing the scream, they ran to get their father. The father called a nearby friend. They both entered the woods where the children were pointing, slowly and with much caution. The carnage was not visible from the oxcart trail they followed, so it was several hours before the remains of the poacher were discovered. Other animals, seizing upon the opportunity of a free feast, left little for identification.

Actually, it was the frenzied feeding sounds that drew the villagers to the scene. The first one to discover what was left of the body fainted. His friend, while helping him up, couldn't control himself and barfed all over the both of them. They finally made it back into the village, and when questioned, the only word that came to their minds and hearts was "foosa."

Sgt. Mankara of the provincial gendarmerie was summoned to the village. "Okay, all right, calm down," he said, as he questioned the villagers one at a time. Some of the townspeople were speaking out of hearsay, just to be noticed. Others hadn't seen the carnage, but were full of theories. The only two who had been to the scene were afraid to speak, but the sergeant, after sorting out all the information, took the two aside in private for further questioning.

"Which one of you saw what happened?" Neither man spoke. "What did you see?" he said, as he looked back and forth at the two of them.

"We saw . . . no, we heard," said the father of the children. He then explained the whole story.

"Now, let me get this straight," said the sergeant. "Your children heard a man scream. They then came and alerted you. You went and got your friend here, and you both entered the woods to investigate." They both nodded affirmatively. "Then what did you do?"

The friend then spoke up. "We followed the trail for maybe a half mile. Then we decided to start back and every 50 feet or so, we would walk into the forest a little ways, look around, and then come back to the road. It was almost when we were at the edge of the forest coming out, when we heard some animals scuffling. It was very noticeable, because up 'til then, the forest was eerily silent. When I saw the blood and torn, shredded body, I collapsed."

The sergeant then looked at the other and said, "What did you do?"

"I reached for my friend, at the same time viewing the carnage and threw up over the both of us."

"You didn't tell me that!" shouted the friend.

Then the father continued, "Then I carried him to my house knowing only one thing could do this."

"And what might that be?" asked the sergeant.

In unison, they both said in fear, "Foosa."

The officer was taken to the scene, whereupon investigation, he concluded that someone had been killed and the animals destroyed most of the evidence. It could have been a homicide or a heart attack. How could one tell? "How do I report this?" he asked himself. The victim didn't have any means of identification. "Someone will show up reporting a missing relative. Just a matter of time," he thought.

When the sergeant returned to his office, there was a notice lying on his desk that had been sent out to all precincts by Inspector Areben. All occurrences of an unusual or suspicious nature were to be reported to the inspector immediately. "Mmmm, this is a good opportunity to dump this off on him," thought the sergeant. "He's been given jurisdiction in this province, as well, so it must be quite important."

He picked up the phone and dialed. "Inspector Areben, please," he said as the call was answered on the other end.

"One moment please."

"René here!" said the voice.

"Inspector, this is Sergeant Mankara."

"Oh, yes, from Mahajanga Province. It's been a long time. What can I do for you?"

"I was just reading over your notice and I thought I should call," said the sergeant. "I was called in to investigate a death in the village of Savutanana. There wasn't much left of the corpse to make any considerable conclusion as to what may have happened. We have two after-the-scene witnesses and nothing else."

"That's about a hundred miles from here, isn't it?" asked the inspector.

"More like one hundred and fifty," answered Mankara.

René continued, "Did you see any large animal tracks, I mean any that are larger than ones you have ever seen around your area?"

"What are you getting at?" asked Mankara.

"Just answer my questions!" rebutted René.

"No, by the time we arrived on the scene, many animals had visited the remains. We couldn't make head or tail; pardon my expression, out of any of it."

"What about blood? Was there a lot of blood?" asked René.

"Everywhere! And one real strange thing I did notice was that there were pieces of viscera clinging to the surrounding shrubs. What's this all about anyway?"

Areben didn't want to expound on anything until he was absolutely sure, and at this point he was more confused than ever. He was, however, becoming more intrigued with Chester Whalton's theory as time passed. He answered the question the best way he knew how.

"We've had a couple of animals slaughtered over in this area in a very bizarre manner. At first we thought it might have been a cult thing. A while later, a man was set upon and cut up viciously. Some believed it to be an animal, but I disregarded that possibility. We had called in a biologist from your province that had some very strange theories and weird ideas as to what may have caused the occurrences. I'd like you to give him a call and invite him over for a look-see."

As René was giving the sergeant the biologist's number, the sergeant remembered something he failed to mention. "Inspector, there's one other detail I failed to convey. My men found two dead lemurs in the same area, apparently killed by poisoned darts. I don't know what significance—"

René cut him off mid-sentence. "Call that American right away and tell him you would appreciate his expertise as soon as possible. I'm on my way now."

Mankara made the call to Chester Whalton and explained the complete story, including his conversation with Inspector Areben.

Somehow, Chett wasn't surprised, merely disturbed that his worst fears were becoming a reality. "I'll leave at daybreak. Please keep the area from any more disturbances, if possible."

"As you say, Mr. Whalton."

"Please, call me Chett, and by the way, exactly where are you located?"

"As you approach the village from your direction, turn left onto the narrow bullock cart trail; it's passable. About a mile up you'll see our vehicle. There'll be a sentry posted. We'll be on the watch for you anyway."

"Thank you," said Chett, and then hung up.

About mid-morning, Sunday July 9th, Chett and Randi arrived at the scene. He brought Randi along because of his strong belief in the present existence of the giant fossa and his keen animal sense. A familiar face greeted them. "Inspector Areben, what are you doing here?" asked Chett in surprise.

"Once again, I have opened my mouth too wide," answered René. "So the central office has placed me in charge of any and all investigations dealing with cases of a bizarre nature, until of course, a definitive explanation is obtained. I also have jurisdiction in all provinces."

"It sounds to me," said Chett, "that you have them convinced there is a madman running loose on the island."

"I have not told them about your theory, otherwise you'd be the one classified as mad."

The biologist and his assistant were permitted to scan the whole scene and examine whatever remains were left abandoned. Bones were scattered around, and Randi found the skull, 20 feet away from the scene.

"Chett, look at this!" he said, pointing to the bite radius on the human skull. Teeth and fangs had left an outline. There were puncture marks just below the cheekbones and on top of the skull, two inches above the forehead.

"Any animal could have made those," said René.

"Not on this island," said Chett. "This was no small carnivore."

They were able to determine that the neck had been snapped cleanly, probably by a tremendous blow from the back, and the flesh initially shredded by razor-like claws. Randi had disappeared for a little while, and when he returned, he said he had found tracks leading off into the forest, of not one animal but two, of significant size.

After taking, once again, blood and scat samples, their attention turned to the two dead lemurs.

"Did anyone find a blowgun on the scene?" asked Chett. The inspector scanned the faces of the gendarmes standing there and not one offered an affirmative.

"Randi," he said, "check around those clumps of thorn bushes."

Several minutes later, Randi shouted, "Got it!" He surfaced from the bushes holding three splintered pieces of what used to be a silent killer, the poacher's blowgun.

"Well, Chett," asked René, "how do you see this one? Or do we wait and see some more?"

"It depends on what you're willing to believe, René, but this is what I believe happened. The victim, a poacher, darted two lemurs from the cover of the shrubs and was then attacked by his competition, which were probably sizing up those lemurs at the same time. They hit him simultaneously with such force that the blowgun was broken into three pieces, and he was thrown and landed several feet away, breaking his neck. The rest is open to conjecture."

"So who or what do you propose made the attack?" asked René.

"Foosa," said Randi, without hesitation.

"I agree," added Chett. "There's nothing else on this island capable of such carnage."

"You have me convinced, almost. I will not believe one hundred percent," said René, "until I see one with my own eyes. In the meantime, what do I tell my superiors?"

"The truth!" suggested Randi.

René thought for a minute then offered, "If we go public with our findings, we'll not only create panic among the populace, but every carnivore will become a target for indiscriminate killing."

"I don't believe so. You see, I doubt if anyone will venture into the forest when this story gets out, not even the poachers. We may be doing a great service to man and animal and make it easier for us to track them down," reasoned the biologist.

René liked what he had to say but asked, "Do you really think my superiors will believe this fossa tale?"

"Not at all," said Chett. "But they may believe a pack of wild dogs is responsible, depending on how you lay it out for them. In the meantime, we'll pursue our quarry and follow tracks. Oh, by the way, before you take pictures, cut up the lemurs to make it look like they were attacked by dogs, as well."

"Good point," said René. He then turned to his subordinates and gave them the order to get it done and cautioned them all, "Not one word to anyone about what you've seen or heard or I'll have your hide!"

"We'll need to make up a hunting party and have a base of operations," offered the biologist, "and I have to contact my superiors, as well. May I suggest using the Batrambady compound as the base?"

"That sounds feasible," replied the inspector. "And why not the five of us as the hunting party?" meaning Chett, Randi, himself and the two officers. Chett nodded his approval. They then discussed what they'd need for gear and agreed to meet at the compound the following morning.

When Chett returned to his office, he immediately called Dr. Lansing and brought him up to date on everything that had transpired. The good doctor was trapped in awe, somewhere between disbelief and traumatic amazement.

"Chett, do you have any substantiation that it's the *giganta?*" asked the doctor.

"Only what I've told you so far; the sanguinary manner of kill, tracks, musky odor and scat identification, but not a soul has seen one, or lived to tell about it, except maybe an old man who's still in shock and incoherent. It's absolutely imperative that we cancel all volunteer teams scheduled to come here from this point on, at least 'til we get this matter cleared up one way or the other. Fossa may have become a man-eater. We're sure he's tasted blood . . . human blood."

"I'll handle this end," said Lansing. "Keep me up to date on any new happenings, as you're able, and don't take any unnecessary chances with this thing."

CHAPTER FOURTEEN

The Mozambique Channel

Wednesday, July 12th

"Okay, good people," shouted Captain Aurelien Andrianaivo, "Shoot the nets!" And after a brief pause . . . "I have a hunch we're going to get rich today!"

According to his deckhands, his hunches were usually right on target, honed by years of fishing with his father and the fact that he loved his work.

That's the one thing Blaine could identify with Aury—his love for the sea. At the present time, he felt right at home. He'd been introduced to the crew, who were surprisingly friendly, and given a rundown of what his duties would be his first day out. Aury believed in breaking in new hands slowly and safely. "Harmony and contentment among the crew make for bigger catches and more money, and that's the name of the game." Aury couldn't remember where he heard that, but he applied it to his boat and it paid off.

"Blaine, pay attention to what everyone suggests," said the captain. "You will be all right." He winked at him, knowing it was his first day and that he was uptight.

"Aye, aye, captain!" responded Blaine. The first day on any job is tough and intimidating for most people, but on a working commercial fishing boat, the confusion and dangers could be doubled. He was very grateful for the light winds and calm seas, so far.

The *Tolura* is a 12 meter (40 foot) craft that uses wide mesh surface nets, designed to catch only what they are after, unlike the large trawlers that drag the bottom for everything. The trawlers stay out for long periods of time, forcing them to freeze their catch. The *Tolura* comes in frequently to sell fishes that are sometimes still quivering.

"Would you explain to me how the overall routine works?" asked Blaine of Aury.

"We only stay out two, three days, at most. Usually, a half day going out, a night and day fishing, if necessary, and a half day coming in. We're only fishing the edge of the channel this trip, but on occasion, we'll venture further, depending on what's running and of course, the weather. As you noticed, we set up the gear on the way out, catch and ice down the fish and sleep on the way in. Naturally, we take turns at the helm. I like to sleep on occasion, myself!" Aury quipped.

"Who sells the catch?" Blaine queried.

"Up until last year, my father would bring in the fish, and the profit-sapping middlemen would sell them. Now we have a new system, thanks to my wife Moira. She came up with a great idea. We briefly inventory our catch, call it into her, and she puts it up for bid on the Internet. Most times she has it sold before we get into port. We keep a portion aside for local sale and distribute some to the poor, my mother's idea. Two trips a week and we sometimes earn as much as 30,000 francs."

Blaine counted on his fingers, "That's over $7,000, American!"

"Somewhere in that vicinity," responded Aury. "The boat and captain take 60 percent. My father gets 7 percent. Each crewmember with a full share gets 11 percent. Understand, my percentage covers insurance, taxes, fuel and repairs. Net repairs are a big item, especially if we run into sharks. Last month, the nets were irreparable, thanks to an ornery Tiger shark. It cost me 10,000 francs ($2500) to replace them."

"Did you catch the shark?" Blaine asked.

Haj, one of the crew, spoke up, "No, he just tore the nets to hell, after gorging himself on our fish, then casually swam away . . . about a 15 footer. Tigers are bad news for fishermen."

Aury continued, "So on a good trip, the crew can earn . . ."

"That's between 700 and 800 dollars a week?" Blaine interjected.

"That sounds about right," said Aury. "You know, to bring this vessel up to date I installed all this fancy equipment: green radar screen, color-coded sonar readings and a computer map that shows every rock and sandbar from Madagascar to France, but I never use it to fish. My instincts and a secret mental map or chart of generations, handed down to me from my father, are all I need. So far, so good! Let's get to work!"

"Blaine," yelled Sabastien, "I need a hand over here!" Blaine accommodated, and then jumped back over to the other side to help Haj.

He worked hard and the crew appreciated him. By early evening, the nets were hauled in for the last time. Blaine had worked the winch, helped with the sorting and storing of the fish and iced them down. The captain was especially pleased. Blaine's back was aching and his hands were sore, but he let on like he was just fine. Haj knew better and had him soak his hands in salt water, while massaging them. Blaine didn't need any urging to sleep on the way back into port.

Aury contacted his wife when they were underway. "Hello, Moira, we did well. We tied into three different schools, but no tuna yet. We'll probably need to go out further next trip."

"You better give me a kiss right away!" she warned.

So he gave her a big smooch on the radio and said, "Wait 'til I get home!"

"Let's get back to business!" she insisted.

Aury gave her a detailed inventory of the catch and said, "We should be in by early A.M. Friday."

"You mean tomorrow morning, don't you darling?" she asked.

"Yes I do."

"Then you mean Thursday A.M., not Friday, my dear one," she said lovingly.

"I'm sorry, you're right," he said. "I guess I'm a little tired."

"Just a little," she agreed. "By the way, how's the new hand working out?"

"He's a keeper. Works hard and learns quickly and gets along with the other guys."

"Can't ask for more than that," she said. "See you in the morning."

Later on, Aury woke up Haj to spell him for a couple of hours at the wheel while he grabbed a nap. "It's been a good day," he thought, as he nodded off.

CHAPTER FIFTEEN

Don't Rattle the Cage

Batrambady Base Camp
Thursday, July 13th

"I can't figure this out," said Inspector Areben. "It's been five days since the last kill and nothing since."

"Patience, René," said Chett.

"Patience is not my strongest suit. Why do you think they made me an inspector? I'm known for getting things done expeditiously, but this . . ."

Chett was leaning over a map of Madagascar and said to René, "Look at this. I've been laying this whole thing out, trying to make sense of it myself, and there's definitely a pattern taking shape."

"Explain," said René.

"Presuming they came out of the Jangala Reservation on the ocean side, which has me puzzled for the moment, they began heading this way, northwest. The first kill, an ox, was on June 24th, as far as we know. Seven days later, July 1st, they killed and ate a cow. Another seven days goes by to July 8th and a man is the victim, which probably would have been lemurs, but that's another story. Now look at the path they're taking and the distance being covered. They're traveling about 75 miles a week. They crossed the Mahajamba River over to the Betsiboka River and are following it northwest. Why?"

"I don't have the slightest idea," answered René. "You tell me!"

Chett thought for a minute and offered, "I believe they're eating fish between meat kills. I found that to be the case in their smaller brethren. Fish is probably a major part of the diet. If my hunch is right, the next day or two will produce a meat kill near here, hopefully in one of the traps."

"Aha," said René, "I knew there was a reason you were stalling around here besides waiting for equipment. You believe they're migrating to this forest, don't you?"

"It would make sense." said Philibert, "There's nothing west of here except the town of Mahajanga, Betsiboka Bay and the Mozambique Channel. This area hasn't been ravaged by storms as the Jangala Reservation has. Then Chett added, "They seem to be averaging about 12 miles a day. That should bring them around here soon. We'll start checking traps tomorrow, and please caution your men to be careful, but not gun happy. If we get one in a trap, I want to dart it for examination."

"Examination, my ass," said René. "These things, according to you, have tasted human blood and need to be destroyed!"

"Yeah, right!" said the biologist in a critical voice. "Kill it off just like everything else on this island. The animals are always the bad guys!"

They argued for a while, and Chett won his point, but only up to the sedated capture, then René would call his superiors for final disposition, taking into account the biological and ecological ramifications of such a discovery. After a couple of cans of Maddy's Pilsener and some light conversation, they retired but kept a guard posted around the clock. Everyone had a turn on duty.

They were all up early in the morning and eager to check traps, except for the two officers René brought, who were still filled with fear from childhood stories of the fossa.

Chett cautioned them all, "Remember the remains of the poacher. Don't take chances. Keep your eyes and ears open and check the traps as well as the ground. Keep your guns at the ready, but I still don't believe human meat is part of their menu. I think that poacher was a victim of circumstance. Anyway, they cast off a strong musky odor, sort of like rancid meat. If you find one in a trap, blow your whistle or use the radio."

They paired off on predetermined mapped routes and trails with the two officers wishing to work together, leaving Chett and René as the other team. Randi was assigned anchor position at the base camp, keeping the perimeter in check and answering the phone and radio messages.

It was noontime and the two officers, who had traveled a few miles on foot, decided to stop for a rest and lunch. One, being a sergeant, offered a suggestion in the form of an order, "I think we should split up. It's hot, and we can cover our assigned route in half the time. Besides, there's nothing around here. We've already checked two traps and nothing has been disturbed."

"I don't think it's a good idea, Sergeant. You heard the American," said the private.

"The American; what does he know about Madagascar? We were born and raised here," said the sergeant.

There were six traps to check by the two officers. The sergeant gave the radio to the private, kept the whistle and was to check traps three and four while the private checked five and six. They would then meet at a designated rendezvous and return to the camp together.

When the sergeant arrived at the third trap, he looked around very carefully and finding it undisturbed, moved on to the next, thinking, "Just as I figured; there's nothing in this area." When he approached the fourth trap, he found it inhabited and couldn't believe his eyes. He blinked a few times and then rubbed his eyes, and sure enough, he was staring at a snarling, beautiful but deadly giant fossa.

"We got you! We got you!" he shouted as he danced up and down. Then he thought of the stories he was told as a little boy of fossas running off with children in the night. He became angry, and instead of blowing his whistle or shooting off a round, he started to taunt the animal and poke at it with his rifle. He obviously forgot it was traveling with a mate. The private heard the sergeant's screams over a half mile away, just prior to his insides being torn out and devoured.

By the time the private arrived at the fourth trap, the caged animal, with the help of its mate, had successfully chewed away two of the wooden bars and fled. The carnage they left behind would've discouraged anyone from taking up the chase, and the private was no exception.

When he recovered his composure to use the radio, he just pressed the button and shouted, "He's dead . . . he's dead . . ." and his voice trailed off.

The inspector yelled into the radio in reply, "Who is this? Speak up!" He repeated again.

Then a voice said, "He's been torn to pieces. I'm here at trap four."

"Don't move and stay alert!" ordered René.

Chett called Randi to alert him and then called back the private. "We're on our way. Stay as calm as possible. We're on our way." They were a good six miles and a half hour away.

The private just pressed his back against a tree and kept his finger on the trigger. He couldn't stop shaking or rolling his eyes from side to side. He even nurtured thoughts of crawling into the broken cage for protection. Chances are that it would be many moons before he would be able to sleep peacefully again.

"So you saw this giant fossa?" asked René when they arrived at the scene.

"No, I didn't," he replied. The private was still shaking.

"Why didn't you? You were together," questioned René.

"We split up. It was the sergeant's order," said the private. "He thought we could cover more ground in less time."

"The only thing that covered the ground here was his blood!" said René. "Maybe now and in the future you will obey orders."

"I was obeying his orders," said the private in his own defense. "When I heard the screams, I came running. This is what I found."

Chett was looking around and opined, "Definitely two animals. It appears as though one was trapped . . . but why didn't he blow his whistle or fire his rifle?" Then, in frustration, "Two bars chewed out and still no positive I.D."

"You still plan on capturing these things?" asked René. "I'll tell you right now, I shoot. I shoot to kill on sight! The sergeant was a friend of mine. How do I tell his family? I'll need to call in and then we do some serious tracking."

"I'll call Randi. We need to bag the remains," said Chett.

The tracks headed for the river and away from Batrambady and this puzzled them, but they stayed on the trail until nightfall and camped out. It seemed, at times, as if they were chasing a wisp of smoke. They added another man to the hunting party and posted an all out alert for all the provinces. The culprits were still listed as wild dogs, and according to René, until a positive identification of the fossa was made, that's the way it would stay. "I don't believe it 'til I see it," he stated.

"It might be a good idea if we rotate the watch. We're all going to need sleep," suggested Chett.

"Two hour shifts," said René. "I'll take first watch." He then walked around a little to stretch and asked himself, "How do we warn them all with such poor communications?"

In the morning, René was back in touch with his superiors, who wanted to beef up the patrols, but René convinced them that it wouldn't be a good idea to have a bunch of novices running around in the woods with guns. They agreed. He suggested a controlled hunt was best. Chett thanked him dearly for that and made a suggestion that they keep a man in a vehicle on the road that ran parallel to the river.

"We can make better time without carrying packs and extra gear," he said. "There's also a good chance he could spot them crossing the trail should they change direction. We'll keep an open channel at all times."

"Very good idea!" praised René. "You should have gone into police work."

Chett gave him a smile and a look that said, "Not on your life!"

For the next couple of days, they stayed on the trail, but the fossa remained elusive. The biologist was gaining more respect for this animal as time went on, but René just became more frustrated. He was beginning to admit to himself that the giant fossa, if that's what it was, had more cunning than he imagined, and every now and then, deep down inside, he felt that he was the one being tracked by the animal.

A study of the map showed they were not following the normal patterns of their offspring, but instead were on a mission or heading for a specific destination. The more Chett rolled it around in his brain, the crazier the thoughts became. He was in frequent communication with Randi, hoping someone would have called in a sighting. He wished Randi were here now, for he was an excellent tracker.

Monday morning, the 17th, they came across the remains of several fish. A short distance from the riverbank, across the trail, the officer in the vehicle found the blood-soaked fur of a recent lemur kill.

"We're getting close!" said Chett excitedly.

"I damn well hope so," said René. "We're only 30 miles from the town of Mahajanga. I would, at least, like to get a glimpse of one."

He no sooner got the words out of his mouth than three shots rang out from the direction of the road. René grabbed the radio and shouted, "What's goin' on over there?" No answer. René asked again.

This time the officer replied, "I'm not sure. I thought I saw something. Now I'm not sure. Something crossed the road about 50 yards ahead of me, I guess."

"Mark the spot where you fired. We're coming over for a look. Stay in the truck!" cautioned René.

As they cut their way through the tangled brush, Chett couldn't help but laugh at the reaction of the inspector every time they encountered an animal of a strange nature. It was bad enough these city boys were all cut up from vines and underbrush, but when René discovered an eight-foot tree boa dangling next to his head, he let out a howl and jumped to the side.

"Hell, you probably scared the fossa into the next province!" Chett said humorously.

Then as an added fright, René thought he had a piece of tree bark on his shoulder, until he went to brush it off. The "bark" jumped and René let out another howl. This time everyone laughed. It was just a leaf-tailed gecko.

Up to now, the hunting party had kept close to the riverbank and established trails. Now they were cutting their way through some tough vegetation, the fossa milieu. The city boys were fascinated and awed by what they were seeing, never realizing before the beauty of their own country.

Chameleons of every bright color imaginable and for the most part, existing nowhere else in the world, orange mantilla frogs, tomato frogs, insects of every description, including the foot-long, winged, walking stick and overhead, the territorial cries of the Indri lemurs, as they leaped 20 feet in the air from tree to tree, sounding like horns of various pitches.

"I never realized there was so much beauty in our land!" said René, in a tone of bewilderment.

"Now you know why I come here, year after year, to help preserve it," said the biologist, "along with all the volunteers from so many countries. If you could only pass on your feelings to every other Madagascan, they'd put an end to the scorching of the forests."

A short while later, they arrived at the road and made their way to the police vehicle, a quarter mile further.

"This is the spot, Inspector," said the officer, as they approached. They scanned the area carefully. Two animals definitely crossed the road at that point.

"What do you think?" asked René

"I think I'd love to . . ." Chett paused as he noticed something else, ". . . get a radio collar on one of those buggers. Look at this!" He pointed to tracks leading away from the direction that they were following. "I've never known them to travel in pairs, so this is all strange to me, as well."

"So what's your point?" asked René.

Chett pulled out his map and sat down on the road. "The only place they could be heading is here," He fingered a spot on the map.

"You think they're heading to Tsingy National Park?" asked René.

"It's the only sensible conclusion!" he offered.

"But they'd have to turn south, eventually, wouldn't they?" suggested René. "Why didn't they just go straight across, east to west?"

"If I knew the answer to that question, I'd have them in cages right now!" retorted Chett. "We have to assume this is where they're going."

"Assuming you're right, there's no need of beating ourselves up any more. Let's all get into the vehicle and follow the road to where it turns west, about 15 miles from here, and that should put us slightly ahead of our quarry, presuming of course, they're heading to the Tsingy."

One of the officers added, "It will get us out of the heat for awhile as well!"

"I like your logic, René," said Philibert. "And I'm hoping that the howls you made and the shots that were fired will steer them away from humans. That would surely be a blessing." So the hunting party headed west.

CHAPTER SIXTEEN

The Docks of Mahajanga

Monday, July 17th

The same morning, 30 miles away, Blaine was helping to make the *Tolura* ready for sea. This would be his third time out, and he was developing the sea legs of an old salt. Captain Aury double-checked on everything, as a safety precaution, and found, when it came to Blaine, few orders had to be repeated.

"The beauty of short trips is . . . less supply!" Aury thought. He always made sure the food was good and plentiful. The safety equipment was kept up to snuff and the icemaker, a very necessary item, was checked and maintained each trip, before and after.

"Are we ready to cast off?" shouted the captain. He received three "Aye-ayes" in succession. "Cast off!" he shouted once more.

The morning was warm, 89 degrees at 7:00 A.M. There was a light breeze, picking up to 15 knots by late afternoon.

"Not bad for the channel," he thought to himself. Aurelien loved the feel of the sun on his back and the warm breeze in his face. He called Blaine up to the wheelhouse. "Want to take her out?"

"Do you trust me?" questioned Blaine.

"I'll be close by!"

He waited 'til Blaine got the feel of the boat and asked, "So, how are you getting on with my sister? Don't look surprised; a fool could see you're attracted to one another."

Blaine winced and kind of looked sideways at Aury and answered in a question form, "It shows that much, does it? We've been dating. She's a wonderful girl."

"She thinks a lot of you, also!" said Aury. Blaine looked at him curiously, and Aury shrugged his shoulders and said, "She told me!"

Changing the subject, Blaine asked, "What course are we to steer?"

"Steer due west, my man; due west." When they cleared the bay, Aury ordered a course change to the south toward the Isle de Chesterfield. "I have a good hunch today. Well, actually, it's my father's idea."

By mid-afternoon they were a little over 100 miles out when he gave the order to shoot the nets. For a couple of hours, nothing stirred, and then all at once the sea started to boil and came alive with tuna, tons of them. Blaine let out a "Yahoo!" and they all turned to.[1]

The decks became busy, slick and dangerous, especially after nightfall. Blaine likened the experience to playing hockey, ice hockey that is, with the lights out.

"This is fantastic!" he said.

Haj added, "We strike the jackpot, no?"

Blaine noticed the other crewman hadn't said anything for awhile and yelled over to him, "Sab, are you okay?"

Sabastien was working the winch with one hand and doing something with the other. "Shush, I'm counting my money," then he laughed.

The rest of the crew laughed with him and Aury yelled down

[1]Seafarer's term for "get-to-work"

to Sab, "Get your hands on those fish and start counting them as well!"

For a long time, the decks were awash with tuna. By midnight the catch was in and iced down. *Tolura* was 90 percent to capacity, and Aury was on the radio to his wife. "Moira, this is *Tolura*. Moira, this is *Tolura*. Over."

"This is Moira; anything wrong?"

"No, all's well. Ninety percent capacity with tuna, I repeat, tuna. We're heading in. Did I wake you?"

"Nice of you to ask," she said. "What's your ETA?"

"About 8:00 A.M.," he answered.

"I'll call Tana before going on line," she said. "A direct sale to the buyer may be more profitable. He may want them all."

"That's your end, dear. See you in the A.M. Out."

They were all exhausted to the man, but Blaine was still filled with the excitement of it all and couldn't sleep. He lay up on deck, hands behind his head, looking at the stars. Through the hum of the engines, he heard a voice. It was Haj.

"Thinking about today and the past at the same time?"

"A little of both; how did you know?" asked Blaine.

"I've lain out on this deck many times. There's something real peaceful about being out here," answered Haj.

"Yes," said Blaine. "You hear the sound of the waves lapping against the hull; the drone of the engines and get to use the stars for a blanket. What memories!"

"Some days the weather and the fishing is not good . . . the memories are not good too, no?" suggested Haj.

Haj is of Arab and Comorian parentage, but speaks French and Malagache fluently and his English is passable. He's 35 years old or young, whatever your slant, and at 5'6" tall, weighing in around 200 pounds, is as strong as an ox with very powerful arms and hands. He has a dark, ruddy complexion, black hair and a well-trimmed moustache. Yet the one thing that commanded attention was the one-half inch wide scar that started just below his right cheekbone and ran under his right ear to about three inches down his neck.

"Mind if I ask you something, Haj?"

"You ask many questions. What is it you don't know?"

"How did you learn all those languages you speak?" asked Blaine.

"My parents, they both speak the French, and they speak their native tongues, too. I pick up the language and accent it too easy. My first boat, the captain, he speak Malagache and the first mate, he was spoken in English. Five years I work with them . . . deep sea, tough work. That's how I own this scar."

"That was my second question."

Haj continued, "Two hundred mile out, I was working winch when the cable, she snap. Slice me like cheese. My fellow mate, not so lucky. Take his arm at the elbow. We were taken by whirly-bird to hospital. They stitch me up, but I don't work winch forever. Aury good captain. He understands."

"Are you married?" asked Blaine.

"I have no more answers. Time for sleep," said Haj and went below.

The first chance Blaine had to talk to Sabastien alone, he found out that Haj lost his wife to the first ever cholera epidemic of Madagascar in May of this year. One hundred and seventy people perished. Since the burial, he's refused to speak about it with anyone. He has no children, and his work on the boat is his life.

Sabastien is one of a kind, equal to a full house. He's a big man and when he walks, it's as though each stride is on a separate mission. At 6'3" tall and 190 pounds, he is as strong as he looks. He is 40 years old and married with three children, of which he always spoke highly. He was given to periodic episodes of braggadocio about himself and past exploits. One would see him as the type of guy that never made mistakes and looked down on those that did.

One time when they were all hauling nets, Blaine turned to Haj and said, "Just once, I'd like to see him slip and fall on his ass! I don't want him injured; just embarrassed enough to be humble."

Haj laughed out loud and said, "Never happen, man, never happen."

The truth be known, Blaine looked up to Sabastien's self-confidence. He was very grateful for all the help that Sab had given him. He wasn't always gentle with his words, but to the point and honest; exactly what Blaine needed his first couple of trips out. Sab saved him a couple of potential injuries. Blaine learned to understand his broken English, mixed with French-laced Malagache. Blaine thought, "This is a good crew."

He asked Aury if he wanted him to take over the wheel, but Aury insisted he get some sleep. "I'll wake you for your shift at 4:00 A.M."

"Aye, aye, Captain," Blaine said and went below. A chorus of snoring greeted him, so he just lay down, closed his eyes and joined the choir.

Aury woke Sab up at 3:00 A.M. to take the wheel and told him to let Blaine sleep in 'til daybreak. He wanted Blaine to earn some experience, but felt he wasn't ready for night navigation in these waters.

They arrived in port at 8:30 A.M., unloaded their catch, hosed down the boat and made some minor repairs. Aury always checked the icemaker himself, and after doing so, conferred with Moira who had all the arrangements made for dispersal and transportation of the cargo.

"How far out did you go?" she asked.

"Isle de Chesterfield, this side. My father gave me the tip. He said if the catch was good, and it was, to go back in two days. That's the plan. The crew can use the rest."

"So can you!" she said.

When Aury was satisfied the *Tolura* was again ready for sea, he called the crew together. "You've got tonight and all day tomorrow to yourselves. We meet here Thursday, 5:00 A.M., take on supplies and head out. You all did a great job."

"I've got you for a whole day and two nights. Oh, lucky me!" said Moira. Then on a serious note, she added, "Isn't that Isle de Chesterfield a long way out? I used to hear your father tell some awful stories concerning the crazy weather in that area. Two ships went down in that channel a few years ago."

"My father taught me how to navigate that area many times. We'll be all right. Besides, it's well worth the effort for catches like this one."

"Oh, I suppose, but I worry."

He countered with, "You're supposed to worry. That's what women do best." She elbowed him in the side, and then put her arm around his waist as they left the dock.

The crew stopped at the local watering hole for a few beers. A little while later, Aury and Moira showed up to buy a round of drinks and congratulate their good work.

"I just want to let you know the tuna brought a price of 20,000 francs," Moira informed the crew.

Sabastien whistled his approval and Blaine and Haj gave each other the high five that Blaine had taught him earlier.

"You know," said Blaine, "I think I'll take Sirana out to some-place nice tonight and spend a few francs. After all, I can sleep in all day tomorrow and get my beauty rest."

"Why don't you buy her a ring?" asked Sabastien.

Blaine looked at him out of the corner of his eye and whis-pered, "Not yet!"

Aury and Moira gave him a ride home and kidded him all the way about settling down in Madagascar and raising a family. He remained silent.

He walked in the house and asked the whole family out to din-ner, all that is, except Sirana. She was at work. The Andrianaivos already had other plans and graciously turned him down, insisting a night out with Sirana would be much more stimulating. Blaine showered and left a note for Sirana to wake him when she arrived home. He made no mention of dining out.

When Sirana entered the house, she found the note from her parents first. "We'll be with friends 'til 10 o'clock or later," signed Mom. Then she found the note from Blaine. She looked in on him. He was sound asleep. She showered, powdered her body, slipped into a lacy nightgown and went in to wake up Blaine.

Though they dated several times, they never had the opportunity to spend any appreciable moments together alone. She sat on the edge of his bed and touching his shoulder said, "You wanted me to wake you?"

Opening one eye and thinking he was dreaming, he reached up and touched her cheek and said, "You're beautiful." When his olfactory senses detected the smell of perfume, he sat straight up and realized Sirana was sitting there with just a nightgown on.

"Are you crazy?" he said to her. "If your father comes in here, I'm a dead man and a homeless one at that!"

"Relax; they're out for the evening, at least until 10 o'clock."

"What time is it now?"

"Does it really matter?" Sirana asked boldly. "We never have any time alone. If you want, I'll leave."

As she went to stand up, Blaine grabbed her wrist gently, took hold of her other hand and said, "Don't go . . . I want you, I mean I don't want you . . . I don't want you to go. Damn it, when I'm around you, I don't know what I mean!"

"That's good," she said. "Slide over."

Blaine cautiously moved to the other side of the twin bed and lay on his side facing Sirana, not knowing what to expect. She put her hand softly on his cheek, tenderly kissed him on the lips, looked deeply into his eyes and allusively whispered, "What shall we talk about?" Blaine was to remember this as the sexiest moment of his life.

She was close enough to realize he was fully aroused and decided to take full advantage of the situation. She reached down and softly caressed his claim to manhood, and when she did, it jumped. Blaine thought she was going to make it leap right out of his skivvies. Her breasts were heaving out of the nightgown, so Blaine saw fit to relieve her of her undergarments. She did the same for him, and they touched each other in passionate exploration, sharing the techniques of their different cultures. Her French side came to dominate the exercise, and he had all he could do to stay in the game.

"You're going to lose me!" he said, sounding as though he were holding his breath.

"Not yet," she whispered, as she came to rest on top of him. They began moving as partners on the dance floor, feeling each other's every contraction until she bit her lip and her eyes rolled back in her head. She quivered . . . then quivered again. Blaine could hold back no longer. They passed through the sea of ecstasy and reached the island of bliss together.

They laid there for a long time, holding each other in silence. They kissed and kissed again, and then Sirana said, "I'm hungry!"

The Betsiboka

"Wait and see . . . wait and see!" said René disgustingly. "I've had it! When do we call it quits? Here it is Wednesday afternoon the . . . 19th is it? Nine . . . 10 days, we've been tracking these things and still no contact. We're as far west as we can go. Look out there the both of you, it's Betsiboka Bay," he said pointing out to the water. "Should I order up some boats?"

"I'm frustrated as well, René," said Chett in somewhat of an apologetic tone.

"I'm beyond frustration!" retorted René.

Then Chett glanced around at the whole hunting party, and seeing they were in agreement with René, suggested, "How about one more day? Let's give it one more day, and if there's nothing positive, we'll head home. There's a small village about five miles south of here where we can get some supplies. I have friends there and maybe they've seen something. What do you say?"

The rest of the party talked among themselves for a minute, then René looked back and uttered, reluctantly, "One more day, but we skip the village. It's just wasting more time."

"Aza mandelo tanana misy havana!" said Chett out loud in the Malagasy tongue.

"Okay, you've made your point," said René. What Chett had quoted is an old saying on the island which, translated means, "You never pass by a village where there is family or friends."

Greetings were passed around as they entered the village, and Chett was told that the local chicken coop was almost destroyed the previous evening, and the remains of 14 chickens were in evidence. He checked it out, and it was impossible to make a positive identification of the perpetrators. The whole area was scuffled.

"We have other carnivores that are capable of eating chickens. There are poachers, as well," offered René. "Don't you find it odd that the tracks were wiped clean?"

"I guess. Maybe, I'm obsessed with the idea of finding and capturing something that is supposed to be extinct," said Chett. He had to admit that they had lost the trail.

The next morning, they hiked back to the vehicle, loaded up and headed home.

"I hope you don't think me ungrateful for your assistance," said René, "I thought we'd have this case wrapped up in a couple of days."

"Inspector," he replied, "I've been tracking, trapping and studying the related species a long time, and if what we're tracking is truly the giant version, I'm in awe. It has to be the most cunning and elusive animal on the planet. My hunch is that it will show up again. They may have even doubled back on us. A big plus is that, up to now, they had remained reclusive. Maybe they'll go back to living that way."

"What bothers me," said René "is now that it's tasted the blood and flesh of humans; can it revert back to its previous diet?"

Chett thought for a moment and stated, "The best possible scenario is that it will find a place of obscurity, away from human intrusion."

"Is there such a place any more, and if so, for how long?" asked René, as he stared out over the forest in wonderment.

CHAPTER SEVENTEEN

Phenomenal Encounter

At 5:00 A.M. sharp, Blaine was sitting at the top of the gang-plank of the *Tolura*, as the other crewmen were arriving. He was up at four o'clock and quietly left the house to walk to the docks. He was trying to sort out his feelings from his aspirations, which he never found troubling in the past.

He knew what his career would be from the time he was a young boy and never let anything take precedence over that goal, that is, up until now. It seemed that Sirana was in his every waking thought, as well as his dreams.

"I don't get it. I was never this confused before in my whole life!" he thought to himself. Then he remembered what the coed from Utah said the last night at the research complex, "When you find the right girl, you'll know it!" Right now, he had a hunch that Sirana might be the right girl, and it frightened the hell out of him. Aury's voice brought him back from his secret thoughts.

"I stopped by to pick you up at the house."

"Oh, I'm sorry," said Blaine. "I needed to clear my head this morning, so I walked."

"That's funny," said Aury. "Sirana answered the door. She was up early as well." Then he lifted his eyebrows twice rapidly, as if to say, "Ooh-la-la!"

Aury called out the list of things that needed to be checked, and after the usual "aye-aye" from each crewman, he shouted, "Let's prepare to get underway. Sabastien, you have the helm!"

"Where are we headed today, Captain?" asked Sab.

"You know better than to ask that now," said Aury sternly. "When we clear the bay, I'll give you the heading. For now, stay on 280 degrees."

None of the captains ever told where they were bound for else the best spots would be over-fished. Not even the crew was given the location or course until they were well underway. When they cleared the bay, Aury took the helm and steered southwest.

"I have a hunch we can find another school of tuna," said Aury to the crew. "Are you with me?" After getting a thumbs-up from them all, he said, "So be it!"

Once again, they headed for Isle de Chesterfield. Sometimes the currents could be very treacherous in this area, especially in bad weather, but the fishing could be excellent, as their last trip confirmed. Aury asked for another weather check on the radio and announced it to the crew. "No storms in the area, clear skies and light winds, diminishing to 10 knots by late afternoon."

Sab breathed a sigh of relief and Haj filled in Blaine, "Bad weather . . . bad news. Last year, strong winds and crazy sea wash us into shoals, pretty close, but Aury good captain. Take no chances. He become, how you say, a sticker for safely."

"A stickler for safety," corrected Blaine.

"Exactly," reaffirmed Haj.

Mid afternoon, they arrived at the general area where Aury wanted to fish and ordered the lines out. The first haul was light with some tuna but more of a mixed bag. As soon as the fish were sorted and iced, Aury decided to head further west, about 30 miles into the channel. This is a move he learned from his father and had never known it to fail. Night was only an hour or so away and sunsets were beautiful out here.

"This is the spot!" said the captain. "Shoot the nets!"

After the nets were let out, an absolute calm befell the area. There was no visible chop in the water and the wind became nonexistent. Eight eyeballs scanned the immediate area around the boat, in eerie anticipation. Then as suddenly as it stopped, the wind picked up again to 15 knots and there was a hissing sound, heard in the distance.

"Listen to that!" said Blaine. "It sounds like a steaming freight train, coming right at us!"

Everyone became apprehensive, including Aury, who had never experienced this type of situation. The waves became irregular and about 50 feet away, formed in lines of convergence. The waves were eddying around the boat, creating a severe banging against the hull. There was a high frequency sound overriding the usual ambient noise from wind, waves and swell.

"Should we haul in the nets, Captain?" asked Haj.

"There's no time!" cautioned Aury. "Stay calm and hang on!"

Sabastien was the only crewman on the side of the boat that was facing the expanse of the channel. He noticed a great amount of matted vegetation and debris traveling on the waves at a very abnormal rate of speed. He wasn't sure, but he estimated, maybe, 40 or 50 knots. He also thought he saw a brown furred animal riding the debris. "I don't say nothing," he thought to himself. "The rest think I'm crazy, maybe lose my mind. I say nothing."

As the winds died down and the calm slowly returned, they all looked at each other in awe. Blaine was in deep thought and after a short while spoke. "I think I know what we just experienced. I believe I know what happened. We just survived a suloy."[1]

"A what?" asked Aury?

"I've got some notes on ocean phenomena that I was compil-

---

[1] A suloy is an unusual state of the sea where the surface is covered by precipitous and irregular waves that form either in lines of convergence, in curved boundaries of eddies, or in rounded patches of water.

ing in one of my courses at school. It's below. I logged some notes in the same book about my experiences on the *Tolura*. Be right back."

In a few moments, Blaine returned with his thick notebook. Inside the book were several computer readouts that he downloaded from the Internet. "Let's get under the light and check this out," he said.

The rest of the men gathered around Blaine. "A suloy . . . see," he pointed to the printout sheet that bore a picture of a shear, taken from a satellite. Then he read from his notes, "It was named by a Russian oceanographer named Federov in 1983. There are fewer than a dozen published articles on the subject, and those are in Soviet literature. The astronauts aboard the *Discovery* took these pictures of the Mozambique Channel on August 30th, 1985."[2]

"What was that date again?" asked Aury. Blaine repeated it, and Aury pulled out his father's logbook. Aury started to scan through the dated pages while he was talking. "When I was only 10 or 11 years old, I remember my father telling my mother about a very strange occurrence in this channel. He logged it and notified the maritime authorities. Here it is! This is dated, 4:12 P.M., August 30th, 1985. 'We have encountered a possible shear with a long narrow line of chaotic seas, preceded by a loud hissing noise resembling a locomotive engine. We experienced severe banging on the hull, which forced us to "heave-to" while the line of waves passed by at an estimated speed of 100 kilometers (62 mph).'"

"So I wasn't imagining things," said Sab in a low tone of voice.

"What did you say?" asked Haj. Sabastien just shrugged his shoulders.

"If it was 1985, that was 18 years ago!" stated Aury. "I wonder how often they occur."

---

[2] Throughout the year, the Mozambique Channel, between Madagascar and Africa, exhibits strong currents and shears. During the summer monsoon season, suloys are often found.

"Nobody seems to know. There's no useful data on frequency, wave spectra or even a hypothesis on their generation. To experience one is absolutely fantastic!" offered Blaine.

"To survive is much better," added Haj.

"I just hope we didn't collect much debris in the nets," said Sabastien. "Hell will be played sorting it together." Blaine understood what he meant.

"No sense guessing," shouted Aury. "Let's haul 'em in!"

The winch began hauling in the lines, and a severe tug was felt off to one side. Aury quickly developed a sick feeling in his gut. The last time he heard that winch squeal like that, they were hauling in a Tiger shark that eventually tore the nets to pieces. Another tug moved the boat 30 degrees starboard.

"Back off on the winch!" Aury shouted, and then he waited. Nothing stirred. He ordered the winch in motion again. It was straining but seemed to be handling the strain okay. The lights from the boat lit up the area, but Haj and Blaine were still not able to see what the drag was.

Aury figured they had a load of fish weighted down with a lot of debris. The winch continued to strain, and then there was a loud clunk and it seized.

"Sab," said Aury, "try backing off and then start it again!" Sabastien followed orders, but after several tries, it was still to no avail. "Okay, shut it down," said Aury. "I've got to think this out."

He went over his options. He could cut and abandon the nets and head for home, which is a no-no. They could try hauling them in by hand, which would take forever and a day, or, God forbid, call for help. He also asked the crew for their thoughts.

Blaine's forte was always a good idea at the right time, and so, he proposed one. "Why don't three of us start to haul while the winch takes up the slack? Once we get it going, it may take over on its own. It's possible that it's not seized but just over-capacitated."

"Aury, it's worth a shoot!" said Haj.

"Okay," replied Aury. "Let's try it. We may be able to get it close enough to see what's binding it up."

Aury thought about it some more, then shouted to Sabastien, "Sab, start it and see if we can back it off about 10 feet. As soon as we start pulling, kick it into gear. I'll give you the word. Keep a sharp eye on that cable. If you see any sign of fraying, shut it down immediately!"

The three pullers got into position and Sabastien started up the winch motor. "Okay, Sab, slowly put it in reverse and back off real easy," ordered Aury. Because of the strain, it clinked into gear and reversed easily. "Okay, stop!" He looked at the crew and said, "Here we go. All right, Sab, as we pull, just put it in forward and inch it along, but don't force it. If it starts squealing again, back off!"

"Thank God the weather is calm and the boat isn't pitching," thought Haj out loud.

Blaine glanced at him and said, "That's the most correct sentence I've ever heard you say in English."

"You scared plenty, Blaine. I was spoken in French," said Haj. They all laughed, and then got down to business.

They all followed orders. Aury definitely commanded respect. Little by little, the nets were coming in until the lights from the boat made visible an awesome sight.

"I don't believe this!" shouted Blaine as he pointed into the water. Everybody stopped and eyes became focused on a shark of great length and girth but apparently void of life. It wasn't stirring at all.

"Tubarão," called out Aury.

"A what?" asked Blaine.

"Grand Requin Blanc," said Haj.

"A Great White," repeated Blaine in English. "It's over 20 feet in length!"

"First we get it out of the nets," said Aury. "Just be careful. I heard of one of these believed to be dead, and when they hauled it on deck, it heaved its head up and took off a man's leg. They're devils."

Blaine couldn't stop staring at it. This was the first he'd ever seen in person. It was awesome! "What do you suppose killed it?" he asked.

"It's possible it became entangled in the net," said Aury. "If they can't swim, they die, but one that size should have been capable of tearing the nets to shreds. He might have been injured to begin with, anyway, here's the plan. We get a line forward of the dorsal fin and behind the pectorals, and then snug it up. Next we get a line around the tail. We'll use chain falls to slowly lift it away from the net. We'll forward it along the starboard side. You all with me so far?" he asked. They nodded. He continued, "Once we get that done, we can haul in the nets, sort and ice down the fish, discard the debris and then decide what to do with this monster."

For the first time on this trip, everything went as planned. The shark was moved forward without any undue problems, and they ended up with more fish than anticipated . . . 60 percent capacity.

"Okay," said Aury. "What do we do with this damn thing?" referring to the Great White.

Blaine was the first to speak, naturally, "It may be worth a lot of money. I heard the jaws of an 18 footer fetched over $30,000 American in an Internet auction. The Japanese pay big francs for the fins and marine biologists will pay a modest fee for the carcass, after they try getting it for nothing. Your wife could lay it out on the Internet for feelers. You just need to check the local laws first."

"Where did you learn all that?" asked Haj.

"I'm studying to be a marine biologist," answered Blaine. "Actually I got that knowledge from the Internet."

"Okay, let's get with it," said Aury. "Maybe we can be home for dinner tonight," as he glanced at the time, 2:05 A.M. Then he thought, "I'd better log every detail as it occurred."

He put a call in to his wife, Moira, explaining the situation and detailing the catch. "We have a Gran Requin Blanc in tow, approximately 7 meters in length and somewhere around 4,000 lbs."

"My God!" exclaimed Moira. "Is everyone all right; any injuries? Are you okay?"

"Slow down, dear, everything's okay. Take notes. First you need to find out if there's any governmental law banning the sale of Whitey's parts and jaws. Blaine believes South Africa has such laws, but doesn't know if they apply to us. Secondly, we did not intentionally capture this animal. It became lodged in our nets, apparently void of life. There are slashes around its snout and around both eyes, and it appears to be bleeding from the mouth. There's no way to get it on board, so we'll lash it to the side of the hull. Naturally, we can't ice it down."

"So what type of sale are we looking for here?" asked Moira. "If I go to my sources, what exactly are we trying to sell and for how much?"

"Well, according to Blaine, the jaws of one this size could bring up to 200,000 francs," said Aury softly.

Moira shot back loudly, "How much did you say?"

"You heard me correctly," replied Aury. "Also the fins can attract a few thousand. Try the oriental market. The rest of the carcass may be of interest to marine biologists. You'll have to shop around for buyers. Just one other thing: make arrangements for refrigerated warehouse space in case we don't sell it off right away."

She repeated everything back for clarification, and Aury said, "You got it, honey." He then added, "The biologists may want to examine the carcass intact, but the deal is we get the jaws and fins when they're through with the autopsy. I don't know what kind of time we can make coming in. I'm guessing late afternoon, early evening."

"Be careful, love you," she said.

"Yeah, love you too. Out."

"That trailing blood will attract every shark in the channel," stated Aury.

"I just had a terrific thought!" said Blaine. He suggested, "We can't ice the shark down, but what if we tilt its head up and fill it with ice? Its throat is big enough to stuff some into the gullet, and then lash the jaws together tightly. That just may keep it from trailing blood and help with preservation."

"What are you waiting for?" asked Aury. "Get it done."

When all was secure, they had some hot chow and rested their weary bones and muscles.

"I'll take the helm 'til daybreak," said Aury. "I want to see how she rides with the extra weight we're towing. The rotation to relieve will be Haj, Blaine and Sabastien . . . three-hour shifts. Get some rest."

CHAPTER EIGHTEEN

A Fish Tale

Nightfall was still a couple of hours away when the *Tolura* was in sight of the dock. "It has to be quite a view from land," said Blaine, "seeing a 40-foot boat with a shark three-fifths of its length, riding sidesaddle!"

"When she hang on the dock, the whole town show up!" offered Haj.

"We charge a few francs each for a look, eh?" added Sabastien.

Aury just shook his head, "Typical pirates . . . what a crew!" he mumbled.

There had been no word from Moira all the way in, but she was standing on the pier when they arrived and had a private conversation with Aury after they tied up. The dock winch was more than able to handle the shark, tail first. There was a lot of picture taking and after many oohs and aahs; the fish was trucked over to the warehouse. It was quite a spectacle. Refrigeration space wasn't cheap, but in this case, necessary.

The regular fish catch had already been sold by Moira to her source in the capital city. After unloading, weighing and packing the fish for shipment, the crew was exhausted.

"I know you guys are tired, so I'll finish up here. Moira and I will see you over at the watering hole for a beer in a half hour. We have something important to discuss before you go home." Aury then proceeded to hose down the deck.

The crew was about to order the third round of drinks when Aury and Moira, accompanied by Rijah, walked in the door.

"This must be important," said Haj in French, "if they bring the old man!"

"Who are you calling old?" asked Rijah, as he jokingly put up his fists.

Aury beckoned them all to a small table in the corner, and after the drinks were served all around, he spoke softly, "Moira has some info for us on the sale of the shark. I'll let her tell you."

"Well, it's like this," she said. "I could find nothing in our constitution that bans the sale of shark parts. I contacted my sources and hinted at the possibility of coming into possession of a Great White over six meters in length and put out some feelers for interested parties on the Internet. I've received three offers so far, the highest being over 200,000 francs. I guess that would be around $50,000 American."

They all became overly excited, and Aury cautioned them to keep their enthusiasm at a low pitch.

Moira continued, "The fins, at last check, were up to 35,000 francs or about $8,000 American. The biologists I've contacted wouldn't make an offer until they viewed the real article. They'll be here Monday morning. That brings us to the regular catch, which brought 11,000 francs. Right now, we're seeing a possibility of making $55,000 to $60,000 American. That's all I have."

"I'd say that was quite enough," said Rijah. "You've done a great job."

Then Aury spoke up, "I think Blaine deserves a full share this trip. Anyone disagree?"

With no dissention, Blaine thanked them all and made a request. "What we have in the warehouse is a marine biologist's dream. I'd like to be in on the dissection. Is it possible?" he asked, looking right at Aury.

"I don't see why not. Do you, Moira?" stated Aury.

"We'll make sure it's in the contract," she said, and then went on, "I caution you all to keep this information to yourselves until all the deals are consummated." Aury raised his glass and they all toasted their forthcoming success.

Rijah and Blaine conveyed the news to Yvette and Sirana when they arrived home. Blaine had been warmly accepted as part of the family, and Sirana wanted to make it permanent. Blaine was still hedging. He and Sirana hadn't found the opportunity to be alone for a while, but it didn't matter to Blaine. As long as they were together, no care of where, he felt comfortable. This was a blessing in disguise, because Rijah and Yvette didn't go out that often.

Sirana thought she'd suggest her parents go out for this particular evening, but before she could ask, Blaine spoke up and said, "Let's all go out and celebrate our good fortune . . . my treat!"

Sirana sighed and said, "Oh, swell."

"It's a great idea!" Rijah seconded the motion. They all went out. The weekend was uneventful, but went by swiftly. Blaine needed the rest.

Monday morning, the 24th, found Blaine down at the warehouse early, waiting for the biologists. After baby-sitting the shark all the way to the port, he somehow felt attached to the beast.

Aury pulled up in front of the warehouse at 9:15 A.M. and asked, "Anyone show up yet?"

"Not yet," answered Blaine. "What time were they supposed to be here? I've been here for two hours."

"You're really excited about this, aren't you?"

"You bet! This is beyond my wildest dreams. I've heard of marine biologists, oceanographers and underwater photographers, who've never seen a great white, except in pictures. I guess the movie *Jaws* really brought this fish into the limelight, but by now, it's been all but forgotten. When news of this baby gets out, beaches throughout the world will be less populated."

"So tell me, Blaine, how are you getting on with my sister?"

"You asked that same question last week," said Blaine. "What is it you want to know? Am I in love with her? Yes, I believe I am!"

"Mmmm," replied Aury. "Does this mean that someday we might be related?"

Blaine changed the subject and said, "What time did you say these guys would be here?"

Aury laughed at his evasiveness and answered, "They're coming a long way. They'll be here this morning."

Blaine just sat there tapping his fingers and decided to keep the conversation going in the same direction, instead of on his love life. "Are these guys Malagasies?" he asked.

"No, actually they're Europeans," replied Aury. "They've been involved in research work over at Toliara on the southern coast. They travel all over the world according to Moira, checking out incidents of shark attack on humans and performing examinations on large sharks that are accidentally killed or captured. I understand that they have healthy financial grants."

"They must be very good at what they do!" observed Blaine.

While they were talking, a large van pulled up in front of the warehouse. "Mr. Andrianaivo?" asked the gentleman, sitting on the driver's side.

Aury stood up, walked to the door of the van and extended his hand. "Aury," he said. "And this is Blaine Gibbons."

"Good morning to you both. I'm Phillipe Fontaine and this is my partner, Werner Klemp."

When the introductions and handshakes were out of the way, Klemp said, "Gibbons . . . isn't that American?"

"Yes it is," and seeing they were both curious as to his presence at this meeting continued, "I'm here for the summer on sort of a working vacation. I study marine biology, University of Florida. I was on board when we hauled in the shark."

"Good work and congratulations on your choice of careers," offered Fontaine. "So what do we have here and exactly how did you come by it?"

Aury started to give the details, "We had the nets out for tuna when we were suddenly overtaken by what appears to have been a suloy."

"You experienced a suloy? Most people, including mariners, have never even heard of the term," said Werner.

Aury let Blaine take over. "We had all the earmarks," he said. Then he went on to explain the happenings, right up to the point where they were winching in the nets.

Aury gave a synopsis and ended by saying, "So what we have is a cadaver, over six meters long and weighing about one and a half to two tons."

Phillipe whistled and Werner said, "Let's see it!"

On the way into the warehouse, Phillipe asked if it would be possible to interview the other crewmen. Aury gave his assent. When he unlocked the door to the inner refrigerated section, the biologists just stood there aghast. They looked at each other and then back at the fish.

"This is quite astonishing. This is a female, and I believe it will weigh in and measure much more than anything on record," said Fontaine.

"How did those deep gashes happen on its snout?" asked Werner.

"That's how it was when we hauled it in," said Aury.

"No matter," said Fontaine. "We'd like to get started on the autopsy as soon as possible." He hesitated for a minute, looked at Klemp and suggested, "How would Thursday be?"

"May we first settle on a price?" asked Aury. After all, he was speaking for the whole crew. They dickered back and forth and finally came to terms. Aury added, "We get the jaws and fins intact and one other request. Blaine here gets to sit in on the dissection." They agreed.

Aury was still unable to give Moira a definite date to release the parts for sale and finalize the details, but the family and crew were very satisfied with the way things were working out, so far. This was the biggest single deal of their lives.

Arrangements had been made for repair of the winch and some other minor irregularities. Aury alerted the crew to a possible sailing Monday next and made them all aware of the nets that needed mending by then. "Regardless of how all this turns out, we're still fishermen on a working vessel."

Thursday morning, July 27th, the biologists arrived early, and Blaine was there to greet them. He helped them to set up a sort of field lab in the warehouse. He was wearing a butcher's apron and rubber fishing boots, offering his services any way he could be used. First to be examined was the deep gash near the shark's left eye and the other cuts around the upper lip and snout. A jelly substance was oozing out of the ampullae or pores, used for tracking prey. They took samples. They asked what the shark's demeanor was at first contact.

"She was quite lethargic," said Blaine. "After a couple of hard tail splashes, she acted sedated."

Whitey, as Blaine called her, measured in at 7.1 meters, the largest authenticated *Carcharodon carcharias* (Great White Shark) on record. The teeth ranged around two and one-quarter inches.

"Seven point one meters!" exclaimed Blaine. "That's over 20 feet long!"

"Twenty-three point twenty-eight feet exactly," said Werner.

"She's a beauty!" said Phillipe.

After several measurements more, including bite radius, girth and fin size, they examined the inside of the mouth that was displaying deep cuts in there, as well. "Looks like it was chewing broken glass!" said Klemp. "I want to see the digestive tract. Let's cut her open."

An incision was made from just below the jaw, all the way to the anus. The smell was putrid, and as they all turned away from the acidic emanation, a few objects fell out on the floor. Distinguishable was a blood-covered tuna of four feet and what appeared to be a fur-bearing animal of larger size, also covered in blood, resembling a giant wet beaver.

"What the hell is that?" shouted Werner, as the large animal fell with a thud right at his feet. The tuna skidded five feet away in the opposite direction. Blaine just stared in amazement at the amount of blood pouring out of the belly cavity.

"This is all new to me!" said an excited Phillipe.

Werner yelled out, "Hose this damn thing down and let's get a look at it!"

Blaine grabbed the hose and washed the fur-covered animal. It was man size with a long tail, massive jaws and teeth and retractable claws as sharp as razors. Conspicuously missing were the two front legs. They had apparently been severed just above the elbows.

"Hose down the stomach cavity of the shark," requested Fontaine. Revealed were deep gashes all throughout the stomach and as far up as the throat. Mystery turned to conjecture.

"It's becoming apparent to me," said Phillipe, "what the cause of death might have been to the shark. But I'm not sure I believe my own reasoning."

"I'm following your line of thought," said Werner. "But what kind of animal do we have here?"

They stared at it in silence for a long time, and then, out of the blue, Blaine said, "I think I know what it is . . . I mean, I know what it looks like."

Both biologists looked at him expectantly, waiting for him to expound on his utterance. "About three weeks ago, I was introduced, by photos, to an animal with similar features, but of much smaller size; a *Cryptoprocta ferox*, better known as the fossa." He went on to tell them the story of his volunteer service at the compound and of Chester Whalton's theory.

"Chett told me that he believed the great granddaddy of the fossa still existed. His guess of the size would be comparable to what we have here. Its species would be called *Cryptoprocta giganta*."

"How do we get in touch with Mr. Whalton?" asked Phillipe.

"I have his number in my wallet. I'll call him now," said Blaine.

Blaine left a message with Chett's assistant to call back A.S.A.P. urgent! Within an hour, Chett returned the call, and Blaine put Werner on the phone. He explained the happenings and the discovery of what may be a giant fossa.

"This is fantastic!" shouted Chett in excitement. "I'll be there in two hours!"

They cleaned up the fossa a little more, and the three of them lifted it onto a table. "I'd like to gut this one," said Klemp, but Blaine reminded him his duty was to the shark.

Chett found Blaine and the two biologists sitting at a table drinking ice cold sodas. They offered, he accepted, and after taking a big swig and going through introductions, he looked at Blaine in anticipation and said, "Where is he?"

Blaine stood up and said, "Follow me!" When he opened the door to the room where the animals were, Chett couldn't do or say anything; he just stared with his mouth agape for several minutes, trying to fathom what his eyes were seeing, but what his mind was not grasping.

"This is truly extraordinary. He's much larger, especially around the neck, than I imagined. Look at these claws . . . and the tail, at least six feet, about the same length as the animal itself! Now I can understand what all the folklore is about, and why all the superstitions survived to this day!"

"I know you're excited about this particular specimen," said

Blaine, "but I'd like you to see where we found him!" Blaine took hold of his arm and walked him around the petition that was separating the two animals and pointed to the huge incision.

"He fell out of there. We couldn't believe it either. At first, we didn't have a clue what it was 'til we hosed it down. It was covered in blood. Look at the gashes throughout the stomach lining and around the snout," offered Blaine.

He shook his head in disbelief as Blaine was speaking and asked, "How . . . how?" And he couldn't finish the sentence. Blaine suggested they get out of the cold for a while and compare notes with the other biologists as well.

Blaine told him about the capture of the shark and the other pertinent details leading up to the dissection. It was at that point that Werner resumed the explanation and ended with, "And so good man, that's why we called you!"

Chett was about to convey the story of his exploits with Inspector Areben, when Aury and the other two crewmen came in the door of the warehouse.

"You desired to speak to the rest of my crew?" Aury said to Fontaine.

"Yes, I do," said Phillipe. "When we hear everyone's point of view, we get a much better picture of the whole incident."

Blaine was anxious to show Aury and the crew what the stomach contents of the shark contained, but they wanted to do the questioning first. So he and Chett stood off to the side, out of the way and almost out of earshot.

"How do you think the fossa ended up in a shark?" asked Blaine.

"Well, we were tracking two of them for several days and the trail went cold at the edge of the bay. We thought they turned south toward Tsingy . . ."

"Wait a minute!" exclaimed Blaine. "Tracking what and who's 'we'?"

Chett motioned him away from the others a little more and filled him in on what had taken place.

"No, no . . . this is so damn bizarre," said Blaine. "Who'd believe it? I'm not sure I believe it. Do you?"

"The facts are in that room!" said Chett. "All we have to do is put them together."

"Oh, is that all?" asked Blaine. "That crew over there, that's being interviewed, hasn't seen a fossa as yet!"

"Maybe they shouldn't," offered Chett.

Blaine quickly replied, "You can't hide that! In less than 24 hours, the whole world will know about it, so you better be thinking of a good explanation."

When the interview came to an end, it was decided by the biologists, to show the *Tolura* crew the fossa. After all, they were the people responsible for it being here. The shark carcass, all but the fins and jaws, belonged to Phillipe and Werner anyway. Chett had no say in the matter.

As they gathered around in fascination, Sabastien spoke something in Malagasy; Chett was the only one to understand him. Keeping the speech in Malagache, he asked him to repeat, but pulled him off to the side.

"What did you mean when you said you weren't crazy or overtired?" asked Chett.

"When the sea became rough and the boat was heaving, I thought I saw a furry animal floating on some matted vegetation, but it was moving very fast and it was almost dark," explained Sabastien.

"What do you mean it was moving fast?" asked Chett

"From the suloy," responded Sab.

"What in God's name is a suloy?"

Sabastien thought for a moment and said, "Ask Blaine . . . conversation over."

After Blaine explained the meaning of a suloy, they were all on even ground, but Chett was still reluctant to tell his side of the story or to make an educated guess as to what he believed happened.

"Gentlemen, if you no longer need us," said Aury, "we have work to do. Are you coming, Blaine?"

"I'll be along in a little while."

Chett spoke up and said, "This is all beginning to make sense to me."

"I'm glad it's making sense to you!" said Werner. "I'm quite lost here."

Chett, after looking at the faces of the others, knew it was the time to expound on his theory. He filled them all in on what had taken place in the forests over the last three weeks.

When he mentioned that the track of the fossa started at the Jangala Reservation National Park, Phillipe, who had some knowledge of the interior, stood up and said, "The Jangala Reservation? Good God, man. That's over 275 kilometers from here! Let me get this straight. Are you suggesting that this animal or animals decided to go for a 170-mile stroll from their proposed home in the forbidden forest, down to Betsiboka Bay, having an occasional meat buffet on the way, then jump in the ocean for a fish meal and for sport, I say for sport, mind you, sharpen its claws on a Great White Shark?"

"A bit bizarre, wouldn't you say?" added Werner.

"Thank God," said Blaine, "that the crew of the *Tolura* went home or this place would be in an uproar."

Chett continued, "Phillipe, what you said is not quite the way I'd put it, but you're not far from what I surmised, and that in itself is disquieting."

"Disquieting?" asked Phillipe. "I've been all over the world checking out shark stories that were bordering bizarre. What you're suggesting here is borderline madness."

"Is there a map of Madagascar in here?" asked Chett

Blaine said there was one in the office, as well as a chart of the channel. "I was looking at it earlier," he said.

"Follow me, gentlemen," said Chett and led the way. He went to the map, and with some thumbtacks that happened to be lying around, marked the spot of exit by the fossa from Jangala Reservation and marked all the known attacks and the direction in which they led the hunting party.

"Please listen to what I have to say. This is the way I believe these events occurred and why:

"In the last 20 years, 85 percent of this island has been deforested . . . 85 percent. Many animals became displaced. When I arrived here in 1997, I became involved in conservation and devoted my study to the lemur population, hopefully to prevent their extinction. One day I came across one that was freshly killed. My Malagasy assistant shouted, 'Foosa, foosa.' I found out later he was referring to the *Cryptoprocta ferox*. I decided to retrieve some info on this animal and found not much had been written except knowledge of its existence and its love for blood. It kills in a very sanguinary manner. I decided to change my study to this animal.

"From my observations, it's a relatively reclusive animal and is not fond of being encroached upon, especially by man. If he is, he'll move. After that last typhoon this year that killed and displaced many people, I observed and noted odd changes of habit among the animal population. Have you gentlemen ever heard of removal migration?"

"Isn't that a one-way permanent move?" asked Blaine.

"Exactly!" said Chett. "Throughout history, animals including man that have their existence threatened or their food supply diminished will move to new locations."

Then Werner interjected, "You're not saying that fossas are acting like salmon or geese on a regular migration pattern?"

"Well," said Chett, "not exactly, and yes . . . in a way. I mean the simplest of animals rely on external forces, such as wind or water currents to propel them to their migratory goals.

"Others use more complex senses to navigate, such as coastlines, mountain ranges, etc. I guess what I'm asking myself and what I want you to ask yourselves is: How do we know this species originated here?

"At one time, the elephant bird, believed to be endemic only to Madagascar, is now believed to have swum over here from mainland Africa centuries ago. It's also believed to be extinct, and yet this year, two of its eggs washed up on a beach in Perth, Australia. Children playing in the sand discovered them. The question that was posed, initially was, 'How did they get there?'"

"And what was the conclusion?" asked Phillipe, who was now becoming much more interested in what was being said.

Chett answered, "The Mozambique Channel has been known to have strange currents, occasional typhoons, and other strange wave and tide movements, not easily understood or explained. This suloy that Blaine and his friends encountered is a great example. He has stated that not one person knows what causes them or how often they occur. I suggest certain animals do!

"Let's say, for the sake of argument, and I know I'll get an argument, that the fossas in question were forced into migration. It's possible they are the last of their species and started out on a trek to a destination known only to them and on a timetable to coincide with that particular suloy."

Blaine said, "You're stretching it a little now. Don't you think that's kind of far out?"

"Well, I've known for a long time now," continued Chett, "that fish constitutes a good part of their diet."

Werner interrupted, "How did you arrive at that conclusion? You've only been aware of granddaddy fossa for three weeks."

Chett went on, "We found evidence along the riverbanks while tracking, but we're getting away from the migration theory. Please, gentlemen, bear with me!" He went back to the map. "I want to point out that they crossed, I repeat, crossed mind you, the Mahajamba River over to the Betsiboka River that led them to the bay. We know so little about the fossa, yet try to refer to it with some sort of scientific exactness.

"Okay, Chett," said Phillipe, "you made your point. They're in the bay; now what?"

"Well from this phase on, your guess is as good as mine, but this is my version: I figure they went out off of Cape Sable because that's where we lost their track. They went in, not only to fish, but to swim out to catch the suloy, knowing that it would propel them to where they wanted to go."

"Which is where?" asked Blaine.

"Hell, if I know!" said Chett. He went on, "Anyway, they start swimming out and in comes Whitey, who is also looking for a meal but gets something she didn't bargain for . . . ferocity at her own level. That would account for the gashes around the eyes and snout."

Phillipe jumped in, "Wait, seriously. I can envision this: after getting slashed by a fossa on initial contact, the shark retreats and the fossa continues swimming out. Whitey attacks from behind, devouring most of fossa except the forelegs, which she severs with the bite. She swallows it whole, which by the way, she's well capable of doing, and that's when the fossa lets loose with all its fury, biting and slashing all the way down. It tore up the mouth, throat and stomach of the shark before it succumbed."

"From what I've seen of your dissected cadaver in the other room," said Chett, "Whitey was already on her way to the happy hunting ground when she was trapped in the net."

"That figures!" added Blaine. "My captain said if the shark were healthy, it would have torn the nets to shreds and been on its way."

"Okay," said Werner, "now that you've helped us make sense of the whole incident, we can put it to bed, Right?"

"Wrong!" answered Chett. "We still have an animal to deal with that, in all probability, has already landed somewhere on mainland Africa."

"Do you really believe that?" asked Blaine.

"Yes, I do! If it hasn't drowned or been taken by another shark. We have a responsibility to report our findings. That animal, if still alive, has tasted human blood and flesh. I believe, if threatened, it will do so again."

"Are you nuts?" exclaimed Phillipe. "You want to report this theory, and that's all it is, a theory, to the authorities? They'll lock us all up in a loony bin."

"Okay," suggested Chett, "I'll say to you the same thing I said to Inspector Areben in the forests, namely, wait and see!"

So he again went to the map. "I believe fossa will head for a river delta somewhere between these two points . . . the Zambezi River and Maputo on the east coast of Africa . . . Mozambique! I think it's going to head upstream to some remote area with a good food supply. My guess is it will stay in close proximity to water. The only thing that concerns me is that it may encounter a human being on its travels, and if it feels threatened, I've seen what this animal's capable of doing. It's not pretty.

"We'll sit on our theory for the time being and keep close tabs on any strange news coming out of Africa. Agreed?" They all agreed.

"Are we going to release what we have to the press?" asked Fontaine.

"I think we should tell all the facts we know and show the evidence. There's no way you're going to keep this find of a record Great White from the scientific community. Let's keep our projections and theories to ourselves for the time being. Let's wait and see!" said Chett, and then turned his attention to the fossa, *Cryptoprocta giganta*, lying on the table.

Phillipe and Werner went back to examining the shark while Blaine assisted Chett with the dissection and measurements of the fossa.

"What a discovery!" thought Chett, "If I could only capture the other one . . . alive?"

Every once in a while Blaine would pop in to see what was happening with the shark. He was in his glory. When they wrapped up the day's events, they agreed to meet back at the warehouse the next morning, along with the crew of the *Tolura*. That evening, Blaine excitedly told Sirana and her parents the whole story, without leaving out the minutest detail, except, of course, the fact that the fossa's mate might be alive and well somewhere on mainland Africa.

Friday morning, July 28th was the dawn of a new day in zoological science. Members of the press were called in and given access to the carcasses of both animals, as well as all the scientific terminology they could handle. They were also given pre-dissection photos; Polaroid pictures. Everyone involved was interviewed and photographed. The whole port section of Mahajanga was bustling with people, hoping to catch a glimpse of the purported beasts and their captors. Chett had cautioned Sabastien about telling of the animal he thought he'd seen riding on matted vegetation.

"It's far too bizarre to mention. Just stick to the facts," he suggested. It was decided by the group to donate the carcass of the fossa to posterity and the scientific community, leaving Chett in charge of the disposition. The shark and all its parts were to be sold, and all proceeds divided among the crew of the *Tolura*.

Once the news reached international presses and was substantiated, offers came in from around the world. Collectors, who were doubling the price of the initial offers, were seeking the jaws of both animals. Aury and the crew were ecstatic, but the biologists were worried that open season would be declared on all sharks and Madagascan predators by poachers hoping to gain a quick dollar.

"Chett," asked Blaine, "do you think we did the right thing, disclosing what we knew to the press?"

"How could we have prevented it?" he answered. "Anyway, for now, it's out of our hands. Besides, I don't think you're going to see a bunch of people searching the Jangala Reservation. That place is its own defense."

CHAPTER NINETEEN

The Other Side of the Channel

Donovan Wildlife Ranch & Medical Mission
Mozambique, Africa

Mozambique stretches for 2500 km (1550 mi.) on the south-eastern coast of Africa, bordered by Tanzania to the north, Malawi and Zambia to the northwest, Zimbabwe to the west and South Africa and Swaziland to the southwest. The island of Madagascar lies directly east, 400 km (250 mi.) across the Mozambique Channel.

Michael Donovan, a field research biologist and doctor from Massachusetts, USA and his wife, Anna, from Lisbon, Portugal, met and worked together in the early sixties among the sick and impoverished of Mozambique. Through their efforts and unselfish devotion, two major plagues were curtailed that saved thousands of lives. It was no surprise that they held carte blanche, not only in this area, but in bordering Malawi, as well.

With some funding from the government and a huge effort by local labor, including some from Malawi, a medical facility became a reality in Ancuaze on the Zambezi River. It was equipped phil-anthropically by a large donation that came from Michael's broth-er, John from Swampscott, Massachusetts. He had won millions in the state lottery, and this was the only way Michael would allow him to share it. He also donated a large tract of land that bordered the facility.

It wasn't until the compound was completed in 1967 that Michael and Anna realized they were in love and soon married. She gave birth to a son the following year. They agreed to name him Diogo after her father who had passed away. So it was, in the spring of 1968, that Diogo Donovan was unleashed to the world!

In 1975, Portugal granted independence to Mozambique and almost immediately, civil war began between two rival political groups, the Frelimo, who controlled most of the major cities, and the Renamo, who operated mostly as a guerilla movement, controlling most of the outside areas. In exchange for medical services and occasional food supplies, the Donovan Complex, as it was known then, was under the "protection" of the Renamo and a safe haven for the family. Shipments that came upriver bearing the Donovan stamp went untouched. South Africa was also giving aid to the Renamo. With the spread of the civil war, health and education systems collapsed and troops from South Africa, Zambia and Tanzania were deployed to protect vital areas.

The Donovans were advised to evacuate and were given safe passage out of the country. They took up residence in Swampscott, Massachusetts, and in 1986, as a result of his parents' tutelage, Diogo passed the entrance exams and was admitted to Boston University.

By 1990, an estimated 900,000 people had been killed in war-torn Mozambique, and another 1.3 million had fled the country.

Anna, reading these facts in the newspaper, became upset and said, "Look at this, Michael. We're needed there now more than ever!"

Michael looked at the news about Mozambique and replied, "We can't go back there now; it would still be too dangerous."

His brother John entered the conversation, "Do the both of

you think you're still in your twenties? You have good jobs here, and you, Anna, have you thought about Diogo?"

"He's his own man. He'll be 22 next month and graduates at the end of the semester."

"But Michael's 52," said John. "And you're close behind. You have a good life here!"

Michael settled Anna and John down, thought for a moment and said, "Anna, let's at least wait 'til they've settled on some kind of peace treaty, then I'll go back with you. There's some negotiations taking place now."

"You promise?" she asked. He nodded affirmatively. They embraced and that was all the assurance she needed.

John became upset with both of them. He just couldn't understand their dedication. "For over 10 years," he said, "I did nothing but worry about all of you, living among rebels, raising a son in that environment and all the while, your lives in constant jeopardy. Now this talk of going back . . . don't you feel you've given enough?"

"There's always more to do," answered Michael. "More to give and besides, it's the life we chose together. Anna is right . . . we need to go back."

Just then Diogo came in the front door, and John took him by the arm and said, "See if you can talk some sense into your parents!"

"What's this all about?" Diogo said looking around the room.

Again his Uncle John spoke up, "They want to go back!"

Anna interjected, "Your father and I have decided to return to the compound as soon as a treaty is negotiated. How do you feel about it, son?"

"Unless they start growing some jungle around Boston, there won't be much use for my knowledge of tropical medicine or the experience I acquired in the bush before we left. I guess we're fish out of water. When do we leave?" They all embraced.

John came to wrap his arms around them all and said, "I give up. God bless you."

In October 1992, a peace treaty was made effective in Mozambique. The Donovans started packing. John was very sad for they were the only family left!

"Why don't you come with us, Uncle?" asked Diogo.

"Just as you feel you must go, I must stay. My roots are here, my wife and son are buried here, and I'm going to miss you people terribly," answered John and gave Diogo a firm hug.

The day of departure came, and after best wishes were given to all, John said, "You people go and get that country squared away and maybe . . . just maybe, I'll come for a visit."

"We'd like that very much," said Anna tearfully.

With extensive courses in chemical and biological technology and majoring in tropical medicine, including one and a half years of field study, Diogo knew his parents expected him to play a major role in the re-establishment of the medical mission and research lab. He didn't want to disappoint, but his heart was more into the African bush.

When he was just a youngster, the tales of the big game hunters and bushmen who would frequent the mission would fascinate him. Even deaths he'd witnessed as a result of lion maulings and snakebites never dampened his enthusiasm or his dreams of some-day becoming a big game hunter and safari guide.

For some time, before they were forced to evacuate, he had participated in game drives with Percy Nolan, a good friend of the family and also a big game hunter. Nolan had taken Diogo under his wing and by age 13, Diogo learned to gut, clean and skin his own kill. By age 17, he was working as Nolan's assistant on safaris when he was away from school in Maputo. Of course, when the civil war spread, most of his schooling had taken place at the medical mission, observing and assisting his parents. He always felt pulled in two directions.

The Donovans arrived in Mozambique and couldn't believe the devastation that the civil war had wrought on the land, its people and animals. Many of the roads were impassable, not yet cleared of mines, so a guide had to be engaged who knew the area well. When they reached the compound, or at least what was left of it, Anna looked around as tears rolled down her cheeks.

"Do you really want to start over again?" asked Michael.

"I don't know," she said. "This is where our life together started and somehow I feel this is where we should be. There is no doubt we are needed here. Diogo, you haven't said a word."

"Just thinking, Mom," he replied. "Once in awhile, I have a hard time sorting things out . . . human frailties, cancer, diseases, natural disasters, traffic accidents, wars and indiscriminate killings by terrorists and street gangs, etc., etc., etc. Shoot 'em up . . . patch 'em up! It's a damn miracle anybody reaches old age! Do we really make a difference? I need to know!"

Michael felt it was time to add a positive note to this tune of doom. "I think we all, as a family, need to remember a few things and one in particular comes to mind." Then he expounded on his memories.

"Anna, I think we all remember how we felt when you were diagnosed with breast cancer . . . from the mammography to the biopsy to the decision between lumpectomy or breast removal. I can never forget the feeling I had when the doctor mentioned the word . . . invasive. Nothing else in the world seemed to matter at that time, nothing . . ."

Anna just lowered her head, reflecting, and Diogo said, "I remember how scared I was . . ."

Michael continued, "You were so brave, Anna, opting for aggressive treatment and therapy. The chemo . . . you became so sick that you wanted to stop the treatments at the halfway point, but you stuck it out."

"It would not have happened without your support, Michael," interjected Anna.

"The toughest time for me, Anna," said Michael, "was seeing you lose your hair, and then you asking me to cut it all off for you. I joked about it at the time, but I know that both of us were dying inside . . . then the radiation treatments, and now the Tamoxifen that you've been taking for the past year. The hot flashes have been unreal and will probably worsen in this heat."

"They've been easing off lately!" announced Anna. "And don't forget all the support and help I received from recovered patients and the nurses and aides. We're all here together because of them also . . . and the prayers that were said for me! This is our chance to give a little bit back. Think of the thousands in need. If we help just one, wouldn't it be worth it?"

"You know, Mike, I was thinking how happy I was when my hair started growing back in. I felt like a whole woman again. Look at it now. It's curly and gray, but I love it!"

Diogo sighed and said, "I hate it when you guys make so much sense. I also hate feeling selfish. What are we waiting for; let's get started!"

Once again they put out a call for help, donations of any sort and volunteers, only this time the Donovans were a lot older and had something they didn't have the first time they built the complex—Diogo!

Many of their old friends were killed in the war, but the ones that were left brought others, and with Diogo as the coordinator, things began shaping up. Diogo had become quite a leader. He asked around about Percy Nolan, the big game hunter, but nobody seemed to know where he could be. Word eventually came to the family that Percy had been killed as a result of the hostilities. Diogo was especially saddened. Nolan had been a good friend and mentor in the ways of the bush.

Further word came that, lacking any family, Percy Nolan

named Diogo sole heir of his estate. The hunting camp and land bordered the medical mission to the south and the country of Malawi to the north. So the expanded complex became known as "The Donovan Wildlife Ranch and Medical Mission." Diogo had the best of both worlds. He divided his attentions and abilities, 50-50. He scheduled safari trips for certain times of the year, and the rest of his time was devoted to fieldwork in tropical medicine.

Warring factions all over the country had laid random land-mines, so it had become quite a job to clear even the well-traveled trails. In any spare time he could muster, Diogo, accompanied by his native guides, gradually opened many trails to safari traffic. The toll in human lives and animals that these landmines had taken was horrendous. There were two times when rogue animals had taken lives. Diogo offered his assistance and disposed of a lion and elephant, pro bono. Word of his feats in the bush, as well as his field research in strains of certain rare diseases, brought some notoriety, which was published in the *Noticias*, the Maputo Capitol News.

Flooding from typhoons occurred in the spring of 2002, and with the help of the Donovans, an epidemic of cholera was shortened dramatically. Incidents of malaria are still prevalent but an accepted phenomenon of the African bush. Larium tablets are a must carry, as well as occasional blood checks for bilharzias, a tropical disease caused by trematode worms that are parasitic to man and mammals. "Snail Fever," as it is sometimes called, is Diogo's pet project under the microscope.

On Tuesday afternoon, July 25, 2003, the Donovan phone rang.

"Medical Mission," said Anna. "How may we be of service?"

"Is this Mrs. Donovan?" the voice on the other end of the line asked.

"Yes it is. To whom am I speaking?" replied Anna.

"I am Nataniel Chicoti of the Provincial Police Command. May I please speak to Diogo?"

Anna, slightly alarmed, asked, "He's not in any trouble is he Nat?"

"Not this time!" answered the commander, laughingly. "We could use his assistance once again identifying a rogue animal."

"He's out in the bush today, but I'm expecting him home by early evening."

"Would you please ask him to call me as soon as possible," requested the commander.

"Will do," said Anna. "Have a nice day!"

"You as well!" said Nataniel.

Diogo called as requested and agreed to investigate the incident in question. Beira is 190 miles away, and the condition of the roads do not permit expedience. Navigating the river by motor launch may be quicker, but Diogo preferred to drive his four-wheel drive, zebra-striped Land Rover, outfitted for his specific needs. "Besides," he thought, "once over the Zambezi, Route EN6 to Beira is a sandy, gravel road, and I can make some good time."

Late afternoon on Wednesday, Diogo pulled up to the police substation, 30 miles outside Beira, and was greeted by the commander. "You made great time . . . were you speeding?"

Diogo just peeked at him over his sunglasses and said, "Nat, this better be a good one. You were awful vague on the phone. What exactly do we have here?"

"I didn't want to spell it out until we spoke in person. A teenager was reported missing, which is not a rare occurrence in these times, but this one turned up dead. Looks like a lion attack."

Nataniel and Diogo attended the same high school together until the war forced the Donovans and thousands more to flee the country. They had remained good friends and had contact several times since Diogo's return.

"What would a lion be doing this far down river?" asked Diogo.

"I don't know . . . that's why we called 'B'wana Dog.'"

"You're still a smart ass!" said Diogo.

"How do you think I got this job? C'mon, I'll show you what we got."

Diogo jumped into the police vehicle and they headed out. When they arrived at the scene, an officer was standing guard.

"Where's the body now?" asked Diogo.

"At the morgue, in town," answered Nat. Handing Diogo some photos, he said, "These were taken before the body was removed."

As Diogo examined the pictures, he exclaimed loudly, "Jesus, Mary and Joseph! This was no lion kill! I don't know of any animal in existence that has this thirst for blood!"

"I was thinking that myself," said Nat. "But I'm no expert on this type of carnage."

"These tracks," offered Diogo, "are similar to those of a large cat, but nothing like I've seen before. From those photos, I'd say the claws are extremely large but obviously retractable. Was the visceral, the entrails, recovered, as well?"

"Yes, I believe they were. Why do you ask?"

Diogo thought for a second before he answered. "It's possible we have a man killer and not a man-eater, at large, unless it was scared off before it had a chance to eat."

He widened his investigation of the area and found a half-eaten carcass of a small antelope, apparently killed in the same manner. He also found animal droppings, which he bagged for identification.

"Nat, I think I've pieced these clues into a scene. I believe that whatever this animal is, it was feeding on a fresh kill of antelope and the boy accidentally surprised it. Obviously, it's not afraid of humans," surmised Diogo.

"So, you're saying it's a case of wrong time . . . wrong place?"

"You got it!" said Diogo. "But I'd still like to put a name on this killer. Did you follow the tracks at all?"

"That's another strange part of this thing," said Nat. "The tracks ended at the river's edge. They just disappeared!"

"I can't see what else I can do here," said Diogo.

"Good, I'll dismiss the guard. We can head for town. I reserved you a room at the Tivoli." Diogo just peaked at him again over his glasses.

"Calm down; it's been renovated top to bottom; newly opened this year with TV, phone, air conditioning and a brand new, completely stocked bar in each room. You'll be a guest of the state."

After a couple of beers in the lounge with Nat recalling old times, Diogo was ready for some serious sleep.

Beira is a port city and the second largest in the country. It's a center of commerce and used for trade by Malawi and Zimbabwe. Because of the civil war much of the city needed restoration, but it is now well on its way of becoming a tourist destination. Much of the town can be reached on foot.

The next morning, Thursday the 27th, Diogo walked over to the morgue to meet Nat. It sickened him to examine the remains, but it had to be done. When he finished he turned to Nat. "I could use something a little stronger than beer."

Nat agreed. "Where do you want to go with this?"

"We need to contact the wire services and even go on line with everything we've got, hoping that someone can help identify this thing, whatever it is!" said Diogo.

"We're liable to start a panic!" replied Nat.

"You want to wait 'til it kills again? The life you save may be your own . . . okay, hold off for a couple of hours. Let me talk with my father. He may know something."

Diogo went to the bar at the hotel, ordered a double shot of old Bushmills Irish Whiskey and called his folks. He assured them that he was okay and living in the lap of luxury, compliments of the commander. When he finished describing to his father what he had seen and examined, his father only had one thing to offer, "I only have knowledge of one animal that fits that M.O., but it's not big enough to take down a human being."

"What is it, Dad?"

"When I was in college, I did some field research in Madagascar, and we happened onto a lemur that was killed in the manner you described. There was also a very heavy smell of rancid meat."

"Yes," said Diogo, "I noticed that here too!"

"Well, like I say, that was a long time ago, and the guide told us its name, but I can't remember. It was very sanguinary, but too small to kill anything as big as a human."

"It may be something to go on. Thanks, Dad, and tell Mom I'll be home in a couple of days, not to worry."

When Nat was off duty, he came into the hotel lounge, and Diogo was sitting and pondering. "Any conclusions?" asked Nat.

"Nothing that makes any sense," answered Diogo. "My father said he knew of an animal in Madagascar that answered the description of our boy, but too small to attack a person."

"Madagascar? That's 250 miles across the channel. Does it fly as well? How big does it grow?" asked Nat.

Diogo just raised his hands and shrugged his shoulders. "I think you better go on the wire services with every detail we got and include Madagascar, as well." Then he thought for a moment, "Did you notice a rancid smell at the kill site?"

"Now that you mention it, I did. I just thought it was coming from the cadaver," replied Nat.

"You better include that tidbit in your report, as well!" said Diogo.

Diogo decided this would be a good time to get drunk and possibly enjoy the company of a female. It had been a long time between kisses.

CHAPTER TWENTY

Power of the Press

Mahajanga, Madagascar
Friday, July 28th

"Dr. Lansing?"

"Chett, how's it going? Do you have any more info on the 'granddaddy'?"

"Sit down, doctor," said Chett. "I've got quite a story for you!"

When he finished conveying to the doctor all that had transpired, the line went silent. "Doctor, are you still there?"

"I'm sorry. I'm still trying to catch my breath!" said Lansing. "And you say all of this has been substantiated? I always believed in their existence but never in my wildest dreams . . ."

Chett interrupted, "Doctor, we're releasing all of the information I've given you to the press sometime this morning, except the possible existence of a mate. Right now, that's just conjecture and theory on my part. I'd like you to treat it in the same way. We're monitoring all the news services on the eastern coast of Africa. If something breaks, we need to be ready for it."

"I understand perfectly," said Lansing. "How can I be of help on this end?"

"Well, there is one favor . . ."

"Speak up man! What is it?" asked Lansing.

"There's a member of the crew that caught the shark who, coincidently, just finished some volunteer work here with me at the station. He displays an unusual talent for field research. He's the one who identified the giant fossa. I could use him on a temporary basis, until you assign someone to assist me."

"No problem," answered Lansing. "Hire him. What's his name and status?"

"He's a senior at Florida U., majoring in marine biology,"

"Marine biology did you say?"

"Trust me on this one," said Chett. "He's going to be a good one. His name is Blaine Gibbons."

"That name sounds familiar," said Lansing. "Anyway, I'll be sending you Karina Wolfson. She's just finished an assignment in Brazil and due for a short leave."

"A woman?" exclaimed Chett. "It's possible at any moment we'll be setting up a field lab on the African continent."

"Relax!" said Lansing. "Karina's 33 years old and has worked with carnivores before you did. She also has three years of field experience in Africa with tropical medicine. She's more than qualified for the assignment. Are you forgetting who the boss is here?"

"I'm sorry," said Chett. "I was out of line."

"Okay, my friend; keep me up to date and spend whatever is necessary for preparation. For God's sake . . . be careful!"

Chett spoke with Blaine about the job offer and the possibility of having to set up a base camp somewhere on the coast of Africa. The one thing he did add that he didn't mention before was, "My intention is to capture it alive, if possible."

"You're serious?" asked Blaine.

"Yes, I am," replied Chett. "That's if it's still breathing now. The possibility of it even existing is a slim one at best. I need to be prepared in any event, in case we get the clues we're looking for."

"Which are?" asked Blaine.

"Let's just wait and see!"

The faith and determination that Chett displayed caused Blaine to give serious consideration to his offer. The rest of the day belonged to the press.

On Saturday morning, the 29th of July, news of the strange death of a teenager in Mozambique by an unknown animal reached the world wire services, but was given small attention. The headlines and the biggest story of the decade were the capture of a world record Great White Shark and its prehistoric stomach contents. Everyone involved was given celebrity status.

Aury's wife, Moira, was deluged with offers, and it was while she was scanning the Net that she noticed the news article from Mozambique. She read the gory details and called in her husband who immediately notified Blaine.

"This kill," said Aury, "sounds a lot like the ones that Chett described when he and his hunting party were chasing the fossa here in Madagascar. No?"

"Yes, it does!" replied Blaine. "I better contact him." Meanwhile, Moira made a copy of the article and handed it to Blaine. He picked up the phone and dialed.

"I didn't think I'd catch you so quickly," said Blaine. "Have you heard the news from Mozambique? It just came over the wire services. Aury's wife downloaded the clipping for me."

"I haven't heard a thing," answered Chett. "Read it to me!"

When Blaine finished giving him all the particulars, he shouted, "I knew it! Not far from the Zambezi and probably near one of the tributaries."

"So what happens now?" asked Blaine.

"We follow the trail!"

"We?" asked Blaine. "I haven't . . . uh . . . I mean . . . I really didn't think I'd need to make a decision on this matter. We're still not sure you're right. After all, something else could be responsible for the boy's death."

"That's why we have to check it out! I have to be sure, and I know you're in deep enough now, that you also want to be sure . . . am I right?"

"You're right," said Blaine. "Count me in."

"Excellent! Give me the number of that police commander in Beira. I'll call him immediately, get all the info that we need to make arrangements, and then I'll get back to you, hopefully, by noon."

Chett spoke directly to Nataniel Chicoti, and after introducing himself as an expert on Madagascan carnivores and giving him a brief synopsis of his theory of what might have happened, offered his assistance in the investigation. Nataniel welcomed any insight that might help to clear this case from the books. A meeting was scheduled for Monday morning, 9:00 A.M. at the Tivoli Hotel in Beira. Nataniel made mention of Diogo, a bush expert and guide, and Chett told Nataniel he would be accompanied by an assistant as well.

"I'll make the necessary arrangements on this end," said Nataniel. "See you on Monday."

Blaine was waiting anxiously for the call. If it was a definite go, he'd owe the Andrianaivos an explanation, especially Sirana. He had been treated as royalty since he arrived, and in no way did he want to offend them. At one o'clock in the afternoon, the phone rang. Moira answered and summoned Blaine.

"Hello," he uttered.

"Blaine, this is Chett. A meeting's been arranged for Monday morning. All the arrangements have been made. We fly out on the 10:00 A.M. flight tomorrow. Pack light; bring your personals and field boots, and I'll take care of the rest. We're just going over to feel the situation out. If we can make a positive I.D., everything we'll need can be acquired there. There's been an expert guide assigned to the case and he'll be in on the meeting."

"Slow down, Chett; you're losing me!"

"What do you mean?" he asked. "I'm losing you? Are you quitting on me?"

"No . . . no," replied Blaine. "You're just talking too damn fast . . . I can't keep up."

"I'm sorry. I'm running ahead of myself." So he repeated all he had said, and then added, "I arranged for transportation from the La Piscine Hotel to the airport. Meet me there around eight. I still have to notify Dr. Lansing of our movements, and then I'll be heading into Mahajanga late this afternoon."

"Okay, from now on, you're the boss."

Blaine walked into the other room and found it very difficult to face Aury and Moira and give his resignation.

"You both have been really great to me, and I don't know how . . ."

Moira interjected, "You're leaving us, aren't you?" Blaine just nodded his head sadly and gave her a big hug.

"So where are you off to?" asked Aury.

"Mozambique. Chett has a hunch that the mate of the fossa we caught is the perpetrator of that news article Moira downloaded. That's all I can say for now."

Aury held out his hand in friendship and said, "There's always a place here for you. Good luck!"

"I hope your sister is as understanding as you are. Thank you."

"As I said before," added Aury, "good luck."

"I have to go over and speak to your folks first. Once again, thanks for everything!"

It was only a short walk from Aury's house to his parents', and all the way over, in a slow walk, Blaine was thinking of the best way to tell them of his change in plans. "Sirana would be another matter of much more difficulty," he thought. "But if she loves me as she says, she'll understand." Somehow, this seemed tougher to Blaine than saying goodbye to his aunt and uncle. He was beginning to fathom how deep his feelings for Sirana and her family had grown. Then it dawned on him . . . "I love her!" he said out loud. "I really love her!"

So Blaine tried, as best he could, to explain his decision to Rijah and Yvette, ending with, "Things happened so fast over the past week, and at this point, Chett needs me more than Aury. I just don't want to seem ungrateful for all this family has done for me."

"Please," replied Rijah, "give the both of us credit for knowing you better than that . . . besides, a man must do what he feels he must. Otherwise, he lives a life of regret."

"Thanks to you both; you've been a great help to me in many ways. I need to speak to Sirana. I'm going over to the hospital."

"I thought you were happy here," sighed Sirana.

"I am. You know I am!"

"So, why are you going to Mozambique?"

"I guess for the same reason I came to Madagascar," he answered, "adventure and field study. I never expected to be in this particular situation."

"Have I been part of your field study?" she inquired.

"I'm not even going to answer that," said Blaine. "If you don't know by now that I'm in love with you . . . I don't know what else I can say or do!"

"Would you repeat that last sentence again?" she asked and he did.

"I don't know what else I can say or do?"

"Don't be a smart ass!" she retorted. "You know what I'm referring to."

"You heard it right," he answered.

She threw her arms around him and said, "Are you telling me you're coming back?"

"I'm coming back to you, for you, or whatever way you prefer. You're definitely in my plans for the future."

She kissed him and said, "I've never been so happy! May I tell my parents?"

"You may shout it to the world, 'cause if you don't, I will!" he said. She kissed him once more, only this time with more gusto. He moved her away at arm's length, cleared his throat, took a deep breath and said, "I'll see you at dinner. I have many things to do this afternoon."

"You'll see me after dinner, as well," she added, as he walked out the door.

Among the many things Blaine had to take care of included shopping for a decent ring for Sirana. The bonus money from the last fishing trip was burning a hole in his pocket, until he saw the price of diamonds. He couldn't afford the one that caught his eye, but second best was very nice also. "If she doesn't like it," he thought to himself, "we can always change it."

When Sirana arrived home from work, her mother couldn't help but notice the ear-to-ear smile that was etched on her face. "Unusual," thought Yvette, considering the fact that Blaine was leaving in the morning. "Are you all right, my dear?" she asked.

"I'm just wonderful, Mother . . . I'm fine," she answered with a lilt, as she went in to shower and change.

While she was gone, Yvette asked Blaine, "Did you tell Sirana you were leaving in the morning?"

"Yes, I did."

"Then, why is she so happy?"

"You'll have to ask her," he replied, and then walked out on the veranda to speak with Rijah.

"How would you feel about having me for a son-in-law?" he asked.

Rijah just looked at Blaine, solemnly, and asked, "How soon?"

"I'm thinking about a year," replied Blaine.

"That sounds reasonable. Does Sirana know about it yet?"

"Not officially," said Blaine. "I was going to make it a formal offer after dinner, with your permission, of course. Yvette doesn't know unless Sirana told her."

"You have my blessing," said Rijah, and they embraced each other warmly.

Sirana was still beaming when dinner was coming to a conclusion and had no idea that Blaine was in possession of a ring. He stood up and spoke.

"I've already spoken with your father," he said, as he looked Sirana straight in the eyes. "I . . . er . . . well; I'm not so good at this sort of thing."

He reached in his pocket and opened the fancy case. "Will . . . you . . . ah . . ."

"Yes!" replied Sirana, before he could say another word.

"Let the man finish," scolded Yvette in a soft tone.

So he just came right out with it, "I want you to share . . . I mean; I want us to share . . . will you marry me?"

Looking at the ring, she announced, "It's beautiful!" and started to cry. Yvette's eyes grew teary as well, and Blaine didn't know what to make of it. It wasn't the reaction he anticipated.

"Sit down, Blaine," said Rijah. "Have some more wine. You see, this is a woman thing."

Sirana handed the ring back to Blaine, and dumbfounded he asked, "You don't want it?"

"Of course I do. I will marry you. I'd like you to place it on my finger." He smiled and complied. She kissed him, and then kept staring at the ring.

Congratulations were extended all around and Yvette asked, "Have you set a date?"

Sirana looked at Blaine questioningly, and he spoke up, "Well, I mentioned to Rijah that maybe a year from today sounded good and he agreed. Is that all right with you Sirana? Yvette?" They both shook their heads in unison.

As though it were pre-planned, Rijah and Yvette left to visit friends, and Sirana volunteered to take care of the dishes and pick up. When she finished, she looked at Blaine very lovingly, and he knew where this was going to lead and developed a case of butterflies in his stomach that he had never experienced before. He absolutely loved these new feelings she brought out in him. The phone rang.

Sirana picked it up. "Hello. Yes, he is." She covered the mouthpiece and whispered, "Don't leave me alone tonight . . . it's Chett."

"Chett?" Blaine asked, as he put the phone up to his ear.

"Just wanted to confirm the details and give you the flight schedule. Everything is set, and we have the green light from Dr. Lansing to follow through and take whatever steps necessary for the capture of the fossa; if, of course, it is the right animal. I contacted Pam and she's not too keen on the idea but understands the thrill of quest."

"You don't think we're on a wild goose chase, do you?" Blaine asked.

"I honestly feel, deep down in my gut," answered Chett, "that this is it. There would be too much of a coincidence for this to be another rare animal and showing up at approximately where I predicted. No . . . this is it!"

"Okay then. I'll see you in the morning."

Sirana started to unbutton her dress, and Blaine said, "Are you sure you wouldn't care for another glass of wine?" She just pointed to the bedroom and said, "This is your last night!"

"That has the sound of finality to it. What do you have planned?" he asked.

She walked up close to him, real close, bit him on the earlobe, put her tongue in his ear and said softly, "I just want to chat for awhile." She stepped back, looked down between his pockets and asked, "What did you have in mind?"

He took her by the hand and said, "Let's chat!"

CHAPTER TWENTY-ONE

Decision Time

Sunday evening, July 30th

Chett and Blaine checked into the Tivoli Hotel in Beira, Mozambique and were quite impressed with the attention, service and furnishings. Chett was handed a message from Dr. Lansing to call him ASAP.

"Yes, Doctor, this is Chett."

"Chett, I'm glad I was able to contact you this evening," said Dr. Lansing. "There's been a slight change in schedule. Dr. Wolfson will be arriving in Johannesburg . . . actually, as we speak. She'll be on the first flight out in the morning to Beira."

"But Doctor, we haven't even made a positive I.D. on this animal involved in the incident."

"I gave her all the particulars and she insisted on being in on the ground floor if it's the real thing. It's the only way I could engage her."

"What about Blaine?" he asked.

"Keep him with you. You'll need all the help you can get if your hunch turns out to be a reality."

"You're the boss!" replied Chett. "I'll just need to change the meeting time to late afternoon and reserve a room for her. We'll give it our best shot!"

"There are many dangers in Africa and other animals just as deadly," offered Dr. Lansing. "Take care of yourself and watch over the others."

"Will do, and I'll call you when I can." He hung up.

He let Blaine in on what was going on, assuring him his status hadn't changed. "We'll need to pick her up in the morning and call the Police Command to change the meeting time."

"Well, for now," answered Blaine, "we can shower, change, get some decent grub and have a drink to relax a little."

"That, my friend, is a capital idea!"

Karina's plane was delayed an hour and arrived shortly after noon. Being the only woman on the charter flight made her easily identifiable. "Dr. Wolfson?" asked Chett, as he approached her.

"You must be Chester Whalton," and looking at Blaine, she asked, "and you are?"

"I'm Blaine Gibbons, the temporary assistant."

"Good afternoon to you both, and please dispense with the 'Doctor' business. I'm sure we are very much on equal ground, as far as qualifications go. I'm Karina."

They both shook her hand and Chett spoke up, "I took the liberty of reserving you a room at our hotel. You have plenty of time for a shower and some lunch before our scheduled meeting with the police commander and a big game hunter/field biologist at 4:00 P.M."

"That sounds kind of interesting. Now fill me in on some of the details," she said.

"Let's get to the vehicle and I'll brief you as we ride. How much of our adventure has Dr. Lansing made available to you?"

She told them that she knew about the hunting party and

deaths in Madagascar, and some theory that a similar animal was responsible for a killing here in Mozambique. Continuing, she said, "He also mentioned the fact that it was or may be a fossa-like carnivore of great size."

"That didn't scare you off?" asked Blaine.

"Fear of the unknown is not one of my frailties," she replied.

"Well," said Chett, "first of all, we're not dealing with an unknown, and when I tell you why, you may just change your mind. I guess the unknown right now is the reason we're here. Have you heard of a *Cryptoprocta giganta?*"

"That's what's believed to be the ancient ancestor of the common fossa of Madagascar," she answered.

"Correct," he said. "So I'll wait 'til I get you all together in the meeting this afternoon before I disclose all that we know."

"Are you suggesting that a living *giganta* is responsible?"

Before she could finish her question, Chett said, "I'll disclose all this afternoon, but for now, tell us about yourself."

All the parties involved showed up for the meeting and were milling around in the Tivoli lounge. Nataniel spoke up, introduced himself and commenced to set the agenda. "I believe the first thing we should do is examine the remains of the victim, then return here for discussion and kick some ideas around. You may all introduce yourselves and your specialties at that time. Please follow me."

Diogo had already viewed the remains and chose to stay at the lounge. Chett was familiar with the fossa's modus operandi from the corpse he had the misfortune of having to view in Madagascar. Blaine and Karina were viewing the results of fossa's fury on a human being for the first time. Barf bags were in order, but with a lack of same, the floor became the recipient of their reactions.

Seeing an animal torn apart is one thing; seeing that type of carnage on a fellow human being has a much different effect.

Chett needed no further convincing of what was responsible for the death.

"If you need to make further tests," said the commander, "the remains will be kept here until this investigation is brought to a satisfactory conclusion. What say we return to the lounge and compare notes? The private meeting room has been reserved for us."

On the walk back to the hotel, Karina was full of questions directed at Chett. Some he answered and other details were saved for the group. Blaine, not known to be a drinker, needed a double-shot screwdriver to settle his nerves, and Karina just had a glass of wine. After introductions by all, the meeting began.

Chett brought everyone up to date with the majority of events, including his trek from the Jangala Reservation to the coast with the inspector and the hunting party. Then Blaine related his experiences aboard the *Tolura*, the capture of the Great White, the suloys, the dissection by the marine biologists, and finally, the discovery of the *ancient* one. Chett went into detail when he described the carnage wrought by the fossa in Madagascar and compared it to the one in Mozambique. Then he expounded on his findings and theories concerning the animal in question.

"We're still not sure our culprit is the same one you described!" said Diogo. "A DNA is needed to be sure."

"That would take too long, and in the meantime, we'd loosen our grip on the objective," offered Chett.

"What objective?" asked Diogo? "It's been six days since the kill and nothing since. We are wasting a lot of time. I admit that the tracks at the scene were strange to me, but I have a hard time buying the 250 mile trans-channel swim by any kind of animal."

"Okay, I can't blame any of you for having doubts; I mean for

God's sake, I had a tough time believing the facts as I was staring at them. From the details and descriptions you and Nataniel gave us, combined with the musky odor and the scat sample, I'm 99 percent sure it's the fossa."

"I've studied this animal, its descendant that is, and I know of no other animal with this method of sanguinary killing. I go along with Chett's theory," interjected Karina.

"Ditto," added Blaine.

Diogo shook his head affirmatively as he looked at Blaine, Chett and then Karina and said, "What about you, Nat?"

Imagining the thought of another kill, Nat said, "I'm for getting on the trail of this thing before it kills again. I don't much care what it is, as long as we put it away."

"I have the authorization to back a safari and equip us with whatever we'll need, and considering your reputation Diogo, according to Nat, I'd like you to lead us," offered Chett.

"I don't come cheap!" said Diogo.

"I'll discuss terms with you later, but for now, when can we get started?"

"With Nataniel's pull as a police commander," said Diogo, "I can arrange for everything we'll need this evening, including guns and ammo. Everybody will carry. We need to cover each other at all times."

"I'll give you a list of our needs, as well," said Karina. "Most can be had at any pharmacy. Items of a personal nature, we'll procure ourselves."

Diogo hadn't been attracted to a woman, in any serious fashion, for a long time and yet found himself hanging onto every word Karina spoke. She couldn't help but notice how he turned away every time their eyes met. She detected a shyness that was unusual in a man of his caliber and good looks, and he disguised it very well. "It adds to his attractiveness," she thought to herself.

Diogo, with his dark hair, tanned complexion and muscular build on his 5'11" frame was no Adonis but very handsome just the same. He appeared to be quite athletic at about, she guessed, 190 pounds.

Karina had dark hair, as well, and though she had a vacationer's tan, she was lightly complexioned, compared to Diogo. Full figured at 130 pounds, she was not what most men considered a raving beauty. She was attractive in a wholesome sort of way and wore little make-up except for a light coat of lipstick. Her hair was worn short, compatible for fieldwork. At 5'6" tall, she had a grace about her when she walked that was very sexy and projected an air of confidence.

Chett, Blaine and Nat were hooked up in deep conversation, and this gave Karina and Diogo a chance to share their personal histories.

"So, are you married?" asked Diogo.

"Was once," she answered. "But it lasted less than a year . . . no kids, thank God. Not that I don't like children; I'm just glad I don't have his. Have you been married?"

"No . . . never," he replied.

"That's hard to believe."

"Well, there was a girl once. We were to be married and . . ." he hesitated.

"You don't have to tell me."

"I want to . . . I guess. Maybe, I need to," he continued. "We were very close in college, and when I came here, she wanted to come with me, but I insisted on her waiting until we got the compound set up, and then I'd send for her . . . I did. She was on her way here in 1994 . . . the plane went down at sea . . . no survivors. I stayed drunk a long time, trying to shake the guilt and the what-ifs. I spent a lot of time here in Beira, and if not for Nataniel keeping an eye on me, who knows where I'd be today. I know my parents are forever grateful to him. I had a few skirmishes here in my drinking days, and he always seemed to be around to save my bacon."

"Are your parents in Mozambique?" she asked.

"Oh, that's right, I mentioned the wildlife ranch but made no reference to the medical mission that they started. It's all one big complex. I'll explain some other time."

Thinking about all he had said, she uttered, "I guess you just have to pick up the pieces and go on. Sometimes, it's really tough. Here I am offering you advice, and all I do is bury myself in work. I jump from one assignment to another."

"What are you running from?" he asked.

"I guess I'm afraid of commitment . . . the permanent kind," she responded. "Have you lived in Mozambique all your life?"

"I was born upriver in Ancuaze at the medical mission. We were forced to evacuate in 1988, due to the civil war. We went to the States and lived with my uncle in Swampscott, Massachusetts. I attended B.U., received my degree, and in 1992, when the treaty was signed, we moved back at my mother's urging. We threw ourselves into rebuilding the complex, and when it was finished, I pursued my real love: big game safaris."

"That's quite a resume," she said. "I hope I get to see this complex some day."

Just then Blaine excused himself and said, "Did I hear you mention Swampscott, Massachusetts?" Diogo nodded. Blaine continued, "I was born in Peabody, Mass. I lived there 'til I was 13. Now my home is in Florida."

"I know Peabody very well," said Diogo, and then changed the subject abruptly. That was the hometown of his lost love.

At dinner, they all discussed plans for the fossa search, and when Chett mentioned using a dart gun and traps, Diogo almost lost his cool. "Are you out of your mind? You're the one that described, in detail, the carnage this animal wreaked. We all saw the remains of that poor kid over at the morgue . . ."

Nat jumped in, "Let's calm down. We can work out a peaceful solution to this."

"No!" said Diogo. "I misunderstood Chett's intent. I thought he was here to save lives. You try to capture this thing alive and there's a good chance people will die. I don't plan on being one of them. We have a killer out there, and it should be wasted!"

"Let me explain," said Chett. "I plan on using traps and then sedating the animal for transportation to an appropriate facility for study. This animal may be the last of its kind!"

"I'm against capture!" said the police commander. "I agree with Diogo. I'm responsible for ridding this province of man-eaters."

"Four of us here are biologists," offered Karina. "We hopefully seek to preserve life, not destroy it!"

"That's true!" replied Diogo. "But isn't our first duty to our fellow man?"

"Okay then," responded Chett. "May we agree on this: if the opportunity presents itself to take the fossa alive, without danger to anyone, we do it? On the other hand, if there's no choice . . . we kill it."

"I'll go along with that," said Diogo, "except for two instances. First of all, if I get an open field shot, I take it. Secondly, I'll be the one to determine capture 'cause I'm the one leading this safari."

"Sounds good to me, B'wana Dog!" replied Nat.

"What's this B'wana Dog stuff or whatever?" asked Karina.

Diogo spoke up, "I was in high school with this clown, and one day I made the mistake of revealing my ambition of being a big-game hunter. He started calling me that; he said it sounded more intimidating than Diogo Donovan. The trouble is everyone else at school picked up on it. Thanks, Nat!"

Everybody agreed that Diogo would call the shots, and plans were made to begin the search at the kill site the following morning, early. As they were leaving the meeting, Karina heard music coming from the lounge, and when she stood in the doorway to investigate, Diogo came up behind her and asked, "Do you dance?"

"Are you asking?" she replied. He held her hand gently and led her to the dance floor. Karina knew instantly that she wanted to be held by this man. After the second dance, they retired to a table and ordered a drink.

Diogo spoke first. "You dance very well!"

"You lead very well," she replied.

"Well, you can thank my mother for that accomplishment. She told me never to forget; women love to dance. She always says, 'Dancing is making love to music playing.' I believe that as well. She also emphasized the fact that wallflowers liked to dance too, so spread yourself around!"

"Your mother is a very wise woman; I'd love to meet her."

"Some day you may. Would you like another drink?"

"No thank you," she answered. "I'm exhausted and tomorrow may prove to be a longer day. Goodnight, Mr. Donovan, I had a real enjoyable time."

"I did as well. Maybe we'll get the chance to do it again." She nodded and left the lounge. Whispering low to himself, he muttered, "I like that girl!" He finished his drink and left.

Morning comes early in Mozambique, for the sun rises at 4:30 A.M. Nataniel waited 'til 6:00 before he had all their rooms called for wake up. After a hardy breakfast, they met out back at Diogo's Land Rover. Nat had an assistant with him and stowed Chett's gear in the police vehicle. Karina and Blaine rode with Diogo. Nat led the way to the kill site and showed them the partly washed away tracks that led to the river. Diogo seemed a little puzzled at this.

"What's bothering you?" asked Chett.

"I don't really know . . . I just . . ." Diogo hesitated while look-ing around.

Chett spoke, "Did I mention that fish is part of a fossa's diet? I believe that's why they stay in close proximity to water."

"I can appreciate that," said Diogo. "But this appears as though it crossed or went fishing and came out, either further upriver or some distance down from here. Let's check for tracks a couple of hundred yards in both directions."

After a careful search for tracks by the team proved fruitless, Diogo turned to Chett and said, "You just may be right. This ani-mal appears to be on a mission. How many miles did you say it was covering in a day?"

"About twelve," stated Chett.

"If we can determine its destination, we shouldn't have any trouble getting ahead of it and setting up some traps. For now, let's make destination our number one priority. I think it best if we split up into two groups of three," offered Diogo.

"There's only going to be five of us," said Nat. "My assistant will not be going on with us."

"That won't be a problem," said Diogo. "I've two guides in my employ who are excellent trackers, and one is an excellent cook, as well. Yes, I'll send for Kapungwe."

"So now, what's the plan?" asked Chett.

"My best thinking is this," responded Diogo. "This thing, by now, has a 75-mile head start and doesn't know it's being followed. I'll call ahead and dispatch Kapungwe to the north side with traps and other gear we'll need. By the time you guys go back down to the ferry, cross and then start heading upriver, my guide will be halfway to you. Don't go further than 75 miles."

"You guys . . . meaning who?" asked Nat.

"You and Chett," answered Diogo. "I'll take Karina and Blaine with me. We'll head west on this side of the river, checking for signs along the way. One of us should run into something. Let's keep each other informed. I have a hunch it's on the north side and headed for, well there's a few different ways it can go. We'll have to wait and see."

It was a slow process checking tracks, especially along the river, so before they split up, Diogo called them all together and gave warning. "I would like you all to heed my cautions. Don't go for a casual swim in the river. We have crocs and the Zambezi shark."

"Sharks in fresh water!" chuckled Chett.

Blaine spoke up, "I've read about them. They've been spotted upriver as far as 200 miles!"

"Yes," confirmed Diogo, "and have taken more lives than the White Pointer. Trust me people; please stay clear of anything that hisses, spits, pisses or shits any way out of the ordinary. I pray you'll excuse my frankness; but I prefer to have you all stay alive and that means constant vigilance. Chett, you have a medical kit with you, correct?"

"I don't leave home without it!"

"I know you're a competent man in the field," said Diogo, "but there are many more dangers here than in Madagascar. Please don't try to capture this thing on your own." Diogo looked at Nat, and they returned a knowing nod to each other and parted company.

Diogo radioed the complex from the Land Rover. "Mom, please set two more places for dinner and a sleepover and have Kapungwe get back to me right away. You guys okay?"

"Everything's fine here. How did it go in Beira with Nat?" she asked.

"Long story," answered Diogo. "Fill you in when we get there. See you then . . . love ya, out."

For the next couple of hours, they intermittently checked for tracks along the bank of the river. The effort drew a blank.

"Okay, you guys," said Diogo, "I'm convinced our quarry has permanently crossed to the other side and is heading north. I'll dispatch my guide to the others with all the gear they'll need. They'll be camping out tonight. We'll connect with them tomorrow. In the meantime, it's smooth sailing. We're off to my house!"

He slipped in a CD of his favorite music, leaned back and said, "The joy is in the journey!"

As the music played for a few minutes, Karina said, "That sounds like Jobim's music."

"You know Tom?" asked Diogo excitedly.

"Tom?" she answered questioningly.

"That's the way friends and enthusiasts refer to him—Antonio Carlos Jobim, noted musician and songwriter from Brazil and originator of bossa nova."

"I never met him," said Karina. "But I love his music!"

"You'll get along great with my mother. She's the one that got me going on this music since I was born!"

"I spent some time in Brazil," stated Karina, "and I've sipped a cold chopps at Gorota de Ipanema bar." (She was referring to the little sidewalk cafe in Rio de Janeiro where Jobim wrote one of his most popular songs, "Girl from Ipanema.")

"You've been there, as well? This is fantastic! Now I know you've got to meet my mother," said Diogo.

"Didn't you say your mother came from Portugal? How did she become a Tom fan?"

"What language do they speak in Rio?" asked Diogo.

Karina slapped her forehead in discovery and said, "Of course, Portuguese."

"My mother spent some time there in the early sixties and met him on a couple of occasions, once at a dinner party, where she spoke to him for quite a while. She has every record he ever made, including the album he sang and played with Frank Sinatra."

"I've never heard it, but I'd love to," said Karina.

Blaine was sitting in the back seat, taking in the whole conversation and said, "I never heard of this bossa nova stuff, but I did hear of Frank Sinatra . . . hasn't everybody?"

"Now I know you both must have heard the song, 'Brazil,' correct?"

Blaine drew a blank on that one too, but Karina knew it.

"Well," said Diogo, "have you ever heard it sung by Johnny Mathis?"

"I thought he just sang love ballads and such," replied Karina. "I didn't know he did anything so upbeat."

"You are definitely in for a treat tonight!" said Diogo.

Kapungwe called in on the radio, and Diogo explained the situation and asked him to cook up one of his fancy dishes for Nat and Chett, then signed off. On the way to Ancuaze, Diogo pointed out sights and animals that, to the novice, would have gone unnoticed. One animal, the Blue Duiker, known as the "phantom of the forest" rarely makes itself conspicuous. It's a small antelope known locally as Kabuluku, and Diogo compared its aloofness and habitat preference to the fossa.

Karina was becoming very impressed with Diogo. She had only been in his company for a few hours, and she was as comfortable around him as if they'd known each other for years. In a conversation with Nataniel, the previous evening, she expressed her concern over Diogo's capabilities.

As they were riding along she thought to herself, "Here is a man, according to Nat, that besides his professional qualifications as a field biologist, debates and parties with volunteer intellectuals, mingles with religious missionaries, battles bureaucracy, plays soccer with street kids and isn't afraid to admit that some of his best friends are prostitutes, though he's never admitted to engaging their services. On top of all this, he runs a wildlife ranch and leads safaris on big game hunts. This is a very interesting man!"

Diogo stopped the vehicle near an area he wanted to check out and invited Blaine and Karina to join him. "Stay close to me," he insisted. "We'll be going through some tall grass up ahead."

Karina had spent time in areas just like this one, camping out while involved in fieldwork. She looked around at the beauty of the wilderness and thought, "The feel of the grass gives me the *tingles*. I wonder if that's why snakes love being in the grass. I bet it awakens their sensory glands and sharpens their height of awareness. I feel so alive . . . yet . . ." Just then Diogo spoke out and broke the trance, "You'd better stay close to me in here, Karina, Cobras love this high grass."

She asked herself, "How did he sense I wanted him close at that precise moment with his arms wrapped securely around me?" She held that thought even after they were safely back in the Land Rover and on their way down the road.

CHAPTER TWENTY-TWO

Positive Identification

Tuesday, August 1st

In May of 2003, gold was found in the northern province of Niassa, Mozambique. At last count, over one thousand prospectors from various countries are illegally trying to extract their share. Local authorities are unable to control the situation.

Roads leading to these gold fields are in very poor condition, and in some sections, there are deep trenches to negotiate. To avoid detection, many of the gold seekers are traveling trails seldom used by the average populace. The central roads are strewn with landmines implanted during the civil war.

Latest information reveals these mines are still taking their toll of men and beasts. A rumor has also been spread that some trails have been secretly de-mined and charted and that copies of these maps can be procured . . . for a price. Obviously, a map of this sort would prove invaluable to foreign prospectors.

"Do you really think it was smart, signing that contract?" asked Medeiros, one of the new prospectors. "And how do we know this map isn't a phony?"

His partner, Valente, tried to reassure him. "First of all, we couldn't get this map without signing. Hell, it's only 10 percent of what we find, and besides, it has to be on the level. It's sanctioned by a top official, for crissakes. Quit worrying, we're going to be rich!"

"When you think about it," stated Medeiros, "this guy's getting rich on our sweat. He controls the border guards and checkpoints and feathers his nest for retirement by selling us maps and supplying fools like us with protection to the gold fields in his own province. According to this map, we're traveling parallel to Lake Niassa. It seems like a round about way to get there . . . I don't like it!"

"C'mon, cheer up," said Valente. "Here we are two fishermen, actually ex-fishermen from Portugal, with a chance to strike it rich and you're complaining."

"I suppose you're right," replied Medeiros. Turning his head sharply, he asked, "What was that?"

"What was what?" asked his partner.

"Over there!" answered Medeiros, pointing into the brush. Valente still couldn't see what Medeiros was pointing at. The sun was going down and the area was covered in shadows.

"Hand me your rifle," said Medeiros. He fired into the brush, and an animal leaped into the tree 30 feet away.

"Did you see that?" Valente said excitedly.

Just then, Medeiros fired again and that proved to be a fatal mistake. The bullet grazed the fossa's shoulder, knocking it to the ground, and in an instant, with one massive thrust, it attacked Medeiros. Its huge jaws went right for the face and buried its fangs deep into his eyes, while the lower teeth found their mark under his chin.

Razor-like retractable claws then tore into the body cavity, splattering blood and viscera all over Valente. The muffled cries of the victim were rendered inaudible by his partner's screams.

Valente passed out and collapsed to the ground. The horror of the incident didn't attach itself to reality, at least not at first. Upon regaining consciousness, in disbelief Valente reached for his flashlight, and when he turned it on, what was left of his partner sent him screaming down the trail in stark terror, clothes stained with dried blood and pieces of flesh.

At approximately the same time, 75 miles away, Diogo and company were pulling into the medical mission parking area. The sun was almost down, but the house and surrounding grounds were quite visible. "It's beautiful!" said Karina, referring to the Donovan home.

The two-level structure was made entirely of logs, and the screened-in porch, wrapped around three sides, overlooked the Zambezi River. The sunset just added to the magnificence of it all.

"There is something very different about Africa to a woman," thought Karina. "It's unbearably romantic!" Then, upon further reflection, "Why haven't I felt this way before?"

Anna and Michael came out of the house to welcome them, and after the intros, Diogo asked, "What time's dinner, Mom?"

"Give me another half hour!"

Michael said, "I'll show you to your rooms. Son, you take Karina's bags. We'll put Karina in the spare room upstairs, and Blaine can use the pull-out on the first floor."

Anna was staring at Karina, and when Karina looked back questioningly, Anna said, "Forgive me, Karina, it's just that you're the first woman Diogo has ever invited here, even on business."

"Are you saying I'm special?" she asked laughingly.

"The odds are in your favor!" replied Anna.

Before dinner, Diogo cautioned Blaine and Karina not to discuss the fossa in detail with his mother. He didn't want her to know the danger they may all be facing soon. "Keep it light!" he ended by saying.

So around the dinner table, Karina's taste in music and her experience in Rio de Janeiro were quickly brought up.

"Oh God!" exclaimed Michael, "this'll be good for at least one hour's worth of expounding!" Anna and Karina hit it off well together and continued conversing while the men retired to the living room.

"We'll leave the dishes to them," said Michael. Upon entering the other room, he asked, "Okay Diogo, what's going on?"

"Well," answered his son, "remember when I called you to describe the kill site? You mentioned a possible suspect animal in Madagascar?"

"Continue," said Mike.

"Blaine is from the States and had been doing some research work in Madagascar. He's got quite a story for you, so I'll turn it over to him."

Blaine related to Michael all that had transpired from the time he left Florida, right up to his presence at the compound.

"This is absolutely incredible," said Mike. "That's quite a tale!"

"I assure you," responded Blaine, "this is no tale! Everything happened just the way I told you. I suppose if I were to write a book, not many would believe it!"

"So where do you go from here?" asked Mike.

Diogo spoke up, "We'll be heading out early in the morning and, hopefully lash up with Kapungwe and the others by noon. I've studied the maps, and I have a hunch the animal will be heading for the Mwabvi Reserve in Malawi, because of its remoteness."

Michael suggested, "There's also the Niassa Reserve. I was reading where Joseph C. Bacon, head of the Wildlife Federation, said Niassa was Africa's last true wilderness with many inaccessible regions and is still one of the most isolated parts of the continent."

"Where's that?" asked Blaine.

"Up north of here. It's real rugged country . . . about 35,000 square kilometers of it!" answered Diogo.

"There's one other problem in that region," Michael added. "Somebody recently struck gold, and there's a whole bunch of illegal, trigger-happy foreigners running around. It was on the news.

The local police can't control the situation. They've called in the Provincials."

"Ah, just what we need!" exclaimed his son. "We'll have a little more excitement to add to this salubrious safari!"

"What's this about a salubrious safari?" asked Anna, as she and Karina entered the room.

"We were just comparing notes between Madagascar and Mozambique on animal diseases and treatments," said Michael.

"Why Madagascar?" asked Anna.

"That's where Blaine just completed some fieldwork," replied Mike.

Karina came to the rescue by changing the subject. "Diogo told me you have an album by Sinatra and Jobim?"

"I do," said Anna. "Would you like to hear it?"

"I think I would first like to hear 'Brazil' by Johnny Mathis or was Diogo just pulling my leg?"

"I'll put it on," said Anna. "You are definitely a girl after my own heart."

When the song was over, Karina just sighed and said, "And I thought he only sang ballads!" Anna then played the album entitled *Francis Albert Sinatra & Antonio Carlos Jobim*.

Somewhere in between songs, Blaine couldn't stop yawning, excused himself and went to bed. The others poured themselves glasses of wine and listened to the soothing tones until the CD ended. Michael and Anna excused themselves and retired. Karina walked out onto the screened veranda, holding a half glass of wine, and looked out over the moonlit Zambezi River.

"I feel as though I could reach up and touch that moon!" she said.

"I suppose, in some ways, you could," said Diogo. "You look like you're enjoying your visit with us."

"Your mom and dad are really special, and I don't think I have ever seen a more beautiful spot." As their eyes met, this time in a longer gaze, they both realized their feelings for each other were something special . . . something that had been missing in their lives for a long time.

For some reason, it momentarily frightened Diogo, and he grabbed for words, "Oh, I have a CD you really might like. It's called a *Twist of Jobim*, put together by Lee Ritenour. They spiced up some of the numbers. You may enjoy it." He put the music on and poured another glass of wine.

As the first few notes played, she said, "I know this one, 'Agua de Beber' . . . water to drink."

He lifted her glass out of her hand and said, "It should be called 'Wine to Drink' . . . it's absolutely intoxicating!" He set her glass down.

She asked, "The wine or you?"

He lifted her to her feet with his right hand, twirled her around, reached out with his left hand, put it on her right hip, pulled her in close to his body and said, "Me and the music!"

She looked him straight in the eye and said sarcastically, "Cute!" Little did she know that it was the first time he made that particular move on any woman.

In a boyish and naive sort of way, he was trying to impress her, when all the time it was his simplicity that she admired. "This is bossa nova with a kick!" In the middle of the number the piano took the lead, and he said, "I was never a lover of piano, but this guy, Dave Grusin, is great!"

She loved the way he was holding her in his arms, firm yet gently. Sensitive to his every move, they danced as if choreographed. He pulled her in close to himself where their lips were just inches apart, and after holding for a few seconds, twirled her out again. Though he wanted to kiss her so badly he ached, he felt it wasn't the right time. In one move, he brought her behind him, from one side to the other where their buttocks touched, and when she arrived on the other side, she enclosed his leg with the both of hers and slid suggestively part way down. Then she stood straight up, threw her head back and spun away.

Embracing her again, he kissed her gently on the tip of the nose, and when she didn't draw back, he moved his lips ever so softly to her earlobe and then slowly down the length of her neck. She responded by biting his ear. He moved her away a little as he quivered, and they stared at each other intently. Simultaneously, their heads moved toward one another, and when their lips touched, they both knew their lives would never be the same again.

The song ended. He picked her up in his arms and carried her to the guest room, at the far side of the house. Sounds of passion emanated from the two lovers a few minutes later . . . "Ooh . . . ooh, Diogo!"

"Sssh, you'll awaken my parents." Another few minutes went by . . . "Oh, Karina!"

"Sssh, you'll wake up your parents!" she said jokingly. The rest of the night, sleep came at a premium, but neither complained, and Diogo managed to be in his room by daybreak.

Just before breakfast, Michael pulled his son aside and asked, "Did you and Karina find each other last night?"

"What do you mean, Dad?"

"Well," said Mike, "sometime during the night, I heard her call out your name and shortly afterwards, I heard you call out her name. Your mother, God bless her, was half asleep and thought you were lost . . . she asked me to get up and find you!"

"That's very funny, Dad, very funny."

"The funny part about it is I almost got up! Ha-ha," laughed Mike.

At breakfast, Karina asked Diogo, "Exactly what is bossa nova?"

"I guess the best way to express it is the way my mom explained it to me. She asked Jobim the same question. In Portuguese, the term could be translated to mean 'new style' or 'new fashion.'

Jobim fashioned a music style of his own combining Brazilian beats, such as samba with jazz. He wanted to break away from the traditional and create a *new wave* . . . Brazilian Jazz.

"That CD I played for you last night that featured 'Agua de Beber' was put together by Lee Ritenour and some other great musicians in 1997 as a tribute to Tom, who died in 1994. Did I explain that correctly, Mom?"

"Son, you even impressed me!" said Anna patronizingly. After breakfast, they loaded up on their equipment, and as they were ready to leave, Anna came running out with a bag full of sandwiches and goodies. "You may need this on your trek," she said.

Blaine spoke up, "You people are really something else . . . thank you!" Karina echoed his sentiments.

Pointing to her son, Anna said warningly, "Keep in touch!"

CHAPTER TWENTY-THREE

The High Price of Gold

Late afternoon, Tuesday August 1st, Diogo's aide Kapungwe met Chett and Nat with tents and supplies, including a couple of good rifles. Chett was not happy with the idea of killing the fossa and still nurtured the thought of a live capture. He kept the notion to himself and fell asleep dreaming of what a spectacular find this would be to the scientific community.

The next morning, while they all were still asleep and before daybreak, Valente staggered into their campsite moaning and then collapsed. Kapungwe, a light sleeper, sprung to his feet and ran out of the tent to investigate. He cradled the unconscious man in his arms and called out to the others, "Bring a canteen!" They came running each with a canteen, and Chett was struggling to get his pants up while he held the strap of the canteen in his mouth. Kapungwe was able to bring the man to consciousness for a brief moment, but upon opening his eyes, Valente screamed out in horror. The vision of his mutilated friend was obviously still on his mind, but he was refusing to admit to reality.

"What is it, man?" asked Chett excitedly. "What's troubling you?" Valente went to speak, but before he could utter a word, he fell back into unconsciousness.

"This guy's been through something terrible," said Nat.

"Yeah, and whatever it was," added Chett, "scared the hell out of him!"

"Look at his clothes!" said Kapungwe.

"I don't see any wounds on him," said Chett.

"So where did all this blood and tissue come from?" asked Nat. "Hopefully, he'll be able to tell us something later. Let's get him into the tent and cover him up. He's obviously in shock."

Chett asked Kapungwe, "What time are we to expect Diogo?"

"He usually likes to be on the road early," answered the guide. "He should be here by early afternoon."

"We'll try questioning this fellow again at that time," said Nat. "In the meantime, let's scout up the road a little ways for a sign."

Diogo was right on schedule, and he and the others were brought up to date on the latest happening. "Let's see if we can get him up!" said Diogo. "It's important to find out what he knows!"

This prompted Chett to voice a question. "You're not thinking this has anything to do with the fossa, are you?"

"We can't afford to overlook anything, at this point in time," answered Diogo. "Did you guys find any sign yesterday?"

Nat answered, "We found tracks on the river bank, this side, and lost it later in the brush. It was definitely heading this direction, and I think we're ahead of him."

"From what angle did this straggler come from?" asked Diogo.

"I don't know," said Chett. "We were all asleep. Kapungwe found him first."

Diogo looked at Kapungwe questioningly, and he just shrugged. Diogo became very upset. "Are you telling me you never posted a guard last night? Are you all losing your minds? Listen to me, all of you. We continue to underestimate our prey and someone's going to die. This thing is a killer, day or night . . . day or night! Goddamn it, wake him up!"

Karina went into the tent and gently shook the stranger to

awaken him. On the second try, he opened his eyes. "Madre mio, an angel!" he exclaimed.

"They're many people that would argue against that statement," said Karina. "Have some water." She helped him to sit up.

He drank a little and asked, "Who are you?"

"I'm Karina and you're called?"

"Pedro . . . Pedro Valente." She helped him onto his feet and out of the tent. He was surprised to see the others. "Where did all of you come from?" he asked.

"This is our campsite, and you wandered into it early this morning," said Diogo. "Right now we're very interested in exactly where you came from. How did you get all that blood on you?"

When he looked around and saw Nat's police uniform, he was reluctant to say anything. Nat spoke to him firmly, "You'll answer our questions now or at police headquarters. The choice is yours."

"I didn't do anything wrong!" cried Valente. Then he continued to tell the whole story. "My partner, Medeiros, and I came here from Portugal just two weeks ago. We heard there was gold to be had in the north country. We are but poor fishermen who scraped together enough money for the trip, hoping to return with wealth."

"Do you know gold smuggling is illegal?" asked Nat.

"We are not smugglers. We were going to dig for it!" answered Valente. "It can't be illegal. We signed a paper."

"What kind of paper?" asked Nat.

He produced the paper. "This is a paper of commitment to a high official. We were given a map to the gold fields and issued a permit of excavation. We agreed to pay 10 percent of our diggings before we left the country."

"You fool!" exclaimed Nat. "Don't you know you never would have been permitted to leave? Once you came with the gold, they'd kill you for smuggling and keep it all! Where's your partner now?"

Panic set in on Valente's facial expressions, and fearfully he related all that happened, at least all that he could remember. "This animal that attacked Medeiros, I have never before seen in my entire life! It was very fierce and had a terrible odor. I will never forget the teeth and claws. Its eyes . . . I will see in nightmares as long as I live!"

"I wonder why it didn't kill you?" questioned Blaine.

"I don't know," said Valente. "I passed out during the attack. When I came awake, I smelled a terrible odor. I found a flashlight, and when I saw what was left of Medeiros, I ran."

"How do you know this animal was wounded?" asked Diogo.

"I saw it with my own eyes! Medeiros fired the gun, and I saw the animal spin around on the branch and fall to the ground. Without hesitation, it bounced back up and attacked with lightning speed. I could do nothing. I'm so sorry. I've never seen the likes of it."

"I think you'll agree, it's a terrible price to pay for gold," said Diogo. "Now we're back to the gospel, according to you Chett. You told us yourself that we are tracking the most vicious animal in the world, and now it's wounded. That makes it twice as dangerous. Are you still harboring notions of capturing this thing with darts?"

Diogo shook his head negatively and walking away said, "Where's the beer?" Kapungwe handed him one, and Diogo looked at him scornfully and said, "And you! Didn't I teach you to always have someone stand guard at night? This man's partner could have been one of you!"

"I'm sorry, Dog," said Kapungwe. "It will never happen again."

Then Diogo approached Valente and asked, "Do you think you can lead us to your dead friend?" He said yes with a nod. They provided him with a change of clothes and some hot food, and before heading out, Diogo brought them together again for another discussion.

"I had a plan when I arrived here at the camp. Now, in the light of recent events, it has to be changed. I was going to split us up into three groups of two, so we could cover more ground. Now, I think it would be a good idea to go with two groups of three, with someone always manning a vehicle. We have radios. Let's use them. And damn it, everybody carries a weapon. If what we find up ahead is evidence of the fossa, there's only one of two places he'll go. One is to the Mwabvi Reserve in southern Malawi, and his other choice, in all probability, will be the Niassa Reserve in northwestern Mozambique. Any questions or gripes? We may as well air them out now."

Blaine spoke up, "Are we going to be able to take the Rovers where we're going?"

"To a point," answered Diogo. "We'll just have to dance to the music."

"And this man, Valente," said Nat, "What do we do with him?"

"He goes back. We'll work that out later. For now, he goes with us." The safari then broke camp and headed out to find Medeiros, or what was left of him.

When they arrived at the scene, Valente was reluctant to go anywhere close and hung back, still shaken from the gruesome events of the previous evening. "This isn't going to tell us much," said Chett. "Other animals fed on the carcass."

"And the vultures picked clean the rest," added Karina.

"Let's gather up what remains are left," said Diogo. "We can, at least, give him a decent burial." Then he walked toward Valente, who was cowering in fear, and asked, "Do you think you can show us where Medeiros wounded the animal?"

"I . . . I think so. It . . . it was over there," Valente said, pointing into a tree. Seeing his friend being buried made him very nervous. He would sneak a quick glance, and then turn away in fear.

Kapungwe climbed the tree to the location where Valente had pointed. "There are blood spots here, Dog!" he called down.

"There are a few here at the base of the tree, as well," said Chett.

"You have your field kit?" asked Diogo.

"Affirmative!"

"Do you think you can identify these blood spots?"

"It's going to take some time," announced Chett.

"That's okay," said Diogo. "We'll camp by the river; it's only a hundred yards from here through the brush. In the meantime, I'll do some tracking."

"Are we still on the Zambezi River?" asked Karina.

"No," replied Diogo. "This is now the Shire.[1] The Zambezi continues west. This is a tributary that runs north through Malawi, and where, I believe, our animal friend is headed. You see this also runs through the Mwabvi Reserve." Then he turned back to Valente and asked, very curiously, "What the hell route were you guys following to get to the north country; and where's your vehicle?"

"The vehicle is just up the trail around the bend," replied Valente. "According to the map we had, we could drive to Lake Niassa without fear of mines or washed out roads. We then follow the shoreline north and turn east, thereby avoiding the tall mountains."

"That's one trick I'd love to see," exclaimed Diogo. "Where's the map?"

"I don't know!" answered Valente. "Medeiros carried it with him."

"Hell, it's probably been eaten," said Diogo, and Valente uttered a shrill in fear.

Diogo walked up the trail and around the bend. There it was a, beat-up Land Rover, vintage 1989. It carried boxes of stores and supplies and extra gas cans in the back, a necessity for this trek.

[1] Pronounced "shir-eee"

There was also a 16-foot aluminum car-top boat and a 9hp engine. He noticed the keys were still in the ignition, but no sign of the map. He continued up the trail and found some tracks resembling the fossa's, heading toward the river. He thought, "If this animal gave up fish in his diet, we'd probably lose the trail. Chett was definitely right; it doesn't stray far from the water. Now if only the DNA is a positive match . . ." He hurried down to the river, gun at the ready, and scouted the bank for signs. His hunch was correct . . . it was headed upriver and was ahead of them! "Was there a shortcut I didn't know about?" he asked himself. He walked slowly back to the others, scanning the area real well for a safe campsite.

"I found a good spot to set up," he announced. "How's Chett doing?"

"I helped a little, and we're almost there . . . he's good. We should know the results soon," answered Karina.

"Hey Valente," shouted Diogo, "I thought you said you were poor fishermen?"

"We are!" answered Valente defensively.

"Then how could you afford a Land Rover, boat and motor, a month's supplies, and extra cans of gas?"

"They advanced that all to us for our signatures on the papers," he said.

"They must have been awful sure you were going to strike it in a big way!" said the Dog.

Blaine was standing by taking notes, when Chett announced, "Bingo! We got a match."

"Great!" said Diogo. "Let's set up camp by the river. We'll move out in the morning."

Diogo found many other tracks on the river's edge, but didn't mention them. Some belonged to a lion or two, so he didn't want to make anyone uneasy, especially Valente. He'd give everyone the jitters. "Tonight and early morning may prove quite interesting," he thought. He established a watch rotation, making sure someone was to be awake at all times. During the night, there was an occasional roar of a lion and the laugh of a hyena that pierced the calm insect-filled air. All, to a man, including Karina, were grateful for tent screening that kept the malaria-ridden mosquitoes at bay. The evening was relatively uneventful.

Once again, sunrise came early, and Diogo, having the last watch, awoke Kapungwe first. He asked him to go back to the kill site and scan the area for the map that Medeiros was supposedly carrying. He then awoke the others.

After a light breakfast, some chat and good coffee, Diogo addressed Valente, "How are you feeling this morning?"

"Much better, thank you," he replied.

"You'll be parting company with us this morning," said Diogo. "So I took the liberty of writing you an introduction. When you reach the main road, turn right. About 20 miles up, you'll come to an Anglican mission. The Reverend Hartley Ashton and his wife, Edna May, are good friends of mine. They'll supply you with directions to a shortcut across the river that will save you a half-day's travel. She also makes great scones! You'll need to stop in at the police outpost in Beira and give a deposition on the happenings here. See Nat for the particulars."

Nat overheard the conversation and spoke up. "He won't have to see me because I'll be going with him. Are you heading into Malawi?"

"Looks like a definite," answered Diogo.

"That puts me out of my jurisdiction and on my way back to Beira. A report of Medeiros' death will have to be made, and without identifiable remains, I'll need depositions from all of you. I'm also anxious to look into this black market gold scam, and Valente can be a key witness."

As Nat and Valente were about to leave, Diogo approached Nat and whispered, "You know, you're leaving us with just one vehicle, four people and a ton of gear." Then he counted on his fingers. "Excuse me, five people. I was really counting on you."

"Oh?" answered Nat. "I thought you were counting on your fingers, B'wana Dog!"

"That's real funny, Nat . . . real funny!"

"Seriously," said Nat, "I thought you knew I was leaving Valente's vehicle with you. I'd have to impound it anyway."

"It may be weeks before we're back!" exclaimed Diogo.

Nat just smiled and shrugged his shoulders. "Okay, Valente, you're with me. Get your personals out of the Rover and stow 'em in here." They bid farewell and left.

Kapungwe came out of the brush as Nat was heading down the road, and they waved to each other. He walked into the campsite and Diogo asked, "Did you find anything?"

"Nothing; where's Nat heading?"

"He's off to Beira with Valente, but left us this vehicle with supplies for as long as we need it."

"That was nice of him," said Kapungwe and added, "You know, B'wana Dog, I saw evidence of many animals in this area, including what looked to be a large herd of wildebeests."

"Yes," replied Diogo. "I noticed that myself yesterday afternoon at the river's edge. There's definitely more wildlife around here than previously estimated by the game commission. That's a very good sign!"

"So where do we go from here?" asked Karina. Chett and Blaine were about to ask the same question. They were all experiencing a touch of anxiety. Blaine thought it time for a quip . . . "I have a riddle for you. How do wildebeests communicate in the wild? They read the gnus-paper." Karina just rolled her eyes up into her head.

"I saw fossa tracks a little ways upriver from here," announced Diogo pretending he didn't hear the joke.

"Why didn't you mention it!" snapped Chett.

"I wanted to be sure of that blood match so we wouldn't be chasing fantasy. Now I'm sure! We're all sure," said Diogo. "Now here are the possibilities we're facing: This Shire River runs through some rough country. It's certainly a suitable home for fossa, going by what you told me. We're almost into Malawi. I have friends there in high places. Border guards will not be a problem. However, if fossa should decide to cross the river and head northeast, we're in for a long campaign. That'll mean he's heading for the Niassa Reserve, which is also a favorable area for him. We've noticed increased animal activity in this area, along with plenty of fish and seclusion. Hopefully, he'll decide to stick around."

"How will we know which way he's going?" asked Blaine. "How do we make certain?"

Diogo went to the Rover and took out a map of the Mwabvi Reserve. "As you can see here, the only way to be positive is to track both sides of the river. I have no idea what the road conditions are from this point on. I also don't know how long Valente's vehicle will hold out. Besides fossa, there are other dangers, as well. It's very risky to split up. But we don't have a choice."

Then Chett came up with an idea. "Why don't you and Karina take this side and the good Rover while the rest of us take the older vehicle and track the other side?"

"The only problem with that is Valente's vehicle doesn't have a radio," said Diogo. "I'm sorry now we sent the compound truck with the other guide . . . we could have used both right now!"

"Couldn't we use flags?" suggested Blaine. "We could use red for emergency; green for all is okay, and yellow for a positive fossa sighting."

"That'll work!" said Diogo. "We just need to know where we can cross in safety to come to each other's aid. We know we can cross down at our last campsite, but that's at least 10 miles from here. I wish we had the Medeiros' map."

"We better get started," stated Chett.

"We'll scout the area for awhile on foot and set up a couple of traps. That'll give you guys time to double back and catch up on the other side," replied Diogo, adding, "This map I have is not detailed but shows a definite narrowing about two miles from here. Why don't we make that our rendezvous point? We may be close enough to shout communication."

"Sounds good!" said Chett. "Kapungwe, you got a good idea of where we are now?"

"I've got the location etched in my brain."

Karina and Diogo headed down to the riverbank, and she asked, "How come you haven't been paying much attention to me on this trip?"

"I thought the worry lines on my face were obvious," replied Dog. "I'm still not too comfortable about you being out here in the bush."

"So you're angry with me?"

"No, I'm just concerned. I know you're capable; it's . . . well, since the other night . . ." he muttered.

"Nothing's changed!" she said sternly. "I'm still a damn good field biologist and a very independent woman!"

"Calm down," he said.

"No . . . I came here looking for fossa . . . not love. But I damn well intend to leave this place with both!" Diogo just threw his hands in the air in a surrender gesture and didn't say another word.

When they arrived at the river's edge, they noticed a few zebra and a small herd of wildebeests cautiously drinking from the river and keeping a keen eye on, not only them, but the two large crocs that were lazing in the morning sun about a hundred yards upstream.

"One can get so occupied keeping an eye open for large animals," said Karina, "that the little ones like birds and butterflies go unnoticed."

"The other side of the coin holds true, as well," said Diogo.

"One can become engrossed chasing a butterfly and end up in the jaws of a lion. Everything's a matter of balance and knowledge of impending dangers. This damn thing we're chasing could pop up anywhere . . . anytime. That's what makes it so unpredictable."

"I believe that when fossa arrives at his destination," said Karina, "if we don't stop him first, he'll submerge himself in the wilderness, just like he did in Madagascar. I don't think it wants anything to do with humanity."

"You may be right," agreed Diogo. "But what if you're not . . . what about the dead bodies he's left behind already?"

"I'm willing to bet that in every case, he was provoked. I can feel it deep down in my gut," said Karina.

"Anyway," said Diogo, "let's stroll casually upriver and look at some tracks." As they moved toward the watering hole, a small backwash in the river, the animals that were drinking were spooked and left. "There are so many tracks here that it's hard to pick them apart," he said. "If this animal is as solitary as you say, he'll probably pick a secluded spot and pick off a stray. Let's get the Rover and move upriver a ways. Chett and the others should be heading up the other side by now. They'll be at this point within an hour."

"What happens if they pick up fossa's track on the other side?" she asked.

"Then we must head him off or we'll be in for one hell of a safari to the north country."

"Why can't we just let him go?"

"Because I'm getting paid by your boss to capture this thing dead or alive, and right now dead seems good to me. I've never known of a man-eater to go back to its former diet.

"Besides, how come you're not siding with Chett on this thing and seeking to capture it?" he said.

"For one reason, I've never cared for putting animals in zoos," she said. "Secondly, this may be the last of its kind. When it dies off, the species dies. So why not just let it live out its life in the wild? I agree with Chett on one point, darting it for field study, but not for taking back for exhibition."

"I'll have to think about that one," he stated.

They drove to where the river narrowed and made camp. "The others should only be a few minutes behind us," he said. "That's if they haven't picked up a trail. We have time to set a few traps. I'd like to place one ahead of us, one behind and one to the west about a hundred yards."

"What do we use for bait?" asked Karina.

"Kapungwe should be taking care of that problem. I told him to pick up a couple of goats at the ferry crossing. There's a village not far from there."

"And how does he get them to us?" she asked.

"We'll figure that out later."

The other side of the river was only 150 yards away; the current was slow and his mind was already working on a plan to get the "bait" across. It wasn't long before Chett showed up on the other side, and in lieu of blowing the horn; he had Blaine hanging out the window waving a green flag. Then to Diogo's amazement, they started driving across!

"What the hell are they doing?" he mumbled. "They'll lose all the gear!"

"What's happening?" said Chett as he brought the vehicle to a stop.

"What the hell kind of stunt was that?" asked Diogo. "What if you hit a deep spot?"

"No chance!" he said, as he produced a map. "We found the lost Medeiros map!"

"Where was it?" inquired Diogo.

"We found it in the side pocket of the door, stuck behind a magazine. Blaine found it, and this thing is detailed like you wouldn't believe! It has the spots of the rivers that can be crossed or portaged over, as well as trails that are mine-free. Best of all, we found a pair of portable two-way radios."

"Excellent!" replied Diogo. "Kapungwe, how did you make out with the goats?"

Kapungwe held up two fingers and said, "Small ones, I'm afraid."

Diogo studied the map. The next good crossing was almost 10 miles ahead. "We still have a few more hours of light," stated Diogo. "I'd like to move upriver another five miles before we settle in for the night. What say you guys?"

"You're calling the shots," said Chett. The others had no comment.

"Okay, leave one of those goats with me. You guys head back to the other side and move up to a spot approximately here," Diogo said, pointing to a location on the map. "Set up a trap ahead of where you plan to camp. We'll do the same on this side. Having those radios gives us more freedom to maneuver. Someone's on watch all the time, right?" They all nodded their agreement, and Chett, Blaine and Kapungwe parted for the other side. Diogo broke the light camp he had set up earlier, stowed the gear and headed upriver.

"This looks like a great place for a camp," said Diogo as he pulled the Rover to a stop. "Help me set up one of these traps!"

Karina wasn't too keen on using a live baby goat for bait, but knew it was necessary. "I don't have to like it!" she said. He just grinned. "So do we pitch one tent or two?" she asked.

"Just one," he replied.

"Mmmm, that sounds interesting. And sleeping bags?"

"Just one," he answered again.

"Do you mean to tell me we're both going to squeeze into one sleeping bag?"

"Yep," he replied. "But not at the same time. One will keep watch while the other sleeps and vice versa."

"You're impossible!" she shouted.

Diogo said, "Yep!"

After the camp was set up, they helped each other with cooking. "This is very romantic. Sitting around the fire under the stars deep in the African jungle, just the two of us in love and by ourselves . . ." She let her voice trail off sexily, intimating her sensual mood.

And Diogo added, "Yep, and waiting for a killer to attack and devour us!" They continued to speak for a while and Diogo volunteered for the first watch, cautioning her to keep the fire going throughout the night on her watches.

"If you see or hear anything out of the ordinary, don't hesitate to use your rifle," he said.

"Everything around here is out of the ordinary for me, including the way you're acting!" she shot back.

"I'm not acting," he replied. "I'm trying to keep all of us alive!" Then he grabbed her by the elbows and kissed her gently on the lips. She kissed him back hard. She wanted him and thought he was being coy.

"Believe me, Karina," he said, "I feel the same way you do. We've got to stay alert. We've got the rest of our lives to . . . well, when this is over."

"The rest of our lives!" she echoed. "That sounds like a commitment."

"Yeah, a commitment that could end very abruptly . . . one encounter with the giant fossa. Get some sleep!" he snapped . . . lovingly.

As the sun was going down on the other side of the river, laughter emanated from around the campfire. Kapungwe was dancing around like a wounded peacock and had the others roaring with laughter as he was enacting his version of a native joke. They were all taking a turn at entertaining, and Chett was next up.

"Well," he started, "there was this elderly fellow who lived alone in a retirement condo in Florida, near where you come from, Blaine. Anyway, he met and started dating a woman of his age, who was still living in her own home. After several dates, this guy began getting sexually frisky, if you know what I mean. The woman said she didn't believe in premarital sex and suggested they take vows. 'What do we have in common?' the man asked. 'We're old and both lonely,' she stated. 'We love to dance and go for walks, and besides, we could save a lot of money.' 'That's all true,' said the man, and then asked, 'What about sex?' 'Infrequently!' answered the woman. He thought for a moment and then asked, "Is that one word or two?'"

Blaine got it right away and almost split a gut, but Kapungwe looked baffled and failed to see the humor until they explained it to him. After a deep sounding jovial chuckle, Blaine took the stage. "I don't know any real funny jokes, but I would like to give my impression of a retired ex-jock."

"What is an ex-jock?" inquired Kapungwe.

"In the United States," explained Blaine, "any male who plays sports is called a 'jock,' because they wear a testicle protector by the same name. (He placed his hands on his crotch to demonstrate.) A plastic cup fits inside this jock and offers protection against accidental contact."

"Oh, I see!" said Kapungwe. "Please continue."

"So an ex-jock," said Blaine, "is someone who, after many years, develops a distinguishable walk. It starts early in one's career as the jock and cup, helped along by perspiration, cause chafing on the inside of the upper thighs. No amount of talcum powder or ointment tends to help the condition. Eventually, it just takes its toll so that the athlete starts to walk with his legs further apart than normal. It happens so gradually that he's not even aware of it. After years of wear and tear, the ankles and knees become weaker, and this poor guy feels like a car that needs ball-joint replacement."

The two-man audience is beginning to laugh aloud now because Blaine is demonstrating while he's talking, and his natural limp adds to the comedy. "Finally," continues Blaine, "he retires and starts to put on a little weight. This really bothers him, so he starts sucking in his gut, trying to hide it, while at the same time, throwing out his chest and pulling back his shoulders with cocked arms. But he cannot accomplish this maneuver without his ass sticking way out in the back. So he walks like this."

As Blaine put more emphasis into the movement, Chett and Kapungwe continued laughing so hard that they were rolling on the ground, holding their stomachs. Blaine pranced around the campfire once more, and then fell to the ground, laughing at himself . . . They were all feeling uptight from the tension of the day and the humor offered a bit of respite.

"Did you ever play sports?" asked Chett.

"I played some college ball . . . third base. I still play . . . for the scholarship; I have one more year. I have a good glove and good batting average, but I'm not fast enough running the bases to play professional. I do love it though."

"What say you turn in?" suggested Kapungwe. "I'll take the first watch."

Yawning, the others said, "Sounds like a good idea."

"I'll wake you first, Chett," said Kapungwe. "Then Blaine can take last watch 'til sunrise."

A short while later, after they had settled into the sleeping bags, Chett started laughing aloud, thinking of Blaine prancing around, doing his impersonation.

CHAPTER TWENTY-FOUR

Without Provocation

August 4th, Friday Morning

Blaine was on watch as the sun was rising, and before waking the others, decided to relieve his bladder behind the bushes. He set his rifle down right on the tail of a startled snake that responded by biting him on the back of his leg. Blaine felt just a bump and looked around to see what it was and didn't realize, at first, he had been bitten. He never saw the culprit that, although protecting itself, could probably cause his demise.

He felt a burning sensation, and when he examined the area, he let out a howl that made Kapungwe jump out of his tent and come running. "What is it?" he asked. Blaine just turned, revealing the back part of his leg. Kapungwe shouted out, "Snake bite!" Chett came out of his tent, looking around in a daze, trying to get his bearings. Kapungwe yelled again, "Snake bite! Over here! Quickly, get the kit!"

He quickly awakened and ran for the kit while Kapungwe tried to keep Blaine calm.

"What kind of snake was it?" he asked, as he arrived with the kit.

"Never saw it," answered Blaine. "I think he nailed me without provocation. All I felt was a bump on the back of my leg."

"How are you feeling now?" asked Kapungwe, who was no stranger to snake venom.

"My nose feels tingly, and I feel like pins and needles on the tips of my fingers," responded Blaine. Kapungwe had applied a tourniquet above the bite immediately. Chett made incisions into the fang holes and applied the suction cups. "I've got a polyvalent antivenin in the truck; do you have any allergies?"

"None that I know of," he answered.

He administered the injection and immediately called Diogo on the radio. "Diogo here . . . what's up?"

"Blaine was just bitten by a snake, type unknown. We applied T.I.S.A."[2]

"What did you use for antivenin?" asked Diogo.

"A polyvalent."

"How bad is the swelling and discoloration and how far apart are the fang marks?"

There was a slight pause . . . "Fang marks are about five-eighths inches apart, swelling and discoloration are minimal at this time," responded Chett.

"You did a good job. Is he experiencing any other symptoms?"

"Let me check." Another pause . . . "Says he has a metallic taste in his mouth, and his vision is kind of tunneled. He's sweating more than normal, so he says."

Diogo looked at Karina and said, "Sounds like a Black Mamba."

"Very dangerous?" she asked.

"Very deadly. Okay," said Diogo again on the radio, "have him keep still and breathe slowly. We should get him back to the Donovan compound ASAP, just in case he has a reaction to the

---

[2]Tourniquet/Incision/Suction/Anti-venin = T.I.S.A.

injection. Drive straight up to the rendezvous point. We'll pick you up there, and Kapungwe can take Blaine back for treatment."

"You're the boss! See you soon."

When they arrived at the meeting place, Diogo and Karina had already crossed the river and were waiting for them. "Let me take a look at Blaine," said Diogo. "Karina, what do you know about snake bite?"

"I treated a few in Brazil," she replied. They both examined Blaine and came to the same conclusion. He was swollen and discolored around the bite and would be sore for a while but not in danger, barring a reaction of some sort.

All of a sudden, Blaine started to laugh out loud, and they thought he was experiencing delirium. "I do know a joke!" he said laughingly. "As a matter of fact, it's a snake joke." The others thought Blaine was losing his grip on reality, but Kapungwe explained to Diogo and Karina about the previous evening when Blaine had announced that he didn't know any jokes. So to ease the tension of the moment, Blaine continued with the joke.

"These two guys were out hunting and one of them was bitten by a snake. He was bitten on the head of the penis by a Diamond-back Rattler. 'Quick! Get some help!' he shouted. The partner, seeing his friend in a lot of pain said, 'I'll carry you to the truck and take you to the doctor.' 'No time for that,' said the victim. 'Drive down to that ranch we passed a mile back and call the doctor from there for first-aid instructions.' The partner left immediately.

"The truck pulled up in front of the house, and he quickly explained the situation. They directed him to the phone. 'Hello Doc?' he said. 'What can I do for you?' asked the doctor. The partner explained the whole story, and the doctor told him he'd have to make two incisions on the fang holes and suck out the poison. 'Do you have suction cups?' asked the doctor. 'No,' was the reply. 'Then you'll have to suck out the poison by mouth,' exclaimed the doctor, 'and quickly!' 'What'll happen if I don't?' asked the partner.

'He'll die!' The partner hung up the phone and thanked the people and left.

"When he arrived back, the victim was laying on the ground, propped up against a boulder, holding his swollen and blue penis in his hand. 'What did the doctor say?' he asked. The partner stared at the penis and calmly whispered, "He said you were going to die."

Everyone, including Blaine had a good laugh that did break the tension of the moment, and then Diogo turned to Kapungwe and announced, "You'll be taking Blaine back to the compound. Explain the situation to my father, and I believe with one look, he'll know what kind of snake it was. Also get a sample of the antivenin from Chett and give that to my father, as well. We'll take the extra gasoline you're carrying; you won't need it."

"You got it!" replied Kapungwe.

"Chett, you're with us!" said Diogo. They all wished Blaine well as he parted their company.

"So, where are we off to?"

"I'm a little puzzled," said Diogo. "Didn't you say that the fossa could make 12 miles a day?"

"That's been the case," replied Chett.

"Well, we just picked up some tracks a ways back, and I figure he's only covering half that distance. It's possible he's wounded a little more than Valente thought. I'd like to back-track a mile or so on this side, and if we don't find any sign, we'll cross over and concentrate on the other side and assume it's heading for the Mwabvi Reserve and set our traps accordingly,"

Chett produced the map and said, "This may make things a little easier for us."

"The going will be a lot rougher from this point on," said Diogo as he scanned the map. "This map would've been a lot more helpful if we were staying on this side of the river and heading for the Niassa Reserve, which is still a possibility. I'm 90 percent sure he's on the other side, and we've got to nail him before he gets lost in that wilderness."

"Wouldn't we have a better chance now of capturing him with a dart, if he's as weak as you think?" asked Chett.

"Being wounded, he'll attack without provocation. It's even more dangerous now."

"Hey! Does my vote count?" asked Karina.

"You're part of this safari," replied Diogo.

"Okay then," she retorted, "if we spot the fossa, why can't he make an attempt with a dart, while you and I cover with rifles? Of course, if we catch it in one of the traps . . ."

"I know, there can't be an argument," said Diogo. "But if you miss, I take the shot. We may never get another chance. Agreed?" They agreed.

They searched the east side of the river for tracks, but to no avail. They came back to the rendezvous spot and crossed at the narrows and headed north. The pace was slow, and the further into the reserve they traveled, the more drastically the scenery changed. "It's a virtual wilderness," said Chett, excitedly. "No wonder he headed this way!" He was looking out over a hilly landscape of sandstone ridges and rocky gorges. This was definitely fossa-type country.

"It gets worse," said Diogo. "Or better, whatever your outlook may be. Up ahead there are fast flowing streams, some with rapids, and dense woodlands."

"You've been here before?" asked Chett.

"Twice . . . and neither time was peaches and cream. There are some areas in here where it's impossible to track. We'll set traps on the perimeter."

"It's really beautiful here, and there seems to be more wildlife than you previously projected," said Karina

"Up to last year," responded Dog, "there was an abundance of poaching taking place in this reserve, and obviously conservation enforcement is working. We'll be on foot soon. We need a plan."

"I haven't seen or heard any lions," said Chett. "There must be cats around. The giant fossa could survive very well on the Blue Duiker antelope and the monkey population, not to mention the access to fish."

"If I have my way, that brute will not be surviving at all. Period," said Diogo.

"Okay, you two," said Karina. "Let's not get into a 'death o' the species' argument that could go on forever. I'm for setting up camp right here!"

Diogo pulled the Land Rover into a small clearing, not far from river's edge. "The sun will be down soon, and I want to check the riverbank for tracks before nightfall. Would you two mind setting up camp?"

"As you wish!" replied Karina. "And would B'wana Dog like me to cook something special?" Diogo just shook his head in surrender and left silently with his rifle.

There were a few crocs around, and though they were on the other bank, Diogo kept an attitude of furtiveness all the same. He went upriver a few hundred yards to the bend. There were many tracks, but none like what he was looking for.

"Maybe we got ahead of him," he thought. He slapped at a bloodsucking fly and said to himself aloud, "You damn fool. If there was something around, it's gone now!" Among the beetles, bugs, snakes, flies, mosquitoes and leeches, one may lose his cool once in a while, even B'wana Dog! An eight-foot python slithered down a tree a short distance away from him, and he said, "I must've annoyed him, as well."

It was just turning dark as Diogo arrived back at the campsite and something smelled good on the fire. "See anything?" asked Chett.

"No, and that's bothering me. You say this thing likes fish also, and yet we haven't seen any leavings or scat anywhere, at least not of our boy.

"It could be he's sick or hurt worse than we thought. That would cut down on his appetite. He's traveling slow and resting more . . . maybe not able to chase game.

"That's what makes us perfect targets for him . . . we don't run fast!" said Diogo.

"C'mon, you guys," called Karina. "Dinner is served . . . get your own plates!"

"This is really good!" said Chett, as he tasted Karina's mulligan.

"Ditto," echoed Diogo.

After dinner, Karina said, "Diogo, we set up and cooked. You pick up and clean."

"Okay, okay. But both of you do me a favor. Keep on your sidearms and keep your rifles within reach!"

"You're awful panicky tonight," said Karina. "What's bothering you?"

"I don't know for sure," he answered. "I just sense danger, and until I find out what that danger is, I'm staying very alert. Two-hour shifts tonight, so that nobody falls asleep during his watch. Let's not take any chances."

Except for the roar of a lion in the far distance, the night was uneventful. Karina had last watch, so at daybreak she woke the others. After a light breakfast, they broke camp and headed out.

Several hours away, Kapungwe was also breaking camp. He had decided to split the travel time to the complex into two days. The roads were rough and Blaine didn't need the bouncing around, at least not in his state of health. When he attempted to awaken Blaine, he found he was incoherent and running a fever. He was very puzzled for he had been a witness to much snakebite and had never seen anyone have a reaction to the antivenin before.

He checked the bite area. It was still slightly swollen and discolored, but nothing looked out of the ordinary.

"I've got to get him to the compound as soon as possible," he thought. "I've still got five hours of travel time." He lifted Blaine in his arms and carried him to the Rover and made him as comfortable as possible, giving him some support on all sides, so he wouldn't get jostled around. He noticed Blaine was perspiring profusely, so he placed a cool, wet cloth on his forehead and, without breaking camp, headed down the road, slightly panicked. He was thinking of things he'd seen Diogo do for fever, etc. He stopped the vehicle, pulled out the first-aid kit and gave Blaine three aspirin with as much water as he could handle. Then he remembered about the tourniquet. "Was I supposed to reapply it?" he said to himself. He found the first-aid book and put his mind at ease. "No, I was to move it up if the swelling increased. The swelling decreased, so he should be okay." Then, after a short pause, he started up the vehicle and with a shout of confidence he said, "Hang on Blaine, we'll be at the compound soon."

Diogo and party reached the bend in the river just above the area he had tracked the previous evening. The trail narrowed and was overgrown with vines and other vegetation. "This is where I begin to earn my money," said Diogo. "It'll be slow going from this point on."

Chett wanted a look around and jumped out of the Rover as it came to a stop. It was as if he had a sixth sense concerning the fossa. "Look at this!" he whispered aloud. He found some scat that he attributed to the fossa. The three of them began searching the area for more signs.

"Here's his track going in the river," said Karina.

And 20 yards upstream Diogo relayed, "Yeah, and here's his track coming out. He's close by. Bring the binoculars."

Chett ran to the Rover and returned with the glasses and his dart gun. "What the hell are you going to do with that?" asked Diogo, sarcastically.

"Look, B'wana Dog, you said I could take a chance with this!"

Diogo looked at Karina, moved his mouth to the side of his face and nodded his head in approval. "Okay, let's find him first." They spread out about 20 feet apart, guns at the ready, and entered the bush.

Just up ahead were some ridges rising out of the growth and several caves were in view. For a second, he thought he saw something, but wasn't sure. Diogo scanned the trees up ahead with the binoculars and then scoped over the caves.

"I think I saw something in one of those caves," he whispered to Karina. She relayed the message to Chett, who was getting very excited. His hands were sweating heavily, and his heart felt like it was going to jump out of his chest.

For the first time on this safari, Karina was feeling very vulnerable and admitted it to herself. "What am I doing here? I'm supposed to be a field biologist, not a damn big game hunter. I'm here now. I've got to keep my cool!"

Diogo was like ice for he was a big game hunter and a good one. His thoughts were collected, and he worried that one of the others would do something stupid. He glanced over at Karina and whispered again, "Tell him to stay abreast of us and start moving slowly toward the left and away from the front of the caves."

She nodded her assent and passed on the word. It was going to be very difficult to get Chett within popgun distance of the giant fossa, but Diogo was going to try. When they cleared the brush out of sight of the caves, Diogo approached the others. "Have either of you ever known this animal to live in a cave?" he asked.

Chett answered first. "Not the ones I've been researching, but that doesn't mean this granddaddy wouldn't."

"I'm of the same opinion," replied Karina.

"But you know," stated Chett, "this could explain why we

found no tracks in the Jangala Reservation. This same kind of terrain exists there, and we never thought of searching caves, at least in the areas we could reach."

Diogo put his arm around him and said, "Do you see how the face of the third cave to your right sets back? Here, check it with the binoculars. There's a three or four foot lip that sticks out."

"Okay; I see what you mean. What's the plan?"

Diogo looked at Karina and asked, "How good are you with that rifle?"

"I shoot well, but I'm a little nervous."

"If you weren't nervous," said Diogo, "there would be something wrong with you. Here's what I want you to do . . . work your way slowly back into the bush and to the right of the cave, staying out of sight of the fossa. Chett, you're going to climb the backside of that ridge, above the cave, and get in position to shoot down at the lip. I'm going to take up a position in that tall tree, just to the rear of us. With this scope, I'll make a good sniper. Now Chett, as soon as you're ready, give us a wave. This will be your signal, Karina, to start raising a hell of a ruckus. Hopefully, it will draw the fossa out for a look-see. Chett, that will be your chance to dart him, and if you miss, I'll be the backup. There's no second chance . . . I take him out!"

"What kind of commotion would you like?" asked Karina.

"Don't fire the rifle. There are some monkeys around. Shake the trees and yell. That should stir them up a little, and the birds will pick up on it as well. A few of the larger, hidden animals may bolt, so keep your rifle handy."

"Oh great! That's just great! Already I feel like a dead woman!"

"Look, Miss Independent, it was your idea to come. If you've a better plan, spit it out. You agreed with him on this dart idea. I'd just as soon knock this animal down for keeps."

"O.K., O.K.," mumbled Karina. "I'm going."

Chett nodded to Diogo and headed for the ridge. Diogo readied his rifle and checked the scope. He double-checked his ammo, loaded and flipped on the safety. When he got to the tree, he loosened the sling and hung the rifle on his back. Quietly and stealthily he climbed into position and readied himself for the kill.

Up to this point, none of them had seen the giant fossa alive. They knew it existed, tracked it and saw the carnage it had left behind, but not seeing made it hard to believe. Diogo brought the vision of Valente's friend to mind and the reality of what they may be facing caused him to tremble.

Karina was almost in position, but cut up and somewhat bug-bitten. It was not easy going through the underbrush. Chett was elated and shaking at the same time as he neared the top of the ridge. He couldn't help but notice how beautiful the whole area was from his vantage point. He checked his dart rifle, got into position to take the shot and waved to the others. He couldn't see them but knew they were there. As a matter of fact, Diogo couldn't see Karina either. She concealed her movements very well. He was impressed.

Karina took several deep breaths, gulped out of nervousness and started shaking branches and yelling at the top of her lungs. She found the yelling somewhat dispelled her fear, at least for the moment. Monkeys started jabbering and leaping through the trees in a mild frenzy. Several larger animals could be heard busting out of the cover of the underbrush and birds were squawking as well. Sweat was pouring into Chett's eyes, causing them to sting and burn, but he wouldn't take his hands off the rifle. Suddenly he caught sight of a brownish figure edging out from the cave and took the shot.

"I got it!" he shouted. "I got it. Hold your fire," he shouted again, fearing that Diogo would kill it.

He had to move around the side of the hill to get to the cave, and at the same time Diogo scooted down the tree and headed in that direction.

As Karina went to make her move, she caught sight of two yellowish, sun-glared eyes staring menacingly in her direction. As her eyes came into full focus, she heard a snarl and the exposed teeth of a huge, foreboding figure propelled her into a state of paralytic fear. "This must be the grand-daddy!" her mind surmised. "I'm dead!" Her rifle was frozen in her hands. Her arms and feet and even her eyelids couldn't move. "This animal's much larger than I ever imagined." Massive chest and shoulders with a long neck and a tail that appeared to be a mile long were all the information she could filter through her brain, as they stared at each other for what seemed like an eternity. She closed her eyes in surrender, shuddered and fainted. The rifle fell to the ground.

A short time later, she opened her eyes and the fossa was gone. Her mind was racing a hundred miles an hour. "Was I imagining all this?" she asked herself. "Tell me I'm dreaming." She stood erect on wobbly legs, and when she tried to walk, it felt as though the blood no longer flowed through them. She slowly headed for the others.

When Diogo reached the cave, Chett was kneeling over a brown colored animal that obviously wasn't the giant fossa. "A lioness?" asked Diogo very surprised.

"She's been wounded," responded Chett. "I think we can treat her before she awakens."

"You better hope so," said Diogo, "because you're going to have one pissed off cat on your hands." Just as he finished talking, he saw Karina coming out of the brush, walking lethargically and dragging her rifle by the sling. "Are you all right?" he yelled down. If she heard him, she gave no acknowledgement and continued to stare into nothingness.

"Can you handle this by yourself?" asked Diogo. Chett nodded affirmatively, Diogo moved in Karina's direction. When he reached her, her eyes seemed to be staring into next week. "What is it?" he asked. When she didn't respond, he took out his canteen, splashed some water on her face and gave her a mild slap.

Her eyes suddenly focused on his and she said, "He's nothing like you think."

"Who?" asked Diogo.

"You just don't know," she mumbled.

"I don't know what about whom?" he queried.

She continued to babble, "When he stared at me, every little thing I've ever done wrong came flashing before my eyes. It was instant confession."

"What in God's name did you see?" he asked, trying to make sense of it all. "Karina, talk to me!" he said in a loud tone, giving her another slap on the cheek. She just buried her head in his chest and wept bitterly.

In the meantime, Chett was finishing up with the lioness. "What's going on?" he shouted down.

"Meet us back at the Rover," Diogo shouted back. Then he put his arm around Karina, shouldered her weapon as well, and headed out. When Chett arrived at the Rover a short time later, Karina was sipping on a glass of brandy and still staring into nowhere. Diogo was taking some gear out of the back, preparing to make camp.

"What happened to her?"

"Don't know yet."

He walked closer to Diogo and whispered, "She's got that same look that Valente had the day he stumbled into our camp."

"Do you think she saw our boy?" asked Diogo.

"It's a good bet. Why don't we give her a mild sedative, and after a little sleep, she may want to talk."

"You do that," said Diogo, "and I'll start setting up camp."

A few hours later around the campfire, the men were discussing the situation. "So what are the chances of finding fossa in this area now?" asked Chett.

"I think all the commotion of the day sent him off in another direction," replied Diogo. "Unless . . ."

"Unless what?" he asked.

"Unless this is the area he picked to live. He might just lay low 'til we leave."

"That would be a trait unlike the fossa I know," said Chett.

Then a voice out of the darkness, behind them, said, "This is not the fossa we know."

It was Karina. Diogo jumped to his feet, put his arm around her and said, "Thank God you're all right!"

"I don't know if I'm all right," said Karina. "I don't know if I'll ever be all right again! I know I'll look at life in a completely different manner from now on. I want you both to promise me one thing." They both looked at her agreeably, before they knew what the promise was to be. She continued, "We stay together from now on . . . no heroics! No friggin' darts . . . no bullshit."

"You saw him!" said Chett excitedly.

"I'd say it was more like he saw me!" Karina said. Then she told them the whole story in detail. They both sat there with their mouths agape, and by the time she had finished, they had a whole new perspective of their mysterious quarry.

CHAPTER TWENTY-FIVE

The Gathering

"It looks like *Dendraspis angusticeps* to me," said Dr. Donovan.
"I agree," added his wife, Anna.

"Meaning exactly what?" asked Blaine. "Am I going to live?"

"You'll be fine," answered Michael, and Blaine looked at Anna for confirmation, and she just nodded. He felt a little more at ease.

"You've had an encounter with a tree snake called the Mamba. There's a green one and a black one, but I'm not exactly sure which one you entertained. I'm giving you a slightly different antivenin. For whatever reason, you've had a bad reaction to the first dose they administered. That does happen on occasion. Actually, it saved your life."

"Just how dangerous is this Mamba snake?" asked Blaine.

"Well," said the doctor, "without immediate treatment, few survive. I have heard there's a possibility of the kidneys filtering out the poison by keeping the victim on large concentrations of oxygen."

Blaine just laid there in silence for a while counting his blessings. Then the doctor added, "We'll keep a close eye on you for a few hours, but you should be all right now."

Anna saw Kapungwe loading supplies onto the old Rover and went out to him. "Where are you going?" she asked.

"B'wana Dog wanted me to return with supplies and two goats as soon as possible," replied Kapungwe.

Anna glared at him while shaking her head to the negative. "You're not going anywhere tonight," she insisted. "You'll get some rest and have a good hot meal. You can head out in the morning."

Kapungwe knew better than to argue with Anna and besides, it would be criminal to pass up her cooking. The conversation was kept light, and Michael and Anna knew their two guests had been cautioned by Diogo not to answer a lot of questions, so they didn't ask any.

First thing the following morning, Kapungwe went out to the Rover, and Blaine was leaning against the vehicle waiting for him. "You should be resting!" said Kapungwe.

"I've rested enough!" countered Blaine. "They're going to need both of us up there."

Anna called them both in for breakfast. Addressing Blaine, she said, "You're taking a risk leaving so soon."

"Really, Mrs. Donovan, I'm feeling fine," offered Blaine.

Michael gave him some pills to take and some different antivenin for Chett's medical kit. "Be sure to tell them about your reaction to the first treatment and make sure they add this vial to their kit."

"Will do; and thank you both for everything!"

As they were driving away, Blaine looked at Kapungwe and stated, "They sure are great people!"

"That, my friend, is a true fact."

"So what did you great white hunters capture in the cave?" asked Karina.

Chett spoke up. "It's a lioness. She had a gash on her right hindquarter. I cleaned it up, stitched her and gave her an antibiotic. She should be all right."

"Truthfully," said Diogo, "she was the last thing I expected to see around here. I had heard lions were long gone from this area, but that's Africa . . . always expect the unexpected."

"I didn't know lions traveled alone," said Karina.

"They don't usually," offered Diogo. "That wound, most likely, slowed her down, and she became separated from the pride. But this is a good sign that wildlife is returning to this area once again."

"Isn't it a coincidence that this giant fossa knows that as well?" asked Karina. "So what are our plans now?"

"We kill on sight!" replied Diogo. "There's no choice now."

"Yes, there is!" shouted Karina. "We could just retreat back to civilization and leave it alone!"

"We could do that," replied Diogo. "But how would you feel picking up the newspaper some day and reading that another human being was torn to pieces by an unknown animal?"

"You don't know that would happen for sure," said Karina.

"The odds are better than even that it could and would," answered Diogo.

"I'm afraid I have to agree with him," added Chett. "We can't gamble with the lives of others."

"You're a hell of a one to speak about gambling with lives. You and your goddamn darts," she retorted. "And I got news for the both of you. Those traps you've got tied to the top of the Rover? You can throw them away. They won't hold what I've seen today!"

"Karina," said Diogo, "I can understand that you want to leave, but this job has to be finished. I can't turn back now. Kapungwe should be back sometime tomorrow with more supplies. You can stay in the Rover until he arrives."

"Alone?" she shouted. "Are you out of your mind? You go out scouting in the morning . . . I'm with you."

"Good girl!" said Chett. "Let's get some sleep."

Karina looked at Diogo and whispered, "Sometimes he's a real asshole!"

Diogo smiled and replied, "Aren't we all? I'll take first watch."

Karina gathered her thoughts and composure for a moment and said, "There's one thing I want to say to the both of you." They looked at her attentively. "Remember how skeptical we were when Blaine told us about the giant fossa taking on a Great White Shark? Well, I believe it now. Goodnight!"

August 6th, Sunday morning

The morning was given to cleaning rifles, checking all the gear, studying the maps and getting some well-needed rest. They all agreed to await Kapungwe's arrival and then develop a plan of attack or entrapment. At this point in time, either or both seemed to be feasible.

During the afternoon, Diogo decided to do a little scouting on his own. Karina lost the argument of safety in numbers. B'wana Dog emphasized the fact that he was still in charge and his movements were not subject to a vote. "I need to see if there is any correlation between my charts and Valente's maps. I'm not going on a hunting expedition!"

"You know my thoughts on this," said Karina. "Please be careful."

Both maps showed a one hundred foot waterfall existed about two miles upriver. The difference was that Valente's map showed a trail around the falls. Diogo's did not. "No matter," he surmised. "It will be all grown over by now."

By the time he found his way to the falls, he had proven his assumptions correct. The trail was still distinguishable, but almost grown over. He had never ventured this far into the reserve before and the view from above the falls was magnificent. "I wish I was here on a different errand!" he said aloud to himself, as he scanned the whole area with the binoculars. He couldn't shake the feeling that somehow he was being watched. He looked back at the trail.

"Damn . . . things grow fast around here!" He took another mental picture of the area, and then headed back to camp.

They were all sitting around the campfire after they ate, quietly discussing what they should do if Kapungwe didn't show up, when they heard the sound of a vehicle in the distance.

"That should be him now!" stated Diogo. "But if it's not, I'll be in the bushes with my rifle. Just sit still and be cool. It could be poachers."

Kapungwe drove into the campsite and parked next to the other Rover. Diogo addressed Karina when he saw Kapungwe, "He can drop the supplies and take you back to the compound. There's no need of you risking your neck anymore. We can handle it from here."

"I'm still part of this team!" she retorted. "I admit I'm scared to death, but I'm in this to the end. That's why I came in the first place."

Chett was first to greet Kapungwe and asked, "What's with the goats?"

"Bait," he replied. "And I have traps to go with them."

Then another voice spoke, "We now have the means for a stakeout!" As Blaine jumped out of the other side of the truck, Chett nearly had a heart attack.

"What are you doing here?" he asked.

"I just figured you'd need all the help you could get," he replied.

"You figured right," added Diogo, with his hand out for a shake. "So, what was it that bit you?"

"Your parents agreed on a Black or Green Mamba. I had a reaction to the antivenin. Your father told me to make you aware of that and to give you this vial to add to the medical kit. He also said you guys saved my life. I give thanks to you all."

Karina asked, "Are you sure you're well enough to be here?"

"I feel strong . . . honest!"

"Did you guys eat?" asked Diogo.

"We left after breakfast," answered Blaine. "This was our first stop."

"Okay, get some food and rest; we'll be pulling out first thing in the morning. You two won't stand guard tonight."

Before everyone turned in for the night, Diogo gathered them all together for a plan he wanted to discuss. He relayed the happenings of the previous day to Blaine and Kapungwe, and they sat and listened in awe.

"If any of you wish to leave for the compound in the morning, you're free to do so. There's no shame attached to common sense; any takers?

"Well, here's what I've been thinking. If you remember, Valente said he passed out as his friend was being attacked. He was left unharmed. Karina fell to the ground, momentarily, and the giant fossa left her untouched, as well. This could be a good thing to remember in case any of us are caught off guard in the future. Faking a faint may save your ass."

"And your pony too!" added Blaine wittily. They laughed. Blaine had a way about him of breaking the tension, and, Lord knows, they were all stressed out.

On a serious note, Blaine asked, "What's the terrain like up ahead; what exactly are we facing?"

Diogo answered, "Rocks, caves, heavy brush and trees with the river running through it all, including falls and rapids. You know, guys, my knowledge of fossa is only what I learned here in Africa and what you've told me. If any of you have ideas contrary to mine, please feel free to opine. Here are the maps. I'll show you what I've come up with so far."

Pointing to the map and holding a flashlight, which he presently handed to Kapungwe, Diogo continued, "There's a large waterfall about two miles from here. The travel's not easy. There's heavy underbrush and vines and the perfect hunting spot for the fossa.

Wildlife is much more abundant than we first projected. We know if he wanted, he could have been 10 miles ahead of us yesterday, but he was here. I'm convinced that this Mwabvi Reserve is where he plans to stay."

"Or," said Chett, "he could be ill or injured; that gunshot wound inflicted by Valente's friend could've become septic."

"Good thought!" said Karina. "That's something that obviously slipped our minds. And I'll add one other possibility . . . 'he' could be pregnant!"

Blaine sat up straight and muttered, "He could be a she!"

Then Chett added, "Of course! Now that gives the migration theory a reason. It fits! The male gave his life and tore up the shark so his mate could escape."

"And he did it all for love!" mumbled Blaine.

"That could also explain why I haven't seen any fossa MO, animal or fish. If this is the case, she'll be more dangerous than ever," offered Diogo.

"Now there's a pleasant thought on which to attempt sleep," uttered Karina.

"Don't worry, honey," said Diogo. "You can have first watch."

They all settled in, and on this particular evening, Karina did sleep in the Rover. No one questioned her prudence. Kapungwe volunteered for watch after a few hours of sleep, so Diogo was able to get a little more rest than he had planned. They let Karina sleep through after her early watch.

The next morning, Monday, August 7th, Blaine kept the rest of the people up to date on the local news front.

"The United States," he said, "coughed up $340 million to repair locomotives and de-mine the rail lines from Tete Province to Beira. There's also a Telecentre being set up in Tete to facilitate communications between Mozambique, Malawi and Zambia. It's called the Triangular Development."

"Well, thank you, Walter Cronkite!" said Diogo and countered with, "We're going to have to backpack it in, goats and all. We'll come up with a setup once we see the lay of the land. Everyone's armed . . . load and lock. Karina, do you want to stay with the trucks?"

"No, thank you. I'm with the rest of you."

When they gathered everything they believed they would need and decided who would carry it, they headed out. This was safari!

CHAPTER TWENTY-SIX

Shoot to Kill!

Mahajanga, Madagascar
August 7th, Monday

Sirana was in the middle of reading a letter from Blaine when her mother, Yvette, asked, "Is that word from someone special?"

"You know it is, Mother," answered Sirana. "I really miss him. I'm also very worried about him. He wrote this letter a week ago from Beira. He says the communications aren't too reliable where he's going, so for me not to worry if I don't hear from him in a while."

"Where is he going?" asked Yvette.

"Into the interior and he says most of the roads are reportedly in bad condition. He's in good hands though. He speaks quite highly of a big game hunter called Diogo Donovan who's lived there for many years."

"Your brother misses him as well," said Yvette. "He's a great hand on the boat. By the way, is it possible he'll be spending some time here on his return?"

"Oh, I pray so, Mama . . . I pray so."

Meanwhile in Englewood, Florida, Linda Gibbons was also

reading a letter from Blaine. He detailed his moves from the last time he called her from Mahajanga.

"I can't believe the excitement and adventure this boy has experienced since he's left home," said Linda to her husband, Ed.

"It's hereditary!" said Ed. "All of us Gibbons had a taste for adventure. Where's he off to now?"

"He wrote this letter from Beira, Mozambique in eastern Africa," related Linda. "Then they had a rendezvous with a female biologist and a big game hunter and were heading out for the Zambezi River basin. He says the consensus of opinion among them is that the animal they're in pursuit of is on some sort of migratory mission that could possibly lead them as far as the bordering country of Malawi. He says everything, so far, is all theory."

"Any mention of when he'll be coming home?" asked Ed.

"He says he'll be stopping in Madagascar first. I gather he's very fond of that sea captain's daughter. In any event, he says not to worry. Communications aren't good, but he'll be in touch whenever possible."

"How about you making us a pot of coffee," said Ed, "while I read the letter for myself?" Ed really missed the boy and tried not to show his worry.

Mwabvi Reserve, Malawi

Diogo kept them all close together on the trail as the waterfall came into view. They were only one and a half miles from base camp, but it seemed like ten to them all. The going was extremely tough. Rest was definitely in order.

"Okay, let's take a break!" shouted Diogo. "No fires, keep the noise down to a minimum, and please, nobody goes wandering off by themselves."

In unison, as if rehearsed, they answered together, "Yes, Daddy Dog!"

Diogo just shook his head and smiled and pulled out his binoculars. He scanned the whole waterfall area and nearby caves. He wanted a closer look, but knew it wouldn't be a smart idea, at least not without backup. "Maybe I should just get some rest," he thought to himself.

Karina came over, sat beside him and asked, "Whatcha thinking? Huh?" sounding like someone from the backwoods.

"About all of you," he responded. "In a short period of time, I've grown fond of every one of you."

"Oh?" said Karina wryly.

"Knock it off!" he said. "You know I'm in love with you."

"Still?" she asked. He just took a deep breath and called the others to gather around.

"I have a plan," said Diogo. "I had Kapungwe bring a couple of shotguns from the compound for very good reason. First of all, they're easy to handle in the brush and you don't need to aim. Secondly, they're semi-automatic. They'll fire five shells as fast as you can pull the trigger."

"That's for me!" announced Blaine.

"After I tell you the plan," said Diogo, "you may not be so anxious to wield the shotgun. There'll be two flushers and three snipers. The snipers will be situated in the highest spots we can find so as to give adequate cover to the flushers, who'll be checking each cave, nook and cranny, as well as backing each other up."

"So what are the goats for?" asked Chett.

"They'll be our attention-getters starting tonight," he answered. "We stake them out and cover the positions with sniper rifles. If there's no luck during the night, the two flushers start out at daybreak for the caves, covered by the snipers. Anyone have anything to offer?"

"Just a question," said Chett. "Are we going to be getting into position at night? And, when do we sleep?"

"That's two questions!" said Diogo. "It'll work something like this: we'll stake out the goats with all of us covering each other until the sun gets low. Then we make like we're leaving and stealthily move into the sniper positions that have been pre-arranged. It'll be a long night. The flushers will make a fire at camp and keep it going throughout the night as a distraction."

"Camp, meaning right here?" asked Karina.

"That's correct," replied Diogo. "At daybreak the fires are squashed and the flushers head out. As for sleep, we'll need to work out a schedule and a quiet means of communication so that one flusher and two snipers are awake at all times. You need to make yourselves as comfortable as possible. There are some good spots in the rocks." He handed Chett the binoculars for a closer look, and Karina scanned the area also.

"Anyway," he said, "this is how I see the situation . . . Kapungwe is definitely on a shotgun. He damaged his eye on a scope last year. Blaine, do you still want a shotgun?"

"Most assuredly!" responded Blaine.

"Good, then that settles it. We'll be the snipers. You two will be the flushers; any questions?"

"Yes," said Blaine. "I know Chett's a crack shot and so are you, but what about Karina? No offense, but our asses are on the line."

"Well, rest easy," answered Diogo. "I've seen her handle a rifle and she can knock a fly off an elephant's ass at a hundred yards. Do you have any other questions? Let's get some rest for about an hour, then we'll stake out the goats."

"I need you to check me out on this scope," said Chett to Diogo. Diogo complied.

Everyone but Kapungwe grabbed a nap. For some reason, he just couldn't keep his eyes closed. He just lay there listening to the hum of the millions of bugs and thinking about his wife and kids. For the first time in years, he was nervous before the hunt. After lying there for an hour, he awoke the rest of the party.

"Why is it necessary for all of us to be in on the goat-staking?" asked Blaine.

Diogo answered, "I want everyone to get familiar with the territory 'cause we may be here for awhile, and at some point in time, we just may have to run."

"Yes," added Chett. "We know what'll be chasing us, but we need to know where to run."

Diogo continued, "Not only that, we may also need to change positions. Each of us has to know where the others are located."

They started out single file with Karina and Blaine each tending a goat. Karina had made friends of the goats and was on a guilt trip for using them as bait and possibly as fossa food. The trail was rugged and overgrown, and in some instances, large swampy areas had to be circumnavigated. The next instant they'd be staring down sheer cliffs. It took approximately one hour to cover five hundred yards. At the base of the falls was a small clearing, and it was chosen for stakeout #1.

From that point, the landscape dropped in altitude rapidly, and the river ran wild over jagged rocks. The beauty of the landscape so overly awed Karina that she relaxed her grip on the rope holding the goat.

An animal, feeling encroached upon, darted from the underbrush and startled Karina. She released her grip on the rope and the goat bolted, slid down the embankment into the river. The current and rocks did the rest. Scratch one goat. It was around the bend and gone before any of the others could react.

"I'm really sorry," she said.

"Don't be," Diogo said. "It couldn't be helped, but please, all of you remember every move we make from now on is critical. If we screw up, someone may not go home. This time it only cost us a goat."

Kapungwe lashed down the other goat while Diogo set spring traps about every 20 feet or so at the edge of the brush.

"What's the purpose of the traps?" asked Chett.

"Well," said Diogo, "Our friend may get leery of the staked-out goat and skirt the edge of the brush for a closer examination. If it's caught in a trap and detained for just a few seconds, one of the snipers will have a chance to nail it. But I don't believe these traps will hold our quarry for any length of time. According to Karina, this fossa is a brute."

"You're right!" said Blaine. "If it's anything like the one we took out of the Great White, we'll have our hands full."

Diogo handed Blaine the binoculars and said, "Scan the caves all around and keep your eyes open for any sign of movement." Then he addressed Kapungwe, "Check the depth of the pool at the base of the falls. I'm going around the bend of the river for a look-see."

"Okay, B'wana Dog." Then he did as asked.

Around the bend, Diogo observed that the current slowed significantly until it reached the next lower plateau where it, once again, turned into roaring rapids. At this point, there were animal signs everywhere, including those of the fossa. They were certainly in the right area. There was no more guesswork. He hustled back to the group and relayed his findings.

"Fossa is nearby!" he said. "I found tracks and remnants of fish. There's also a good way of getting to high ground by circling around. Blaine, did you spot any movement at all?"

"Nothing," Blaine replied.

"What about you, Kapungwe? How deep is the pool?"

"It's twenty feet at center and not shallowing 'til right next to the bank."

"Great! Okay, everyone's on me. We'll pick out the sniper positions so we all know the locations. Write them down if you have to, and then Blaine and Kapungwe can continue on to the camp. You guys will find the going a lot easier taking the high ground. And Blaine, watch out for snakes!"

Blaine threw Diogo a look that said, "You don't have to remind me!"

"Oh, by the way, only use the radio if necessary," said Diogo. "We'll contact you when we're in position."

They split up. The snipers had the best possible vantage points overlooking the whole area, including the staked-out goat. Their prearranged signals included a line going from one position to the other, used as a wake-up call or alert. The flushers kept a fire going all night and spelled each other every three hours. They were going to need the most sleep, for their job would require a lot of footwork in the brush.

Daybreak arrived without incident, and Diogo said to himself, "This has to be the first night since I've been in Africa, that I didn't detect any sound . . . no insects humming, no roaring lions or elephant calls . . . not even the familiar hyena laugh . . . nothing . . . except the roar of the falls. I have to admit, they are magnificent. I guess I can't blame Karina for getting caught up in the vista. I must apologize for being a little rough on her yesterday. But I won't tell her that the crocs got the goat. She feels bad enough." He awoke the others by tugging the rope that connected the positions.

Once again, he scanned the area around the falls, only this time he used the riflescope instead. He spotted the fossa on a ledge near the falls and fired immediately. He scared the hell out of the other snipers and startled the flushers as well, who were getting ready to start out. Diogo fired again and once again the round ricocheted off the granite walls on a near miss. The speed of the animal amazed him. The other snipers each got off a shot before fossa disappeared behind the falls, apparently unharmed.

Blaine came on the radio, "What's going on up there?"

"We spotted fossa!" was the reply.

"Did you get him?" he asked.

The reply was, "No luck. It disappeared behind the falls carrying something in its mouth. You're going to have to flush him out; ergo, your job description."

"Oh, whoopee-ding!" said Blaine sarcastically. "Now I know why we're flushers!"

"You got it!" answered Diogo. "There's a ledge about 10 feet down from the top of the falls that runs left and right. Most likely, there's a cave behind the falls, but there's only one way to be sure."

"Don't tell me . . . Let me guess . . . you want us on the ledge!"

"Naturally!" responded Diogo. "Listen, the noise from the falls is deafening, so you'll need to use hand signals when you get near the cave. We're going to move in closer. One of us will stay in position for cover."

"Gotcha!" replied Blaine. "I just hope you guys put on a little better display of marksmanship than previously shown."

"Point well taken!" said Diogo.

He then got close to the others and explained the plan. He wanted Karina to stay in her position. She argued the point, but Diogo was adamant. She stayed, and then spent a few minutes on her scope to zero in on the ledge behind the falls. Chett and Dog made their way to the trap site only to find that the fossa had been there ahead of them. The shredded remains of the staked-out goat and the vast amount of blood were definite clues. The roar of the falls had assured the certainty of a silent kill.

There was a tall tree just to the left of the falls, about a hundred yards away. Diogo suggested Chett take his position about halfway up while he chose a spot on the hill behind them, in between the rocks. Both positions offered good coverage of the ledge and surrounding terrain. Karina was in a great spot to cover their backs.

As she scanned the area with her scope, she saw Blaine and Kapungwe coming into view to the right of the falls overlooking the ledge and hand signaled Diogo. Kapungwe tied off a rope and dropped it over the cliff. He slid down the rope to the ledge and Blaine passed down the shotguns and followed. The roar of the falls was deafening, but the good part was that the fossa couldn't hear either. The confrontation had to be face to face. Blaine became very nervous. His hands were trembling uncontrollably, his palms were sweating and his mouth felt like it was filled with cotton.

He continued to inch his way to the mouth of the cave with Kapungwe close behind, and with the feeling of impending doom, nodded to his partner and slowly entered the cave. Just as Blaine's full shape became visible, the fossa, taken completely by surprise, lunged out of the darkness at the intruder. Instantaneously, Blaine fired from the hip and then experienced the same feeling a pedestrian would have if struck by a moving vehicle.

The report of the muffled shotgun blast drew all eyes to the falls where all witnessed two figures hurtling through the cascading waters and falling into the pool below.

Diogo scrambled from his nearby position and rushed to the edge of the river. As he arrived at the bank, a limp body emerged and he grabbed an arm, hauling him onto the shore. Chett arrived in time to help him drag Blaine up onto the embankment. They both noticed another figure partially submerged, being pulled downriver by the swift current. The "Giant of the Jangala" was apparently dead.

Upon close examination, Blaine was alive but unconscious and covered in blood, his own. He had deep lacerations in his lower chest and stomach from the fossa's slashing claws and a couple of broken ribs, either caused from the fall or the impact of the fossa's charge. But he was alive, and it definitely was a miracle.

"A one hundred foot fall with jagged rocks all around and he missed them all," said Chett, "The boy is absolutely blessed!"

Karina arrived, out of breath, took one look at Blaine and said, "Oh, my God! Is he alive?"

"He's not good, but he's breathing . . . maybe a couple of broken ribs and a concussion. We need to tend these wounds right away. They're from fossa's claws and most certainly septic. Can you handle it?" Diogo asked.

"I don't see a problem," said Karina, "if your kit's well supplied."

"Everything you'll need is in there," he said. "We have to make sure the fossa's dead . . . c'mon Chett!"

Kapungwe showed up shortly after they left and gave assistance to Karina. They stitched Blaine up and bound his ribs. She administered an antibiotic and gave him something for pain in case he regained consciousness sooner than expected, and in his case, when and if he would come around was anybody's guess.

When Chett and Diogo got around the bend; they saw what looked like the fossa's carcass washed up onto a small sandbar in the middle of the river where the current slowed.

"I don't see any movement."

"Yeah," responded Diogo. "But we have to make sure. The trick is going to be retrieving the son-of-a-bitch. I left that rope up in the sniper's position. I'll go up and get it. Use you rifle if you have to keep the crocs away." Diogo left and found the rope then double-checked on Karina and Blaine.

"Is the fossa dead?" she asked.

"It looks that way. The carcass is washed up on a sandbar in the middle of the river. We're going after it. How's Blaine doin'?"

"Still out, but fixed up. Kapungwe is a godsend," she said.

"He always has been. I'll leave him here with you two."

"Be careful!" she said with a worried tone. He nodded and left.

"How are we going to accomplish this feat?" asked Chett.

"Simple," responded Diogo. "I just tie this rope around my middle and jump into the current about 50 feet above the sandbar. You hang on to the other end, better known as 'the bitter end,' which it would be for me if you were to let go."

"Are you crazy!" asked Chett excitedly. "What if you miss the bar? You'll float right pass the crocs."

"Not if you pull me in fast enough!" stated Diogo assuredly. He then continued, "Here's the plan: I make it to the sandbar, tie the rope onto the fossa, after I make sure he or she is alive no more, you haul it in. Then you throw the rope back to me and haul me in."

"It's at least 50 feet to that bar. That's a long damn throw," said Chett doubtfully.

"I've got faith in you," responded Diogo assuredly but added, "just make sure you get a turn with the rope around a rock or a tree. Don't depend on only your grip."

"Losing faith are we?" quipped Chett.

They both walked back upriver to a point where Diogo thought he could make it and tied the rope around his waist. Chett grabbed a good hold of the coil of rope and wrapped the end several times around his arm.

"Ready?" asked Diogo.

"Ready!" was the reply. Then he added, "I'll run alongside as the current's pulling you and feed out the rope as you need it."

Diogo took a running start and dove headlong into the raging current. He was swimming full strength toward the sandbar while the current was pulling him unmercifully toward the riff on the other side. Chett ran as fast as he could to get a little ahead, took one turn of the rope around a felled stump and jerked the rope as hard as hell. The force of the tug around Diogo's waist took the breath right out of him as he hit the sandbar with a thump that spun him around.

He lay there for a few moments until he caught his breath, and when he opened his eyes, he was staring right into the open jaws of the giant fossa! Diogo was very pleased it was dead.

"You all right?" shouted Chett.

"Yeah, and awful glad I didn't meet her when she was alive!" yelled Diogo.

"She?" queried Chett.

"You heard me. And she looks like she's a very recent mother!"

He studied her wounds and surmised it was Blaine's shotgun blast that did her in. He tied the rope around the carcass and shouted over "Haul her in!"

Chett pulled with everything he had and let the current swing her into the bank. "You're a big one lady, maybe bigger than your mate."

He untied the rope, coiled it and headed back upstream for Diogo. With a running start, he let the rope fly from his hand. It landed 10 feet short.

"Not bad for a rookie," shouted Diogo, as he looked down the river at the crocs that were sizing him up for their evening meal. He retrieved the rope and tried again. Once more it fell short.

Diogo yelled over to him, "Chett, go further upriver, heave it out as far as you can, and the current may help push it over."

He did so, but the current was pulling it away from the sand-bar. Diogo saw it was going to miss by another 10 feet and compulsively dove in headfirst and grabbed hold of the rope . . . barely.

"You crazy son-of-a-bitch," screamed Chett. "Do you have a death wish?"

"Time's running out," said Diogo. "We've got this girl's offspring to worry about."

They cut a pole and tied the carcass on and headed back to the others. Blaine was still unconscious but resting comfortably in a makeshift cot that Kapungwe had put together.

"You guys do good work!" said Diogo, and while he checked over Blaine, Karina and Kapungwe checked out the giant mama.

"B'wana Dog, we have a problem."

Karina took a second look. "It's been breast feeding!" she exclaimed.

"You both have now entered into the wonderful world of reality and dilemma," said Chett. "Diogo and I have been discussing the situation, and naturally, we can't come to an agreement."

"That's not very difficult to understand," stated Karina. "You want to keep whatever offspring that's found alive for posterity, and Diogo wants them dead."

"And what would Karina have us do?" asked Diogo.

"Set them or it free to the wild!" she responded. "We sure as hell can't flip a coin!"

"I'll make the decision for all of us," said Diogo. "Kapungwe, bring the shotgun." He started up to the falls.

Chett and Karina watched as the others made their way to the ledge and disappeared behind the falls. They waited for the report of gunfire. Five minutes . . . 10 minutes . . . nothing. Then two figures emerged from the mist, each holding a small animal by the scruff of the neck. They appeared to be alive.

Diogo and Kapungwe cradled the baby animals in their arms and made their way down the cliff and when they reached the others, Karina exclaimed, "You didn't do it . . . you didn't kill them . . . they're adorable!"

"Yep, two adorable killers-to-be," said Diogo.

"Kapungwe reminded me of something; we can't blame the sons for the sins of the father!"

"Or in this case," said Karina, "for the sins of the mother!"

"I'm sure my father would agree. I wouldn't kill lion cubs because the father was a rogue," related Diogo. "Question is now, what do we do with them; any ideas?"

Karina spoke up, "Well, the mother was making a home for them here."

"We're not sure of that fact, if it's a fact," stated Chett. "What I mean is that maybe this was just a layover until she fully recovered from her wound and childbirth."

"You may have something there!" exclaimed Diogo. "This area is still on the way to Niassa Reserve in western Mozambique. If you guys recall, my father mentioned the vast remoteness of the region. It could be the ideal place for them to be . . . but . . ." He hesitated for a moment then continued, "They're too young right now. They'd never make it on their own."

"Well," suggested Chett, "we've got to get Blaine back for treatment right away, and I think I need to bring Professor Lansing up to date. After all, he is financing this expedition, and he may just want to present these cubs to posterity." He was actually hinting about bringing the pair of fossa back for scientific study.

"Do you hear what he's suggesting?" said Karina.

"It's out of my hands!" said Diogo. "I was hired to trap and/or kill *Mama Fossa*. My job is finished once I get you all back safely, and right now those cubs do not present any danger to this party. Let's get them in a cage."

CHAPTER TWENTY-SEVEN

Recovery and Decision

They arrived back at base camp weary and worn, somewhat relieved from the demise of their quarry and very worried about Blaine. He was still in a coma.

Kapungwe had no sooner set down his load, when he immediately started a fire and began putting a meal together. The others pitched in where they could, making Blaine as comfortable as possible and tending to the newly acquired offspring.

Kapungwe was definitely a godsend and Diogo realized it more each day. He wasn't just one of his hired hands, but a good friend and companion. He was also a damn good cook. Diogo knew he could take scat in a tough situation, and make it palatable, hoping of course, that it would never come to pass.

"I suppose you're going to expect a bonus after this job is completed, Kapungwe," stated Diogo.

"Not one kwacha!"[1] replied Kapungwe.

"Well, you're wrong. It would have been most difficult, if not impossible, to complete this mission without you. You get a bonus!"

Kapungwe smiled and sang while he washed the cookware. He

---

[1] There are 80 to 90 kwacha to the dollar (Malawi currency).

seemed so tireless. Karina wondered where he got all his energy. She went to check on Blaine's wounds. While changing one of the dressings, she heard a whisper.

"I'm very thirsty," moaned Blaine.

"Thank God!" she shouted. "He's out of the coma!" The others came running to see him. She held up his head and told him to sip slowly.

"Are you hungry as well?" asked the cook.

"A little . . . but I have a splitting headache," whispered Blaine.

Diogo had just arrived to hear Blaine's last sentence and said, "No doubt! That was one hell of a fall!"

"And the fossa?" asked Blaine.

"Dead," replied Karina. "You got her with the shotgun blast."

"Her?" he asked.

"That's another story," said Diogo. "We'll fill you in tomorrow morning. Right now, have a little soup and rest easy. We'll be heading out to the compound in the morning. You're still not out of the woods, so to speak. How's the pain?" Blaine just winced a little. "Karina will give you something. The most important thing right now is rest."

The next morning, Wednesday the ninth, they broke camp after a light breakfast and explained all to Blaine. He was amazed at all that had taken place after his fall. And wrapping up the informative details, Diogo finished with, "That's why we had Kapungwe skin out the fossa. Now we're the only ones who know she was a mother, should the decision be to turn the offspring into the wild."

"Why would the decision be otherwise?" asked Blaine.

"Chett pays the tab, and he answers to his boss. It's his call. In any event, the babies go with us 'til they're old enough to fend for themselves."

They traveled all day, making occasional stops to check on Blaine and nurture the fossas. Karina fed them milk from a stray goat they picked up along the way. She fashioned a nursing bottle out of a rubber glove.

Early evening they pulled into the Donovan compound, completely worn out. Diogo pulled Kapungwe aside and whispered, "Put the cage with the animals behind the last hut . . . I don't want my parents to know about them just yet." He also cautioned the others to leave that part out of the story for now.

Just then, the Donovans came out to greet the returning safari. Michael and Anna were very happy to see everyone back safe and sound. Well, not so sound; they saw the condition of Blaine. "Oh, my God!" exclaimed Anna. "What happened to him? We just fixed him up."

"I knew we shouldn't have let him go back in the bush in his weakened state," added Michael.

"His condition has nothing to do with the snake bite," said Diogo. "He fell from a hundred foot ledge into the water. He's got a concussion, a few deep wounds and possibly, a few broken ribs."

"Oh, is that all?" asked Michael sarcastically.

"How are you feeling?" asked Anna.

With all the strength he could muster, Blaine answered, "Terrible."

"Let's get him inside!" urged Anna. Then she put her arm around Karina and said, "You look exhausted."

"And hungry," added Karina.

"Let's get Blaine tended to and then I'll get on some food."

"You're a nice lady!" said Karina. Anna just squeezed her shoulder.

They were introduced to Chester Whalton and after a brief conversation were already calling him Chett.

Upon examination, Michael announced, "You guys did a very fine job of stitching Blaine up. There's no apparent infection, so I'll just leave that be for now. He does have two broken ribs, and there is some swelling of the brain.

"Anna, these guys look famished. Why don't you get dinner started and I'll finish up here."

As Anna was leaving, Karina spoke up, "Let me help. Besides, I need a woman to talk with."

After the women left, Michael grabbed hold of Diogo and asked urgently, "What the hell clawed this kid? I'm surprised his intestines didn't fall out!"

"We didn't want to say anything in front of Mom," answered Diogo, and then relayed the whole story to his father.

"Why am I not surprised?" asked Michael, as he administered antibiotics and a pain medication. "You're a very fortunate man, if you want to call your condition fortunate. I suppose it beats being dead. How's your vision?"

"Seems okay," replied Blaine. "No blurriness at all."

"That's truly amazing!" said Michael. "But I'm telling you straight out . . . you need lots of rest and quiet and a restricted diet. You screw up and pull open those sutures . . ." He just shook his head. "Well, it's your life. How are the rest of you?" the doctor asked, scanning their faces. They just nodded in the affirmative. "Show me the animals."

They went behind the hut, and Chett showed him the skinned out fossa.

"Awesome!" exclaimed Michael. "Where are the cubs?"

"In Chicago!" replied Diogo quickly, and then added, "Just kidding, Dad."

Michael exhaled loudly and looked over the animals. They showed no sign of aggression. "They appear to be very healthy. What have you been feeding them?"

"Goat's milk; Karina has been taking care of them."

"She's quite a girl," said Michael, "but why all the hush-hush?"

"We didn't want Mom upset and worried."

"Over what?" he asked. "The danger's over now. Besides, your mother isn't as sensitive as you think she is; after all, she raised you!"

"Okay, we'll give her the whole story after breakfast," Diogo ceded.

After dinner, not one member of the safari needed coaxing to turn in, and when morning arrived, the smell of fresh coffee brewing and Anna's cooking acted as an alarm clock. Anna rang the "call to meal" bell, and one by one they arrived to see mounds of scrambled eggs and toast and what seemed like a whole side of bush pig.

After grace was said, Karina asked, "Anna would you like me to take Blaine some food?"

"Already taken care of, and the animals were given milk," replied Anna. "But, thank you dear for asking. The animals are cute, but not familiar to me. Now do I get the whole story?"

Michael never ceased to be astonished at Anna's intuition. "Okay guys, give her the whole story."

As they each took their turn and told their version of what occurred, she just sat speechless, in awe, until Karina relayed her confrontation with Mama Fossa. She gasped and stared at her son with somewhat of an evil eye. "It's a good thing for you, son, that nothing happened to her.

"This whole story is fantastic! Chett, you must be terribly proud to have brought this whole thing into fruition. Imagine, from all your work in Madagascar to the culmination here, and all of your lives touching each other as they have. It's truly amazing. So what becomes of the baby animals?"

"I'm not quite sure," answered Chett. "I need to check with my benefactor, Dr. Lansing. After all, he subsidized this whole expedition."

"Does this mean they'll be caged in a zoo?" asked Michael. "Or worse yet, be used in lab experiments?"

"It's not for me to say," answered Chett.

"Oh, yes it is!" retorted Anna. "We're the only ones who know those babies exist. Look at what their parents went through just to have them born here! Now you're going to bring them back to Madagascar. They'll probably end up in a foreign zoo." Then Anna turned to her son and said, "For God sakes, Diogo say something!"

"There's nothing I can say, Mom. When I discovered their existence, my first thought was to kill them. I couldn't do it."

"Why would you want to do that?" she queried.

"The mother and father were killers and most probably, human flesh eaters," said Diogo.

"So you're assuming the cubs would be man-eaters as well?" asked Anna. "Do you go around shooting all the lion cubs that are out of a rogue's loins?"

Michael then asked, "In their natural environment, in Madagascar, was the animal ever implicated in any human death?"

"Not that we know of, at least not until it started the migration," answered Chett.

"But those incidents could have been provoked," said the doctor.

"It's possible; what are you getting at?"

Michael continued, "Who's to say that if you placed them in an environment similar to Jangala Reservation, that human contact would ever take place?"

"There is no such place," said Chett.

"Oh, but there is!" offered Michael, "The Niassa Reserve. There's plenty of wildlife and areas that are inaccessible to humankind. These animals, being *cryptoprocta*, would naturally seek out this type of territory, wouldn't they?"

Chett turned to Karina and asked, "What are your thoughts? Lansing pays your salary as well."

"Well," she stated, "we've proven the existence of *Cryptoprocta giganta*. We have a frozen male carcass intact in Madagascar, and a skinned out female carcass here, and who knows? There could be others in Jangala Reservation yet. Those facts alone will certainly call for more funding and exploration . . . let's set them free!"

Chett got up and paced back and forth and paced some more. He started nodding his head as if speaking to himself and finally asked, "Who's going to do it? If I report the fossa as dead, I'll be expected to report to my duties in a short time and so will you," he said addressing Karina.

Diogo spoke up, "Obviously, Blaine can't do it. That leaves me."

"Are you willing to give up more of your time, Diogo?" asked Chett.

"I may be persuaded. I've still got that gold miner's map to the area. It will be at least three weeks before we could turn them loose. Blaine needs time to recover. You could convince Lansing you need at least two more weeks here. Then, travel time back to the coast and back to Madagascar. By that time, our little friends will be ready for meat.

"I'll also need to speak with Kapungwe and his wife. It's hard to make major decisions when you're exhausted. Let's rest up for a few days and we'll discuss it again. Agreed?" All agreed.

Diogo was beginning to feel over-committed. He went for a long walk down the trail along the Zambezi River. He did this whenever he had something pressing on his mind or a big decision to make. His mother watched him disappear around the bend from her kitchen window, as she'd done many times before, and knew something was really bothering him.

"Mike . . . is something going on with our son that I'm unaware of?" she asked.

"He has a bad gut feeling about turning those animals into the wild for one thing, and the other may be . . . I think . . . well, he may be in love," answered Michael.

"Why doesn't he want to release the animals?" she asked.

"I asked the same question last night during our private conversation. His answer was, 'Dad, you would have had to see the carnage this animal is capable of wreaking on a human being. I can't get the pictures out of my mind. Now I'm beginning to feel the decision is resting on my shoulders.'

"Then he mentioned something about working on a plan to keep Karina from leaving. I believe there's only one way you can interpret that thought."

"We worked it out, and I believe, they will as well," she said.

There was much to consider concerning the disposition of the young fossas, but what was foremost on Diogo's mind was his relationship with Karina. As he walked, he thought, "I honestly can't expect her to give up her career and stay in Africa. What kind of a life would that be with me on safari half the year?" He continued to ask himself crazy questions and considered concessions he could make just to keep her here. He wanted to ask her to marry him, but he lacked any sound or even sensible suggestions that could possibly make it work. "I need rest!"

A few days later found Diogo walking the same path, but well rested and able to think much better. He and Karina hadn't much chance to be alone. She was helping out Anna at the clinic and taking care of the baby fossas, while he was getting caught up on his correspondence with prospective trophy seekers and visiting sick villagers with his father. The sleeping arrangements had been changed to accommodate Chett, who wasn't with them on the first visit. Chett was now temporarily bunking with Diogo.

"A penny for your thoughts!" said Karina, startling Diogo, as she came up behind him.

"Only a penny?" he asked.

"Are you thinking about us?" she queried. He just nodded and avoiding her eyes, looked out over the river. "I haven't been able to come up with a solution either," she said.

He answered by asking, "How do you know what I've been thinking?"

"We love each other!" she retorted. "Or haven't you noticed? It's obvious to everyone else."

He turned and faced her. Lacking the right words to say, he just pulled her into his arms and after a lover's moment, whispered in her ear, "There's got to be a way of working this out . . ."

"Maybe there is," she said. "At least your mother put some ideas in my head."

"Well, continue!"

"She suggested, as well as your father, that I could stay on and help them with their work here. They were/are hoping that at some point in time, you'll come out of the bush and take over the compound."

"And what did you say to that?" he asked.

"I said I would give the idea serious consideration. But first, I asked if you had anything to do with influencing their offer. Your mother laughed and said she was hoping that I would influence you. I like her a lot. Besides, I have a pet research project that could be completed here in Africa."

"Does that mean you're going to stay?" he asked excitedly.

"No . . . it just means I may come back. I've got some loose ends to tie up, and I've yet to hear what you're willing to trade off. I can't be expected to do all the giving."

"I'm aware of that fact, but I'll need some time as well, to work it out." He sort of went into deep thought as he gently held her hand, and they walked back to the house in silence.

"How long do you think I'll be laid up?" Blaine asked Anna.

"Don't rush it!" she replied. "You're welcome here for as long as you need or want to stay. Right now, the needs outweigh the wants."

"Now that you put it that way," said Blaine, "I have this girl in Madagascar . . . I really need to let her know what's going on."

"Would you like to call her this evening?" asked Anna.

"Oh, Mrs. Donovan, that would be great! I know she's worried. I haven't spoken to her in quite awhile."

"Well, there's no need to worry her further. You're out of the woods, but you need lots of rest . . . at least, another week or so. I'll let you try calling your aunt later, as well."

As they spoke, Chett was on the phone in the house, relaying to Dr. Lansing all that had transpired, except for the existence of the fossa's offspring. "Well, it's all just about tied up here . . . the *giganta* is dead."

"It's a pity," said Lansing. "I wish we could have had it alive for study." As Chett heard those words, he was glad they'd made the decision to free the cubs. Lansing continued, "When will I see you?"

"Blaine's on the mend but needs, at the minimum, seven to 10 more days of rest. Karina's well but also in need of some rest, and as for myself, I can't leave 'til Blaine's well enough to travel. His first stop is Madagascar, and I may as well wrap things up there before I see you." He got that all out before Lansing could get another word in.

"How's your physical condition?" asked Lansing, knowing that Chett was evasive.

"My malaria was kicking up a bit, but I'm fine now. A little rest wouldn't hurt me either," he answered in truth.

"Then I'll figure on three weeks?" asked Lansing.

"That sounds about right."

"Tell Karina and Blaine and all concerned, they have a well-done coming in the form of a bonus. What are Karina's plans?"

"I believe we'll be parting in Beira," said Chett "When Blaine and I board for Tana, she'll be heading to the States."

"Tell Mr. Donovan he'll be on the payroll 'til you leave," added Lansing.

"Thank you, sir; he'll appreciate that . . . see you then."

Karina and Diogo came into the house just as he hung up the phone.

"It's done!" he exclaimed. "I told Lansing the fossa was dead, and we'd be here at least another week, minimum."

"Well, that takes care of everything," said Diogo, "except for one minor detail. What about our two little friends in the cage out there?"

Chett answered, "If we stay more than a week, Lansing will definitely get suspicious. I have no doubt he'll have dates set up for presentations of our discovery and safari to the scientific community. This could be the ideal situation."

"How do you figure that?" asked Karina.

He continued, "Diogo will be the only one to know the whereabouts of the drop site of the animals. He can choose the area without our interference."

"That's not the point!" interjected Diogo. "This project was your baby. You made that a point right from the start. Now you're dumping it on me. Remember, you guys are the ones who wanted these babies kept alive." When Diogo presented his side of the situation, Chett felt ashamed and guilty.

"I hadn't looked at it from your point of view; I guess I've been caught up in all the hoopla of the whole project. I'm sorry, Diogo. Taking you for granted was not my intention. Your help has been invaluable to all of us."

"Apology accepted; and believe me, I do understand your situation, but I have a business to run here as well."

"Lansing told me to relay to all of you a well-done, and that a bonus to all, including Diogo, was forthcoming. Also, he told me that you, Diogo, would be on the payroll 'til we leave. I'll have to pad the books a little, but you'll be on the payroll until the package is delivered."

"So is Kapungwe!" added Diogo. Chett nodded his assent. During the next few days, all were making plans, and on one occasion of feeding, Karina was snapped at by the male fossa. Kapungwe assumed feeding responsibilities.

"These animals were not meant for cages," said Diogo to Kapungwe. "They're starting to snap at each other."

"We'll split them up," said the guide, and prepared another cage.

Michael offered that they just might be ready for a change of diet. Diogo thought about that and decided to start feeding them fish and an occasional live chicken. It seemed to quell their aggressiveness, at least for the time being.

"Kapungwe," said Diogo, "how would you like to take another trip into the bush?"

"You are the boss, B'wana Dog," he answered.

"No, you don't understand, Kapungwe. This is not part of your duties, but a volunteer mission. You will be compensated."

"I talk to my wife," said Kapungwe, "but I sure she like the extra kwacha. How far in the bush?"

"Niassa," said Diogo.

"Oooowee, long trip . . . maybe two weeks," surmised Kapungwe.

"That's about right," replied Diogo. "So when you're putting supplies together, don't forget to pack some fish on dry-ice and maybe cage half dozen chickens. I'll take care of the guns and ammo and the usual paraphernalia. I'll let you know when."

CHAPTER TWENTY-EIGHT

The Joy Is in the Journey

A few days before the date of departure set by the group, Michael desired a private conversation with his son, and seeing him alone checking gear by the Rover, he approached.

"Hi, Dad; out for a walk?" asked Diogo.

"No, son; actually I came out to have a word with you. It's been difficult to corner you alone lately."

"What's the problem, Dad?"

"I don't know exactly, well I do know. I . . . guess what I'm trying to say is . . . I don't have any . . ." Mike was having a problem getting the words out.

"Spit it out, Dad! What's bothering you?"

"Son, we've always been able to talk things out, and now I just feel like I'm stepping over the line. Your mother and I are very concerned about this upcoming venture into Niassa land."

"There's really nothing to be concerned about," he assured his father.

"Right!" said Michael. "Poachers, illegal prospectors and unfamiliar territory . . . nothing to worry about."

"I've a detailed map of the whole region I'm going into, and I've got Kapungwe. Besides, we'll be taking the new radio, and I'll keep in touch . . . promise. You can reassure Mom," Diogo said.

Then changing the subject, he said, "Did I mention the return of the wildlife I'd seen in the reserve? Hartebeest, antelope, zebra, buffalo, some elephant and even a black rhino. The upper river was boiling with hippo in the Shire."

Getting back on track, Michael asked, "What's your destination?"

"Northwest of Lichinga. The east coast of Lake Niassa is, for the most part, uninhabited. A few miles into the reserve we found a way across the river leading to a trail north. It will save a couple of day's travel. As the crow flies, we're only speaking about 200 miles, maybe 250. If the trail's good, we can make excellent time and may even be back within a week."

"So let me get this straight," said Michael. "You leave here and enter Malawi from the south, move northeast across the Shire, then north once you've crossed the Mozambique border to an area you've never tracked, counting on a map that was made up by God knows who, God knows when. There was a time, Son, when you displayed a lot of sense. What if you're discovered taking those animals across the borders?"

"That's why we're taking this trail designated on this map, and I've got the signed pass that gives me free passage to Mount Binga, if it becomes necessary to travel that far. They won't have any reason to search the Rover."

"Sounds like you've thought this whole thing out very well," said Michael. "That was my gravest concern. I feel better talking it over with you. When I explain it to your mother, she'll feel better as well."

Diogo gave his father a hug and said, "I know you guys care and so does Karina. She may come back to stay, and if she does, this could prove to be my last venture into the bush on safari."

Michael shook his head approvingly, put his arm around his son and made light conversation as they walked back to the house.

The following day, Karina and Diogo were out walking and discussing the possible obstacles to their future together when she asked, "I just thought of some basic questions. Where does the power come from that feeds the compound?"

"Just upriver," answered Diogo. "The Cabora Bassa Dam and Hydroelectric Project. It's the main source of power in the country. We're in the province of Tete, and just across the river a little north is the main town and telephone connection. So power and communication have never been a problem here, except during the war. We're luckier than most. It also contributes a great deal to our effectiveness working with the populace here and in Malawi."

"And if the bridges are out?" she asked.

"There's a ferry across the Shire and across the Zambezi, as well. The motor launch allows the river to become a highway for us, should the occasion arise. Supplies come up the Zambezi on a regular basis."

"Thank you," she said. "All these things will have a bearing on my decision to come back."

"Oh, I see," replied Diogo. "You want to make sure you have an out."

"You got it!" she stated smugly.

The evening meal was Zambezian chicken grilled in palm oil and very spicy which Anna had learned from one of her patients in the Nampula area. As usual, it drew raves from the guests, as well as the vegetable concoction Chett prepared with a Malagasy accent. Karina pitched in with a form of German potato salad, and the meal was topped off with a Portuguese wine that Anna had saved for such an occasion as this. She was thrilled with the company and the joking and the sounds of laughter that filled her home.

"I can't remember when I've had so much fun at a dinner table. It's a shame you'll all be leaving so soon." As her voiced trailed off in a note of sadness, the others took time for a moment of reflection, and then Blaine spoke, "I'd like to take this opportunity . . ." he cleared his throat to choke back his feelings, "to tell you all how grateful I am. I've had my life saved twice and have been treated with the greatest care, and I'm not only accepted as an equal, but taken in and treated like one of the family. I've lived an adventure that only the boldest would dare to dream and very few would experience. I'm still alive to go back and tell about it, thanks to all of you."

Karina interjected, "We owe you as well, Blaine. You put your life on the line for us!"

"Believe me," said Blaine, "it was by no means intentional."

Diogo added, "I've never seen braver!"

"Coming from you," replied Blaine, "that's quite a statement."

Chett was silent for a long while, but then finally spoke up. "All of you humble me. This was my project from the start, and without the help of any one of you, the difficulties we faced would have been insurmountable. Kapungwe's not here, and I owe him a special debt of gratitude . . . and what can I say about you, Michael and Anna Donovan? Even with the evidence we have, who will believe the whole story? Only Diogo and Kapungwe will know how it truly ends." He stood, raised his glass of wine and said, "I toast all of you!"

Diogo made it known that he and Kapungwe were leaving in the morning. "I decided, after consulting with my guide and noting the increasing contumeliousness of my cargo, that the sooner we leave the better it will be for all concerned. Sun is up at 4:30 A.M. and we'll be off." Karina just stared at him in disbelief. She thought they would, at the least, have one more night together before they parted. She began to miss him already.

When they found themselves alone, Diogo spoke first, "I know I kind of shocked you, but I had to make this decision. My folks are unduly worried about this trek I'm making. I know they've worried before, but this is the first time they've ever made it known. I need to complete this mission."

He pulled her into his arms and kissed her like they had never kissed before. She kissed him back, looked right into his eyes and said, "Damn you . . . stay in touch!" Then she ran a few steps, turned backed, then turned away again and ran to her room.

"I'll never understand women," said Diogo to himself.

Light filtered through the trees in broken rays as the sun began another day. Diogo made his way to the Rover, and in the dim surroundings, picked out the form of Kapungwe standing by the rear door. The animals were already loaded and two crates of live chickens adorned the top of the vehicle. "What would I do without him?" whispered Diogo. Then off to the side two other figures appeared. Blaine and Chett came out to say goodbye.

"Karina said she had to skip this scene," said Chett. "But told me to give her best . . . well, you know what I mean. Women are strange."

"This is a real welcomed surprise," exclaimed Diogo. "And, yeah, women are strange but wonderful."

Blaine put out his hand to shake, and Diogo just pulled him in for a hug. No other words needed to be said. The Rover headed down the road.

The rest of that day at the compound was spent packing and getting ready for an early departure to the airport at Beira. The three guests still found time to help out the Donovans in their daily tasks of treating villagers of various maladies and administering vaccinations for one thing or another. As Karina treated some of the children, she observed the gratitude in their eyes and the smiles on their faces. It gave her a very strong sense of belonging.

Not long after the evening meal, Diogo made contact stating that they had reached the river crossing and were making camp.

The call put everyone at ease, including Michael. Toasting and joking by all filled the time 'til the need for sleep won precedence.

Jonas Kumani was to be the driver to the airport, and two days travel was the plan. Kumani was Diogo's second choice in guides and companions. As the trio was boarding, Anna had a few words with Karina, and Michael shared pleasantries with the guys. "I hope you decide to return to us," said Anna. "All of us feel you'd be a godsend in our work here. You're a natural!"

"Anna," replied Karina, "you've been a good friend to me, and I admit I feel a sense of belonging, but there's still much to think about. I'll definitely stay in touch." After farewells and hugs, the party was off to Beira.

Around the same time, Diogo and Kapungwe were crossing the Shire River, and once on the other side, they found the partially overgrown trail designated on the map. "It's not traveled much," noted Kapungwe who, by the way, had relatives in Malawi but was not familiar with this border area.

"That could be a blessing in a lot of ways," replied Diogo. "And I'm glad you came along to help me interpret the language."

"But, B'wana Dog, they speak English in this country!"

"I know," answered Diogo sarcastically. "Let's push on."

Three hours down the road, they found the going a little trickier and the trail harder to distinguish. By this time they had crossed out of Malawi into Western Mozambique and were heading straight north. They'd make good time for a while, but then would hit a glitch.

"The trails cross here," related Kapungwe. "I not sure what's the right way. What you think, boss?" Diogo was poring over the map and couldn't find two intersecting trails at this point.

"I'm not sure either. We've made much better time than I figured. We're near the Lugenda River area. The trail to the left, if it stays left, will bring us where we need to go along Lake Niassa.

The other heads true north away from our destination. Let's follow the northwestern trail for a few miles, and we'll make another evaluation then."

No more than 200 yards down the trail, there was an explosion. The right front wheel of the Rover hit a landmine, sent the front of the vehicle 10 feet into the air, twisting to the left as it made contact with the ground, and rolling over twice down into a culvert.

Kapungwe was thrown from the Rover on the first roll and pinned by the falling axle, which crushed his left leg. He lay motionless. Diogo was trapped between the front seat and dashboard. His head was bleeding profusely from somewhere on top, covering his face in crimson. His right arm was pinned, twisted behind his back and obviously broken. He was unconscious.

The clouds of dust and smoke, tainted by the smell of oil and residue from the explosion, permeated the still air. Surrounding the scene of twisted bodies and metal were the blooms of various proteases, aloes, gladioli, helichrysums, known as everlastings, and a wide variety of orchids. The trail they were on bordered evergreen forest on one side and montane grass on the other. Whatever animals happened to be in the immediate vicinity, were temporarily scared away. Except for one of the wheels spinning a wobbly course on an upturned axle, all was silent. Nature had been interrupted for a brief moment in time. A lazy Bateleur eagle glided down over the scene for a quick inspection, and then soared out of sight beyond the trees.

Two animal cages were lying 10 feet away, each containing a confused and pissed-off fossa. Chicken feathers covered the ground where moments before they were flying in the air, ejected from screeching hens frightened by the explosion and impact. If not for the two injured and unconscious men, the scene could have been one of mirth.

Many hours went by before the silence was broken once more.

"Base to Diogo . . . Base to Diogo . . . Come in please. Diogo, do you read me?" It was Michael on the radio. The message was repeated three times. On the third repetition, Diogo started to come around. His right arm was not available for use to reach for the microphone. He made a try with his left hand, but it was too much of a strain. When he tried to stretch, his right arm exploded with pain and caused him to withdraw. He called out for Kapungwe. No answer.

He was wide awake now and trying to gather his thoughts. "What the hell happened?" he thought aloud. He tried moving his right arm again, "Aaaagh! Forget that thought." He could feel his legs and had movement in his toes, but they were pinned and he couldn't swing them out. He called out for Kapungwe again. Still no answer. The temperature had dropped to about 50 degrees and he felt cold. July and August are winter months in Mozambique.

His pistol was still in its holster but strapped to his right hip. The sun was going down. He started to think of the possible danger of foraging animals. He could hear jackals in the distance. "Where the hell is Kapungwe?" he thought.

The Rover was turned up on its side and Kapungwe lay no further than 15 feet away, but totally obscured from Diogo's view, still unconscious. "Maybe he went for help . . . no . . . he wouldn't have left me like this. He must be dead or hurt real bad . . . maybe he was thrown into those trees."

He checked the headlights . . . they worked. He turned them off. "They might come in handy," he said to himself. "What about the horn?" He gave it a light tap . . . it worked, as well. He made a reach for the holster flap, and a shockwave of pain came from his right shoulder. "Aaaagh!" He knew he had to reach the pistol. Nighttime in the bush can make the mind play all sorts of games. "The hell with it," he yelled and grabbed for the gun. "Aaaagh, sonofabetchu thought I was going to swear!" He quipped to himself to ease the pain. He had hold of the pistol!

He heard a noise off to his left and stretched his neck to the side. There laid the fossa cages. "At least they're okay for now. A lot of good it's going to do if I don't find a way out of here. Good thing we put locks on those cage doors." His thoughts were running all over the place as the sun sank behind the trees, "What if . . . what if . . . what if . . .?"

Karina was lying in her sleeping bag in the tent thinking about Diogo and the whole adventure. "Blaine was right," she thought. "Who would believe it?" Her group had decided to drive most of the day and travel two-thirds of the distance. The following day would only be a half-day's ride to the airport, where they would spend the night in the hotel and fly out the following morning to their respective destinations.

"I do love him," she thought. "And I know he loves me . . . isn't this what I've been dreaming about my whole life? Or . . . am I in love with my career? I know I need to work and feel useful . . . I'll have that opportunity at the compound and time for my research. My research is important. He's willing to give up big game safaris to make it work, but what kind of a woman would I be if I demanded such a thing? I'm running away . . . but why?" She had a hard time falling asleep. She was worried, but didn't know why.

Blaine was also tossing and turning. His thoughts were all on Sirana. So much so that he couldn't lie on his stomach. They were apart much too long. "I couldn't lie on my stomach anyway, my insides aren't fully healed," he thought. "I have enough pain, and now I have to add growing pains . . . I give up!" Then he fell asleep.

Michael and Anna were getting ready for bed. "I know something's gone wrong," said Michael worriedly. "He promised he'd call every night."

"He called last night, didn't he?" asked Anna. "Besides, it

wouldn't be the first time he's forgotten. He gets out there in the bush and he's in another world."

"But why wouldn't he have answered my call?"

"Maybe they were out of range or had the radio off. They might've been afraid to make a lot of unnecessary noise. There could be a thousand reasons. Try to relax Mike. He'll be okay."

Knowing he had the pistol, Diogo felt a little safer, but he still couldn't figure how to get out of his predicament. Besides his arm being broken and twisted behind him, the steering wheel inhibited his every move. It too was bent out of shape. "If I could only free my legs!" He tried once more. "Damn it! I'm not dying like this!" he shouted out loud.

Night fell and he couldn't keep his eyes open. He was feeling cold. There was an old rag stuffed under the seat that they used on occasion as a seat cover when they came out of a muddy situation. He was able to reach it and pulled it over himself to some degree. "Better than nothing," he thought. "At least I don't have to decide what position to sleep in," he quipped.

He tried making the twisted arm more comfortable. Nothing worked. "I've got all kinds of pain killers in my bag," he thought, "and I can't reach the damn thing. If I ever get out of this, I'm going to redesign this layout." He thought of Karina, and it eased his pain until the thought came that he may not see her again . . . He fell asleep.

Sometime during the night he heard a scuffle close by that startled him and caused the chickens to squawk. He turned on the lights quickly. An animal disappeared into the darkness. He couldn't make out what it was. He fired a round to scare it off. "I've got to save the battery," he said to himself. "I may need the horn . . . only five shots left in the pistol. I've got to save one for myself . . . just in case." He knew there was the distinct possibility of becoming some animal's dinner, but he didn't want to be alive for the start of the feast. He heard another noise. It sounded more like a moan. Then he heard a voice in a tone just above a whisper.

"B'wana . . ." and it trailed off.

"Kapungwe!" said Diogo softly. "It's got to be . . ." Then he shouted, "Kapungwe!" and waited for a reply.

"Can't speak good, Bwana," he whispered.

"Can you move?" asked Diogo.

A faint "no" was the response. Diogo surmised that Kapungwe was pinned down as well, and probably under the vehicle.

"Kapungwe, I'll ask some questions . . . just answer yes or no." Diogo gathered, from what the answers were that his friend was unable to move from the waist down, and his breathing was labored. As far as he knew, there were no emanations of blood coming from his body. Diogo's head wound was superficial, and the bleeding had stopped hours ago. No scent of blood outside the vehicle was a good thing. "How am I going to protect Kapungwe?" Diogo asked himself. "If I sleep, I'll never hear his cry. I must stay awake."

Before the night was over, he was forced to fire two more rounds to scare off predators. He had three shots left.

Jonas Kumani, driver of Chett's party, pulled up in front of the hotel. It was just past noon. They all checked in and reserved a room, one for Jonas as well. The plan was a shower, a nap, the lounge for drinks before dinner, and then a good night's sleep for the long plane ride home.

At seven P.M., Karina was on her second glass of wine when she came to a final decision on her future. She raised her glass in a toast and addressed the others. "I'm not leaving!"

The others had stood for the toast, and Blaine asked, "Where are you going?"

"I'm marrying Diogo! This is where I belong." She looked at Jonas and announced, "I'll be riding back with you in the morning." They celebrated with a couple more rounds, and then went in for dinner.

That same day out in the bush was a very long one for Diogo and Kapungwe. They were both more thirsty than hungry, for even though it wasn't summer, the sun was bright and hot. Diogo kept constant contact with his companion to keep abreast of his condition. He surmised it wasn't good. They welcomed the cool evening.

Shortly after dark, the stillness was broken by the radio once again. "Base to Diogo . . . base to Diogo . . . come in Diogo. Do you read me?" This time it was Anna. Diogo could detect the fear in her voice, and it hurt him that he couldn't answer. She repeated her call three times.

Except for the sound of the insects, silence returned. It was a cloudless night and the moon shone brightly, affording Diogo good vision in the area he could see. The fossas were lying quietly and unusually calm. "They must be hungry and thirsty as well. I'll make a decision on them in the morning," he thought.

The radio came on again, and as Michael was repeating for the third time, his voice faded to nothing. The radio was "gonzo," completely unusable.

After dinner, Karina went to her room and placed a call to the Donovan Compound to relate the news of her decision to return immediately. Anna answered, "Hello. This is the medical center. How can I help you?" Karina noted that her voice was a little strained and sensed she was trying to choke off a sob.

"Anna, this is Karina. Are you all right?"

"Oh Karina, it's good to hear your voice," she replied.

Karina asked again, "What's wrong?"

"Diogo failed to call in last night. Michael called him and there was no response. I wasn't too alarmed for it wouldn't have been the first time. But he failed to call tonight as well. We called twice . . . no response. I'm afraid. . ." Her voice trailed off in sobbing, and she handed the phone to Michael.

"Hello, Karina? Forgive Anna. As parents, we have this sixth sense, well, you know."

"Don't apologize," said Karina. "I felt unduly worried myself the last couple of days and couldn't put my finger on it. I dismissed it as trauma in trying to make a decision which by the way, is why I called."

"What was it you were trying to decide?" asked Mike.

"I'm staying!"

"Good for you!" replied Mike and relayed the message to Anna. "All we have to do now is get our boy back here."

"I know approximately where they crossed the Shire," said Karina. "And Diogo told me Jonas is as good as Kapungwe when it comes to tracking. Why don't we try to find them?"

"I know if you can get Jonas anywhere near where he can pick up a trail, he will find them. In the meantime, let's pray they are both okay," said Michael.

"We'll leave first thing in the morning," said Karina.

"Good," replied Mike. "Have Jonas call me tonight. I'll give him the okay to pick up whatever you'll need."

Karina found the boys in the lounge, briefed them on the happenings and had Jonas call the compound immediately. Unsurprisingly, Blaine wanted to be in on any distress call concerning Diogo.

"We'll be fine," Karina assured him. "You're still on the mend and definitely needed elsewhere. I just want a commitment from both of you to attend our wedding!"

"You got it!" Chett and Blaine echoed together. It was settled.

As hard as Diogo tried to stay awake, he just couldn't prevent his eyelids from closing. He couldn't afford to waste any more rounds. "I can probably flash the lights on and off quickly," he thought "and blast the horn a few times to scare anything away. That'll save the battery, and I'll have the bullets for an emergency."

All through the night he kept watch, nodding off occasionally, but not going into a dead sleep and keeping tabs on Kapungwe. He never knew a night could be so long. Near daybreak there was a terrible racket near the rear of the Rover. Something was trying to get at the chickens. Diogo screamed out, and whatever it was scooted away. At sunup, he notified Kapungwe that he was closing his eyes for a while. The sun was nearly high before he awoke.

"Kapungwe!" shouted Diogo upon awakening. "You all right?"

"I'm okay, Dog," he answered in a raspy voice.

"I just woke up," announced Diogo.

"Mmmm," uttered his companion.

"I wish I could move . . ." said Diogo. "I can't do a thing to help you."

"I am the same," replied the raspy voice.

Then, Diogo's attention went to the fossa cages where the animals were quiet and listless. They needed water and food, soon. He couldn't let them suffer the same fate that was obviously in store for Kapungwe and himself. He grasped his revolver, braced his arm against the truck and took careful aim. As he squeezed the trigger, he wondered if he had made the right decision. There was a loud report, "BLAM!" The loud noise startled the hell out of Kapungwe and made him lunge. Diogo's arm kicked back, and he writhed in agony as pain shot through his broken arm. The female fossa flipped upside down in the cage. Diogo didn't miss . . . he blew the lock right off! The door swung open, but she just sat there, looking around in all directions.

"Dog, what is wrong?" asked Kapungwe.

"I'm freeing the animals . . . they are on their own," answered Diogo. "There's not much hope for us, maybe they'll make it." He raised the pistol once again and aimed at the second cage, but the lock was at a bad angle, and he couldn't stretch any more to get in a better position. There were only two rounds left.

"Oh, what the hell!" said Diogo to himself. "We're going to die anyway." He raised his arm once again and aimed at the lower corner of the cage, "BLAM!" The loud report sent the female fossa scrambling into the bush. A real good shot moved the cage about two inches, just enough to give him a clear shot at the lock. He didn't waste any time, "BLAM!" The last round did the job. They were both free. The male fossa didn't stick around to ask directions. He lit out after the female, and as is common to their species, they disappeared like a wisp of smoke. "*Cryptoprocta giganta*, if it finds life in the wilderness, may never be seen again by human eyes," he thought.

Karina and Jonas spent some time on the maps and studied the ferry schedules for both the Zambezi and Shire Rivers. Karina showed Jonas the approximate area where Diogo had crossed the Shire, and he was positive he knew a shortcut to the eastern shore of Lake Niassa.

"The trails in some spots," said Jonas, "may be grown over, but the main roads leading there are in good condition. Our first leg will be on tarred road. Then we go to hard gravel. You say you saw the map he is using?"

"Yes, it showed a trail running right along the border all the way to the high country."

Jonas pointed to an area on the map and said, "They couldn't have gone further than here. We'll head for that destination then backtrack."

"How far do you figure it is from here?" she asked.

"Three hundred to 350 miles to Americans. Over 500 kilometers to us."

"Why do you say they couldn't have gone further than that area?" she asked.

"If they are further than where I figure, their radio must be dead, but they must be okay and still moving," answered Jonas knowingly, his tone denoting many years of experience in the bush. "If something gone wrong . . . we find them on backtrack."

At sunrise, 4:30 A.M., they were on the move, and by noon were across the Zambezi heading northwest. This was all new scenery for Karina. She just wished the circumstances were different so she could enjoy it. Her initial visit was on the southern side of the river. Then Diogo was her big game hunter guide and she had felt somewhat secure. Right now, her insides felt like mush. She trusted Jonas, but he wasn't Diogo. "Please God, let him be okay!" she prayed. It was just loud enough for Jonas to hear, and he added, "AAA-men!" They both laughed and she felt more comfortable.

Diogo had never in his life felt as insecure as he did at this moment. The pain that he was experiencing deep down in his gut was one of helplessness for not being able to save his friend. Despair had not set in, as yet.

"What's worse," Diogo asked himself, "starvation or being eaten alive?" He and Kapungwe had witnessed both alternatives firsthand. He wished there was another option, but the bullets were gone. There was no instant escape.

Kapungwe was lying out there in the open, more susceptible to danger than Diogo and in worse physical condition. "Can you hear me?" asked Diogo.

"I . . . hear . . . you, Dog," answered Kapungwe.

"Our chances are not too good," said Diogo. Then he strained to hear the response.

A weaker voice answered, "I . . . under . . . stand."

Karina and Jonas traveled nonstop, and by nightfall had come within 30 miles of their destination where they would begin backtracking. This was wilderness. They had passed the last village over three hours ago.

"Not much out here is there?" asked Karina.

"The animals like it that way," replied Jonas. "Less people . . . more animals."

They made camp and started a fire. Ten Celsius is cool at night, if one's not prepared for it. Instead of cooking, they decided to eat some of the sandwiches that were left from the huge lunch that was packed for them at the hotel. "Nothing but the best for Mr. Donovan," was the oft-used phrase. Jonas and Karina talked about many things around the fire, but most of the conversation was on Diogo, his family and Kapungwe.

"Kapungwe been my friend for many years!" said Jonas. "We grow up together and get a job together at the compound. We know Diogo when he was a small boy. Good people. I remember one time during the floods a woman was in labor and sitting up in a tree. Michael climb the tree from the boat and deliver the baby . . . Anna drove the boat!! They have done much for my people"

Karina listened to many tales with interest then volunteered for first watch, since Jonas did all the driving and was quite tired. She kept the fire going and kept her rifle at the ready. "I don't know how he kept us on that trail for the last 50 miles!" she thought to herself. "He's a damn good tracker."

The sounds of different animals were all around but nothing close enough to be of any major concern. Karina had come into her own, in a manner of speaking. After her encounter with grand-mamma fossa, she was confident of being able to handle any situation. A few hours went by and she woke Jonas.

"I think I'm losing it, but I thought I heard a car horn in the distance," she related.

"Could be an echo in the head from all the driving, and then out here . . . silent," suggested Jonas.

A large animal wandered through the area near Diogo and Kapungwe. Diogo caught a glimpse and turned on and off the headlights and blew the horn.

"You still okay?" he asked. His companion acknowledged. They were getting more frequent visits now that noise was being made, probably out of curiosity more than anything. A couple more hours went by, and then he heard scurrying. He saw one jackal. "Where there's one . . ." Then he saw another. "They've got us zeroed in now . . . or maybe they're after the chickens . . . we're in the way. Once they know we can't move . . ." He flashed on the headlights. He saw four. He blew the horn once shortly . . . then again. "Kapungwe, are they near you?"

"Circling," he whispered raspy.

Diogo flashed the lights once more, and this time laid on the horn for 30 seconds. They disappeared to the edge of the wooded area, but he knew they weren't leaving. Every few minutes he'd flash and then blow the horn. He had to protect his friend. This was all he had to fight with. "At least we can go down swinging."

Jonas woke Karina and she said, "Time for watch already?"

"No, I heard the sound of a car horn as well!" he stated. "We need to investigate."

"In the dark?" she queried.

"You drive . . . I'll walk ahead of the Rover to identify the trail. Headlights on and follow me . . . slowly." They broke camp, packed up and started out.

The roar of a lion close by sent chills up Diogo's back. He believed that the sound of the jackals alerted the larger animals of the possibility of an easy meal. Leopards could be a little spooky and leery of an unfamiliar scene, but the lion was not always predictable.

"I'm sorry, Kapungwe," said Diogo with great sadness, for he knew that his friend was thinking on the same wavelength. This could be their last night.

Then Kapungwe spoke with reference to his life, "It has been a good journey." Diogo just smiled. He was forgiven.

There was more animal activity in the area now, and they both knew it was just a matter of time. "That's what life is," thought Diogo. "Just a matter of time." The jackals came in for another close inspection, and he flashed the lights on and off and blew the horn. They lit out, but it wasn't the commotion that Diogo made that scared them off. A couple of lions made their presence known. They made their approach from the tall grass off to Diogo's right, barely in his line of sight. He flashed on the lights once again, and this time left them on while his hand pressed down on the horn continuously. Temporarily, it worked. The lions were confused.

Jonas heard the sound of the horn much more clearly now and could see lights shining in the distance. He surmised someone was in deep trouble. He picked up the pace, and Karina followed close behind. When they arrived, almost at a right angle with the lights and horn blaring, there was no way to gain access through the heavy brush, so Jonas went further down the trail and found where the other trail intersected. Without hesitation, he ran toward the lights gun in hand. Karina skidded around the turn, trying to keep up. A lion was in full view of the headlights, and Jonas fired in the air to scare it off, "BLAM!" He fired again, "BLAM!" The female retreated but the male came on. That's when Jonas noticed the figure of a man lying on the ground. From behind him, two more shots rang out, "BLAM! BLAM!" Karina dropped the lion. One of its front paws came to rest on Kapungwe's foot. "Damn good thing those lights were on!" she said.

In the morning, a radio message was being received at the Donovan Complex: "Michael, this is Karina . . . we found them.

Their Rover hit a landmine and they're injured, but alive! They'll need some patching up, so we're putting a band-aid on them and bringing them in."

"God bless you!" said Anna.

"Jonas deserves all the credit. He did a fantastic tracking job," added Karina.

"Bless him, too!" exclaimed Michael.

Before Karina signed off, she said, "Diogo requests that you send cables to Chett and Blaine reading just two words . . . Mission Accomplished!"

As they were ready to leave, Diogo looked out in the direction the fossas were headed, the Niassa wilderness, and the words of naturalist William Beebe came into mind: "When the last individual of a race of living things breathes no more, another heaven and another earth must pass away, before such a one can be again . . ."

CHAPTER TWENTY-NINE

Mission Accomplished

Mahajanga Airport

Sirana was waiting at the gate when the flight from Tana arrived. Blaine was leaning sort of heavily on Chett for support as they disembarked. He was still a little sore and unsteady on his feet. After they cleared customs, Sirana moved closer, and when Blaine got within hugging distance, she threw herself at him. He let out a yelp; she quickly backed away asking, "What did I do?"

Blaine responded, "I'm still a little sensitive around the ribs, but my lips are still in working order." She came closer, kissed him gently, first on the upper and then the lower lip. He looked into her eyes and said, "The hell with it!" He pulled her in tightly, making the hunger of the two lovers obvious to all passersby.

"Ahem!" Chett cleared his throat.

"Oh, excuse me, Mr. Whalton," said Sirana. "I didn't mean to ignore you." She gave Chett a light hug and kissed him softly on the cheek. "Thank you for watching out for Blaine."

"Please, call me Chett, and I didn't really do a good job of taking care of him. Look at him! He's all banged up and scarred."

"Scarred?" she asked.

Blaine hadn't told her about being clawed and almost disemboweled by the fossa. He merely said he broke a couple of ribs in a fall. Blaine knew she'd find out sooner or later, and so decided this was as good a time as any to divulge the whole story, leaving out of course, the part about the baby animals.

"Let's get to the car first," he said. "Then I'll tell you about our adventure. Better still, let's wait 'til dinner and we'll tell the whole family. We are invited to dinner . . . are we not?"

"Of course," replied Sirana. "But you could have allowed me the pleasure of asking."

Chett just looked at Blaine and shrugged his shoulders in an "I'm sorry" manner for letting the cat out of the bag. As they were getting into the car, Blaine whispered to him, "Should I tell her about the Mamba, as well?"

Chett just rolled his eyes and said, "Sirana, do you think I could possibly get a ride to the La Piscine after dinner? If the answer is affirmative, I cordially accept your invitation."

"My brother will be going right by there on his way home. I'm sure he'll be glad to take you."

As they pulled up to the Andrianaivo residence, Rijah and Yvette came out to greet them. Blaine thought to himself, "This is truly a wonderful family and I'm a lucky guy." He slowly eased himself out of the car and reveled in the warmth of the greeting. Chett was impressed as well, for he really didn't get to know the family due to the urgency of the situation and sudden departure. He was looking forward to dinner and conversation, as well.

As always, Yvette set a fine table and outdid herself in the meal preparation. Rijah bragged about her, as usual, adding that Sirana had helped. Sirana smiled and in Blaine's eyes, she was the belle of the ball.

"So, are you married, Chett?" asked Rijah.

"Yes I am. My wife works with me here in Madagascar but is in the States now on sick leave."

"I'm sorry," she uttered, "I pray she will be well soon."

"Oh, she's not the one who is sick: it's her mother . . . or was her mother. I guess what I'm trying to say is that her mother is now feeling fine after her sickness. I just spoke with her yesterday. With all the traveling I've been doing, it's hard to keep track of all the details."

The conversation naturally drifted to their African adventure, and just then the doorbell rang.

"Hi, everyone!" shouted Aurelien. His wife, Moira, just waved hello and smiled.

"You're just in time," pronounced Rijah. "They're going to tell us about the trip to Mozambique and beyond!"

"We wouldn't want to miss this," said Moira. "But can we eat first? I'm starving!"

Yvette added, "So am I." Sirana was given the honor of establishing the seating arrangements and dinner was served.

After being poured a glass of French wine, the guests toasted the Andrianaivos for their hospitality and offered kudos to the chef, seconded by all. After dinner, Chett was given the floor.

"About our journey, where should I begin?"

"Karina Wolfson would be a good start," offered Blaine.

"Perfect!" said Chett. Then he began to expound on how the whole safari was organized, beginning with their introductions to Nataniel Chicoti, head of the National Police Command and Diogo Donovan, alias B'wana Dog. When he got to Anna and Michael Donovan, Blaine echoed his praise for them as well.

Blaine kept skirting around his near brush with death, especially on two occasions, until he mentioned how Kapungwe and the others saved his life. At this point, they all stared at him in eager anticipation. "O.K., O.K.," said Blaine. "I'll let Chett tell this part of the story because he saw it all."

Chett began with the Portuguese gold miner who wandered into their camp, and the bloody demise of his companion. Next was telling the incident of the snakebite and Blaine's remarkable recovery. He detailed the pursuit of the fossa, right up to the cave above the falls. He then looked at Blaine for permission to continue. Blaine nodded his assent.

"It just happened all at once," he continued. "There was a shotgun blast and then two bodies were hurling through the falls and plunging into the water below. At first we thought Blaine was a goner."

"What's a goner?" inquired Sirana.

"A dead man," offered Blaine.

"Oh my God!" she responded, pressing her hand to her lips.

He finished the story at the point where they retrieved the fossa carcass downriver. "Blaine was unconscious at that time."

Blaine then grabbed center stage and ran on about the Donovan Compound and the great work being accomplished among the people. "I hope you don't mind, but I invited them all to our wedding."

"Excellent," responded Rijah. "Ah, the world abounds with wonderful people." He loved meeting new people from different walks of life and relished conversation.

"But we are also invited to the wedding of Karina and Diogo. They will bring us up to date on when that will be. She left Beira determined to be his wife and made us promise we'd attend. We all parted the next morning."

Blaine and Chett had no way of knowing what had happened to Diogo and Kapungwe and their brush with death. The conversation then went to wedding ceremonies and traveling times, and then Moira offered news of monetary interest. "I thought you'd all like to know the final tally on the shark parts etc. It was $75,000, American." Blaine just whistled and she continued, "We decided on a better split for the crew, because you must admit, circumstances were quite bizarre, and the crew was outstanding."

Blaine stood and bowed saying, "I accept the praise for the whole crew."

Aury then took the floor. "We figured $12,000 each and $6,000 for you, Dad." To that news Rijah held up his wine glass in praise of a better retirement.

Blaine was quite surprised. "I was hoping to make just enough to cover expenses and get some hands-on experience when I arrived. Now I have a fiancé, extra cash and experiences beyond belief."

"Hang onto the money!" said Aury, "Once you're married, there's no such thing as extra cash." He laughed and Moira elbowed him in the ribs.

"I'd love to see the expressions on the faces of Haji and Sabastien when you give them the news." He liked them a lot, and Blaine wished he could go back to work with them.

"I can see it in your face, young man," said Rijah. "You want to be back on the boat!"

"That's very true, sir," replied Blaine. "But I have much to consider now. First I need to heal and get my strength back." As he said that, he opened his shirt, revealing the massive scar tissue across his whole midsection. Except for Chett, they all gasped, the fury of the fossa becoming real for the first time.

"I don't imagine you'll want contact with another one of those anytime soon?" said Aury.

"Have you heard of others?" inquired Blaine

"Oh, no," said Aury. "I was just sort of propounding. I couldn't begin to imagine what you guys have been through."

"Blaine, why don't you recuperate here," said Rijah. "As a matter of fact, I insist."

"I appreciate your offer, Captain, but I'm sure both my aunt and uncle are worried about me. I've kept them in the dark concerning my injuries. Telling them the truth is not going to be easy, but necessary. Besides, I've another year of school which begins in a couple of weeks."

The doorbell rang. "Who could that be at this time of the

evening?" wondered Yvette aloud. Rijah went to the door and after signing for a cablegram, returned and handed it to Blaine. He tore it open quickly, thinking it might be bad news from home. It read: RELAYING MESSAGE FROM DIOGO . . . STOP . . . MISSION ACCOMPLISHED . . . STOP . . . DIOGO AND KAPUNGWE DOING WELL . . . STOP . . . ANNA DONOVAN.

As Blaine read the message, he wondered what Mrs. Donovan meant by "Diogo and Kapungwe doing well." He showed the cable to Chett.

"We need to call them," said Chett. "But it keeps until the morning. I'll call from the hotel."

"I'll meet you there early," said Blaine. Turning to the others, he said, "Nothing to worry about . . . they want depositions from us concerning the miner's death." It was a lie, but a necessary one.

Chett had a room reserved at the La Piscine hotel, and Aury offered to drop him there when the evening had concluded. They all sat around awhile longer, and he and Blaine were brought up to date on local happenings. Aury, Moira and Chett left first, and after cleaning up, Rijah and Yvette retired. Sirana stared at Blaine with that come hither look, and Blaine said, "No way!"

"Kiss me?" she asked sexily.

He obliged to the point of losing his willpower and pushed her away gently saying, "Not with your parents here, and please . . . no early morning visits. I really need some rest."

She just threw up her eyebrows and said, "Your loss!" Then she went to bed.

After breakfast Chett finally got through to the Donovan compound. Communications aren't exactly first rate in that area. He spoke to Diogo who gave him the whole story, promising to keep in touch if circumstances changed in any way. Blaine showed up a short while later and Chett related the happenings in Mozambique after their departure.

"They were near Lake Niassa which is somewhere near the edge of the Niassa Reserve, using the map that was supposed to steer them away from danger. Anyway, Diogo admits he may have taken the wrong turn at a fork. They ran over a landmine."

"Oh, Jesus!" exclaimed Blaine. "Go on . . . go on."

"They were both hurt pretty bad. Kapungwe was thrown from the Rover. The front axle that had flown skyward, on impact crushed his leg. Diogo was trapped inside the vehicle with a broken ankle and an arm that was broken and twisted behind his back. I guess Kapungwe also suffered a couple of broken ribs.

"Michael feels he can save Kapungwe's leg, and they'll both be on the mend for quite awhile. You'll all be soul mates, so to speak."

"That's not very funny!" retorted Blaine.

"It wasn't meant to be. I just alluded to the fact you'll have company in your healing process," answered Chett.

"So what did he mean by 'mission accomplished'?" asked Blaine.

"He told me he felt that both of them were going to end up as meat for the scavengers. The fossas were still locked in their cages, but within sight. They had been thrown from the top of the vehicle as well, and would have starved to death. So, with the good arm he took aim and blew the locks from the cages with the last two bullets and set them free. Last he saw of them, they were heading into the denseness of the reserve."

"That took a lot of balls . . . using up the ammo like that," said Blaine. "I would have saved at least two bullets to die in dignity."

"I asked that same question," said Chett. "And it seems Kapungwe was out of his sight and reach, and he wouldn't let him die alone."

"That's the Dog!" said Blaine. "I wouldn't expect anything different. So how did they get out?"

"That's another whole story in itself." He went on to explain Anna's intuition and how Karina followed up on it with the help of Jonas. "Anyway, just as Jonas and Karina arrived on the scene, a pair of lions was coming in to make Kapungwe their dinner. Jonas dropped the first one, and Karina, firing over his shoulder, nailed the other. It died right at Kapungwe's feet."

"Wow!" said Blaine. "We missed all the action!"

"Yeah, your mangled body looks like it missed all the action. As for me, I've had enough excitement for a while. I'm all out of adrenaline," he stated.

"And what about that Karina," Blaine continued, still awed at the scene. "Do women have instincts or what?"

"Well, that's about it," said Chett. "I'm heading up to the compound when Randi gets here, finish up some paperwork and probably head home in a few days."

"I'll be heading out as well," said Blaine. Chett reminded him that he always had a job with him if he wished. They gave each other a brotherly hug and parted.

Blaine wanted to stay in Mahajanga with Sirana, but knew deep in his heart there was no way he could be in close proximity to her, under the present living conditions, without abusing her parents' welcome and trust. "So much to think about . . . school, marriage, my aunt and uncle, the future uncertainties . . . everything's just swirling around in my head at once. I think I'll walk home, slowly." Hoping his head would clear by the time he arrived home was a demand on wishful thinking.

"Boy, are you in deep thought!" came a voice from the shadows of the huge jacaranda tree next to the house.

"Oh, Aury, it's you!" said Blaine. "You startled me!"

"Apparently; I have a good idea where you're at. Let me guess . . . you want to marry my sister and come back to work on the boat, and heaven knows we need you . . . but, you also miss your parents and you have to finish school, etc., etc., etc."

"Aury, you're a psychic," pronounced Blaine.

"One does not need be a genius to understand the dilemma of a friend," said Aury.

"Do you have any suggestions?"

"Are you sure you want to hear them?" Blaine shrugged his shoulders and nodded, so Aury continued.

"For starters, stick with the plans you had before you became involved with my sister. There's no doubt, she'll wait for as long as it takes. That's a fact, and one you never have to worry about. You want to be a marine biologist, go for it. Everything else will fall into place."

"I remember your father telling me something similar years ago," said Blaine. "He told me to hang on to my dreams and make them reality."

Aury interjected, "Sirana's dedicated to her profession . . . be dedicated to yours. You'll both find a way to work it out."

Blaine smiled, saying, "You mean love conquers all and all that stuff?"

"Well, that's my advice," said Aury.

"And good advice it is. Thank you. I guess I have to sit down with Sirana and have a good heart-to-heart."

"She may surprise you with her understanding," said Aury. "I've got to get down to the boat. She's dry docked for a couple of days. I'll say hello to the crew for you."

"Thanks again," said Blaine. "See you before I leave?"

"Of course; we'll tip a couple of brews."

It was midmorning and hot when Randi arrived at the hotel to collect Chett. Somehow the heat didn't bother him; he was happy to be in familiar surroundings. All the way back to Batrambady he expounded to Randi on the adventures that took place in Mozambique. Randi just listened with his mouth agape until Chett got to the part when they left the Donovan Compound to head home, then Randi exclaimed, "What happens to the baby foosas?"

"We're not exactly sure," he answered. "The hope is that somehow they'll find their way in the world, far away from man." He then went on and explained his conversation with Diogo that morning. "So you see, they've been given a chance to survive, at great risk I might add."

After giving Randi a chance to digest all he had heard, he asked, "So what's been going on here?"

Randi shrugged and answered, "Many reports throughout the island of strange happenings, but I think most of it jumpy nerves and superstition. Since all the publicity, we even have many visitors coming to the Compound for a look-see and asking foolish questions. Many wanted a picture with you!"

"Wow, that's cool. I'm a celebrity, huh?"

"Dr. Lansing call yesterday to see if you arrived," said the assistant. "But I told him today. He very excited!"

"He received the carcass of the first *giganta*," said Chett. "No doubt he'll expect me to return soon. I'll call him this evening. Is there anything else?"

"Everything same, same," said Randi as they pulled into the research station.

It wasn't long before the phone started ringing. "This is Chett."

"Chett, Dr. Lansing here; how are you feeling, boy?"

"I'm in need of some rest and good food, although I had one heck of a meal last night. How've you been?" asked Chett.

"Never better," answered Lansing. "You wouldn't believe the stir going on in the scientific community over the fossa and the record-breaking Great White that swallowed it. What a fantastic story."

"You should have seen what the fossa did to the shark!" said Chett. "That's a story in itself."

"And you'll have ample opportunity to tell it on the lecture circuit," added the doctor. "We've been deluged with requests by students who want to get in on the voluntary fieldwork."

"Doctor, we're not even sure if it's completely safe here yet. There could be more of these animals on the move."

"I've already checked with the authorities, and they assure me that outside of a few rumors, there's been no physical evidence of further migrations. Besides, those were probably the last two of its kind in existence." The good doctor was sounding very sure of himself.

Chett countered with, "You may be right, Doctor, but there's always the unexpected, isn't there?"

"You've done a hell of a job. Come on back for a rest."

"O.K., Doc, you're the boss . . . see you soon." He then called in Randi and cautioned him never to mention to anyone his knowledge of the existence of the baby fossas.

Blaine found a few occasions to be alone with Sirana, and on each one, made the most of it. They both knew it would be a long time between . . . kisses. Blaine was packing when Sirana walked into his room. "Four months is a long time apart for lovers; sure you still want to marry me?" she asked.

"I'd marry you right now if I could. It's important to our future that I get that degree. I have to finish school first."

"And after school," asked Sirana, "what then?"

"What do you mean?" he queried.

"Well, do we live here? Do we live in Florida? Where do you work? Where do I work? Who travels where to the wedding?"

"I can't answer any of those questions right now!" he exclaimed.

She put her fingers on his lips in a quieting gesture and said, "God is good. That is why he has given us four months to be apart to think about these things and another eight months to be sure. The answers will come."

"How come I get so mixed up and you seem so wise?" he asked.

"Women are smarter!" As she said it, she rolled her eyes and raised her eyebrows. Blaine thought of a response, but kept silent. He was certainly gaining wisdom.

CHAPTER THIRTY

Life Is Good

Englewood, Florida

"Have you heard from Blaine at all?" asked Ed, as he was docking the boat.

Linda was waiting to greet him and she said, "I just got off the phone. What are you, psychic?"

"No! I'm a psycho. Now what did he have to say?"

"He's well, so he says, and he asked about you."

"What do you mean by 'so he says'?"

She thought for a moment and said, "I don't know for sure, but I have a feeling he's hiding something or at least leaving something out."

"Is this one of your woman's intuition things or you just reading something into it?"

"I can't put my finger on it, I just feel it. Anyway, he's on his way home and sounds determined to get his degree."

Ed shouted, "That's great; both for his heading home and the degree! Gosh, I really miss him."

"Is it him you miss or not having a dependable mate and fishing partner around? Anyway, he'd like you to pick him up at the airport, if you didn't mind."

"Mind?" he said. "Why would I mind picking up a celebrity? He's been in all the news services. What gets me is that he never told us; we had to see him on TV!"

"He's never been one for braggadocio," she reminded him. Stuttering a little bit, she added, "Oh . . . er . . . ah, there's just one more thing." Then she spit the words out rapidly, "He's proposed to Sirana, the captain's daughter. The date is set for next July 4th."

"She must be quite a girl if she's captured Blaine in that short a time. I can't wait to meet her. I love her already!"

"You may not have to wait too long to meet her," said Linda. "She's planning a Christmas visit."

"You don't sound too enthusiastic about the whole idea," noted Ed.

Linda hesitated before she spoke too quickly, "I have mixed emotions. Naturally, I'm happy for him, and I'm sure she's a wonderful girl, after all she wrote to him constantly in his time of need. She was certainly a great help. I . . . well . . . what if they decide to live in Madagascar?"

"Now let me see," answered Ed, while rubbing his chin. "I guess you'll just have to let go! We need to be grateful for the time we've spent with him. He'll be here for almost a year before he makes any kind of definite plan. Let's enjoy every day of it. Sooner or later, he has to make his way in the world. Let us be the springboard for his launch!"

"Sometimes you make too much damn sense," she said. "Give me a hug!"

"Is that all?" he asked in a sexual overtone. She gave him a shove, and since he was standing on the edge of the dock anyway, the momentum carried him in. SPLASH! She was laughing so hard that she could hardly help him back up. So he pulled her in too. "Life is good," she said laughingly. Even while choking, he agreed.

Donovan Compound, Mozambique

"Next time a parent expresses concern, you'd better listen!" said Michael to his son. "I'm just so damn glad to see you alive, but it's hard for me not to belt you one."

"Dad, you don't have any idea how glad I am to be home. I most certainly appreciate your concern and Mom's," said Diogo. "I perish the thought of what would have happened if Mom hadn't called Karina in Beira. Dad, I want to share something with you truthfully. I got to the point out there where I could accept my death, but, son of a bitch, I couldn't handle the thought of Kapungwe dying. I felt it was my fault. The fact that I was trying everything in my power to keep him alive kept me going. Isn't that strange?"

"No, not so strange," answered Michael. "That's love and true friendship. You were tested on one of the hardest decisions in life and you passed. I'm proud of you. Now follow my orders and get some rest. I'm going to operate on that ankle in the morning."

"Dad, how's Kapungwe doing?"

Michael shook his head affirmingly and said, "Your mother and I are operating on him tonight. I believe we can save the leg. Karina is going to assist. Your mother and Karina stopped in to see his wife earlier and explained the whole situation. They brought her some supplies as well."

"Thanks, Dad, I needed to hear that. I'll get some rest."

That night the operation on Kapungwe went touch and go, but they were able to save the leg.

"He may have a slight limp," said Michael. "We did all we could do."

"Honey," said Anna, "I thought you did one heck of a job on the reconstruction of his knee. I'll be amazed if he can walk."

"He'll walk," said Mike under his breath. "Diogo will see to that."

Anna and Karina were swiftly becoming good friends. The fact that Karina helped to save her son's life didn't hurt the bond between them. "I know it's none of my business, Karina, but you seem to have the 'noodgies,'" said Anna.

"The what?" asked Karina?

"The 'noodgies.' I guess it's a Massachusetts coined word. It means anxiety or a sort of uneasiness, jitters or maybe just a need to tie up loose ends," replied Anna.

"I think you've got me figured out. I need to make a decision on my career. One way or another, I need to speak with my boss and let him know what's going on. He's expecting me back sometime this week," answered Karina.

"I thought you already made that decision when you decided to marry my son?" asked Anna somewhat puzzled. "Have you changed your mind?"

"Anna, I want that more than anything else in the world. I just have some issues I need to deal with. I . . ." She hesitated as though she wanted to share something, but just hung her head down.

"You know," said Anna, "I've been around a few 24 hours, and I'm a fairly good listener. Why don't you give me a try?" Anna put her arm around Karina and steered her over to the picnic table and remained silent waiting for Karina to say the next word.

"Anna, there are things I've never discussed with a living soul," said Karina. "I guess I thought if I buried them deep enough, they would never surface. Since meeting and falling in love with your son—at least I believe I'm in love—I find myself questioning every emotion, every intention and every thought, wondering if I'm being honest with myself. I've been running away for a long time, that's why I came to an abrupt stop in Beira and decided to follow my heart."

"Thank God you did or Diogo and Kapungwe wouldn't be alive!" interjected Anna. "But go on, dear, I didn't mean to interrupt."

Karina continued. "I guess I was in my third year of college when my parents were involved in a terrible automobile accident. My mother suffered a terrible trauma to the head, leaving her quite incapacitated. She was in a coma for three weeks, came out of it for a short time and fell back in again. My father only suffered broken bones, and for him it was a matter of a short rehab stay. When he had recovered, he spent every waking hour at my mother's bedside. At the time, I felt very sorry for him and wanted to leave school to take care of them both. He insisted I stay in college for he said that's what my mother would want.

"When my mother regained consciousness, she had no idea who she was, or for that matter, where she was. She needed 24-hour care and was placed in a nursing home. Though my father visited her every day, he began drinking heavily. I saw my mother every chance I could get. It never seemed like enough to me. She passed away three months before my graduation. I didn't even have the heart to continue. Somehow I got through it, and on the day when they were handing me my diploma, my father showed up quite intoxicated, made a fool of himself and just about ruined my day."

"I had no idea you lost your mother," said Anna. "Diogo never mentioned it."

"I never told him," said Karina. "And when I had heard what happened to Blaine's parents, the wound just opened up again. You see, my father was responsible for the accident, and consequently, my mother's death."

"You can't just assume something like that, child!" said Anna very sympathetically.

"It's not an assumption, Anna. He admitted to me a short time after graduation. It seems he was drinking much more than I had known about. My mother must have been covering for him. Anyway, the night of the accident he had a few too many, but insisted on driving home anyway. He got loud and, to avoid a scene, she let him drive. The rest is history.

"I never wanted him near me again. I just wanted to run away. I ran into the arms of a man whom I ended up marrying, and in six months, we both came to the conclusion that it was a big mistake. So I buried myself in my work, became involved in field research and here I am. Anna, I just want to be sure I'm not using Diogo and you also as a means of escape."

"I think you're being kind of rough on yourself and possibly on your father, as well," offered Anna.

"Explain that, Anna?"

Anna hesitated a second to choose the right words. "It just seems to me that forgiveness is needed all around. First of all, you need to forgive yourself. There was nothing more you could do for your mother, even if you knew the truth from the beginning. I think that's what's eating away at you. Secondly, you need to forgive your father. Obviously, he's laying enough guilt on himself. It sounds like the poor man's gone through hell. He not only lost his wife, he lost you as well. He didn't abandon your mother, but stayed by her constantly to the end. That says a lot for his character, and maybe he needs a second chance."

"It's been quite a few years since I've seen him. I've been in touch with some neighborhood friends, and they say he's been sober for over a year. He's in a self-help program. I still have a mountain of anger to deal with."

"It may best be resolved with a face to face meeting with him. I imagine he misses you terribly," said Anna. "And if my hunch is right, that program he's in is teaching him to forgive himself."

"So one way or the other," said Karina, "I have to make the trip to the States before I make the trip down the aisle. Do you agree?"

Anna offered one more tidbit of wisdom. "Someone once told me that you had to say goodbye to the past, or at the very least, resolve it, before you could say hello to the future happily. What say we have a cup of coffee?"

"Did anyone get in touch with Nataniel?" asked Diogo of his father. Looking a little puzzled, Michael asked, "Nataniel who?"

"Chicoti . . . Nat," said Diogo, "of the Police Command."

"Oh! You mean the guy that kept you out of trouble when you went on that binge?"

"Thanks for bringing that up again, but yes, he's the one and the same. I believe I owe him an explanation."

"Well then," said Mike, "you're the one that should get in touch with him. You're on the mend now. Use the good arm." Michael handed him the phone.

"Hello, Nat?"

"Diogo, how are you doing? Did you nail that animal? What was it, a fossa? Anyone else get hurt?"

"Slow down!" said Diogo. He then commenced to explain the whole chase, including the kill and all incidents leading up to it. He felt a little guilty for not telling him about the baby animals, and led Nat to believe that he and Kapungwe were injured on the return trip from the Niassa Reserve.

"Niassa Reserve?" shouted Nat. "What in hell's name were you doing there? You said you were going into Malawi."

"That's where the chase ended, but we went through Malawi to get there. Some steps should be taken to rid that area of those damn mines," said Diogo.

"Well," said Nat, "with you two laid up for a while, the country and wildlife will probably get some rest."

Diogo countered with, "You're the one that got us into this expedition in the first place. We have Valente's vehicle here, minus a few supplies."

"There's no hurry on the wheels," said Nat. "Valente was deported. Thank God you won't be making that trip again. Also we looked into that mining scam. There really is gold in them hills."

"What are you saying, Nat?"

"It seems there are miners pouring into that whole sector from all different countries. My people can't control the flow. You nailed that fossa just in time."

"That's terrific," said Diogo in a low tone, as if speaking to himself.

"What was that?" inquired Nat.

"Oh, nothing; I was just thinking to myself. I'll let you go now, and I'll return the wheels as soon as I'm up and around."

"Get well," said Nat. "See you soon."

Diogo related to his father the illegal goldmine situation that was in close proximity of where he determined the fossas to be.

"Well, my son, only time will tell. You did your part."

Karina came in to speak with Diogo about taking some time to straighten out her affairs before becoming a permanent fixture around the Donovan compound.

"So you definitely decided you want me?" asked Diogo.

"No!" she said. "I definitely decided I want to be here at the Donovan ranch. I'll decide on you when I get back!" She laughed as Diogo reached out for her from the hospital bed in a failed attempt.

His face changed expressions and in a serious tone he asked, "When are you leaving?"

"I want to wait until you can get around. I figure about three to four weeks. In the meantime, I have to call Professor Lansing and explain the situation. He's been good to me and deserves more than a letter of resignation. Your parents can use me around here until you're back on your feet. Kapungwe will be laid up a lot longer than you."

"I spoke with Nat this morning," said Diogo with worry in his tone.

"And?" asked Karina.

"Valente has been deported, and the gold mining is running rampant. He says his people are unable to control the flow of illegals coming into the Niassa Reserve."

"Isn't that where you released the babies?" she asked. He just nodded. She kissed him with a quick peck to the lips, knowing he'd wrestle her down with the good arm if he had the chance.

"It's been a while since we . . . well you know"

Before he could finish the sentence, she said, "It's good for your character, besides you need your strength. Recover, my darling, recover."

Diogo with one last request asked, "Will you ask my folks if Kapungwe and I can share the same room?"

"By order of your father, these are the arrangements, at least 'til the end of the week. He knows if he puts you two together, no one will rest. Maybe I'll come back this evening to see what's up."

"Don't tease!" he said.

As she was walking out the door, she looked back around and said, "Who's teasing?"

Niassa Reserve, Mozambique, Africa
Several Months Later

"What seems to be the problem, Kolongo?" asked the Portuguese miner, Ilidio.

"Something is not right," he answered.

"Would you like to explain that?" asked Ilidio.

Kolongo seemed very nervous, which was out of character for him for he was known to keep his composure, even in stressful situations. He was the tale-teller around the campfires in the evenings.

"A very strange happening have I witnessed this day!" he whispered.

"Go on . . . go on," urged Ilidio.

Kolongo reluctantly continued. "I was on the trail heading back to base camp from the mine when I noticed a young antelope taking a cool drink at the river below. It was quiet, and the scene made me feel so peaceful. Suddenly two animals, the like of which

I have never seen, rushed at the young buck from two different directions. The antelope did not know which way to run. His lack of decision was fatal. The other two animals tore him to pieces. It was as if the predators had practiced their attack. I have never seen such a thing."

"It was probably a couple of lions," said Ilidio.

"These were not lions!" exclaimed Kolongo. "I know what lions look like!"

"Come, show me where it was," said the miner. "I think your superstitious native mind is running wild. But we'll take guns anyway."

Kolongo led the way. He was born a member of the Shangaan or Tsonga tribe, one of the Bantu speaking peoples. He learned to speak Portuguese and English in a missionary school in the southern province.

The Shangaan people were known for their ability to adapt well to working in the mines for gold and diamonds. Two freelance Portuguese miners hired Kolongo, along with several other tribesmen of different backgrounds. The tribesmen had no idea they were mining illegally.

When they reached the spot on the trail where Kolongo said he saw the attack, nothing was visible.

"I don't see nothing, you crazy Shangaan. That river is over 200 feet from here, and I don't see how you could possibly identify one animal from another with trees and ledges in the way."

Kolongo suggested they go down for a closer look. This time Ilidio led the way. It took them about 15 minutes to descend down the slope.

"Good grief!" shouted Ilidio. "What the . . ." He couldn't finish the sentence. He was looking around at the massive amount of blood spattered around the area, some with tufts of animal hair stuck to it. "What is that smell?"

Kolongo's color had lightened several shades from fear. "I think we should part from this area," said Kolongo.

"Look at these tracks!" said Ilidio. "Have you ever seen such as these?"

"We must go! Now!" insisted Kolongo. He started back up the hill. Ilidio looked around a little more and noticed the carcass had been dragged off out of sight. "Must be a strong animal," he thought to himself, and then he followed Kolongo up the cliff side. When they reached the top, Ilidio asked him why he was so upset.

"Ancients tell of such a one being a spirit god. His thirst is only for blood."

Later back at the camp, head miner Eduardo reproached Ilidio. "Ilidio, Ilidio, you know how superstitious these people are. Do you want to spook the whole countryside with tales of a blood-thirsty monster?"

"Eduardo, I've seen the site and the blood. I know of no animal that kills like that! It's as if the killing was for sport."

"But, my friend, you did not see or witness the act; you're only taking a spooky native's word for it. You know he's a taleteller. Why, it wouldn't surprise me if he set the whole thing up just so he could laugh at you. Loosen up. There is always something killing something else in the bush. That's the way life is around here. Remember why we are here. Have a drink, think of the gold and forget these native rantings."

Around the campfire that evening, Kolongo began relating the gory tale. Speculation spread rapidly from ancient spirit curses to punishing gods in the form of bloodthirsty beasts. Eduardo had to think of something quickly before they all ran off in fear, so he sought to discredit Kolongo in the eyes of the others.

"This taleteller is conjuring up a fantasy just to gain your attention. He's always telling crazy stories. We have guns, and guns will protect you from any animal. So I urge you to get rest and put these fairy tales from your minds. It's a long day in the mines and much fortune to be made." After a little bit of mumbling, Eduardo promised them a bigger percentage of the take if they would trust him. Eventually they all gave in to exhaustion and fell asleep.

Ilidio went into his tent, raised the flap and looked up at the stars, wondering how he would spend his share of the gold. Then his mind drifted back to the blood. "Maybe Eduardo is right, but I wonder what kind of animal it was? Besides, if it were dangerous to man, we would have heard about it by now. Hah, it can only be superstition!" Then he dozed off to the sound of the rapids of the Rio Ruvuma River.